S0-AHO-767

MARIEL OF REDWALL

Gabool the Wild is the most feared rat ever to sail the high seas. As the pirate king he rules with a quick temper and a swift sword, terrorizing all who cross his path. Joseph the Bellmaker and his daughter, the mousemaid Mariel, are his latest victims. When their ship is attacked by the searats, Gabool takes Joseph's marvelous bell among his booty, and casts him and his daughter overboard. Washed ashore, and suffering from memory loss, Mariel finds a home at Redwall Abbey. And when she recalls what happened to her and her father, she sets off with three Mossflower companions to confront Gabool—and make him pay for his crimes . . .

READ ALL OF THE BESTSELLING NOVELS OF REDWALL . . .

Redwall

The book that inspired a legend—the first novel in the bestselling saga of Redwall! The epic story of a bumbling young mouse who rises up, fights back . . . and becomes a legend himself . . .

Mossflower

Brave mouse Martin and quick-talking mousethief Gonff unite to end the tyrannical reign of Tsarmina—who has set out to rule all of Mossflower Woods with an iron paw . . .

Mattimeo

Slagar the fox embarks on a terrible quest for vengeance against the fearless mouse warrior Matthias, cunningly stealing away what he most cherishes: his headstrong son, Mattimeo . . .

Mariel of Redwall

After she and her father are tossed overboard by pirates, the mousemaid Mariel seeks revenge against searat Gabool the Wild . . .

continued . . .

Salamandastron

When the mountain stronghold of Salamandastron comes under attack, only the bold badger Lord Urthstripe stands able to protect the creatures of Redwall . . .

Martin the Warrior

The triumphant saga of a young mouse destined to become Redwall's most glorious hero . . .

The Bellmaker

The epic quest of Joseph the Bellmaker to join his daughter, Mariel the Warriormouse, in a heroic battle against a vicious Foxwolf . . .

Outcast of Redwall

The abandoned son of a ferret warlord must choose his destiny beyond the walls of Redwall Abbey . . .

Pearls of Lutra

A young hedgehog maid sets out to solve the riddle of the missing pearls of legend—and faces an evil emperor and his reptilian warriors . . .

The Long Patrol

The Long Patrol unit of perilous hares is called out to draw off the murderous Rapscallion army—in one of the most ferocious battles Redwall has ever faced . . .

Marlfox

Two brave children of warrior squirrels embark upon a quest to recover Redwall's most priceless treasure from the villainous Marlfoxes . . .

The Legend of Luke

Martin the Warrior sets out on a journey to trace his heroic legacy: the legendary exploits of his father, Luke . . .

Lord Brocktree

The mighty badger warrior Lord Brocktree must reclaim the

mountain land of Salamandastron from the army of a villainous wildcat . . .

Taggerung

The otter Taggerung, realizing he's not cut from the same cloth as the vermin clan who raised him, embarks on a journey to find his true home and family . . .

Triss

The brave squirrelmaid Triss plans a daring escape from the enslavement of the evil ferret King Agarnu and his daughter Princess Kurda . . .

Loamhedge

Young haremaid Martha Braebuck, wheelchair-bound since infancy, embarks on a quest to the mysterious abbey of Loamhedge to find a cure for her condition . . .

Rakkety Tam

Mercenary warrior squirrel Rakkety Tam MacBurl quests to rescue kidnapped Redwall maidens and thwart the plans of the murderous wolverine known as Gulo the Savage . . .

High Rhulain

Young ottermaid Tiria Wildlough travels to the mysterious Green Isle, where she joins a band of outlaw otters to rid the land of the villainous wildcat chieftain Riggu Felis . . .

Eulalia!

A young haremaid embarks on a quest to find Gorath—the heir to the lordship of Salamandastron—held captive by the Sea Raider Vizka Longtooth . . .

Doomwyte

The young mouse Bisky leads his friends on a quest for the jeweled eyes of the Great Doomwyte Idol—into the realm of the fearsome Korvus Skurr, the black-feathered raven . . .

Also by Brian Jacques

The Redwall Chronicles

REDWALL
MOSSFLOWER
MATTIMEO
MARIEL OF REDWALL
SALAMANDASTRON
MARTIN THE WARRIOR
THE BELLMAKER
OUTCAST OF REDWALL
PEARLS OF LUTRA
THE LONG PATROL
MARLFOX
THE LEGEND OF LUKE
LORD BROCKTREE
TAGGERUNG
TRISS
LOAMHEDGE
RAKKETY TAM
HIGH RHULAIN
EULALIA!
DOOMWYTE
THE SABLE QUEAN
THE ROGUE CREW

Redwall Picture Books

THE GREAT REDWALL FEAST
A REDWALL WINTER'S TALE

The Tribes of Redwall Series

THE TRIBES OF REDWALL: BADGERS
THE TRIBES OF REDWALL: OTTERS
THE TRIBES OF REDWALL: MICE

Other Redwall Books

REDWALL MAP AND RIDDLER
BUILD YOUR OWN REDWALL ABBEY
REDWALL FRIEND AND FOE
A REDWALL JOURNAL
THE REDWALL COOKBOOK

The Flying Dutchman Series

CASTAWAYS OF THE FLYING DUTCHMAN
THE ANGEL'S COMMAND
VOYAGE OF SLAVES

Other Books by Brian Jacques

SEVEN STRANGE & GHOSTLY TALES
THE TALE OF URSO BRUNOV
THE RIBBAJACK
URSO BRUNOV AND THE WHITE EMPEROR

Mariel of Redwall

Brian Jacques

ACE BOOKS, NEW YORK

THE BERKLEY PUBLISHING GROUP
Published by the Penguin Group
Penguin Group (USA) Inc.
375 Hudson Street, New York, New York 10014, USA
Penguin Group (Canada), 90 Eglinton Avenue East, Suite 700, Toronto, Ontario M4P 2Y3, Canada
(a division of Pearson Penguin Canada Inc.)
Penguin Books Ltd., 80 Strand, London WC2R 0RL, England
Penguin Group Ireland, 25 St. Stephen's Green, Dublin 2, Ireland (a division of Penguin Books Ltd.)
Penguin Group (Australia), 250 Camberwell Road, Camberwell, Victoria 3124, Australia
(a division of Pearson Australia Group Pty. Ltd.)
Penguin Books India Pvt. Ltd., 11 Community Centre, Panchsheel Park, New Delhi—110 017, India
Penguin Group (NZ), 67 Apollo Drive, Rosedale, North Shore 0632, New Zealand
(a division of Pearson New Zealand Ltd.)
Penguin Books (South Africa) (Pty.) Ltd., 24 Sturdee Avenue, Rosebank, Johannesburg 2196,
South Africa

Penguin Books Ltd., Registered Offices: 80 Strand, London WC2R 0RL, England

MARIEL OF REDWALL

An Ace Book / published by arrangement with Hutchinson Children's Books

PRINTING HISTORY
Hutchinson Children's Books, London / 1991
Philomel hardcover edition / 1992
Ace mass-market edition / March 2000

Cover art by Troy Howell.
Hand lettering by Iskra Johnson.

For information, address: The Berkley Publishing Group,
a division of Penguin Group (USA) Inc.,
375 Hudson Street, New York, New York 10014.

ISBN: 978-0-441-00694-6

ACE
Ace Books are published by The Berkley Publishing Group,
a division of Penguin Group (USA) Inc.,
375 Hudson Street, New York, New York 10014.
ACE and the "A" design are trademarks of Penguin Group (USA) Inc.

PRINTED IN THE UNITED STATES OF AMERICA

20 19 18 17 16

To Liz —B.J.

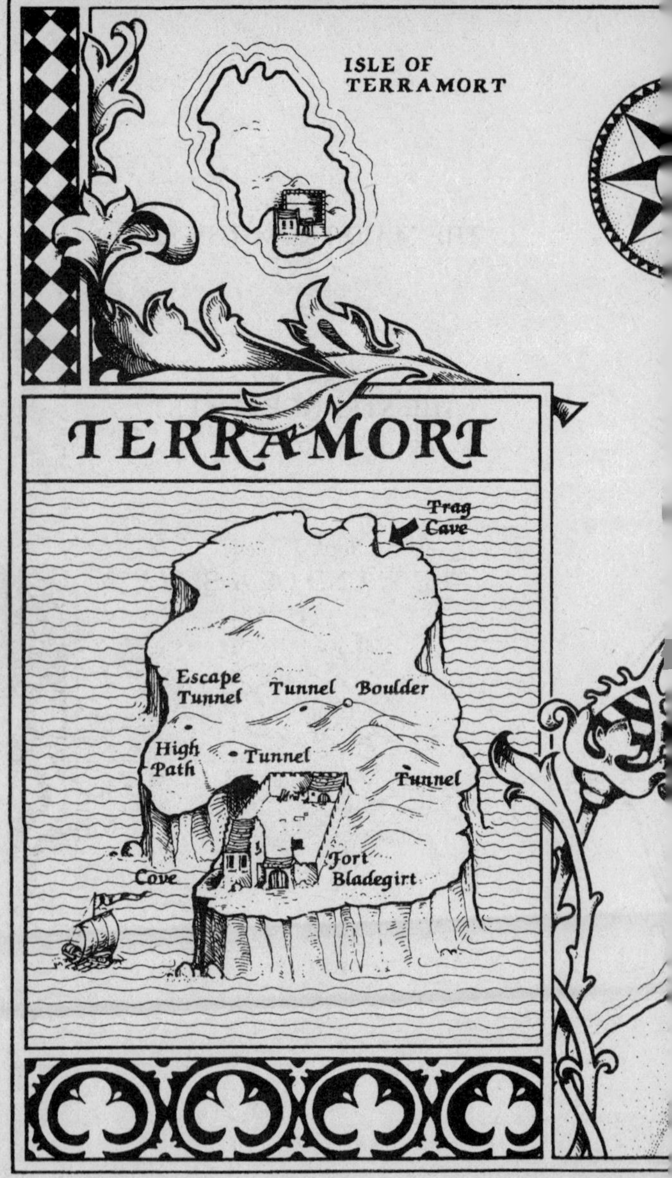
ISLE OF
TERRAMORT
TERRAMORT
Trag
Cave
Escape
Tunnel
Tunnel
Boulder
High
Path
Tunnel
Tunnel
Cove
Fort
Bladegirt

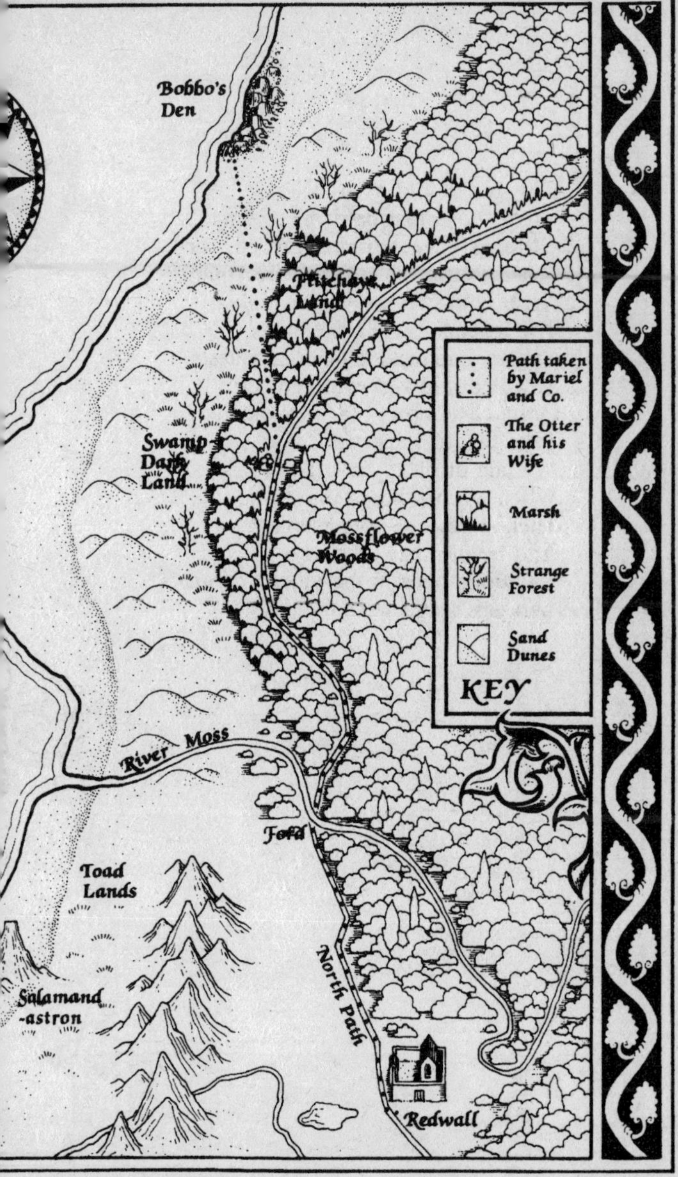

Bobbo's Den
Flitchaye Land
Swamp Dark Land
Mossflower Woods
River Moss
Ford
Toad Lands
Salamand-astron
North Path
Redwall
Path taken by Mariel and Co.
The Otter and his Wife
Marsh
Strange Forest
Sand Dunes
KEY

Old stories told by travelers,
Great songs that bards have sung,
Of Mossflower summers, faded, gone,
When Redwall's stones were young.
Great Hall fires on winter nights,
The legends, who remembers,
Battles, banquets, comrades, quests,
Recalled midst glowing embers.
Draw close now, little woodlander,
Take this to sleep with you,
My tale of dusty far-off times,
When warrior hearts were true.
Then store it in your memory,
And be the sage who says
To young ones in the years to come:
"Ah yes, those were the days."

BOOK ONE

The Maid from the Sea

1

Abbot Bernard folded his paws deep into the wide sleeves of his garb.

From a viewpoint on the threshold of Redwall Abbey's west ramparts he watched the hot midsummer day drawing to a glorious close. Late evening light mellowed the red sandstone Abbey walls, turning them to dusty scarlet; across the flatlands, cloud layers striped the horizon in long billows of purple, amber, rose and cerise. Bernard turned to his friend Simeon, the blind herbalist.

"The sun is sinking, like the tip of a sugar plum dipping into honey. A perfect summer evening, eh, Simeon?"

The two mice stood silent awhile before Simeon turned his sightless face toward the Abbot.

"Father Abbot, how is it that you see so much yet feel so little? Do you not know there is a mighty storm coming tonight?"

The Abbot shook his head, disbelieving, yet unwilling to deny Simeon's unerring instinct. "A storm? Surely not!"

Simeon chided Abbot Bernard gently. "Perhaps you have other things on your mind, my friend. Maybe you have not felt the cooling breezes die away. The air has become still and hot, the birds stopped their evensong much earlier than usual, even the grasshoppers and the buzzing bees have ceased what little noise they make. Listen!"

The Abbot cocked his head on one side, perplexed. "I hear nothing."

Simeon chuckled dryly. "That is because you are hearing the sound of silence, Bernard. One thing I have learned in my life is to listen to the sounds of Mossflower country. Every sound carries information; so does every silence. This is going to be a mighty storm, one that we have not seen the like of in many a long season."

Taking Simeon by the paw, Abbot Bernard led his blind companion down the rampart steps and across the lawn toward the main Abbey building.

Simeon sniffed the air. "Mmmm! I smell hot apple pie and raspberry cream pudding, and scones, fresh from the oven too, with damson preserve spread on them. We'd best hurry before the moles get here or there'll be none left."

The Abbot quickened his pace. "How d'you know the moles are coming?"

"Bernard, Bernard, did you ever know Sister Sage to serve raspberry cream pudding and no moles to arrive?"

"Right again, Simeon. Your powers of observation leave me in the shade. Oh, I must tell young Dandin to beat the log alarm. It'll warn anybeast still outdoors to come in."

Simeon grimaced. "Oh dear, do we have to suffer that noise again? Young Dandin is a bit overenthusiastic at beating a hollow log with two clubs."

Abbot Bernard smiled reflectively. "Yes, he does rather put his heart into it, doesn't he. Still, I wish everyone were as willing in their duties as our Dandin. If ever Redwall Abbey gets a bell, I'll be the first to vote him as bellringer."

The two mice made their way between the flowerbeds

which dotted the dark greensward. An ominous grumble of thunder muffled its way over the far horizon to the northwest. Abbot Bernard turned in the doorway of the Abbey, attempting to conjure up his powers of smell.

"Hmmm, cider poured cold from the cask, eh, Simeon?"

The blind herbalist wrinkled his nose. "Wrong, it's pear cordial."

The Father Abbot of all Redwall tried not to look amazed. Even though Simeon could not see him, he might sense his Abbot's expression.

Far, far over the horizon, far to the northwest, far across the oily blue green billows which were rising, lashing their tops into rippling white peaks of foam, far over the abysses and deeps of the heaving seas, far from the peace and calm of Redwall Abbey, stood Gabool the Wild.

Clouds of jet black and slate gray boiled down out of the sky to meet the lashing waves. A blast of hot wind like the gust from hell-furnace doors set Gabool's scarlet cape fluttering as he stood on the high cliffs of his island, defying the elements. Thunder boomed out, forked lightning ripped through the lowering vault of the sky. Gabool drew his jewel-hilted sword and waved it at the storm as he roared and laughed in exultation. The deadly curved blade with its sharp double edges hummed and sang against the wind.

Gabool the Wild ruled the seas, he was the dread Lord of Terramort Island, King of the Searats, Warlord of all Rodent Corsairs, Captain of Captains. No creature alive was a fiercer fighter than Gabool. From the lowly position of a young scullyrat he had fought his way up to be the biggest, the most savage, the cruelest and the most ruthless. In all the seas and oceans there had never been a rat like Gabool the Wild. Huge gold hoops dangled from his ears, his fangs (which he had lost long ago in hard-fought combat) were replaced by sharp jutting gold canines, each one set with a glinting green emerald. Below his weird yellow blood-flecked eyes, an enormous dark beard sprouted and curled, spilling down to his broad chest, silk ribbons of blue and red woven through it. Whenever Gabool moved, his rings, bracelets, medals and buckles jangled. Gold, turquoise, silver, ivory—plunder from the far places of the high seas. Strange weapons with shimmering twisted blades were thrust into the purple sash about his waist. Dangerous to serve and deadly to trust, he stood laughing in the teeth of the gale, satisfied that the creature who had dared go against him was now fish bait on the seabed. Thunder crashed overhead as the skies released a deluge of whipping, lashing rain. Lightning crackled around the rocky tor, illuminating the barbaric figure as if even the high heavens were challenging him.

The Warlord of all Waters threw back his huge head and shrieked out his battle cry to the storm.

"Gaaaaboooool!"

The pitifully tiny figure of a mousemaid was hurled about like a chip of bark in the eastward rush of high roaring seas. Tormented rolling waves, whipped to a frenzy by the screeching wind, billowed and swelled, long combing chariots pulled fiercely along by tossing white stallions of foam and spray.

The mousemaid, partially stunned, dared not even let one paw free to undo the rope about her neck. Her numbed paws clung grimly to a jagged spar of driftwood as she plunged wildly about in the maddened waters, now on top of a wave high as a castle, hurtling down blue green valleys into a trough that yawned like a deep, dark monster mouth, now being spun sideways with the spume, now being flung backwards from greater heights to vaster depths.

The rope became tangled around the wooden spar; painfully the little maid tried to bite at the hemp. Seawater gushed into her mouth, and she retched as the water threatened to choke her. A flailing end of rope struck her across the eyes. Unthinkingly she let go of the spar; it whipped off in a different direction from her. With both paws tearing feebly at the rope circling her neck, she was shaken about like a small fish upon rod and line.

All consciousness was finally beaten from her body when the spar struck her across the head, and the helpless figure was lost amid the pounding crashing seas. Obscured by the boiling cloud curtains above the maelstrom, not even the stars or moon were witness to the fate of the little mousemaid, victim of Gabool's cruel whim.

2

Close to the north side of the Abbey building, a new construction was under way.

Astride the wooden scaffolding of a half-finished bell tower, young Dandin pounded doggedly away at the hollow beech log.

Thonkthonkthonkthonk!

Though he was a sturdily built little mouse, he felt himself driven aback by the blasting wind. Shaking rainwater from his eyes, he bent his head against the onslaught of the storm and continued stubbornly thwacking the log with two hefty yew clubs. Whenever Dandin raised his gaze slightly he could see the fringe of surrounding Mossflower Woods swaying and hissing, rustling and sighing, like a restless ocean.

"Dandin, come down, you'll catch your death up there!"

The young mouse peered over the scaffold, shielding his eyes against the deluge. Draped about with a clean worn-out floursack, Mother Mellus, the Redwall badger, stamped a huge paw upon the wet sward.

"D'you hear me, young mouse? I said down, this instant!"

Dandin blew rainwater from his whiskers, smiling roguishly he called back, "Right this instant, marm, just like you say."

Without a backward glance Dandin threw himself from the tower and came plunging earthward to the accompaniment of the badger's startled growls. Not more than a fraction from the ground, he stopped falling and swung there, dangling by a strong vinerope harnessed about his waist. Dandin touched his nose with a wet paw.

"Came as quick as I could, marm . . ."

A huge paw cuffed him roughly about the ears as Mother Mellus freed him from the encircling vinerope. Tucking him firmly in her elbow crook like a baby, she hurried in out of the rain, scolding Dandin as he complained loud and long.

"Put me down. I'm not a baby, I can walk . . ."

"No, you're not a baby, you're a young pickle, d'you hear, and you should know better. Throwing yourself from a high tower like that! By the weasel's whiskers, you scared me out of ten seasons' growth!"

"I know what I'm doing; it was completely safe. Now will you put me down? I can stand on my own paws, you know . . ."

"I'll put you down, you young rip. Next time I'll tan your hide so hard you won't be able to sit down until berrypicking. Just let me catch you jumping from high places like that again! What'd you do if the vines snapped, eh? Then we wouldn't have to dig a grave. You'd go so far into the earth when you hit the ground you'd be able to shake paws with the taproots of an oak. Be still, you little blaggard, or you'll feel the back of my paw. Young Abbey beasts these days, I don't know . . ."

Scolding and arguing by turns, the young mouse and the old badger went inside the Abbey. Mother Mellus kicked the huge door shut behind her, leaving the storm to rage on outside. Across Great Hall in the cozy surroundings of Cavern Hole, Abbot Bernard sat at head of table with Brother Simeon on his left paw and Foremole, the mole leader, on his right. Lanterns twinkled around the homely festive board, moles jostled shoulders with mice, hedgehogs sat next to otters and squirrels. The Abbey infants were allowed to sit at table with their elders; they were mainly woodland orphans gathered in by Mother Mellus—baby mice, small hedgehogs, a young squirrel and twin otters who had been brought by their parents. Little ones who were known as Dibbuns, they were sat on the table edges, facing the Brothers and Sisters of Redwall, the good mice who tended and cared for them.

Redwall fare was famous throughout the length and breadth of Mossflower. The Abbey grew all its own produce, and Redwall cooks were experts.

Foremole had his nose buried in a raspberry cream pudding, speaking in the rustic mole language through mouthfuls of his favorite sweet.

"Hohurr, baint nuthen loik rabserry pudden, no zurr. Oi could eat this yurr pudden till next moleday an' still ax furr more."

Gabe Quill, the hedgehog cellar-keeper, held a noggin of pear cordial up to a lantern, swishing it about as he inspected its bright amber color critically.

"Hmm, what d'you think of that for a touch of good cellar-keepin'?"

A big male otter named Flagg relieved Gabe of the drink and slurped it down in one gulp.

"Very nice, sir. Too good to swill cellars down with."

Gabe's face was a picture of indignation. "Why you 'orrible otter!"

Grubb, a baby mole, looked up at the general laughter. Wiping damson jam from his snout, he shook a small digging paw at Gabe Quill.

"You'm can 'ave an 'orrible owl, but otters is orful, buhurr aye."

Sister Serena, a rotund mouse who ran the Abbey infirmary and sickbay, wiped the jam from Grubb's whiskers and passed him a bowl of honeyed milk as she reprimanded him.

"Hush now, Grubb. Don't correct your elders."

Grubb sucked noisily at the milk, coming up with a cream-coated chin.

"Burr elders, Dandin says oi'm a liddle owd feller, that be maken oi an elder too. Betcher oi'm elder'n they, an' woiser may'ap."

At the head of the table the Abbot paused with a hot scone between paw and mouth. "The log pounding's stopped. Where is Dandin?"

Simeon took a sip from a foaming tankard of October ale. "In the kitchen. Can't you hear him? He's getting a drying-down, dry clothes and a good telling-off from Mellus."

The reprimands of Mellus and the protests of Dandin echoed loudly down the corridor between the kitchen and Cavern Hole.

"Keep still, your ears are saturated!"

"Owow! I won't have any ears left, the way you're going. Ouch! And I'm not wearing that great big habit, it belongs to fatty Brother John."

"Ooh, you ungrateful little scamp! How dare you call Brother John a fatty when he was good enough to lend you his spare robe! Hey, come here, come back, I say . . ."

The smack of wet paws on the floor of the passage of Cavern Hole announced the culprit's escape. Dandin scampered in. He sat between Foremole and a squirrel named Rufe Brush. Grabbing a wedge of speckled nut-cheese, he jammed it between two slices of oat farl and began munching, pouring himself a beaker of cold strawberry cordial as he did. Flagg, the big otter, winked at Dandin and passed him a bowl of otters' hotroot sauce to dip his farl into.

"Aye aye, matey, run a-foul of Ma Mellus again, have 'ee? Quick an' dip yer bows now—yonder she comes."

Dandin ducked beneath the table just in time. Mother Mellus came bustling by, a clean linen bonnet tied about her great striped head. She nodded to the Abbot and took her place at the far end of the table in a large armchair. Sitting two young mice on her lap and a baby mole on the arm of the chair, she soon forgot Dandin as she occupied herself feeding the Dibbuns, wiping chins and generally taking charge.

"Come on now, little one, eat up your woodland salad. Pudding later."

"No, don't lika sala', wanna pudden."

"Salad first, pudding later. You want to grow up big and strong like me, don't you?"

"No, wanna stay lickle an' eat pudden alla time!"

Abbot Bernard reached beneath the table and nudged Dandin.

"You can come out now, young mouse. Mother Mellus has her paws full with those Dibbuns. You did a fine job as log banger, Dandin, though there was no need to stay out in the storm so long."

Dandin sat up proudly and reached for a raspberry cream pudding.

"Thank you, Father Abbot. I stayed out until I knew all our Abbey creatures were inside, safe and dry. It's my job."

Blind Simeon smiled. "Well done, young Dandin. You're just the type of mouse Redwall Abbey needs. One day when the Abbey is fully built and completed, who knows, you could be our next Abbot."

Dandin wrinkled his nose, not too pleased with the idea. Abbot Bernard laughed heartily.

"No Abbotship for you, eh, young rip? It's easy to see that you come from the line of Gonff the Mousethief. I wish that Martin the Warrior had left ancestors behind."

Simeon held up a paw. "Maybe he did, my friend—not direct descendants, but spiritual ones. Martin was a Warrior and the founder of Redwall; his presence is all around us in these very stones. I have never talked with a creature whom I felt was actually touched by Martin's spirit, but then we have never needed such a one in this time of peace. However, I feel that one day before my seasons have run, I will meet some creature whose life has been touched by the shadow of our Warrior."

Rufe Brush looked up from a plate of hazelnut cream and apple pie.

"Not on a night like this you won't, Simeon. Listen to

that rainstorm. Any creature out on a night like this must be drowned by now."

Simeon was about to answer when he suddenly turned his face aside and clasped a table napkin to his nose.

"Whaaaw! Somebeast's eating wild garlic!"

A fat mole named Burgo several places down with a clothespin fitted snugly upon his nose was tucking into a big basin with a spoon. He waved a paw at Simeon.

"Burr, nor c'n oi stan' the smell o' garleck. Oi do dearly luvs the taste of it tho'. At's whoi oi keeps moi snowt pegged! Garleck woild soup! Nuthin' loik et, zurr."

Amid the laughter that followed, Dandin turned to Rufe Brush.

"By the fur, Rufe, that rain sounds as if it were trying to knock our Abbey down. You were right, anybeast out in this must be well drowned by now!"

3

Fort Bladegrit stood at the edge of the high rocks which towered above Terramort cove, the big window of its banqueting hall facing out to sea. It had a courtyard and a high wall which ran around its perimeter where the ground was open, though part of the actual fort building integrated with the outer wall where it overhung the cove. The entire structure was built from solid rock with heavy wooden doors at the entrances both to the fort and courtyard. On three sides it was overlooked by hills. Gabool the Wild had taken it as his by right; indeed whoever owned Bladegirt was absolute King of Searats, as long as he could hold it. Inside the fort chaos and misrule were the order of the day. Corsair rats left their ships to come ashore after long plundering voyages. They made their way to Bladegirt in droves, leaving their ships at anchor in the cove. Roistering, fighting, gambling and drinking, the searats enjoyed their shore leave after the hardships of a life at sea.

In the high banqueting chamber Gabool sprawled on a carved rock throne, which he had made more comfortable by covering it with the skins of his slain enemies. He stared with loving fascination at a great bell dominating the center of the floor; monumental in its size the prize stood, reflecting the torchlights and revelry through its burnished sheen. Copper, silver, brass and gold had been used in its casting. Heaving himself up, Gabool strode forward, sword in one claw, a chalice of wine in the other as he traversed the perimeter of his greatest prize. Grinning like a child with a new toy, he tapped his swordblade against the marvelous bell; the soft musical note vibrated gently like a giant harp strummed by the wind. As he walked, Gabool's restless eyes roved up and down, from the strange figures embossed around the top to the intricate words ranging around the wide base of the great bell.

Gabool was puzzled as to their meaning, but they were pretty decorations which made his prize all the more fascinating to look upon.

"Blood 'n' thunder, Cap'n. Give it a good belt an' let's hear it ring out!" A burly drunken searat named Halfnose pulled a wooden cudgel from his belt and thrust it toward Gabool. With lightning speed the Warlord grabbed the club and crashed it down on Half-nose's skull, at the same time landing a thrusting kick into the drunkard's belly, which sent him reeling into an open cask of wine. Halfnose slumped across the wine, his head submerged. Gabool roared with laughter.

"Drink or drown, seascum. Nobeast comes near Gabool's bell!"

The carousing searats shrieked their appreciation at his joke. Gabool pointed at Halfnose with his sword.

"If he ever gets out o' there, give him a cup of wine t' revive him."

This caused further merriment, except from the table where Bludrigg, Captain of the ship *Greenfang*, sat with his mates. Though Gabool laughed as heartily as the others, Bludrigg had not escaped his notice. Everyone was laughing, but not Bludrigg—Bludrigg the surly, Bludrigg the argumentative, Bludrigg the trouble-causer, the seadeck lawyer. Gabool watched him closely. Bludrigg, who could sense the scheming mind behind his King's false merriment.

Things between the King of Searats and his Captain had been building to a head for a long time; Gabool decided to settle accounts with Bludrigg now. Gulping wine from the chalice and allowing it to spill freely into his beard, Gabool pretended to stagger drunkenly. He winked in a friendly manner and thrust his sword point down into a chest of booty. Tottering over to the table, Gabool banged the half-empty chalice down in front of the *Greenfang*'s Captain.

"Bludrigg, me old matey, c'mon, drink up!"

Bludrigg's face was sullen as he thrust the chalice aside.

"Don't want no wine. I can drink all I want aboard me ship."

All around the hall they stopped drinking, singing and gambling; an air of expectancy settled over the searats. Gabool blinked, as if trying to shake off the effects of the wine, and swayed slightly.

"Food then. Can't have my Captain starvin'. Roast meat, fruit, fish, sugared preserves? Here, bring m' friend Bludrigg some vittles."

Bludrigg's swordclaw fondled the hilt of his sheathed scimitar.

"Leave the food, Gabool. I eat well enough."

Gabool sighed, shaking his head as if in puzzlement. He sat next to Bludrigg and threw a comradely claw about his shoulders.

"Hmmm, no wine, no food, no smile on me old shipmate's face. What d'you want then, bucko?"

Bludrigg shook Gabool's claw off. He stood upright, knocking the chair over behind him, his eyes blazing with suppressed rage at the drunken Warlord.

"I want my share of the plunder. There's been none from the last three sailings. I'm tellin' you, Gabool, I want my portion of the booty—an' I'll have it tonight, come hell or high water!"

From around the packed hall there were murmurs of agreement. Gabool spread his arms wide and smiled.

"Blow me down! Is that all? Why didn't you say so sooner?"

Bludrigg was lost for words; the expected clash had not come. Now he felt slightly foolish in front of his crew. He shrugged, mumbling halfheartedly; he tried excusing himself as if he were complaining on behalf of his searats.

"Well, I never thought. . . . It's just that my crew were startin' to complain, they thought you'd forgotten us . . ."

Gabool looked injured. He went over to the chest of booty, where his sword stood upright amid a heap of armlets, goblets, baubles and shiny stones. Drawing forth the sword, he turned one or two items over with its point until he found what he sought. Gabool flicked the sword up as a shiny gold coronet studded with gems slid along its blade.

"Aharr, friend Bludrigg, the best for you. A crown fit for a King!"

Bludrigg felt a sudden rush of confidence; he had done it! Gabool was notoriously mean with plunder, but he, Bludrigg, Captain of the *Greenfang*, had actually got the better of Gabool. The King of Searats had backed down before him. Bludrigg's chest swelled as he accepted the beautiful coronet from Gabool's sword-blade and placed it on his head. A cheer rose from the company as Gabool spread his arms wide. Extending the sword away from Bludrigg, he addressed them.

"See, yer scurvy wave-riders. Pay attention, you jetsam of the oceans, I am Gabool the Wild, this is how I repay me friends. . . ." Without warning Gabool swung a powerfully savage blow with his sword. "And reward my enemies!"

Even the hardened searats moaned in horror as the head of Bludrigg thudded to the floor. The coronet rolled in front of Gabool. He picked it up on the dripping sword blade and held it forth to the assembly.

"Would anyone else like to wear the crown, mateys?"

Heralded by the call of seabirds, eastern sunrays flooded warm and golden into a sky of calm blue reflected in the millpond sea below. The angry storm had passed, leaving summer serenity in its wake. The sun warmed the wet bundle on the flotsam-strewn tideline until it stirred. Seawater and bile flooded from the mousemaid's mouth as she coughed feebly. The damp paw set tiny flies buzzing as it reached for her throat and began weakly grappling with the knotted rope. The wooden spar lay across her back. A seabird landed upon it; the added weight caused the mousemaid to vomit more salt water forth with a gurgling groan. Startled, the bird rose noisily into the air, cheated of the carcass it had taken for dead. Other seabirds began to wheel and circle overhead. A tiny crab tried nibbling at the maid's rough wet burlap dress, gave up and scuttled away.

Finally undone, the rope fell away from her bruised neck. Painfully she shifted the spar and rolled over onto her back. The mousemaid lay still awhile; some of the more venturesome seabirds spiraled lower. Rubbing sand and grit from her face with the back of a paw, she opened both eyes, immediately shutting them again against the glare of sunlight. Small wavelets trickled and lapped gently away from the shore; the tide was ebbing. The mousemaid ventured to explore the wound that the spar had inflicted upon her head. She winced and left it alone. Turning over again, she shielded her eyes with her paws and rested on the firm damp sand, soaking up the life-giving rays of the comforting sun. A large speckled gull landed close to her. Readying its dangerous beak, it stalked slowly forward; the mousemaid watched it from between her paws. Within a neck-length of her prostrate body the sea gull stood upon one webbed foot and began bringing its beak down in an exploratory peck.

Thwack!

She swung the wet-sand-weighted end of the rope. It was knotted and her aim was good. The rope's end thudded solidly into the bird's right eye. With a squawk of pain and distress the sea gull did an awkward running takeoff, flopping into the air and dispersing its alarmed companions.

The little mousemaid began dragging herself laboriously up the beach, her throat parched, mouth dry, head aching, limbs battered almost numb by the pounding seas. She reached a tussock of reedgrass in the dry sand above the tideline. Pulling the grass about her, she lay down in the safety of its shelter. As sleep descended upon her weary body, strange thoughts flooded her mind. She could not remember who she was, she had no name she could recall; apart from the stormy seas that had tossed her up, there was no memory of anything—it was all a cloudy gray void. Where had she come from? Where was she now? What was she doing here? Where was she going? Her last thought before sleep enveloped her brain was that she was a fighter. She could beat off a large sea gull with a rope's end, even lying stranded and half-dead from exhaustion, and she had survived the sea.

She was alive!

4

Dawn arrived clad in hushed rosiness upon the wake of storm-torn night. Abbot Bernard had not lain abed, he was up and about. Concern for his beloved Redwall had driven sleep from his mind; the ravages of gale-force winds and rain would need repairing. He made a swift tour of inspection, finishing up on the east battlements. Leaning back upon the strongly hewn stones, Bernard allowed himself a sigh of relief. There was not much that any weather conditions, no matter how severe, could do to the Abbey. However, there were broken branches and wrecked tree limbs overhanging the ramparts to the east and north, with here and there some ill-fated sapling or hollow woodland monarch toppled against the walls. Inside, the grounds had largely been protected by the outer structure—a few crops flattened, fruit bushes in disarray and a loose window shutter on the gatehouse blown awry. The Father Abbot descended the wallsteps thankfully and went to summon Foremole to head a repair crew. They could attend to the damage after breakfast.

The calm after the storm also had its effect upon the

inmates of Redwall Abbey. Young creatures tumbled out of the Abbey building into the sunlit morning. Whooping and shouting, they teemed into the orchard to gather fruit brought down by the winds of the gale. The otter twins Bagg and Runn frisked and bounded around the apple and pear trees to the strawberry patch, then lay on their backs, squeaking with laughter as they gobbled up the juicy fruit, inventing fictitious reasons as to why the berries were lying there.

"Heehee, look what was blown down from the strawberry trees by the wind last night. Heeheehee!"

Durry Quill, Gabe Quill's little nephew, joined them. He sat in the strawberry patch, trying to decide which was the biggest berry, eating all the possible candidates as he listened to the otters. Durry was not at all sure whether he should believe they had come from a strawberry tree.

"Strawb'rry trees, I don't see no strawb'rry trees. Where be they?"

Bagg coughed hard to stop himself tittering. He put on a serious face as he explained the logic of fictitious strawberry trees to the puzzled little Durry.

"Teehee, er harumph! What? You never see'd a strawb'rry tree. Dear oh dear. Why, they're great giant things with blue speckly leaves, very light of course, only weigh as much as two goosefeathers. That's why the wind blowed 'em all away. Whoosh! Straight o'er the top of the Abbey walls."

The gullible Durry looked from one to the other, half convinced.

Runn nodded serious agreement and continued the story. "Sright, I see'd it meself from the dormitory window. Way away they blowed, all those poor old great strawb'rry trees, carried off by the wind to the Gongleboo mountains where the Grunglypodds live."

A half-eaten strawberry dropped from Durry's open mouth. "Grunglyboo's mountain where Gronglepodds live, where be that?"

Under a nearby pear tree Dandin stood paws on hips with his friend, young Saxtus the harvest mouse. Both smiled as they listened to the two otters leading Durry Quill astray with their tall tales. Saxtus bit into a windfall pear and grimaced.

"Don't know why we came out here to eat fruit. Most of these windfalls aren't even ripe yet. Taste this pear, hard as a rock."

Dandin sat down with the otters and Durry. "No, thanks, I'll try my luck with all these berries that fell from the strawberry trees." He looked over the top of a large strawberry at Bagg and Runn. "Strawberry trees indeed! You two should be ashamed of yourselves, telling a poor little hedgehog such whopping great fibs."

Saxtus sat down with them, keeping his normally solemn face quite straight. "Dandin's right, y'know. Otters that tell lies get carried off by the big pink Waterbogle."

Bagg tossed a strawberry into the air. It missed his mouth and bounced off his nose as he remarked airily, "Oh the pink Waterbogle. We've been carried off twice this summer by him, haven't we, Runn?"

Runn giggled. "Teeheehee! I'll say we have. We told him so many whoppers he said he's not carrying us off anymore."

From the direction of the damson and plum trees Simeon's voice interrupted.

"Saxtus! Dandin! Brother Hubert wants you for your Redwall history and recording lessons. He is not getting any younger, and someday we will need a new recorder; traditions must be upheld. Come on, young scamps, I know you're there!"

The two young mice dropped flat in the strawberry patch, Dandin holding a paw to his lips.

"Shush! It's Simeon. Lie low—he might go away."

The steady pawsteps of the blind herbalist came nearer. Simeon called again.

"Come on, you two. I know you're hiding in the strawberry patch."

Saxtus tugged Bagg's tail and winked at the young otter. Bagg winked back as he called out, "It's Bagg and Runn, Simeon. We're the only ones here."

Simeon appeared, chuckling. "I'm going to count to

three, and if you two otters and that nephew of Quill's aren't off to the Abbey kitchen to help with the chores, I'll tell Mother Mellus to come and fetch you with a hazel twig. As for Saxtus and Dandin, unless you want me to give you an extra lecture on the value of nightshade and campion as herbs, you'll come out now and stop lying there trying to breathe lightly. I may not have eyesight but my ears and nose have never deceived me yet."

Saxtus and Dandin stood up ruefully, wiping away dew from their novices' habits. Wordlessly they followed Simeon to the gatehouse at the entrance to the outer walls. Simeon strode boldly ahead, a smile hovering about his lips.

"Hmm, pity the strawberry trees got blown away in the storm. You could have climbed up one and hidden in its branches."

Brother Hubert sat at his desk in the gatehouse. Though Redwall Abbey was of no great age, he was surrounded by old books, parchments and scrolls. Dust was everywhere. It settled in layers on furniture and shelf alike, providing a fine patina to the tomes and volumes piled willy-nilly, coating the yellowed parchments and writing materials, lazily drifting in a slow swirl around the morning sunlight shafts flooding through the window. Hubert kept his head bent to the task of recording the Abbey's daily life, the long feathered quill pen waving back and forth as he wrote. Saxtus and Dandin stood in front of him, listening to the scratch of quill on parchment, keeping a respectful silence until Brother Hubert spoke to them. Looking over the top of his spectacles, Hubert blinked severely.

"What is punctuality?"

Saxtus spoke out. "The respect we show other creatures by being on time."

"Hmm, you two young Brothers have more respect for strawberries than you do for me, is that not right?"

Saxtus and Dandin stood in silence. Brother Hubert put aside his pen.

"Tell me in turn our Abbey charter. Dandin, you may begin."

Dandin swallowed hard, looked at the ceiling for inspiration, shuffled his paws and began hesitantly.

"Er, to be Brothers and Sisters of peace and goodwill, er, living together in harmony under the protection of Redwall Abbey, er, er, forsaking all unnecessary forms of violence, not only to Mossflower, its trees, grasses, flowers and insects, but to all living creatures . . ."

Brother Hubert nodded at Saxtus to continue. He did so with much more confidence and less hesitancy than Dandin.

"To help and comfort the dispossessed, harbor orphans and waifs, offer shelter to all creatures alike, give clothing, warmth and food to any beast or creature that is deemed in need of such. To educate and learn, particularly in the healing arts, comfort the sick, nurse the injured and help the wounded . . ."

Dandin received Brother Hubert's nod to continue from Saxtus.

"Er, er, help the wounded. . . . Er, lessee now, er. . . . Oh yes! To take our food from the earth and replenish the land by caring for it, er, husbanding crops and living in harmony with the, er, seasons always. To honor and protect our friends and brethren, only raising paw to do battle when our life at Redwall is threatened by treachery and the shadow of war; at these times every Redwall creature should show courage, fortitude and obedience to the Father Abbot. Albeit the taking of another life must always be justified and never carried out in a wanton manner."

Brother Hubert came out from behind his desk.

"Well done, Saxtus, and very clearly spoken. As for you, young Dandin, you stammer and hesitate, you seem to have difficulty in remembering—except, that is, until you come to the part that deals with treachery, war and battle."

Dandin looked down at the floor, gnawing at the side hairs of his paw.

Brother Hubert leaned back against the desk, took a

beaker of cordial, blew some dust from its rim and took a sip before continuing.

"Right, Saxtus. Tell me what has been going on in Great Hall for three seasons now."

Saxtus stroked his chin thoughtfully.

"Going on . . . Great Hall . . . er, er. Oh, is it the making of some cloth picture? Is that what you mean, Brother Hubert?"

Brother Hubert polished his spectacles upon his habit sleeve.

"I don't know, are you asking me or telling me? My my, what a pair of little puddenheads. See if you can tell him, Dandin."

This time it was Dandin's turn to brighten up.

"In Great Hall for the past three seasons, actually it's three and a half, the Brothers and Sisters, also many woodlanders, are combining their skills to make a wonderful tapestry. This will depict our founder, Martin the Warrior, showing how he battled with villainous vermin, foxes, rats, stoats, ferrets and weasels, even a huge wildcat like that awful Tsarmina. Martin the Warrior wasn't bothered by those evil beasts, oho no; he got his famous sword and buckled on his bright armor, took up his shield and drove them from Mossflower country. Wham! Blatt! He whirled his deadly blade, the rats screamed, the foxes dived into hiding. *Swish! Chop*! Martin was right after them and he whirled his sword an—"

"Enough, enough, you bloodthirsty young scamp. How do you know all this?"

Dandin smiled. A reckless light burned in his bright eyes.

"Because the father of my father's father was Gonff the Prince of Mousethieves, Martin the Warrior's famous companion. He could steal the nose from under your eyes while you were watching and he was a great balladmaker."

Brother Hubert nodded wisely. "Yes indeed, an unusual fellow, by all accounts—thief, rogue, warrior, questor, but all for the good of other creatures. He married the lovely Columbine, if my memory serves me rightly, so he could not have been too bad a creature. Never let me catch you stealing, young Dandin. Wait, there was something I meant to tell you. Ah yes, I have it here somewhere."

He began rummaging among piles of old records until the dust flew, finally coming up with a small object. By this time all three were coughing and spluttering amid the dust. Hubert shepherded them outside into the cool shadow of the ramparts before he presented Dandin with the item. It was a small flute, beautifully made from a piece of straight applewood, bored out by a red-hot iron rod and wonderfully carved, and it had an ornamental letter "G" near the mouthpiece.

"I was looking through some ancient records," Brother Hubert explained. "They said that the family of Gonff lived down at old Saint Ninian's church for six generations. Before Gonff moved away from Redwall Abbey, however, he was presented with a flute by Abbess Germaine, our first Abbey Mother. But apparently Gonff thought it was far too splendid and fancy for him—he preferred a reed flute—so he left this behind. I think this is the flute; it carries his initial and looks very old. I'm sure it belongs rightly to you, Dandin. Do you think you can play it?"

Dandin gazed at the flute, his eyes shining. "I'll certainly try, Brother."

Hubert dusted his habit before returning to the gatehouse.

"Good, perhaps we'll hear you at the Abbot's Midsummer Jubilee feast?"

Saxtus squinted at the sun. "When's that, Brother?"

"Three days hence, though some of the older Brothers and Sisters have been planning it for quite a while now. Our Father Abbot is very modest and does not want to cause too much fuss, so we have kept it quiet; we didn't want to get you young ones too excited. Still, I suppose you've got to know at some point . . ."

Both young mice leapt for joy, hugging each other and laughing aloud at the prospect of the great event.

"Hurray! Abbot Bernard's Jubilee feast. Redwaaaaaaalll!"

Brother Hubert's dry, dusty old features broke into a wide grin.

"Go on now, be off with the pair of you. No doubt you'll be needed to help with the preparations."

Sister Sage was not on duty serving breakfast that morning. She took herself off for a breath of fresh air on the ramparts, enjoying the soft breeze that drifted over Mossflower Woods.

She came down from her morning stroll along the walltop to join Brother Hubert, and together they watched the two young mice hopping and leaping like wild crickets, across the sunlit lawns and flower beds, toward the Abbey kitchens.

Sister Sage chuckled and shook her head. "Cowslips! Look at those two young 'uns, would you! It makes you feel good to be alive on a summertide."

With that, she hopped off after them, capering madly despite her long seasons. Brother Hubert attempted a small caper, until dust arose from his habit and his glasses fell off. He looked about quickly to see no creature had been watching, then hurried into his gatehouse.

5

The midday sun glinted off the waters of the far northwest sea as thick-headed revelers from the previous night hauled anchors to sail out and scour the seas or range the coasts in their constant search for plunder and booty, slaves and trinkets. Gabool the Wild watched them from the high window of his banqueting hall, *Waveblade, Blacksail, Rathelm* and *Greenfang*, four good craft laden with the rakings and scrapings of seas and oceans, murderers all.

Gabool had conferred captaincy of the *Greenfang* on Garrtail, an up-and-coming member of the searat brethren, but dull and wholly servile to his master Gabool, Lord of all Waters. Dull Garrtail might be, but Gabool knew that it would not stop him gossiping to the master of the *Darkqueen*, Saltar, brother of Bludrigg. Garrtail knew that the *Darkqueen* habitually ranged the seas to the south; he would make sure his path crossed with Saltar. There was little doubt the corsair master of *Darkqueen* would hear the tale of his brother's death, chapter and verse.

Gabool tore at a leg of roasted kittiwake and chewed reflectively. Saltar had the reputation of being a hard searat to cross. Though they had never matched blades, Gabool knew Saltar to be a corsair hook fighter, using a vicious metal hook to impale opponents before slaying them with his curved sword. Gabool spat the meat away and hurled the kittiwake leg out of the window, watching it bounce off rocks on the sheer face until it hit the sea below.

He laughed slyly. Two could play at that game!

Taking a long dagger from his waist sash, Gabool went to the far end of the hall. A colored cloth wall hanging, held outward by a wooden rail near the ceiling, reached from on high down to the floor. Gabool pushed it to one side and found the crack in the stonework behind it. He jammed the long dagger, handle first, into the crack so that it was wedged, with the blade pointing outward, then let the wall hanging fall back into place. Though he was a renowned fighter and a fearless one, Gabool never took chances, particularly since the incident with the mousemaid. Standing back, Gabool surveyed the trap. Good, the wall hanging looked like any other in the hall, perfectly harmless.

Now his restless eye was caught by the great bell. He wandered around its wide perimeter, fascinated by the object. Surely no Searat King had ever taken such a magnificent prize. Gabool pinged it with his long curving claws, sounded it by banging his rings and bracelets upon its brazen surface, amazed by the clear musical noises it made, tingling, humming and vibrating. He bared his lips. Leaning close in, he bit lightly at it, making his gold teeth reverberate with the echoes from the bell. Gabool stroked the cool curving object as he crooned softly.

"Speak to me, beauty, we must get to know each other well. I am Gabool the Wild, your owner, but you need not fear me. Your voice will call to my feet one day, your tones will terrify my enemies. You will be the voice of Gabool when I set you atop of my fort and let your tongue swing free. Then, ah then, you will boom out across the waves so that all the seas will know Gabool is King."

On a sudden impulse Gabool dashed off. Slamming the door behind him, he took the downward stairs three at a time, deeper and deeper into the depths of his own lair. Two guards were standing at the entrance to the prison cells. Gabool whirled upon them with a snarl.

"Get out of my sight and leave me alone here!"

As the guards fled, Gabool made his way to a cell that was little more than a cage. He lounged against the bars, grinning at the pitiful creature locked up inside.

"Well, bellmaker, ready to work for me yet?"

Joseph the Bellmaker was chained by his waist to the wall. The floor of the subterranean cell was awash with sea water which seeped through from outside. Joseph had once been a powerful, well-fleshed mouse, but now his cheeks were sunken and dark circles formed around his eyes. Starvation and ill treatment had taken their ruthless toll on the bellmaker, though as he raised his head, both eyes burned with remorseless hatred for his captor.

"I would sooner be eaten by the fishes of the sea than serve you, rat."

Gabool continued as if he had not heard the prisoner. "You can do it, Joseph, I know you can. A bell tower strong enough to hold the great bell, right on top of my fort, where the whole world will hear it."

Joseph pulled forward, straining at the chain in the enclosed space, his voice shaking with pent-up rage.

"Never. I would not soil my paws with your mad ideas and evil schemes. That bell was made for the badger, the Lord of Salamandastron, enemy of all sea-scum. It will never ring for you!"

Gabool drew his sword and clashed it against the cell bars.

"Hell's guts! D'you think I care who it was made for, you fool? The bell is mine now, mine to do what I like with. Its voice will sound for me alone. I, Gabool, Warlord of the Waves, say this!"

Joseph slumped down, shaking his head in despair.

"You're mad, completely insane and evil. Kill me, do

what you want with me, I don't care anymore."

Gabool sheathed his sword. Drawing close to the bars he whispered low, "And your daughter?"

The bellmaker's face betrayed the agony his mind was suffering.

"No, please! You wouldn't harm her, you couldn't! She's so young and, and. . . . Don't you dare hurt my daughter!"

Gabool now sorely regretted drowning the bellmaker's daughter. Still, if the old buffoon thought she was alive, there might be a bit of fun here. Gabool decided to toy with his victim.

"If you build my bell tower I will let you see her again, but not until you've carried out the work."

Joseph tugged at the chain. He bit his lip until blood showed, torn by the decision he knew he had to make.

"Gabool, listen. I would not put a single stone atop another for you. Why? Because it would mean death, torture or slavery for countless other good creatures. Don't you understand, rat, my conscience would not let me, after I saw what they did to the Captain and crew of our ship when searats captured us. I know it means that I may never see my young one again. It tears my heart apart, but I must do the right thing for the sake of others."

Gabool summoned up all his cunning, his black soul driving him on to wickedness, belying the smile on his face as he threw his claws wide.

"Haharr, very stubborn, Joseph, but I can see that you're a good creature. Sometimes I wish that I'd never been born wicked, but decent like you. I suppose I'll have to think of somethin' else now. But hark, bellmaker, I'm sure you'd like to see your daughter again, wouldn't you, matey?"

Tears of gratitude beaded in the unsuspecting prisoner's eyes. "She means more to me than anything. Please let me see her!"

Gabool took the keys from a wallspike. "Hell's gates! I must be getting soft in me old age. Come on, then."

They stood in the banqueting hall, barbarian and bellmaker. Joseph looked around him, dragging his chains as he did.

"Where is she?"

Gabool touched the great bell with his sword. "Not so fast, shipmate. If you won't build me a bell tower, then at least tell me what these little pictures and strange words round the top 'n' bottom of my bell mean."

Joseph shuffled anxiously around the bell, his mind preoccupied with thoughts of his daughter as he reluctantly read off the rhyme at its base.

"I will ring for wedding times, when two hearts unite.
I will toll the hours out, all daytime and through night.
I will wake good creatures up, from their beds each morning,
Or toll when they're in danger, a clear and brazen warning.
For all the family, son and daughter, husband and goodwife,
I will boom a sad farewell, when they must leave this life.
For many great occasions, for many different reasons,
Listen and my voice you'll hear, throughout the changing seasons.
Though I may boom, clang, peal or toll, command and use me well.
But hark, beware the evil ones who would misuse the bell."

Gabool stared hard at Joseph. "Trash! I'll have it filed off one day. What about the little drawin's an' pictures round the top, what do they mean, bellmaker?"

Joseph spread his shackled paws. "Only the Lord of Salamandastron knows that. He gave me a parchment with those drawn upon it. Who knows what goes through the minds of the great badger rulers of the fire mountain;

they are creatures of destiny. I've told you all I know, now can I see my daughter?"

Gabool led him to the open window.

"Of course, matey, I can't show you the exact spot where she lies, but I can show you how to find her . . ."

For Gabool it was but the work of a moment, one swift push!

In the late afternoon the mousemaid cast a long shadow as she wandered the deserted beach alone. Hunger, thirst and attacks of myriad gnats and sandflies had wakened and forced her to desert the hiding place. Over one shoulder she still carried the knotted rope. A long line of pawprints in the sand behind her emphasized the desolation of sea, sand and sky, seemingly inhabited only by predatory seabirds. She had tried gnawing at some young seaweed washed up on the tideline, but the heavy salt taste in the maiden's dry swollen mouth caused her to spit it away. Swaying slightly, she shielded her eyes from the hot orb of the sun and gazed about. Fresh water was nowhere to be had. Turning inland, she made her weary way toward a large outcrop of sand dunes to the south.

Some perverse dogged spirit drove the mousemaid onward, though often she would be toppled over by the hot shifting sand of the dunes. Rolling downhill, she would pick herself up, wipe grit from her eyes and begin climbing again. It was on top of one difficult dune she encountered the first sign of life that was not a seabird. It was a small lizard, eyes half-closed, basking in the heat. The reptile did a sideways shuffle, watching her warily. The maiden tried several times to communicate, managing only a croaking noise. The lizard's head weaved from side to side as it snapped bad-temperedly at her.

"You norra frog, you make frognoise, wharra you want?"

The mousemaid managed to gasp out a single word: "Water."

The small lizard moved its head up and down, its throat pulsating.

"Water faraway. You norra lizard, you die soon, never

make it to drinkwater, too far. Soon now they eat you."

She followed the creature's upward nod. Gulls were beginning to circle overhead; the scavengers of the shore, sensing when a living thing was becoming weaker and more defenseless. The maid grasped the knotted rope and swung it, calling at the sky in a hoarse voice, "I'm not finished yet. You'll see!"

When she looked down, the lizard had gone. Without a backward glance she descended the other side of the dune, half stumbling, half falling. The foot of the dune was in shadow. Before her lay a sandy flatland dotted with scrub and coarse grass. The little mousemaid rested awhile in the welcoming shade. Idly her paw sank into the sand as she leaned back. Suddenly she sat bolt upright. The sand was firm and damp just beneath the surface. Realization that she was not on the seaward side of the dunes brought with it the shining hope of one precious thing. Water!

Scrabbling dizzily, her strength failing rapidly, the maid began digging with all paws. Soon she was rewarded by darker, damp sand. Her paws made a delicious scraping noise as she tossed sand out of the shallow hole. Digging with the urgency of desperation, she was finally rewarded with one wet paw. She sat sucking her paw as the moisture seeped through the ground into the hole, forming a small muddy pool. Throwing herself flat, the little mousemaid shoved her head into the hole and drank greedily, disregarding the gritty sand and ooze, as life-giving water flowed down her throat. New vitality surged through her. Gurgling with delight, she lifted her head and found herself staring into the predatory eye of a gannet that had been sneaking up on her.

Thwack! Thwop!

With eye-blurring speed she belted the knotted rope twice into the bird's face. It stumbled, fell over, sticklike legs buckling under it. The mousemaid advanced, swinging her weapon, with battle light in her eyes and a clear angry voice.

"Come on! What d'you want, the water or me? Come on. I'll fight you, you great featherbed!"

The twirling knot struck the gannet a further three times before it managed to flop off into the air with a half-stunned squawk. The little mousemaid felt the blood thrumming in her veins. She tore up a nearby plant and shook it at the sky.

"That goes for all of you. I'll kill the next one that comes after me. D'you hear?"

She found herself shouting at an empty evening sky. The birds had gone in search of less ferocious prey. Inspecting the plant she had pulled from the ground, she noticed that the root was attached to a fat white tuber. Without further hesitation she began munching upon it. The tuber tasted good, something like raw turnip.

Evening gave way to night as the maid sat at the foot of the dune, bathing the wound on her head with a corner of her burlap smock which she had soaked in water from her newfound well. Dabbing at the cut with one paw and devouring a root held in the other, the mousemaid talked aloud to herself, enjoying the sound of her own voice.

"No name, no memory, no idea where I am. Ha! I know, I'll call myself Storm, because it was the storm that brought me here. Yes, Storm, I like that . . ."

She held the rope up and twirled it. "And you are my faithful Gullwhacker. There, we've both got new names now. This is good—I've got you, the shade from my sandhill, water and food."

Storm settled down in the sand as the warm summer night closed in on her. "Wish I knew who I really was, though . . ." Her voice sounded small and lonely amid the scrub and desolation.

A pale golden moon peeped over the dunes at the little mousemaid sleeping by the foot of the hill, clutching a piece of knotted rope, for all the world like some infant in slumber nursing a favorite toy.

6

The famous kitchens of Redwall Abbey were abustle with activity that night. Friar Alder, the thin, lanky mouse in charge of it all, added wild plumjuice to an enormous hazelnut crumble he had just pulled from the oven. Alder blew on a scorched paw, complaining loudly.

"Not enough time. That's all I've been given, just not enough time. Who do they think I am, a magician? Less than three days hence and I've got to supervise a full-blown Abbot's Midsummer Jubilee. Berry tarts, cream puddings, twelve different kinds of breads, cheeses and salads, not to mention a surprise cake . . ."

Bagg and Runn, the otter twins, followed Alder, waving their paws and repeating his every word in comic imitation.

"Breads, cheeses and salads, not to mention a surprise cake. . . . Owch!"

Friar Alder had turned quickly and dotted them both between the ears with a wooden spoon. "I told you not to mention a surprise cake. Now off you pop, the pair of you. Go and help Dandin and Saxtus."

Dandin and Saxtus were being taught the art of woodland summercream pudding-making by a charming little red squirrelmaid named Treerose, though they were paying far more attention to the pretty cook than to the recipe.

"Now, to make woodland summercream pudding we need a deep earthenware bowl. Pass me that one, please."

Dandin and Saxtus fought each other to grab the bowl and give it to Treerose. Calmly she took it from them with a disarming smile.

"Great sillies, you nearly broke it, fighting like that. Right, now pay attention. First a thick coating of redcurrant jelly inside the bowl. Next, roll out your sweet chestnut pastry very thin, like this. . . . Bagg! Runn! Stop eating those blackberries—I need them for the pudding!"

The twin otters bounded away to torment some other creature, their mouths stained purple from the berries. They caught a young bankvole named Petunia and kissed her cheeks until she was covered in purple otter-lip marks. Petunia's mother grabbed them and set about them with a soggy dishcloth. Dandin and Saxtus roared laughing, but Treerose merely pursed her mouth primly and reprimanded them.

"There's nothing funny about those two ruffians. Watch me, or you'll never learn. Now, make sure the sweet chestnut pastry is well bedded into the redcurrant jelly around the sides of the bowl, then we coat the pastry with an extra-thick layer of yellow primrose cream. Having done that, we take the blackberries and, starting from the bottom of the basin, we place them on the cream, pressing just lightly enough to make them stick to the cream. Tch tch, you great clumsy fellows, not like that. You'll burst the berries. Wipe your paws and watch me."

Blushing furiously, Dandin and Saxtus wiped their paws as the young charmer carried on efficiently.

"Now I'm going to coat these thick almond wafers with some light honeycream, like so. . . . You see how easily they stick to the blackberries when I use them as the next layer. There, that's that. All that remains now is for me to spoon the applecream into the center until the basin is full. To finish off, cover the whole thing with a short hazelnut pastry glazed with clear honey to give it a nice shiny crust. Open that bottom oven door, please."

"Owch! Ooch! Yagh! Woop!"

"Great silly mice! Use oven cloths to protect your paws. Out of the way! I'll see to it. You two are as much use as moles up a tree."

Dandin and Saxtus sucked their scorched paws and stood watching, red with embarrassment as Treerose, the perfect little Miss Efficiency, swung the oven door wide, popped the pudding inside and shut the door with a few deft movements.

Mother Mellus wandered over, trimming the edges from a strawberry flan. "Hello, Treerose. How are the two star pupils doing?"

"Clumsy as ducks on an iced pond, Mother Mellus."

Treerose turned and flounced off. The badger ruffled the ears of the crestfallen mice.

"Never mind. Tell you what—if you get me some cider from Gabriel Quill to bake my horse chestnuts in, I'll let you try one each."

The pair dashed off happily to the wine cellars. Mellus chuckled as she helped herself to a pawful of apple, cheese and nut salad that Sister Sage was chopping.

"Poor old Dandin and Saxtus. That young Treerose is enough to turn any novice's head and set him on his tail. She does it all the time."

Sister Sage topped the salad off with crushed mint dressing. "Yes, I can remember a young mouse being like that about me when I was a snip of a mousemaid. Brother Hubert, would you believe."

Mellus chuckled deeply. "What? You mean old dusty drawers Hubert? Surely not!"

"Oh, he was quite a handsome young dog at one time. We studied together under Sister Verity. She was a stern old stickler; 'Hubert,' she'd say, 'stop staring like a hungry owl at Sage and get on with your work.' " Sister Sage patted her rotund little waist. "That was when I fell out of love with Hubert and into love with food. Ah well, that's the salad. What's next? Pears in custard with wild cherries. Mmmm, my favorite!"

In the wine cellars, Dandin and Saxtus followed Gabe Quill. His nephew Durry carried the lantern for them as Gabe pointed out some of his specialities.

"See that liddle keg yonder—aye, that un. Well, that's the best wild plum brandy ever fermented in these cellars. They do say it was made by big Brown-spike O'Quill, my ancestor. Marvelous stuff it is, one tot of that'd cure a drownin' fish. That's why Sister Sage or Simeon are the only beasts who use it—medicinal purposes. That big tun barrel at the back now, that's dandelion beer. Very good of a cold winter's night with toasted cheese. This one here, haha, you must try this rascal. Funniest drink I ever did make. It was meant to be buttercup 'n' honey cordial, but I made it too sweet, so I takes a herb here an' a plant there an' chucks 'em in to bitter it a touch. Mercy me! It didn't go any less sweet, no sir, it started a-fizzin' an' bubblin'. Little uns do love it dearly. Here, try some."

Dandin, Saxtus and Durry stood wide-eyed as Gabe Quill tapped the barrel and drew three small beakers off. The bright yellow cordial popped, fizzed and gurgled as if it were alive. Drinking it proved almost impossible. Gabe Quill stood by, quaking with mirth as the three young ones tried.

"Whah! Ooh, it's gone right up my nose!"

"Heeheehee! It tickles all the way down!"

"Woogolly! It's like having a tummyful of mad butterflies!"

Gabe took a jug over to his cider barrels. "D'you want a drinkin' cider or a cookin' cider?"

"Oh, a cooking one, I s'pose. Whoops, heehee! Er, sorry. It's for Mother Mellus. She's baking horse, teehee, chestnuts, whoo! For the Jubilee, phwaw! That stuff could tickle you to death, Mr. Quill. Hahaha!"

"Well, it's certainly got you young uns all of a-wiggle. You'd never make it upstairs carryin' a jug o' cider. Siddown now an' sip some of this cold motherwort tea. That'll calm you a bit."

Above stairs in the kitchens, Friar Alder was at his wits' end. The Foremole and his team had decided to make the biggest raspberry cream pudding ever seen in Mossflower country. Alder threw his hat down and danced upon it.

"Flour, raspberries, honey and cream everywhere. I can't stand it!"

Foremole ignored him, but a fat mole named Buxton waved a reassuring paw at the harassed Alder. "Burr, doant you a-froight yerself, maister. Us'ns knows wot we're about."

A young mole named Danty, white with flour from tail to tip, climbed into one of the huge copper stock-pots.

"Hurr aye, doant 'ee fret thoi whiskers, zurr Alder. Yurr, Burgo, tipple some o' they rabserries in yurr, an' moind that garleck doant go near 'em."

Burgo turned indignantly to Foremole, who blanched at the smell of the wild garlic Burgo always carried. His voice sounded squeaky through the peg he wore at the tip of his snout. "Yurr, wot's Danty rubblin' on about? Oi doant loik the smell o' garleck noither. 'At's whoi oi allus pegs me nose up toight. Oh lookit, liddle Grubb's fell in 'ee honey."

Foremole fished Baby Grubb out of the panful of warm honey. "Gurr you'm toiny rascal, wot do 'ee want ter fallen in honey furr?"

Grubb waved a sticky carefree paw. "Hurr, better fallen in honey than mud, oi allus says. Baint nothen wrong wi' honey. Bees makes et."

Foremole wrinkled his button nose, nodding in agreement. "Ho urr, the choild be roight, he'm be growen up wisely clever. Stan' o'er thurr an' lick thoiself off, liddle Grubb. Buxton, Drubber, see wot you'm c'n do for zurr Alder—he'm fainted roight away. Doant leave 'im alyin' thurr in yon rabserry pudden mixture."

From the kitchen doors Abbot Bernard stood watching the proceedings, with Simeon chuckling beside him.

"My my, those moles are certainly teaching Friar Alder a thing or two, Bernard. His kitchen will never be the same again."

"Indeed, Simeon. Excuse me a moment, will you? Brother Ash, would you help those little mice to roll that great cheese they're trying to move? If it falls on one of them he'll be flattened. Oh, Treerose, I don't wish to interfere, but is that a woodland summercream pudding I can smell beginning to burn in the ovens?"

Treerose had been bustling about, efficiently attending to several things at once. However, she had forgotten the woodland summercream pudding she had put in the oven some time before. Panic-faced, she dashed off to attend to it.

Simeon nodded in admiration. "Your sense of smell is getting better, Bernard."

"Thank you, Simeon, but I had a double motive. Treerose is very pretty but far too efficient and snippy. It will teach her that even the best of us can make mistakes. Also, I would hate a woodland summercream pudding to be burnt in the ovens, especially hers. To tell the truth—and I wouldn't tell her—Treerose does make the best woodland summercream I've ever tasted."

Treerose arrived at the ovens, grabbed up a cloth and swung the door wide.

"My pudding. . . . It's gone!"

"I smelled the crust edges just begin to scorch so I pulled it out for you."

She turned to see Rufe Brush standing by her pudding, which was set on the big flat cooling slate. Rufe was a rough-looking squirrel, not given overmuch to hanging about kitchens or joining the growing band of Treerose's admirers. He sniffed at the pudding before sauntering off. "Looks all right to me."

Treerose watched him go. What a fine bushy tail, well-pointed ears and powerful shoulders . . .

Mother Mellus banged a ladle upon a saucepan. "Come on, all you Dibbuns. Bedtime now."

Abbot Bernard yawned. "I think I'll join the Dibbuns, Simeon."

"Me too, Bernard. It's been a long day and we're getting no younger, my friend. I'll just take a stroll first and check that all the outer gates are secured." Simeon the blind herbalist placed a paw on his friend's shoulder.

"Right, I'll come with you."

"No you won't. I can sense your weariness. Besides, what could you see in the dark that I could not feel ten times better? Day and night are alike to me."

"You are right, of course. Good night, Simeon."

"Good night, Bernard. Sleep well."

The Abbot went off to his room, knowing that shortly the kitchen fires would be damped for the night, the cooks would retire and peace would settle over his beloved Redwall Abbey.

As Gabool predicted, the ship *Greenfang* had crossed bows with *Darkqueen*, the huge black galley commanded by Saltar. Upon hearing of the death of his brother Bludrigg, the corsair Captain put about, piling on sail and oars as he set course for Terramort Isle. The whips cracked belowdecks as drivers flogged the galley slaves on to greater efforts. The searat atop of the mizzenmast scoured the waves for sight of land; below his claws the wide sails bellied out on the night breeze. Saltar stood in the bows putting a fine edge to his curved sword on an oilstone. Bleak-eyed and grim-faced, the searat muttered beneath his breath.

"I'll send you down where the fish will eat your flesh and the sea water rot your bones, Gabool the Wild. There was never any love lost between me and Bludrigg, but he was my brother, and blood must be repaid with blood."

"Terramort rocks sighted off the starb'd bow, Cap'n," the lookout called down. "We can drop anchor in the cove afore dawn with this wind behind us."

Saltar sheathed his sword and began polishing the needletip of his cruel gaff hook, scowling at the dark lump on the horizon which marked the black forbidding rocks of Gabool's pirate kingdom.

"Ledder, douse all lights. When we're close enough to

harbor, furl in all sails. Tell the crew to arm up and stand ready. There's killin' to be done tomorrow."

Saltar's first mate Ledder went aft to carry out his orders.

With the hook swinging from a neck cord and his sword at his side, Saltar stood leaning on the forward rail. He had never lost a fight or left an enemy alive. Gabool the Wild might rule Terramort and Fort Bladegirt, but Saltar had heard, as had every other salty searat, the story of how he was nearly bested by a mousemaid.

The corsair spat viciously over the side at the curving bow wave. "Lord of all Seas, King of Searats! Huh! You'll find out tomorrow, Gabool. You'll learn that Saltar the Corsair is no mousemaid!"

In the banqueting hall of Fort Bladegirt, Gabool stood giving instructions to three fortslaves, dormice who had been captured in a land raid.

"Stand on his shoulders, you. Polish up round the top where the ring is. You, be still, and don't put yer bare paws on the metal—you'll have pawmarks all over me bell. Of course, you know what that means, don't you?"

Doing his best to stand still and not to touch the bell, the ragged slave called over his shoulder, "Yes, Master. Pawmarks all over the bell mean whipmarks all over our backs."

Gabool slouched down on his throne. He picked idly at a dish of fruits crystallized in sugared honey and poured a goblet of wine.

"That's right, three lashes each for every pawmark. If I were you, I'd rip me shirt up and wrap it round me paws—save yerself a lot of whipping."

The three slaves hurried to comply with the suggestion, tearing up the pitiful remnants of tattered shirts and bandaging their paws with the strips.

A thin gray rat with a patch over one eye came running. "Lord, the *Darkqueen*'s sails have been sighted."

"Where away?"

"To the north. She should drop anchor here by dawn."

Gabool stroked his beard thoughtfully. "Good, are the troops standin' ready, mate?"

"Aye, Lord. Five score to board the *Darkqueen* and sail her off once Saltar and his crew step ashore, fifty archers halfway up the cliff and a hundred more fully armed with pikes and spears to form his reception committee, just as you ordered."

"You've done well, Graypatch. Have a cup o' wine and some of these sweetmeats with me. Dawn will soon be here."

Graypatch pulled out a mean-looking dagger and tested its edge. "Last dawn Saltar'll ever see, eh, Lord."

"Aye, he can go and visit his brother Bludrigg at Hellgates, and you, me old shipmate, you can wear a velvet patch when you're Captain of the *Darkqueen*. Hey, you! Polish harder, put your skinny back into it."

"Yes, Master." The unfortunate slave polished harder.

Gabool laughed. "Maybe you're hungry. D'you like eating fish?"

"Yes, master. I like eating fish."

Gabool winked at Graypatch as he called back to the dormouse slave. "Well, if you don't rub harder, the fish'll like eating you. Hahaha!"

The thin bodies of the slaves shook and quivered with effort as they rubbed and polished at the great bell with all their might. Gabool's jokes were not to be taken lightly.

Gabool and Graypatch took their wine and sweetmeats over to the window, where they could watch the *Darkqueen* sail in upon the tide.

Graypatch watched the savage Searat Ruler and reflected as he sipped his wine that Gabool was becoming more difficult to tread around. They had been ship-rats together since their young days, Gabool commanding, Graypatch obeying—that was the way it had always been. However, for some time now Graypatch had been looking more to his own ends. When a Searat King began murdering his Captains on the slightest pretext, times were becoming perilous; now the patch-eyed rat was sure of it. Gabool was drunk with his own power and had become dangerous; anybeast could be slain at his whim. But not Graypatch. Offers of Captaincy and velvet patches did not impress him—such offers could easily turn into a blade between the ribs if Gabool saw fit. In his fertile brain Graypatch began forming his own plans as he laughed and joked with his unpredictable companion, while all the time the *Darkqueen* rode the waves to Terramort.

7

Dawn broke mistily over the dunes, promising another hot summer day. The mousemaid Storm awoke to find herself surrounded by toads. During the night the well she had dug had filled up with water, and all around Storm the toads were closing in on her and the precious water. She closed her eyes again, feigning sleep. Her paw grasped Gullwhacker, the knotted rope, as she watched them through partially closed eyes. It was a dangerous situation; many of the toads were armed with tridents. She waited until a large male natterjack was practically standing over her before springing into action.

Whop!

Gullwhacker came down with such a resounding force upon the toad's head that he was laid out senseless. Storm whirled the rope, shouting aloud. "Back off, slimyskins, or I'll whack you into the middle of next season!"

A huge overweight speckled toad hopped heavily forward, flanked by two tough-looking young ones armed with the fearsome three-pointed tridents. The fat one blinked several times, his throat bulging and quivering.

"Grroikl! This is our land, this is our water. Grrokk! You are not allowed to stop here. Go now or die, Oykamon has spoken. Rrrebb!"

Storm was not about to go and she did not mince her words. "You can speak all you want, fatface. This is my land and my water, this little bit right here. I am called Storm Gullwhacker. I come from the sea and I'm going nowhere. But I'll fight to stay here!"

Oykamon puffed himself up to full swell. "Grriokk! You are very insolent for a mouse. Krrrr! We are too many for you. If you fight you will die here. Grakk!"

Storm sprang forward with a yell, swinging her rope. The toads backed off slightly. She laughed scornfully.

"Right then, I'll die here, but I'll take a few of you with me. Well, come on, froggies. Who's first? Or are you going to sit there clicking and grocking until I die of old age!"

At a signal from Oykamon the toads advanced. Storm dipped the knotted end of Gullwhacker into the well water to make it heavier. Two toads sprang at her. Recklessly she jumped upon one, knocking the wind completely out of him as she scored a bull's-eye on his companion's snout with her weapon. Two more rushed from behind her. Storm thwacked at them wildly. As she did, one young toad ran in on her blind side and stabbed her footpaw with his trident. Maddened with pain, she hurled herself upon him, throttling with one paw and belaboring with the rope in the other. Now toads began hopping in on top of her, their weight carrying her to the ground, although she fought ferociously every bit of the way. Suddenly a cry rang from the dunetops.

"Eeeeuuulaliaaa!"

There was a croak of alarm from the attackers, followed by the pounding of swift paws. In the next moment toads were flying through the air like birds as three hares attacked with lance butts. Teeth bared and eyes wide, the three tall creatures moved with the practiced ease of natural fighters, their long ears streaming out behind them as they skillfully kicked with big supple hindlegs, each a sandy-colored seasoned warrior, brooking no nonsense from their flabby adversaries. Thudding, thwacking and tossing with immense energy, they drove the toads from Storm. Belaboring and punishing without once using their lance points, the hares defeated the toad band swiftly. Storm sat up nursing her wounded paw as the oldest of the hare trio strode lankily to the well.

"Good egg! I say, young 'un, is this your water? May I?"

Storm nodded dumbly. The hare drank his fill, spitting out the grit.

He pulled a wry face, and made a leggy old-fashioned bow. "Pshaw! Tastes pretty yucky, don't it. Allow me to introduce us. I am Colonel Clary, family name's Meadowclary, of course, but you can call me Clary, everybeast does. This young wag over here is none other than the celebrated Brigadier Thyme, and the young gel is our ward the Honorable Rosemary, Hon Rosie to you. Capital! Now, pray tell me whom I have the honor of addressing, marm, though you're a bit young to be a marm, aren't you."

Storm stood up, favoring her uninjured footpaw. She threw the rope across her shoulders, squinting at the odd trio.

"My name's Storm Gullwhacker. This is my Gullwhacker—d'you like it?"

"Hmph!" Brigadier Thyme snorted through his stiffly waxed whiskers. "Adequate for the purpose, I suppose, but there's nothing like a lance butt for dealing with toads, young mouse—you take it from me."

The toads had begun to regroup indignantly. Oykamon repuffed himself.

"Grrogg! I will collect many more toads, we will be as many as the sands of the shore, then you will all die. Krrrrik!"

Hon Rosie had an earsplitting laugh; every creature present winced as she launched into it.

"Whooyahahahah! 'Fraid we'll be long gone by then, you old frogwalloper. Sorry we can't stop around and be slain, wot! Duty calls."

Oykamon spat bad-temperedly. "Krroik! Go then.

Death awaits you if you return to this place!"

The other toads shuffled forward aggressively, shaking their tridents.

Colonel Clary strode decisively forward. He twirled his lancetip, disarming the leading toad with a flick. Clary's eyes grew hard.

"Right, pay attention, you slimy rabble! We are the long patrol from Lord Rawnblade of Salamandastron. Nobeast stops us—we range where we please and when, carrying out orders. If you take one more step forward, we will use our lancetips, not the blunt ends. Then you will really see death visit this spot. Back off now, marshspawn. You there, leader chappie, tell all ranks to retreat, or you'll be the first to have your gizzard decorated by lancepoint."

Oykamon croaked out some sullen orders, and the toads retreated hastily.

Hon Rosie turned to Storm. "I say, can you walk on that bally hoof?"

Storm tested her injured footpaw. "I'll be all right. Where are we going?"

"Somewhere you can get proper fodder 'n' drink, old gel. You don't want to be hangin' about this thumpin' great wasteland twiddlin' your paws."

Brigadier Thyme inspected the paw. "Hmm. Not much wrong with that fetlock, young mouse."

The three hares carried satchels across their backs. Hon Rosie took hers off.

"Righto, first-aider Rosie to the rescue, wot? Whoohahahahah! I can't resist bandaging things, jolly good at it. Now, some hart's tongue fern, staghorn clubmoss, dab of salt and bind the blinkin' lot up with a few strands of maidenhair fern. There! I'll bet you could trip a mouse mazurka with that little lot on. Try it."

Storm tested the footpaw. It felt very comfortable and easy. "Thank you, Rosie. It feels as good as new."

Colonel Clary had been pacing restlessly up and down. He shielded his eyes and took some bearings from the sun.

"Good egg, ladies. Got all the latest in shrubbery foot

fashions sorted out now? Top-hole, then we can get going. Actually I was thinking of heading nor'east into the woodland fringes. We could have lunch there and visit old Pakatugg. What d'you say, Thyme?"

"Hmmm, yes, why ever not. Best idea under present circs, wot!"

It took some time for Storm to fall in with the hares' mode of speech. They seemed to treat everything in a very casual offpaw sort of way, but they were usually correct in their judgments.

By early noon they had left the flatlands. Behind them the gritty expanses mottled with sparse vegetation shimmered in the summer heat, with the dunes a hazy half-mirage in the distance. More dunes stood out ahead, paw-sinking shifting sand dunes that were difficult to surmount. Topping one such sandhill, they found themselves facing a fringe of pine-clad woodland, dark green and shady, a haven from the glare of the midday sun.

Brigadier Thyme marked out a vast hornbeam and led them to it. He held up a cautionary paw.

"Keep mum, chaps. Old Pakatugg's close—I can feel it in m' whiskers."

A pointed dart whistled past Thyme's ear, burying itself in the hornbeam. From somewhere close by a gruff angry voice rang out.

"You're a-trespassin' on Pakatugg's land. Who be yer?"

"Clary, Thyme and Rosie, the long patrol of the foot 'n' fur Rangers," Colonel Clary answered. "Oh, and we've got a young thingummy with us. . . . A mousegel."

Though Storm tried to see who it was, she could make out no sign of a living creature.

"Thingummy mousegel," the gruff voice answered. "What sorta thingummy? Anyhow, how do I know you're you? What's the password?"

Clary snorted impatiently. "Oh, come out, you old buffoon, you know it's us. Listen, I'll even give you the bally password. 'Pakatugg Treefleet, we bring you good things to eat.' There, now come out, you old barkwalloper."

Storm had to bite her lip so as not to laugh at the odd creature who dropped down from a nearby spruce.

Pakatugg Treefleet was a fat old squirrel. He carried a long hollow blowpipe and a pouch of darts. Sticking out of his ears, wound about his tail and paws and covering all his body were leafy twigs. He resembled a small moving bush with eyes.

"Huh, landotters, what've you brought Paka for lunch?" Pakatugg growled fiercely through the two teeth remaining in his mouth.

Brigadier Thyme sniffed. "We're not landotters, we're hares, and if your manners don't improve, laddie, you won't be dining on oatscones and mountain cheese, followed by berry 'n' barley bake."

Pakatugg nearly tore the knapsack from Thyme's back. "Oatscones, mount'n cheese, where?"

"Hoho, not so fast, laddie buck. Take us to your hideout first. We want to put the old nosebag on in comfort, y'know."

Pakatugg led them into the woodland to a small gurgling stream. Lilacs, wildrose, shrubs and trees overhung the spot, turning it into a shady green grotto, and the rocky outcrop which edged the stream was covered in soft moss. Gratefully they sat down. The old squirrel went to fetch them water.

"Real son of the land, old Pakatugg," Colonel Clary whispered to Storm. "No harm in the blighter as long as you feed him and obey his silly little rules. The chap's an absolute fanatic on secrecy, passwords, blindfolds, secret signs—the bally lot. We'll see if he can get you to Redwall."

Storm echoed the strange word. "Redwall, what's that?"

"Oh, it's a jolly place—you'd love it, all the best mice live there. Hush, here comes Pakatugg."

The odd squirrel set a steaming kettle and five beakers out.

"Rosebay willow'erb tea. Put the kettle on when I saw

you comin' a while back. Now, out wi' the grub, landotters."

Digging in their packs, the trio turned out the promised repast, together with some extra delicacies they had brought along. Storm could not recall when she had tasted a meal so delicious. The hares sipped gratefully at the fragrant rosebay willowherb tea, nibbling at this and that. Pakatugg, however, launched himself upon the food, as did the hungry Storm. They practically ended up fighting over candied apple rings. The old squirrel glared at her.

"Yer a tough 'un, mouselet. By my brush y'are."

"Whoohawhawhawhah!" Hon Rosie gurgled as she poured more tea. "I'll say she is. We caught her tryin' to battle with a full toad army, single pawed. Storm Gullwhacker's not short of grit, by a long chalk. By the by, Storm old sport, where d'you come from?"

Storm stuffed the apple ring into her mouth. "Mmmmfff, that's good! Where'm I from? Don't know really, don't know where I was bound either before I met you. Can't remember my name. Called myself Storm 'cos I was thrown ashore by the storm. Came from the sea, I s'pose, me and Gullwhacker here."

Pakatugg chewed on an oatscone and stared hard at the young mouse. "Y'mean you ain't got no name, no home, you can't remember nothin'?"

Clary coughed politely, struck by a sudden idea. "Ahem! Sad, isn't it? That's why we brought her here. We thought you might be able to take her to Redwall. They'd probably find out who she is jolly soon—good at riddles an' mysteries, those Abbey thingummies."

Pakatugg stood up, dusting his paws off. "Whohoa! Don't get ahead of yer tail there, landotter. You ain't landin' me with no mousegel as can't remember which season it be."

Storm jumped up indignantly. "Who said I want to be left anywhere with anyone? I've got some say in this, you know. Besides, who needs a squirrel that can't make up his mind whether he's a beast or a tree . . ."

Hon Rosie pulled Storm down beside her. "Steady on,

old gel. We know you're the bravest of the brave, and all that rot, but you're in a strange land now, among strange creatures; this is dangerous territory. We're only trying to get you back to your own bally kind. I mean, what better for one than to be with one's own creatures, eh?"

Pakatugg gathered up the kettle and beakers. "Huh, y'can dress it up whichway you likes, I'm not bein' saddled with no mindless mouse, by the great' ornbeam I'm not!"

For the first time, Storm felt alone and unwanted. She walked off out of the squirrel's bower into the surrounding trees, swinging her rope.

"Me and Gullwhacker don't need anybeast. We're all right."

Brigadier Thyme eyed the squirrel coldly. "Now see what you've done, bucko."

Pakatugg pulled his tail over his head and chewed the end. "Oh, all right, then. But mark, you landotters ain't havin' things all yer own way, by cracky yer not!" Cupping his paws he called to Storm: "Come on back 'ere, mouse, afore you ferget who we are. I'll take you to Redwall Abbey, but only on certain conditions . . ."

Storm had turned and was walking back. "Conditions, what conditions?"

Pakatugg turned to the hares. "Grub! I need food fer the journey, nice grub like you landotters carry, so I'll take her if you give me all the food out o' those havvysacks."

Clary twitched his whiskers. "I say, steady on. What'll we eat?"

"Oh, we can live off the jolly old land until we make it back to Salamandastron," Hon Rosie interrupted. "We've done it before."

Brigadier Thyme emptied his knapsack out. "So be it. What else, squirrel?"

"Hah well, I don't want everybeast in the world knowin' where my gaff is, see—my home's me own secret. So I want the mouse blindfolded when I take 'er to Redwall, so's she can't find the way back to this place."

Hon Rosie looked at Storm. "You can use your Gullwhacker as a blindfold."

Storm nodded agreement. She was becoming curious about this place called Redwall Abbey. Pakatugg made his final demand.

"Lastly, I don't stir paw until tomorrow dawn cracks—take it or leave it."

Clary waited for Storm's nod of assent before he spoke.

"Righto, you old vagabond, but you take jolly good care of this mousegel, d'you hear. She's got all the makin's of a top-flight warrior."

Within a very short time Pakatugg had settled down on the mossy bank and was snoring loudly. Clary shrugged as he, too, lay down.

"Cool and snug here. If old Pakatugg says it's a secret place, then y'can bet a bee to an ant it is. We might as well have a rousin' good snooze; tomorrow we travel to Salamandastron. As for you, young Storm, you're bound for a new life at jolly old Redwall Abbey. What d'you think of that?"

But no answer came from the young mouse. She was curled up asleep on the moss in the green stillness, with Gullwhacker her rope weapon clutched tight in both paws.

8

Dandin was composing songs for the Abbot's feast. He sat in the shade of a great spreading oak, trilling on his flute, running through old songs, tunes and ditties. Saxtus sat with him, as did several of the moles and Redwall creatures. They joined in choruses of well-known songs and called for Dandin to sing more. The moles would not be satisfied until Dandin rendered their particular favorite.

"Sing us 'ee song 'bout zur Gonffen an' 'ee gurt cake, Dandin."

Dandin nodded and picked up his flute. It was one of his own special ballads, telling of how his ancestor Gonff, Prince of Mousethieves, stole a cake baked by Abbess Germaine, first Mother of Redwall Abbey. He trilled an introduction on Gonff's own flute before launching into song.

"It happened in the springing time,
When all the leaves were green,
And once again Abbess Germaine,

A-baking cakes had been.
She stirred them good and mixed them fine,
With honey, nuts and flour,
Then put them out to cool awhile,
Until the teatime hour.
But then along came bold Sir Gonff,
His eyes a-twinkling bright.
A cake he'd set his heart upon,
For suppertime that night.
He took the greatest cake of all, from off the window ledge
And hid it in a secret place, close by the forest edge.
The Abbess came to check her cakes, about the mid-noontide
And found the mousethief with a bow, and arrows at his side.
'Why stand you there, O Gonff,' said she,
'With bow and arrows armed?'
'My good Abbess,' the thief replied, 'You must not be alarmed.
I saw an eagle steal your cake, he swooped then flew away.
So I stand guard upon your cakes lest he returns today.'
The Abbess chose another cake, which to Sir Gonff she gave,
'Take this reward, young mouse,' she said, 'because you were so brave.
And when upon each baking day, my lovely cakes I make,
I'll save a special one for you, for your kind action's sake.' "

The moles fell about, rolling on the grass with helpless merriment.

"Ahurr hurr hurr! Yon zur Gonffen, 'ee wurr a tricky un!"

"Boi 'ecky, 'ee wurr a villyun aroight, a scrumpin' 'ee gurt cake. Hohurrhurr!"

"Come on there," Saxtus called to a mole named Willyum. "What about a song from you, Willyum? You're the champion mole singer, aren't you?"

Willyum heaved his tiny fat body up from the grass; he needed no second bidding. Smoothing down his velvety coat and polishing his nose, he clasped his huge digging paws in front of him and began singing in the traditional manner of the moles, his voice a deep rusty bass, surprising in one so small.

"Oi luvs a woodland stew, oi do; oi do loik apple tart,
An' good October ale that foams is dear unto moi 'eart.
Of rabs'rry cream oi oft do dream, et makes moi eyes to shine,
'Tis a fact that oi loiks anythin, when oi sets daown to dine.
O mole, mole, daown thee 'ole, doant you'm eat none o' mine,
Else oi won't get a bite to ate, when oi sets down to diiiiiiinnnnneeee."

He bowed and kissed his paws to the company as they applauded, wrinkling his nose until his round black eyes were almost lost behind chubby cheeks.

Turning to Saxtus, Willyum returned the compliment. "Now et be thoi turn to sing a song, zurr Sackuz."

Saxtus waved his paws, blushing modestly. "No no, I'm the worst singer in the Abbey, my voice sounds like a mad owl with his beak trapped in a log."

Dandin clapped his friend upon the back. "Go on, you dusty old bookworm, you're as dry as Brother Hubert. Ah, I've got an idea! Why don't you recite us a poem? You've learned lots of them from those old books and parchments in the gatehouse. Go on, Saxtus. Have a go!"

Saxtus remained seated, he shuffled and coughed nervously.

"Oh, all right, if you really must, but I'm not too good at this sort of thing. Right, here goes. This is a rhyme I found on a scroll in the gatehouse some seasons ago, I'm not sure what it means, but I like the words." Saxtus summoned up his courage and began reciting.

"The wind's icy breath o'er the land of death
Tells a tale of the yet to come.
'Cross the heaving waves which mark ships' graves
Lies an island known to some,
Where seas pound loud and rocks stand proud
And blood flows free as water,
To the far northwest, which knows no rest,
Came a father and his daughter.
The mind was numb, and the heart struck dumb,
When the night seas took the child,
Hurled to her fate, by a son of Hellgate,
The dark one called The Wild.
You whom they seek, though you do not speak,
The legend is yet to be born;
One day you will sing over stones that are red,
In the misty summer dawn."

An eerie silence had fallen over the young creatures sitting beneath the oak in the sunlit midday grounds of the Abbey. Saxtus fidgeted with embarrassment as they stared at him. Treerose, the pretty squirrel, was the first to break the silence.

"Well, that was a silly, nasty little rhyme. I didn't like it one bit—there's no story and no point to it. What a load of old mumbo jumbo!"

She shot off up the trunk of the oak, showering them with leaves and twigs as she did. To break the mood Dandin began applauding loudly.

"Hurray! Well done, Saxtus. Very good!"

The others joined in until they were interrupted by Mother Mellus.

"Come on, young 'uns. Bring any of those Dibbuns you can find along with you. Lunchtime! Come on, it's being served in the orchard—turnip 'n' mushroom flan with beetroot and scallions, followed by honeysuckle sauce and acorn dumplings. And I want to see clean paws before anybeast gets served!"

As they washed their paws in a rain barrel by the Abbey's south wall, Dandin questioned Saxtus.

"Where in the name of fur did you learn that poem? It was very strange."

"Told you, didn't I? It was on some dusty old scroll in the gatehouse. I read it when Brother Hubert dozed off, now the confounded thing seems to have burnt itself into my memory."

Blind Simeon joined the friends, dipping his paws into the butt with them.

"Yes, some things have a habit of doing that, don't they? Still, who knows, they may come in useful through the seasons to come. I'd be glad I remembered it, if I were you, young Saxtus."

"Would you, Brother?"

"I certainly would. There is much knowledge in ancient writings. Actually, I was standing near the oak when you recited it. You were right, the words do have a certain ring to them. Oh, and Dandin, would you like something to remember also?"

"Yes please, Brother Simeon. What is it?"

"Remember to leave some of those acorn dumplings for us old ones. We can't make it to table as fast as you young 'uns."

Dandin smiled as he winked at Saxtus. "Come on then, Brother. Hold our paws. We'll lead you round to lunch and you'll get as much as anybeast—we'll see to it."

The two young friends led the blind herbalist off to the orchard, astounded by his perception of their movements.

"Dandin, why did you wink at Saxtus when you said you would take me to lunch?"

"I meant nothing, Brother. Why do you ask?"

"Because I remember a similar wink passing between those two little villains Bagg and Runn, when they said they would assist me in to supper. I ended up in the dusty old gatehouse while they dashed off and scoffed up all the oat muffins with clover butter. But you wouldn't do a thing like that to me, would you?"

This time it was Saxtus who winked at Dandin.

"We couldn't, Brother. You're holding our paws far too tight!"

Earlier that same morn the *Darkqueen* had nosed her bows into Terramort cove. As Ledder gave the order, a double-fluked anchor splashed into the clear water. Saltar the Corsair came ashore with his crew. They were fully armed, but relaxed by the sight of the empty cove. The searats were still wading through the shallows to the shingled beach when the rocks in front of them came alive with a hundred of Gabool's fighters, armed with long spears and cross-hilted pikes. Saltar cursed beneath his breath, but showed no alarm. Standing with his crew, knee-deep in the shallows, he faced the bristling pikes boldly.

"Bilgerats! What's all this about? Where's Gabool?"

Blaggtail, the leader of the shore party shrugged. "In Fort Bladegirt. He said you're to come up."

Ledder waded up level with Saltar, drawing his scimitar. "And what if we choose not to?"

Blaggtail waved his pike twice in the air. Fifty archers stood up in the rocks above his head, each one with a shaft notched to his taut bowstring.

"Gabool said to tell you he only wishes to be hospitable."

The sound of *Darkqueen*'s anchor being hauled up caused Saltar to turn around. His worst suspicions were confirmed—the ship was drifting gently out into open water. Graypatch and five score grinning searats lined the decks.

"Don't worry, shipmate," he called out to Saltar in a mocking voice. "She'll come to no harm. We'll take her for a sail around the bay, while you're jawin' an' chattin' with Gabool."

Ledder made as if to hurl his sword at the sneering Graypatch, but Saltar muttered in his ear, "Stow it, mate. Leave this to me."

Saltar strode up the beach, pushing Blaggtail's pike to one side as he went.

"Come on, let's go and see what his High Lordship wants."

The banqueting hall tables were piled high with food and drink. Gabool threw himself down in his throne at the head of the biggest table. He was wearing no sword and smiling expansively.

"Hey, you seascum, here comes the best Captain in me fleet and his brave crew. Sit down, Saltar old messmate, and you, me favorite waverobbers, pull some chairs up and fill those bellies. Only the best for the best."

Saltar's crew fell to with a will, splashing wine, tearing meat, grabbing and stuffing for all they were worth. The King of Searats indicated that Saltar sit next to him. The corsair did as he was bid, one claw on his saber, eating and drinking nothing.

Gabool laughed aloud, ripping a bite from a cooked fish and hurling it over his shoulder. He quaffed wine, slopping it over the table.

"Haharr! Nought like good food and wine, eh, Saltar? I suppose you heard about your brother Bludrigg?"

"No, what about my brother Bludrigg?" Saltar lied with a straight face.

Gabool tore a roasted seabird apart in his claws, burying his face into the carcass as he gnawed through it, and came up grinning.

"Had to kill 'im. Whipped his head off with me sword."

Saltar's expression never altered a flicker. "What for?"

Gabool wiped his greasy claws in his beard. "Disobedience, bein' too greedy, wantin' to take my place as King. Had to kill 'im. Swish! That was that, old Bludrigg lost his head."

Gabool and Saltar's eyes met, betraying nothing, but each waiting for the right moment. Saltar toyed with a goblet of wine.

"Was he armed when you killed him?"

"No, he was tryin' a crown on for size. Haharr!"

Slowly Saltar stood up, his claw grasping the curved

sword at his side. "I've heard you're very good at killin' unarmed beasts. How about trying one who's got a weapon?"

Gabool's claw began reaching for a sword hidden beneath the table. "Give us a chance, matey. You can see I'm not carryin' a sword—look."

Now it was Saltar's turn to laugh. "Hoho! Then hurry and get yourself one, King of Searats, although I heard that even armed with a sword you were beaten by a little mousemaid . . ."

Gabool sent the table toppling as he kicked it and freed his swordblade, his face a mask of ugliness and cruelty as he launched himself forward.

"That's a lie! A black-hearted lie, and you'll die for it, Saltar!"

Automatically the searats stood back; this was not only a battle to the death between two famous fighters, it was also a contest to decide Kingship.

Gabool the Wild slashed viciously at Saltar; the corsair dodged nimbly to one side, swinging his sword in one claw as he wound the cord of the steel hook around his other and beckoned with it, insulting and taunting in the manner of searats to goad his victim into a false move.

"My brother could've taken you with a cooking ladle, coward!"

Gabool circled, the light glinting off his golden, emerald-studded fangs. "I'm goin' to hang you by your hook and let the gulls rip out your lyin' tongue, crabsbait!"

Suddenly they clashed, sword ringing upon sword. Saltar's hook ripped through Gabool's cloak, pulling him inward. Quick as a flash, Gabool cut his cloak loose with one of the daggers from his waist sash, staggering back as Saltar's clanging blade drove him down the hall.

"You'll die screaming, Gabool. I'll make you call me King before I put you out of your misery."

Smiling inwardly, Gabool allowed Saltar's onslaught to press him backward down the hall, though outwardly the Warlord's expression was grim and he acted as though he were hard-pressed, panting, parrying and dodging the cleaving blade and pointed hooktip. This gave Saltar the feeling that he had gained the upper claw.

"Not as easy as fighting my unarmed brother, eh, Your Majesty?" he taunted Gabool. "But no matter, Saltar the Corsair isn't a mousemaid. I'll finish the job properly, so that when you're hacked to dollrags you'll know it was me who did it!"

Stumbling over footstools, bumping into tables, reeling off walls, Gabool seemed to blunder backward, Saltar's sword threatening to spit him at each thrust, the flailing hook coming to within a hair's-breadth of his throat. Now the King of Searats was down on one knee, a short distance from the hanging wall curtain. Saltar smashed mercilessly downward at him. Gabool's sword, held sideways deflecting the blows, seemed to quaver for one desperate moment. A gasp arose from the piratical assembly. Suddenly Gabool fell, rolled over and, leaping high, snatched a walltorch from its brackets. He regained his stance on the other side of Saltar. Like lightning the corsair turned.

"Aaaaiiieeee!"

Gabool struck Saltar with the blazing torch, driving him backward into the hidden blade behind the wall hanging. The trap worked efficiently; Saltar died instantly, an expression of pained surprise stamped indelibly upon his brutal features.

Silence fell over the banqueting hall. Gabool spat carelessly at the impaled carcass of his one-time enemy. Turning on his heel, he sprang up on the largest dining table. Scattering cups, food, plates and drink with a series of resounding smashes, the Warlord turned upon the gathering of searats. Gabool's eyes blazed, his rings and bracelets jangled, the gold emerald-studded teeth showed in a ferocious grin through his matted and beribboned beard. Pointing to all corners of the hall with his curving sword, he roared at the top of his lungs:

"I am Gabool the Wild, King of all Searats! Who am I, you carrion of the water? Speak my name, you vermin of the main!"

Swords, daggers, spears and pikes waved in the air.

There was not one in all the crowd who dared not shout out aloud: “Gabool the Wild! King of all Searats!”

A pounding upon the hall doors echoed in the silence which followed. Blaggtail threw the doors open, to reveal one of the *Darkqueen*’s prize crew, Shornear, wounded and half-drowned. He staggered in, collapsing in an exhausted heap upon the floor. Raising himself on one claw, he pointed out of the window.

“Lord, Graypatch has sailed off with the *Darkqueen*!”

Gabool came off the table like a springing panther. Seizing the wretched Shornear, he hoisted him to his paws.

“What! How did this happen?”

“Lord, he had it all planned with the others. I would not go along with his wishes so I was thrown overboard . . .”

“Graypatch, my faithful old shipmate—why would he do this to me?”

“He said that you were too dangerous, too wild and treacherous. Graypatch said to us all that anyrat who followed him would at least be able to sleep at night without fearing a knife in his back. He said that you were death to any creature your shadow fell upon, friend and enemy alike. I heard him say that he would take his crew to a place of safety where none could follow.”

Gabool absently let Shornear drop to the floor.

“Well well, who would have thought it, eh? Me old messmate Graypatch, the one searat I thought I could trust, turned traitor on me. The *Darkqueen* was my best ship. Blaggtail, is there any more of my fleet anchored around the coves?”

Blaggtail scratched his chin. “*Nightwake* and *Seatalon* are beached in the north cove, Lord. They both need careening and recaulking. *Crabclaw* too, but she was holed and lost her rudder on the rocks. None of them are seaworthy.”

Gabool scowled. “Where are the rest of my ships?”

“*Waveblade, Blacksail, Rathelm* and *Greenfang* are all on the high seas, Lord, but they should be back by the next full moon.”

The Warlord banged the table to emphasize each of his words. "As soon as they come in, turn 'em round and get 'em out to sea again. I want the *Darkqueen* back, I want to see her heading into Terramort cove with Graypatch's head stuck on the bowsprit and his crew in chains. Whoever does this for me will be made Seacaptain of all me fleet, next only in rank to me." Immediately three rats sprang forward. Gabool hailed them. "Riptung, Catseyes, Grimtooth, pick yourself a crew each. Get those three craft in north cove shipshape again. I want them seaworthy two days from now. Take my houseslaves and chain 'em up as your oarcrews in the galleys. I will hunt Graypatch down, do you hear me! My fleet will track him across the main from tide-send to Hellwaters. There will be no place on land or sea where he will hide from the wrath of Gabool. Now go!"

9

Just over half a day of being tugged about blindfolded by the ill-tempered Pakatugg was quite enough for Storm. She had been scratched by nettles, poked by branches and bumped by trees, when finally the recluse squirrel called a halt for lunch. They sat down beneath a wide-trunked sycamore which had pushed itself a fair living space in the dense forest. Storm unbound Gullwhacker from where Pakatugg had placed it about her eyes.

"Hoi! Get that blin'fold back on right now, d'you hear!"

The mousemaid blinked and rubbed her eyes at the shafting sunlight of the green woodland aisles.

"Oh, go and boil your tail, squirrel. How do you expect me to eat lunch with a rope round my eyes?"

Pakatugg pulled food and drink from his knapsack and sniffed. "Leave it off then, but only for mealtimes—and don't be gazin' all round, tryin' t' get a fix on your bearin's, eh?"

Storm saw that the hares had left a small stone medallion threaded about her neck as she slept. It bore a badger's head and a flat-peaked mountain insignia. She looked up, countering the squirrel's remark.

"Huh, who wants to see your silly old forest! It's not yours, anyhow. It'd take more than a squirrel dressed as a tree to rule all this. What's for lunch?"

Pakatugg sat on the rucksack, clutching the oatscones and flask he had taken from it.

"Well, I'm havin' these oatcakes and a sup o' this, though I don't know what you're dinin' on. I only said I'd take you t' Redwall, never said I'd feed you as well. That weren't part o' the bargain."

Storm could not believe her ears. She watched Pakatugg smugly munching away at a scone.

"I'd share half of anything I had with a hungry creature, you . . . you greedy branchbound old miser!"

"Right, that's it! I've tooken enough cheek from you, mouse! Shut your mouth an' get yon blin'fold back on, right now!"

Storm tried hard to keep her voice level. "No! I'm not going blindfolded and hungry for you or anybeast!"

Swiftly Pakatugg leaped up and fitted a dart to his blowpipe. "Gotcha now, missie. Do as I bid or I'll deaden your paw fer a season wi' this dart."

As Storm stood up and reached for her rope, the squirrel fired. She threw herself sideways, hearing the thud as a sharp dart buried itself deep in the bark of a nearby pine. Launching herself forward, the mousemaid thwacked out with her Gullwhacker.

The blowpipe was knocked from Pakatugg's mouth. He sat down hard, his eyes watering copiously as he clutched the end of his nose where the knotted rope had belted him. Storm stood over him, the light of battle in her eyes.

"First you blindfold me, then you starve me, now you try to wound me. Sit still and don't make a move, squirrel, I don't trust you anymore."

Hungrily munching alternate bites from an apple and a scone, she watched the squirrel applying a leaf poultice to his swollen snout. He was muttering fiercely.

"Huh, me, Pakatugg, lettin' a slip of a mouse break me nose!"

Storm shook her weapon grimly. "Listen, squirrel. I'm no slip of a mouse, I'm Storm Gullwhacker, so don't think you can bully and trick a creature smaller than yourself. I've split this food into two equal halves. You can go where you want and take yours with you. I'll find Redwall Abbey on my own, without having to protect my back against you."

Grumpily Pakatugg stuffed half of the provisions into his knapsack. He hurried off down the dim trail, yelling back derisively, "Yah! I'm glad you did that, you liddle fool. You'll never find Redwall alone; you'll die in this forest wi'out Pakatugg to guide you."

Storm saw the slight humor of the situation. "Aye, and I'd never have reached Redwall being blinded, starved and wounded," she called back. "On your way, you nasty old fleabag!"

The mousemaid ate a leisurely meal and rested awhile before packing the remainder of her provisions and setting off to find Redwall alone. There was no trace of Pakatugg, nor any living creature, just the still, green summer forest. Storm tossed her Gullwhacker high in the air. It landed with the knotted end pointing in the opposite direction to that taken by the squirrel. Trusting to luck, she strode off in the direction the knot had pointed.

The afternoon wore on. Hardly a breeze stirred the leafy canopy overhead as the tiny figure trekked resolutely through the maze of tree, bush and fern, noting from time to time the position of the sun, which she tried always to keep at her back, knowing that if it set in the west she must be traveling east. To restore her confidence, in the enveloping silence Storm tried to hum odd snatches of songs, but she could not remember any. With a careless shrug she pushed on, the soft swish of her paws through grass and occasional birdsong the only sound that fell upon her ears. Once, she came on a small stream. The mousemaid drank and bathed her paws, wondering what Redwall would look like, if ever she was fortunate enough to find it.

Shades of evening turned the forest to a gloomy black-green vault as Storm plodded on, not sure whether she was going in the direction of her goal or traveling in circles. Gradually every tree, leaf and bush began to look the same. Night closed in on the forest and the mousemaid lost her way completely. She strayed from the dim trail and into impenetrable shrouds of wood and vegetation. Storm kept her confidence up by telling herself that being lost in a wood was better than being lost at sea, but the surrounding night and oppressive silence sat heavily upon her spirit. She fervently wished that it was daylight, or that she could meet another living creature. Sitting despondently at the foot of an elm she sipped mintwater from a flask, ate some white cheese studded with dark roast acorns and decided to await the dawn.

Then she saw the light.

Faintly at first, like an elusive will-o'-the-wisp faraway amid the trees. Swiftly and silently Storm made her way toward it. Still some distance away, she could tell it was a campfire of some sort. There was music too. Some creature was playing a stringed instrument and singing a song in a raucous voice.

"If I were a stone I'd lie alone
Amid the earth and clay-o,
'Til some good beastie picked me up
And threw me faraway-o.
Lolly too diddle um
Rinky doo skiddle dum.
There's bread 'n' cheese 'n' cider,
Said the hedgehog maid who sat to supper,
But now 'tis all inside 'er."

It was a funny-looking hare dressed in jester's attire, half green, half yellow. He sat by a small campfire, tinkling a curious stringed instrument.

Storm decided there was no use beating about the bush; she had already met some hares who were friendly. Boldly she strode in and sat down on the opposite side of the fire. The hare winked at her and continued.

"Now my grandpa, he was by far
A dreadful fat old liar.
'It's cold in the river tonight,' he said,
As he sat upon the fire,
'Til my old grandma came along
And hit him with the ladle.
'There's another egg been cracked,' she laughed,
As she set him on the table.
Doodle oo lolly tum
Tiddly oodly iddly um.
I loved a rabbit's daughter,
And she fed me on pots of tea
Made out of boiling water."

Storm laughed at the odd creature and his comical ditty. He twitched his floppy ears.

"Now then, young mouse me gel, what can we do for you?"

Storm shrugged. "Not a lot, sir. I'm lost, you see. Perhaps I could rest by your fire until dawn."

The hare shook his head sadly. "Lost! I knew a woodpecker once who got lost."

"Oh, I'm sorry. Did you find him again?"

"Find him? Of course I found the blighter—that's how he came to get lost in the first place. Who lost you—or better still, who do you want to be found by?"

"Nobody lost me, and I'm looking for Redwall Abbey, so how could an Abbey find me?"

"Hmm, good question. But no need to fret your mousy little heart, young whatsyourname. I'm going to Redwall, so we can both get lost together."

"You mean you're lost too?"

"Who said I am? Don't talk ridiculous. Never been lost in m' life, young thingy. Do I look lost? Sittin' here by my own campfire, singin' away and twangin' m'little harolina . . ."

To stop any further indignation, Storm commented on the instrument. "Ah, so that's what it's called, a harolina. What a nice instrument. I've never seen one before."

"Never seen a blinkin' harolina? Corks, no wonder

you're lost. I say, is that a long patrol medal you happen t' be wearing?"

"This? Oh yes, it was given to me by Colonel Clary, Brigadier Thyme and Hon Rosie . . ."

Before Storm could say any more, a dreamy look crossed the jester hare's face, making him look extra foolish.

"Egads! Hon Rosie, the Honorable Rosemary—exquisite creature, completely adorable gel, doncha know. Did she mention my name by the way?"

"I don't know. What is your name?"

"Tarquin L. Woodsorrel, though she may have called me Tarkers or jolly old Tark. She did mention me, didn't she? You wouldn't kid a chap, would you? Go on, say she did."

Storm saw that the poor fellow was so agitated that she had to lie a bit. "Oh, Tarkers, yes, she did nothing but talk about you."

"Good egg. I knew it. Go on, go on, what'd she say?"

"Er, let me see. She said you were very handsome, a fine singer and a wonderful player, and she wished you were on patrol with her."

Tarquin L. Woodsorrel fell flat on his back, kicking his long legs ecstatically into the air.

"Absolutelyballyspiffinhunkydory! Whoohoo!"

Storm coughed politely. "Does this mean you'll take me to Redwall Abbey, Mr. Woodsorrel?"

"Abbwall Reddymouse, 'course I will. You can call me Tarquin. I'll call you early. D'y'know I couldn't eat a thing right now. Rosie, ah Rosie, I could live on that sweet name the rest of my life without eating."

Storm curled up by the fire, yawning loudly. She did not fancy an entire night listening to a lovelorn hare singing the praises of his beloved.

"Oh well, I'd best get some sleep. By the way, my name's Storm Gullwhacker. This rope is my weapon—actually the rope's called Gullwhacker."

Sleep was some time coming to the mousemaid as she had to lie there listening to Tarquin composing dreadful love songs and plunking odd chords on his harolina.

"O Rosie the Hon, you're certainly the one,
I'll bet my bally life,
With your cute little nosie, beautiful Rosie
You'd make a lovely wife . . .

Hmm, lessee now, what rhymes with wife? Strife, knife . . . life. That's it!"

The fire burned to white ash and red embers in the deep nighttime forest.

10

Almost an hour before he was usually up and about, Abbot Bernard was wakened by the first rays of dawn and a loud knocking on his bedroom door. Hastily stowing his nightcap beneath the pillows, he rubbed sleep from his eyes and tried to look as dignified as a Redwall Abbot should.

"Ahem, the door's open, come right in, please."

Bagg and Runn entered, bearing a tray between them.

"Good mornin', Father Habbot, an' a happy Jubilee to you, sir."

The Abbot hid a smile as he propped himself into a sitting position.

"And good morning to you, young otters. I'd completely forgotten about my Jubilee. It's a good job you reminded me. Now, what's all this?"

"It's your breakfast, Father. Meadowsweet and sage tea."

"Aye, and arrowroot curd with strawberries."

"And barleytoast spreaded with honey."

"Some hot blackberry muffins too."

"And cold willowcake and greengage jam . . ."

The Abbot held up his paws. "Oh, my goodness, how will I get through it all? It's far too much for me. I'll just have the meadowsweet tea for now. How kind and thoughtful of you. I'll bet you haven't had your own breakfast yet. How about you two helping me to finish all this?"

It was no sooner a word than a bite with two hungry young otters. Bagg and Runn sat on the bed as morning sunlight filled the room, doing full justice to the good breakfast they had prepared while showing the Abbot a barkpaper card they had made for him.

"See, there's you, Father, standing on the lawn by the pond."

"Oh yes. What a good likeness, and that's a splendid tree I'm standing by."

"That's not a tree, it's Mother Mellus. Can't you see her stripes?"

"Of course. I thought this one over here was Mother Mellus."

"No, that's Simeon looking for herbs, and this one is Gabe Quill rolling out a barrel of October ale for your feast."

"Why, so it is. Well done indeed!"

The morning blossomed into sunlight fullness, Redwall Abbey stirred itself into life, lazy blue smoke from its kitchen chimneys drifting toward the woods, where it tangled gently to blend in with tendrils of white mist hanging in the trees. Preparations were well under way, flower garlands decked the long tables set out in the orchard. Creatures from the outlying woodlands and fields began arriving, bringing gifts, food and their families with them. Brother Hubert stationed Dandin and Saxtus on the ramparts over the gatehouse.

"Do a slow patrol of the walls. If you see any creatures coming in who might need assistance, then run down and help them."

Both young mice nodded importantly, proud to be helping in such an adult way. They puffed out their chests, frowned intently and with swinging paws set out on tour of the high ramparts around the outer Abbey walls.

Friar Alder put the finishing touch to his great masterpiece. Knowing the Abbot's taste for the savory rather than the sweet, he had concocted an invention of his own, Bernard Bread. It was a vast loaf of wheat-and-oat bread, almost the size of a grown badger. Alder opened the big oven doors as he called to his assistant, Cockleburr.

"Lend a paw here, Cockles. The Abbot's surprise is almost done."

A small hedgehog came running, stumbling and tripping over a long white apron, his assistant-cook's hat falling over his eyes.

"Simmerin' seasons, lookit the size of it. Comin', Friar!"

Together they inserted the long wooden paddles and set them in the grooves either side of the bread tray. Sweating and panting, they heaved with might and main until the Bernard Loaf began moving slowly and majestically toward the oven doors.

"Steady! Easy now, here it comes. Push that stonemason's trolley over here. We'll need something to land it on."

With a gentle thud the trolley received its precious burden. Cockleburr stood back, wiping his brow on the corner of his apron.

"Perishin' puddens, Friar. It's a monster! Lookit that crust. It's like a shiny golden mountain, all crispy an' steamin'."

Friar Alder seated himself upon a sack of flour. "So it is, Cockles. So it is. There's leeks, sage, rosemary, bay, turnip, beetroot, onions, mushrooms of six varieties, young cabbage, fennel, cucumber and corn, all floating in a mildpepper and cream gravy. What d'you think of that, young 'un?"

"Frizzlin' frypans, there's no doubt 'bout it, you're a fantastic Friar, a colossal cook, a stupendous stewer, a . . . a . . ."

"All right, Cockles, that's quite enough. I know I do have a certain skill. All that remains is to heat it slightly before we bring it to the table this evening. Now, is everything else in order, preserved fruits, berry flans, oh, and the Four Seasons Forest Trifle?"

"Just finishin' the pipin', Friar. I got up early and did the pink rosettes and green leaf shapes with the mint cream, and now all I've got to do is the twirly bits along the edges with yellow buttercup cream."

"Good, you carry on with that while I go and check the wine, ales and cordial lists with Gabriel Quill. Always remember, Cockleburr, the right drinks complement the right food. Right food, right drink—success. Wrong food, wrong drink—disaster. Always remember that, m'lad."

The excitement of events to come increased with the advance of late afternoon. A pleasant breeze ruffled the grass, taking the edge off the intense summer heat. The young Redwallers and woodland creatures, joined by some of the more active elders, began an impromptu sports day in the Abbey grounds. Dandin and Saxtus, however, stayed faithfully patrolling the walltops, peering over battlements, scanning woodland, path and flatland, highly conscious of their responsible position. Several times that day they had unbarred the main gates to assist with carrying babies, helping the old ones and other useful tasks. Now they rested awhile together on the northern corner of the west wall, watching their companions at play.

"Haha, look at Bagg and Runn. Trust two otters to win the three-legged race. What a pair of scallywags, eh, Dandin."

Dandin had turned. He was shielding his eyes, gazing up the path to the north.

"Here, look at this, Saxtus. There's two creatures coming toward the Abbey. D'you know them?"

Saxtus peered at the odd pair of figures dogtrotting along the dusty path. "Hmmm, can't say I've ever seen them before. Looks like a hare and a mouse dressed as a ragbag."

"Go and tell Mother Mellus, will you, Saxtus. I'll stand by with the gate open. She'll prob'ly want to speak with them."

Trudging silently along beside Tarquin, the mousemaid had her first view of Redwall Abbey. She liked what she saw. With the dusty brown path running across its front, the late afternoon sunlight played over the structure, giving it a faded rosy glow. Behind the stout outer wall with its battlements and ramparts, she could see the high spired Abbey roof, flanked by lower sloping ones, peaceful and serene, standing homely and solid with the summer green forest at its back. Redwall. Now she knew why creatures talked of it with a reverence; it appeared to blend with the surrounding Mossflower country as a haven of rest and tranquillity, in harmony with all nature, like some gentle giant of a mother, sheltering and protecting her children.

The badger and the two young mice stood out upon the path as Tarquin and Storm walked up. Mother Mellus and the hare clasped paws.

"Well well, Tarquin Longleap Woodsorrel, you old bounder!"

"Stap me vitals, Mellus, are you still alive and growlin', you old stripedog?"

Saxtus and Dandin stood watching as the two old friends greeted each other. Dandin eyed the ragged mousemaid. She stood by, swinging a thick knotted length of rope. Unconcerned by her filthy appearance or the sea-scoured, sand-worn, forest-torn, loose burlap sacking dress she wore, the maid stared boldly back at Dandin as badger and hare conversed.

"So, how goes it at Salamandastron? Who rules there now?"

"Oh, the old fire mountain's still there y'know, strong as ever. The Lord badger there is Rawnblade, biggest dog badger you've ever set eyes upon. Some say he's the image of his great-grandsire Sunstripe the Mace. Ha, what a warrior! He can flay a crew of searats before breakfast, and that's on a bad day. But enough of all this fiddle faddle, old stripehead. You'd remember me at old Abbot Thomas's final jubilee—I was only a bobtailed leveret then."

"Of course, I remember it well. You were with your father Lorquin. Ah, those were the seasons, eh. Who's your young friend?"

The mousemaid stepped up and spoke for herself. "I'm Storm Gullwhacker. This is my weapon, the Gullwhacker."

Mellus nodded courteously, hiding her amusement at the newcomer's confident and forthright manner. "Welcome to Redwall Abbey, Storm Gullwhacker. Perhaps you'd like to be shown around our home. Dandin, Saxtus, take this young mousemaid inside and see if you can get her some decent clothing and a bath."

While Mellus and Tarquin continued their conversation in the open gateway, Dandin and Saxtus walked inside, accompanied by Storm. Saxtus noticed some of the young ones staring open-mouthed at Storm.

"Er, I say, Storm, we'd best go and find Sister Sage. She'll get you cleaned up and dressed nicely."

Storm swung Gullwhacker deftly, flicking the head off a daisy. "Nobody's washin' an' dressin' me up, mouse. I'm all right as I am."

Saxtus disagreed. "No no, you must do as Mother Mellus says!"

Dandin saw something in the mousemaid's face, something which reminded him of himself. He turned to Saxtus.

"Leave Storm alone, friend. If she says she's all right, then she is. Let her be."

As they strolled through the grounds together, young Redwallers sported and cavorted everywhere. Storm watched them with amusement in her eyes.

"What are they doing, Dandin?"

"They're playing. It's a sort of sports day."

"Sports day, playing—what's that mean?"

Saxtus was about to explain when a twine-tied leafball rolled in front of them. A baby hedgehog came chasing it. Storm picked up the ball.

"Is this something for playing?"

The little hedgehog stood smiling at her with all the innocence of a Dibbun. "Gorra see how high you c'n frow it."

Storm spun the ball in her paw. "How high I can throw it . . . let's see." She tossed the ball into the air. As it came down, she swung with the knotted end of Gullwhacker. It struck the ball spot on, sending it soaring into the sky until it was a mere dot.

Dandin, Saxtus and the Dibbun hedgehog gasped in admiration. Storm smiled.

"Good. I like playing. What'll we play next?"

"Yeek!"

Some distance away, Treerose was struck on the back by the falling ball.

Rufe Brush came sauntering over. "What's the matter, squirrel?"

Treerose was furious. She grabbed the ball and came marching over to where the three mice stood. Holding the ball out, she chattered fiercely.

"Who did that? Come on, own up."

Storm did not realize the ball had struck Treerose. She stood forward, grinning cheerfully, and nodded at the squirrel in a friendly way. "I hit the ball high. It's called playing. D'you want to play?"

Treerose went red with temper. "You dirty filthy little ragamuffin, I'll teach you a lesson!"

Swiftly she lashed out, scratching the side of Storm's face with her sharp little dewclaws. Before anybeast could stop her, Storm whacked the knotted rope squarely between Treerose's ears. The squirrel sat flat on her tail in the dust, tears pouring from her eyes.

Storm was perplexed, she rubbed her cheek as she turned to Saxtus. "What's the matter with her? What did she scratch me for?"

Treerose saw Rufe Brush watching and set up a wail.

"Waah! She hit me! What are you going to do about it, Rufe Brush?"

Rufe shrugged. "Dunno really. S'pose I'd better shake 'er paw!"

"Boohoohoo! That dirty little scruffbag has broken my skull. Boohoohoo!"

Mother Mellus's huge paw swept Treerose upright and dusted her down. "Stop that wailing or you'll bring on the rain, miss. Stoppit! You're not really hurt, and if I ever hear you insulting a guest of Redwall I'll dust your tail so hard you won't sit down for a season. Now go and get washed with cold water. Your eyes are all squidgy with whining. Be off with you!"

Mother Mellus turned on Dandin and Saxtus. "And as for you two pickles, didn't I tell you to get this mousemaid a bath and some proper clothes?"

"She said she doesn't want any," Dandin protested.

Mother Mellus eyed the rebellious Storm. "Oh, doesn't she. Well, we'll see about that!"

Mellus took a step forward; the mousemaid took a step backward.

"Keep your paws off me, y'great stripy lump, or I'll Gullwhack you!"

"You'll what?"

Storm swung the Gullwhacker. "You heard me, badger. Now back off!"

Mother Mellus looked over Storm's shoulder. She smiled and curtsied. "Good afternoon, Father Abbot."

Storm turned to see who the badger was addressing. Mellus pounced! The mousemaid was pinioned by two large badger paws, the rope dangling uselessly at her side as Mother Mellus whispered in her ear, "Gotcha, missy! Now let's see if soap and water and a dress will civilize you, you little savage."

Saxtus and Dandin fell about laughing as Mother Mellus carried off a kicking, yelling Storm.

"Yah, lemmego! Paws off, you great lump of an Abbeydog. Fight fair like a warrior, you big stripy trickster. Lemmego. Yaaaaaahhhh. Grr!"

Tarquin joined them, tinkling away on his harolina.

"Oh, corks! Old Mellus has her work cut out there, no mistake. Well then, you chaps—Dandin and Saxtus, isn't it? Allow me to introduce myself, Tarquin L. Woodsorrel at y'service. I remember Redwall Abbey quite fondly y'know. Of course, I was only a little sprog last time I was here. D'y'know, I think a chap could do a lot worse than stop here an' become the jolly old resident hare, wot?"

The two young mice immediately took to the garrulous Tarquin. Dandin especially admired the harolina and the skillful way the hare played it.

"That's a beautiful instrument, Mr. Tarquin. I play the flute—see, this is a whistle that belonged to my ancestor. Do you know 'Frog in the Rushes' or 'Otter Hornpipe'? I like 'Fieldmouse Frolic' myself."

In a very short while, young Redwallers had gathered round Dandin and Tarquin, clapping their paws, hopping and dancing as the pair played merrily, complementing each other with instrumental harmonies.

Tarquin's words proved true; Storm was no easy mousemaid to deal with, as Mother Mellus, Sister Sage and Sister Serena soon found out.

"Garrr! Sputch! Gerrat soap out of me face, you murderers!"

Mellus held Storm firmly by the scruff of her neck as she kicked and lashed about in the tub. Sage and Serena battled gallantly with soap and loofah as bathwater splashed and sprayed all over them and the infirmary floor. Mellus ducked Storm's head under the warm sudsy water, hauling her up for Sister Sage to scrub away at the mousemaid's neck.

"Good golly! You could grow a crop in the muck we're getting off you, missy. Here, give me the soap, Serena. Go and get another bucket of water."

"Arragh! This is worse'n bein' drowned at sea. Grrrmmmfff! Lemmego!"

"Be still, you young rip. I'm soaked to the hide here. Keep her away from that Gullwhacky rope thing, Sage, or she'll cause havoc!"

"Whooshplut! Just lemme get me paws on my rope. I'll show you three torturers . . ."

Slipping and sploshing, the three battled furiously with slippery Storm.

Abbot Bernard and Simeon passed the infirmary door on their way to Cavern Hole.

"My stars, Simeon, it sounds like a fully fledged massacre in there."

"Well guessed, Bernard. You're not far wrong!"

"Still, who knows, young Storm Gullwhacker may prove a clean and valuable member of our little community."

"Yes, clean at least when Mellus, Sage and Serena have finished with her. What about the other one, the hare?"

"Oh, you mean Tarquin. He's to be our first resident hare. He brought a scroll with him from Lord Rawnblade, the Master of Salamandastron. Here, I'll read it to you. It says, 'To Abbot Bernard of Redwall, from Rawnblade Protector of the Shores. It comes to my mind that ties between your Abbey and my mountain should be strengthened, therefore I send this hare, Tarquin L. Woodsorrel, to you. He is frivolous, a glutton, lovesick and prone to composing dreadful ballads; added to this he has an odd sense of humor, a strange idea of dress and is disruptive with other hares. Be that as it may, he is a fearless fighter, an excellent scout and totally honest. I hope you will find his services satisfactory. Give my good wishes to Mellus and all the good creatures at Redwall. May the seasons be kind and bring you peace with long prosperity. Rawnblade Widestripe, Lord of Salamandastron.' There, what d'you think of that for a reference, Simeon?"

The blind herbalist gathered up his habit for the stairs ahead. "At least Rawnblade is truthful. The hare has his faults, but he also has good features. The badger Lord would not send him to us if there was not something in his clever mind. Maybe he fears the approach of trouble and has decided that we need a link with Salamandastron.

I like the sound of this Tarquin L. Woodsorrel. Maybe Rawnblade's loss will turn out to be Redwall's gain."

"I hope you are right, my friend. Your intuition has never let us down."

Early evening found Storm Gullwhacker being propelled forcibly out of the main Abbey doors to mingle with the other young creatures of Redwall. She fought half-heartedly as Mellus shooed her out.

"There now, go and play. My my, you look very pretty now, Storm."

"Pretty? What's that supposed to mean? I feel stupid with this dress on and half the hide scrubbed from me. Couldn't I wear my old burlap smock. Please?"

"What? That scruffy old thing? Certainly not, child. I told Sister Sage to burn it."

"Where's my Gullwhacker? You haven't burnt that too, have you?"

"No, don't worry, Storm. We gave it a good scrub in what was left of your bathwater, and it's hanging out of the infirmary window to dry. You can have it back to-morrow. Now play outside with the young ones, but don't get yourself all messed up again. It's nearly time for the Abbot's feast."

Dandin could hardly believe his eyes. Was this pretty mousemaid in the light green linen habit the frowsy-looking terror he had encountered earlier that day? It seemed hardly possible. He held out his paw to her.

"Come on, Storm. I'll take you round to the orchard. You can sit between me and Saxtus at the Abbot's Jubilee feast tonight."

"What's an Abbot's Jubilee feast?"

"Listen, do you like singing, dancing and as much of the very best food and drink as you can swallow?"

"Yes. Is that what it's all about?"

"You'll soon find out. Come on, let's run. There's Durry Quill—we'll race him."

The two young mice dashed off across the lengthening shadows of the Abbey lawn as the birds trilled their even-song to the setting sun.

11

Rawnblade Widestripe's massive form dwarfed the hares who stood in front of him. The blood of many Salamandastron badger Lords flowed in his veins, and he seemed to fit perfectly into the vast rocky hall of the mountain, seated on his throne with the huge broad-sword Verminfate resting lightly in his hefty paw. The wise brown eyes partially closed as he digested the information from the returning hares of his long patrols. Torches flickered in rockwall sconces of the roughly hewn hall, blending with dying rays of the sun as its fiery orb sank into the western seaward horizon. Silence would follow each report until Rawnblade questioned his scouts.

"So, you sent this mousemaid Storm Gullwhacker with Pakatugg to Redwall. A wise move, Clary. They may cross trails with Tarquin Woodsorrel; the Abbey will be a good place for them both. What news of my bell, Shorebuck?"

"None, Lord," a sandy-hued hare leaning upon his spear replied. "No creature we spoke with knows where the great bell may be."

Rawnblade sighed, resting his chin on the sword handle. "Hmmm, three seasons late and nobeast knows the whereabouts of Joseph or the bell. Searats have the answer, I know it. Only time will tell. Fleetleg, any more about the ship from the northwest?"

A tall, saturnine hare stood forward. "We sighted her earlier this evening, Lord. She was sailing too far off to be certain, but Longeyes says that it could be the *Darkqueen*."

Rawnblade sat up straight. "Are you sure of this, Longeyes?"

The hare called Longeyes lounged at the window, scanning the horizon. He turned to address Rawnblade.

"I'm practically certain, Lord. My eyes see farther than others. It looked to me like *Darkqueen*; no other ship in Gabool's fleet has red sails. If she had cut in closer to land, I would have been able to tell you more, but she tacked off windward and traveled north by east."

"Did you see who was at the helm?"

"It was not Saltar, Lord—of that I'm sure. I didn't get much of a glimpse, but I'd guess by his build it was the one called Graypatch."

"Graypatch? He's Gabool's best steersrat. It could mean that Gabool has left his island. *Darkqueen* is the only ship he would sail in if he did."

Brigadier Thyme ventured an opinion. "M'Lord, if old Gabool has taken to sailin' again, there could be trouble."

Rawnblade arose. He strode across to the window, where he stood gazing at the restless sea ebbing and flowing eternally.

"The prophecies carved on Salamandastron's walls tell of a time coming soon when trouble will become a byword; my destiny and trouble walk the same path paw in paw. Eat and sleep now, my faithful patrols. Our fortunes and fates are written in these rocks. Leave the worrying and wondering to the waves and clouds."

A night mist had fallen when Graypatch anchored offshore. A longboat was lowered to take the reconnaissance crew ashore. Graypatch stayed aboard with Frink, his lookout, always watching north and west for signs of Gabool in pursuit.

Graypatch called down to Deadglim, his bosun, "See if you can find a likely spot, mate—fresh water and cover in plenty."

Deadglim took the scimitar from between his teeth long enough to answer. "Leave it t' me, Skipper. I've got a nose for likely coves."

Mist-shrouded moonless night enveloped Deadglim as he led the shore party forward into the dunes. He peered into the darkness.

"Not much 'ereabouts, lads. Nought but sandhills. Here, Gurd, gerrup on yer paws—time fer sleepin' when we're back aboard *Darkqueen*. Gurd?"

Gurd lay still, unable to answer because of the toad trident lodged in his throat. Immediately a score of tridents descended amid the unsuspecting searats. The screams of two wounded pierced the still night.

Deadglim waved his scimitar, yelling at the silent dunes, "Come out an' fight! Show yerselves, you creepin' bilgewashers!"

Suddenly the dunes echoed to thunderous croaking as countless toads hopped out, armed with tridents. Deadglim knew his challenge had been a foolish one. Throwing valor to the winds, he took to his paws shouting, "Retreat! Retreat! Back to the longboat!"

From the ship's rail, Graypatch and Deadglim could see the tideline teeming with trident-waving natterjacks. Deadglim shuddered.

"Cap'n, if anybeast ever tells you a toad is slow, don't believe it. We barely made it t' the longboat ahead of those slimy devils. There must be thousands of the croakin' scum."

Graypatch turned from the rail. "Set another course nor' an' east, Fishgill. We'll try our luck farther up the coast. Jump to it now, you swab. I don't want Gabool hovin' over the briny at our wake!"

• • •

Gabool the Wild could not sleep. He paced around and around the bell, chopping at midair with his sword, relating his thoughts to the brazen prize.

"Graypatch'll curse the day he was spawned when I catch up with him. I'll boil his skull an' bring it here for you to see, my beauty—see if I don't. Haharr, first Bludrigg an' then his mizzuble brother Saltar. Corsair, huh! He's nothin' but fishbait now. Like the other two, the scratchy liddle mousemaid an' her dear daddy Joseph, haharr! He's the one that made you, isn't he? Gone to fishbait for his foolishness."

Bongggggg!

Gabool jumped back with a yell, then he ran around the bell in a wide circle, searching and seeking, but there was nobeast in the room save for himself. Gradually he became calm.

"Haharr, 'twas only the wind playin' tricks."

Striding back to the bell he stroked it fondly. "Belay! So what if yer do talk, you can tell old Gabool all your secrets."

The bell remained silent. The King of Searats gazed up with narrowed eyes at the figures embossed around the top of the bellskirt.

"Hellsteeth! What do it all mean? Tell me, what's all those pretty liddle pictures, mice, badgers, rats, ships, an' all manner o'things? You tell me; I'm your master now. Speak! D'you hear me? Speak!"

But the bell remained still and voiceless, an inanimate metal object.

Gabool's wild temper rose. He spat upon the bell and kicked it. Still no sound came forth. In high bad mood he strode from the room, turning in the doorway and brandishing his sword at the great bell.

"Hell 'n' gullbait! You'll talk to me afore I'm done with yer!"

He slammed the door furiously and strode off to his bedchamber.

Behind him in the empty room the bell tolled one booming knell.

Gabool's nerve deserted him. He cut and ran. Leaping

into bed, he threw the covers over his head and lay there shivering.

Sleep was a long time coming to Gabool the Wild, but when it did he wished that he had stayed awake. Badgers, mice, searats and spectral ships sailing upon phantom waves pursued him down the corridors of his restless imagination. The figures around the bell had come to life to torment him throughout the long dark night.

Lord Rawnblade too was sleeping. His vast form lay sprawled upon the bed near his armorer's forge in Salamandastron mountain. The sword Verminfate lay upon the bed, close to paw as it always was. In his dream the badger Lord found he was looking at the bell that he had commissioned Joseph the Bellmaker to cast for him. It was beautiful, just as he had imagined it would be, shining with a dull sheen, graven round top and bottom with the poem and the mysterious pictures which only badger Lords could interpret. Now a shape was materializing through the burnished curve of the bell metal—his archenemy Gabool the Wild. Curving sword in claw, the Searat King advanced, ornaments jangling, golden emerald-studded teeth glinting in a fiendish smile. Rawnblade's reaction, even in sleep, was instantaneous; he seized his broadsword and leaped from the bed, striking out with savage force.

Clangggggg!

"Er, I say, M'lord, old chap, are you all right?"

Colonel Clary was at his side. Rawnblade came fully awake, rubbing his eyes with one paw, he gazed down at the sword in the other.

"What? Er, oh, yes, thank you, Clary. It was merely a dream."

"My aunt's kittens! That must have been rather a jolly dream, M'lud. Look what you did to that shield!"

Rawnblade stared at the shield which had been in the way of his swordswing. The thick metal plate had been sheared in half. It lay on the floor, completely severed.

Absentmindedly the badger Lord tested the unmarked blade of Verminfate.

"No alarm, old friend. Go back to your rest—it was only a dream."

"A dream, eh? Something out of the past, perhaps?"

Rawnblade lay back on the bed and held the formidable blade tightly.

"No, this was something from the future. I know it."

Gabriel Quill stood up amid the tables and multicolored lanterns that graced the orchard. He held a tankard of best October ale high and cried, "Righto, everybeast. Let's give a real Redwall toast to our Abbot!"

Every creature stood, raising bowls, beakers, tankards, cups and flagons. The soft summer night echoed as the multitude called aloud in one voice, "Abbot Bernard! Father of Redwall Abbey! Hurraaaaaaah!"

Saxtus sat down with a groan, holding his middle. "Whoof! Shouldn't be yelling like that on an overfull stomach."

Tarquin scoffed as he relieved Saxtus of his plate. Emptying the Forest Trifle, strawberry flan, pear gateau and hazelnut cream junket into his own oversized wooden bowl, he grabbed a spoon and tucked in.

"Haw haw! What's the matter, laddie buck? Little tum too full, is it? Scrumff! Old Tarkers'll show you how to navigate yer way round a bowl of tucker, mmm! I say, any more of that summercream pudden stuff left?"

Grubb the Dibbun mole replied as he nodded sleepily forward toward an overheaped plate of woodland summercream pudding, "Burr, baint no more pudden, zur. Oi snaffled 'ee last o' it. Snurr!"

Buxton and Willyum mole immediately left off eating huge portions of steaming Bernard Bread and dug into either side of Grubb's plate, eating furiously as the baby mole's sleepy head drooped nearer the pudding.

"Ho, save the choild, 'urry up an scoff quick now, lest the hinfant be drownded in yon pudden. Hurr hurr!"

Tarquin joined them indignantly. "I say, you chaps, chew each mouthful twenty times and leave this to me.

Bally unthinkable, poor little blighter bein' drowned in a plate of pudden. Do not worry, young sire, help is at spoon. I'll save you. Gromff!"

Storm tried to stop spluttering Gabe Quill's giggly buttercup 'n' honey cordial across the table. She shook with unbridled laughter at the antics of Tarquin and the two moles rescuing the dozing Grubb. The mousemaid had never been so happy in any of the life she could remember—the food, the delicious drinks, the food, the kind Abbey creatures, the food, the good friends about her, and, of course . . . the food. Never had she tasted such marvelous things. Alternating between Bernard Bread, blackcurrant pie, summer salad, cheese 'n' nut flan, mint-cream cakes and honeyglazed preserved fruits, she held her own with the best trencherbeasts.

Dandin was showing off slightly for her benefit, tossing redcurrants up and catching them in his mouth. He was quite good at it.

"Here, watch this, Storm. Betcher can't catch redcurrants like me."

"Haha! Who can't? I'll show you. Watch!"

Unfortunately the giggly cordial had got the better of her. Storm tossed a redcurrant high and missed it completely. It bounced off Foremole's head and lodged in the ear of Treerose, who was feeling tired and sulky.

"Whahaah! I've gone deaf in one ear. She threw something at me!"

Foremole flicked the offending redcurrant out onto the grass. Taking up a great spoonful of otter's hotroot soup, he held Treerose's nose and poured it down her open mouth.

"Yurr, missie, 'ee doant eat vittles boi stickin' 'em in 'ee earlugs. Daown thy mouth et should be a-goen, loik this, liddle missus."

Treerose was not heard to complain again that night. She was too busy pouring cold water down her throat to kill off the taste of the otter hotroot soup, which it was said could thaw out an icy river in midwinter.

• • •

Most of the eating was now over, and speeches began. Abbot Bernard thanked the Friar for supervising the wonderful feast, also the helpers, layers of table, Gabe Quill for the excellence of the drinks and all present for attending. In response various creatures stood up to thank the Abbot, toast Redwall and congratulate their hosts. Rufe Brush called for some dancing but was silenced by an oat scone; dancing and jigging was out of the question after having eaten so much. So the singing began. Never being backward at coming forward, Tarquin was up on his paws, chewing the last of a celery surprise as he turned his harolina. Finishing the food, he launched into the song of the long patrols.

"Oh, it's hard and dry, when the sun is high
And dust is in your throat,
When the rain pours down, near fit to drown,
And soaks right through your coat.
But the hares of the long patrol, my lads,
Stouthearts they walk with me,
Over hill and plain, and back again,
By the shores of the wide blue sea.
Through mud and mire to a warm campfire,
I'll trek with you, old friend,
O'er lea and dale, in a roaring gale,
Right to our journey's end.
Yes, the hares of the long patrol, my lads,
Love friendship more than gold.
We'll share good days, and tread long ways,
Good comrades brave and bold."

Drubber mole banged his tankard upon the table amid the applause. "Gurr! That'n be a gurt ballad, bringen tears to moi eyes, it do."

Then it was Willyum mole's turn to get up and sing the mole song. He did it solemnly in the correct mole manner and was cheered loudly, though this time it did bring Drubber to tears. He wept unashamedly.

"Burrhoohurr! B'aint nothen loik music to soften a hanimal's 'eart."

Dandin was called upon. He rose and performed a newly written tribute to Abbot Bernard, accompanied by Tarquin on the harolina.

"Long may you rule, Father Abbot,
Long may you reign over all
The woodlands of Mossflower
And the Abbey of Redwall.
When I was a young mouse I learnt at the knee
Of the Father of Redwall,
The lessons for you and the lessons for me
From the Father of us all.
In those good Dibbun days, I learnt many kind ways,
To be honest, strong and true,
And wherever I go, I'll remember always,
That I learned them, sir, from you.
Long may you rule, Father Abbot,
Over all of these creatures and me,
And may we all say in our own simple way,
Have a happy Jubilee."

Every creature present insisted on singing the song again, with Tarquin calling out the words from a scroll. It was a huge success, though Drubber broke down completely and had to be comforted by Danty and Buxton.

"Yurr now, doant 'ee take on so, Drub, owd lad. Et be on'y a song."

"Hurr aye, doant be a-sobben naow. Take moi 'ankerchiefy."

Several more singers were called on to perform. Durry Quill sang the comic song "Why Can't Hedgehogs Fly?" The otter twins Bagg and Runn recited the epic poem, "Otter Bill and the Shaking Shrimp." This led to more demand for poems, and Saxtus was finally coaxed up to recite the poem he had memorized in the gatehouse. Nervously Saxtus stood up, clasping and unclasping his paws as he began falteringly.

"The wind's icy breath o'er the land of death
Tells a tale of the yet to come.

'Cross the heaving waves which mark ships' graves
Lies an island known to some,
Where seas pound loud and rocks stand proud
And blood flows free as water,
To the far northwest, which knows no rest,
Came a father and his daughter.
The mind was numb, and the heart struck dumb,
When the night seas took the child,
Hurled to her fate, by a son of Hellgate,
The dark one called The Wild.
You whom they seek, though you do not speak,
The legend is yet to be born;
One day you will sing over stones that are red,
In the misty summer dawn."

In the silence that followed before the applause, Storm Gullwhacker gave vent to a hoarse strangled sob, which echoed amid the startled revelers.

12

A light morning sea mist hung over the waters around Terramort Isle. The last four ships of Gabool's fleet were returning. They silently nosed into the cove, sails hanging slack, oars shipped as the oily swell carried them noiselessly into harbor. The King of Searats knew they had returned; he had watched them break the night horizon, hours before the mist started to descend. Now Gabool would need all his cunning and slyness if he were to win his Captains over completely. Saltar had never been a popular Captain, neither had his brother Bludrigg; but the fact remained, they were both Captains and he had slain them. Naturally the other four shipmasters, Orgeye, Hookfin, Flogga and Garrtail, would feel their position threatened—they would need reassuring. Once they were happy with Gabool's continuing rule, their crews would follow them into the very fangs of Hellgates. The Warlord knew all this and set his plans accordingly.

The morning remained gray and uncertain as hordes of searats marched past the rock portals into Fort Bladegirt. Gabool watched them from the banqueting hall window, voicing his thoughts aloud. "Look at 'em, the rakin's an' scrapin's of the earth, scum from the wharves, taverns an' cellars, their mothers were bilgerats an' their fathers were barrelsloppers. Murderers, thieves, pillagers, all of 'em. Haharr, they'd steal the very fires of hell to keep 'em warm of a winter night and singe the Dark One's whiskers. Vermin after me own black heart. Haharrhahaharr!"

The Warlord's description fit every searat from the tip of his ragged tail to the point of his scarred nose. They were clad in motley rags, some wearing worn-out seaboots and threadbare frock coats, others dressed in the tattered silks of corsairs. Brass ear, nose and tail rings were much in evidence, eyepatches, skull bandages, missing ears and fearsome scars. But every searat was armed to the teeth; cutlasses, scimitars, straight swords, sabers, claymores, daggers, dirks, bodkins, spears and pikes bristled everywhere throughout the barbaric mob.

Gabool sat grim-faced on his throne, facing the great bell. All around, the banqueting tables were piled high with food and drink; nervous slaves stood waiting, ready to serve their savage captors. The searat crews crowded in. Those who could not find seating leaned against the walls or slouched upon the floor. Nobody touched a morsel of food. An expectant hush settled over all; the King of Searats was not his usual roaring commanding self. Claws settled upon weapons, ready to fight at a moment's notice; it was a taut and perilous situation. The Captains grouped together at one table, Orgeye of the *Waveblade*, Hookfin of the *Blacksail*, Flogga of the *Rathelm* and Garrtail of the *Greenfang*. They were joined by the masters of the three ships that were under repair, Riptung of the *Nightwake*, Catseyes of the *Seatalon* and Grimtooth of the *Crabclaw*. Against these seven Gabool was facing mighty odds, their cold, quick eyes watched him mistrustingly—even Garrtail, who now had his own ship and felt equal to other Captains. The threat of instant death hung heavy in the air.

Gabool's heavy sigh broke the stillness. He stood up,

slowly drawing his curved sword. He dropped it; the bright blade clattered on the floor in front of him as he pointed to the nearest rat.

"You there, matey. You've got the look of a poor old searat who don't have two crusts to rub together. What's yer name, shipmate?"

"Weltskin, sire," the ragged searat said in a puzzled voice.

Gabool nodded. "Well, you pick up that fine blade, Weltskin. My sword belongs to you now. Go on, take it, matey."

The searat Weltskin picked up the sword, his eyes shining. No common crewrat had ever owned such a weapon.

Gabool faced the assembly. Throwing his arms wide, he appealed to them.

"Aaahh, shipmates, what's it all come to? Treachery, deceit an' lies, aye, that's the sad fact, mateys. A Cap'n who scorned me, Bludrigg, an' his brother Saltar out fer revenge, who tried to slay me when I was unarmed in me own home . . ."

Gabool shook his head sadly. "Aharr, bad weather 'n' black days, lads, though I knew all the time those two searobbers was plottin' against me. Still an' all, I offered 'em welcome an' vittles in Fort Bladegirt—their crews too. Why, some of you was there an' ate the same food an' drank the same drink an' saw it all happen. Base traitors they were, messmates. I'd heard them whisperin' together; they wanted it all—my island an' your ships. You Cap'ns there, aharr, I wish you'd been here to see it—you would've sided with old Gabool, I know you would. Faithfulness always has its reward."

Gabool struck the side of the bell with a drinking cup. Twenty slaves bearing chests of plunder staggered in and turned out the glittering contents at Gabool's feet. Necklaces, stones, bracelets, goblets, silks and fine weapons cascaded out across the floor in a sparkling heap. Gabool's quick eyes noted the greedy glances the plunder attracted. He held out his claws to the seven Captains.

"Every bright star has seven true points. You, my shipmasters, my good an' trusty mates, come an' take what you want from this lot. What use is booty an' plunder if a rat ain't got friends he can trust?"

The Captains stumbled and tripped over other searats in their haste to grab what they could. Ripping silks and tossing all they could hold into makeshift carriers, the seven shipmasters bit, scratched and jostled silently as each strove to grab what he thought was more than his fair share. When they drew back, dragging their portions with them, there was still a large mound of loot upon the floor.

"Why, you greedy old plunderers," Gabool laughingly upbraided the Captains. "Snafflin' away without a thought for your crewrats. See if you can clear this lot away, lads. Come on, it's all yours!"

With a wild howl, the searat crews threw themselves upon the remainder of the booty. Scrabbling, kicking, screeching, clawing and ripping, they fought for baubles all over the hall. Gabool laughed madly as he plowed among them. He had won. The plan was working like a charm. Now he sowed the seeds of dissension as he roved among the crews, whispering, "Is that all you got, matey, a few earrings an' a dagger? If I was your Cap'n I would have given you first pick. Ah, but Cap'ns is Cap'ns—they was ever the greedy ones. Hoho, Halfnose, me ol' messmate, did you see that Cap'n Hookfin? He was a-shovin' an' a-pushing your Cap'n Orgeye like he didn't want him to get his proper share. I'd tell Orgeye that if I was you, mate. 'Here, Shornear, what good is two earrings to you, eh? You 'ark t' me, shipmate—that Garrtail, he looked as if he were tryin' to grab everythin' for hisself, an' him only a new Cap'n. I'm sorry I chose him now. If I'd been thinkin' aright at the time, I'd have made you master of the *Greenfang*. Never mind, matey. There'll always be another day, eh?"

When the plunder had all been claimed, the searats threw themselves upon the food ravenously, each one mistrusting the other and all of them feeling more loyal to Gabool than to their own Captains.

The Warlord had yet to play his final card. He banged the bell for silence.

"Now, me lucky rats, I'm goin' to let you in on a secret, so cock yer lungs! There's another traitor, more black'earted than any, but he ain't here this day. What's his name? I 'ear you ask . . .'Tis Graypatch—aye, Graypatch. There's a name for the Dark One's book. We sailed fair seas an' foul together since we was both liddle sloprats, an' now the foul blaggard has robbed the best craft in the fleet for hisself. Aye, the *Darkqueen*, Saltar's ship. Graypatch crewed her an' sailed off in *Darkqueen* behind me back, an' I trusted him like a brother. But here's the worst of it, lads—that ship's carryin' three times the loot in her hold, on my affidavy it is, more plunder'n you could clap eyes on. . . . And I want Graypatch's scurvy head! You can do what you will with the booty—first one to it gets it all—as long as you bring me back the *Darkqueen* with Graypatch's head nailed to the bowsprit. How's that fer an offer, you hellscrapin's?"

Tables were overturned, food scattered, furniture smashed as the Captains and their crews made a hasty exodus from the hall, jamming in the doorway, cursing and fighting in an effort to be first to weigh anchor and hunt down Graypatch and the *Darkqueen*.

"Hoist sail, Ledder. I'll be down straightways!"

"Weigh anchor, Froat. We'll get 'im first!"

"Get the crew aboard, Bullfang. Hurry!"

"Come on, you wavescum. Stir yer stumps—there's prize to be had!"

Weltskin was one of the last to leave, striding importantly with Gabool's fine curved sword over his shoulder. Gabool called him back.

"Weltskin, matey, c'mere."

The searat marched back and saluted his King with the sword.

"D'you want somethin', sire?"

Gabool stroked his beard thoughtfully. "Let's see you swing that sword."

Weltskin swung the sword several times. Gabool looked worried.

"No, matey, no. That's no way to twirl a blade. Here, let me show yer how to use that sword."

Weltskin gave the sword to Gabool. He watched fascinated as the Warlord wove patterns in the air with the glittering weapon. Weltskin's fascination suddenly turned to agonized shock as Gabool snicked the tip from his ear with the sword. Smiling wickedly, Gabool flashed the blade a little closer to Weltskin's throat.

"That's how t'do it, matey. Now do you want to lay about while I does another liddle trick with yer neck, or do yer want t'board ship an' leave this 'ere carver with ol' Gabool?"

A second later the Searat King was listening to the mad patter of Weltskin's paws as he dashed headlong for the harbor and the safety of the open sea. Thrusting his regained weapon into its waist sash, Gabool threw back his head and roared with laughter.

Redwallers gathered in the open doorway of the infirmary sickbay, anxiously peeping in at the still figure of Storm laid upon a truckle bed. Saxtus gnawed at his lip.

"It must have been something I said in that poem. Oh, I wish I hadn't recited the blinking thing now. In fact, I wish that I'd never seen it!"

Dandin patted his friend reassuringly. "Don't be silly. You weren't to know that the poem would have that effect upon her. It's not your fault. Though I must say, Storm is the last creature you'd expect to fall in a faint like that. I've never met a rougher, tougher mousemaid in my life."

Simeon turned from a corner table where he was concocting something from strange-looking herbs and roots.

"Rough and tough she is indeed. I think Storm has been through things that would have killed a lesser creature. She has tremendous spirit."

The Abbot agreed. "She has indeed, though I don't think her real name is Storm Gullwhacker. I wonder who she really is."

Simeon turned back to his bowl and pestle. "That's

what we're about to find out if we can. Are you ready, Sister Sage?"

Sage went to the door. "Mother Mellus, Abbot and Brother Hubert, you'd better come in and watch. Saxtus and Dandin, you can come in also, and you too, Tarquin, but you'll have to be very quiet. Now the rest of you, please go to bed. It's only two hours until dawn. There are visitors' beds set up in Cavern Hole for the woodlanders."

Storm lay very still. Sister Sage placed a fresh damp cloth across her brow, noting the deep scar which ran across her skull. Sage lifted Storm's head slightly as Simeon administered a small dose of the mixture from a beaker. The mousemaid licked her lips, made a small noise of satisfaction, then settled back as if in a calm sleep.

Simeon took a seat near Storm's head and spoke gently into her ear.

"You are with friends, little one—good friends. I want you to tell us what happened to you. Go back to the beginning and tell us all. Can you hear me? Do you understand what I am saying?"

Storm's eyelids flickered. She sighed and then began talking as if she were telling a story to a friend. At his table in the corner, Brother Hubert wrote swiftly with quill on parchment, recording the strange tale.

> *The mousemaid called Storm Gullwhacker. Her story written down by Hubert, Brother Recorder of Redwall Abbey.*

After moving about restlessly for a short while, the mousemaid appeared calm and spoke quite clearly.

> We are half a season out from the deep coasts in the far south, my father Joseph and I. The ship we are sailing in is called *Periwinkle*. It is crewed by shrews. They are a bit scared because they have never sailed upon blue waters before, but Captain Ash is bold and adventurous. He says the only way

we can get the great bell to Salamandastron is by sea. I have never sailed the deep waters before, nor has my father. Every day we see new wonders—great fish, huge seabirds and wonderful sunsets.

The great bell is tied on deck; my father and I sit to watch the sun's dying rays reflected in its shining metal. I can hear the pride in his voice as he speaks to me.

"Mariel," he says. "Surely this is a bell fit for Rawnblade Widestripe, the great badger Lord. See how the sun sinking in the west turns it to a fiery color. That is the copper, brass and gold, Mariel; the silver I put in to make its voice sweet."

My father is strong and very wise; he is the cleverest bellmaker in the world. When I tell him this he laughs and says, "No no, the nicest thing I ever made was your name—Mariel. It sounds like a bell ringing clear across meadows on a soft spring morn. Can't you hear it . . . Mariel! Mariel!"

Now we have had to stop hugging the coast and put out to sea because of the reefs inshore. All around me is nothing but waves and water. It is a bit frightening at times when the big billows ride high with the wind. The crew are not very happy now they have lost sight of land. My father says everything is shipshape—he learned that from Captain Ash. I like the Captain and I am sure he will deliver us safely to the mountain of the badger Lord.

Something is wrong. A great black ship with red sails has been following us since dawn. I heard Captain Ash whisper to my father the word "searats." My father has taken me below to a cabin. I have to lie on the deck underneath a bunk and hide behind some blankets. My father tells me to lie still and not move. I am not afraid now; I am angry. I do not think I will like searats. I want to come out and fight them if they try to harm us, but my father has forbidden me.

Crashing above on deck, screaming, yelling,

paws pounding everywhere, harsh voices shouting bad things! Clashing of metal, splintering of wood, moaning, horrible cries. I must get out of this place to help against the searats. Silence now, just some cries of injured creatures and the creak of ropes. I am trying to lie still but I tremble and shake with rage. Why am I lying here doing nothing?

Pawsteps, banging, the cabin door crashes open! As I peep between the blankets, I can see three big rats fighting over some wine on the cabin table. One called Gripper snatches the wineflask, but the biggest one, called Saltar, kicks him hard and grabs the wine. Gripper falls to the floor. As the ship heaves he rolls under the bunk and bumps into me. I yell, he rips the blankets off and says, "Hellseyes, look what I found—a pretty mousemaid!"

He tries to grab me but I bite him, kicking him hard in the neck. Gripper makes strange sounds and clutches at his throat where I kicked him. His eyes turn up and he is still. Saltar laughs and says to the other rat, "A warrior maid, eh, Ledder. She's slain old Gripper. What a wild one!"

They both pounce on me. I cannot fight back because the dead rat is in my way. Saltar and Ledder throw the blankets over me. I am bundled up, and they punch and kick at the blankets until I go still, but I am half conscious.

Now they have taken me on deck. I can see through a rip in the blanket that my father and Captain Ash are tied to the bell. They must have fought hard because they are both covered with cuts and bruises. The crew are all lying about, dead, wounded or tied up. Saltar is saying something to Ledder about feeding the fishes. Now they are . . . Oh no! . . . No, please! . . . Noooooooooo!!!

Note by Brother Hubert. *Here the mousemaid became very upset, thrashing about until Mother Mellus held her down and Simeon the herbalist administered more of his potion. The mousemaid lay calm for a while then started to speak again. I record her words as best as I can.*

Cold winter, hungry, cold, oh so cold! My father is ill—I have seen him once when he was brought up to talk with Gabool the Wild. He will not build a bell tower for Gabool to hang the great bell in. Gabool is very angry. He sends my father away, back to the cells, where he must stay locked up until he agrees to build a bell tower. A rat named Graypatch says that I should be used to make my father obey. But Gabool says that he is King of Terramort Isle, he alone gives the orders. If hunger, cold and illness do not bend my father to his will then he might use me to force him, but that is his decision and not Graypatch's. I do not think Graypatch likes Gabool. I hate him. Gabool the Wild is the cruelest of all searats. He is a fearsome sight—strange wild eyes, golden greenstone-studded teeth and a long straggly beard—every beast on Terramort fears him. Gabool calls me Skiv. He makes me serve all his meals. If I am lucky he throws me the scraps from his plate; other times when he is in a cruel mood he will say, "Are you thirsty, Skiv?" Then he pours wine on the floor and makes me lick it up. Many times I have tried to escape, but there are too many guards; I am brought back and beaten. Gabool has threatened to kill my father if I try running away once more. But there must be a way, I've got to find a way . . .

Note by Brother Hubert: *Here the mousemaid started weeping and grinding her teeth. Simeon said it was pure rage at her helpless position. He soothed her with a drop more of potion. She is resting now and beginning to relate another incident. I wish she would speak more slowly as I am unaccustomed to recording in this speedy manner.*

I am serving at table, laying Gabool's food out. He likes roasted seabird and strong wine. Gabool is in a very bad temper and I know the reason. Our ship *Periwinkle* was renamed *Crabclaw* by Gabool. He made a rat named Skullgor Captain of it. But on the first day he sailed it from Terramort he was driven back onto the rocks by a sudden squall. The ship was holed and lost its rudder. Gabool has got Skullgor in front of him and he is insulting him, goading him to fight, I think, though Gabool is unarmed. Gabool says, "Skullgor, a dead frog would be a better Captain than you. You are a blunderer and a fool. You let that ship run on to the rocks because you did not want to put to sea, you yellow-livered coward!"

Skullgor draws his sword. He is shouting, "King or no King, nobeast calls Skullgor a coward. Go and get your sword, Gabool. We'll see who's the coward then!"

Gabool reaches for a hidden sword he has stowed beneath the table. He draws it and makes a leap, surprising Skullgor. I am passing, laden with dishes, and I bump straight into Gabool by accident. Like a flash Skullgor is on him, but Gabool shouts out and a rat named Garrtail stabs Skullgor in the back with a dagger. Gabool jumps up and finishes Skullgor off, then he turns on me, yelling, "You've collected your last plate, Skiv. I saw your little game—trying to get me killed by Skullgor, eh? Then go and join him at Hellgates!"

Now Gabool is coming at me with his sword, I know he is determined to slay me. Suddenly I feel a great anger. I must live; he has no right to take my life. I must act fast. I snatch up Skullgor's sword and leap onto the table, kicking a jug of wine into Gabool's face. I slash at him with my sword but he has staggered close in, his eyes full of wine. The sword handle catches him on the skull, stunning him. He falls beneath the table, but as I jump down to slay him they are on me, Garrtail and a half-dozen others. They hit me with something, everything goes black . . .

Note by Brother Hubert: *We thought the mousemaid needed calming down, but she lay still momentarily then started to speak again.*

Black darkness. . . . Wind, rain! I am bound with a rope, a heavy rope. Outside on the high cliffs; we are outside the fort. I can hear waves crashing against the rocks far below. My head aches. I am balanced tottering on the cliff edge. Gabool is with me. He is saying something. I can hardly hear it for the wind and storm. . . . Wait!

"A mousemaid bringing Gabool down—we can't have that, can't we, little Skiv? Saltar said you were a warrior maid. He was right, you are a born fighter—too much of a fighter for your own good. Let's see how good you are at battling with the sea!"

He pushes me. I am falling over the cliff! There is a large rock tied to the rope. It smashes to bits on another rock as I fall. . . . Father, Father, the water is cold as ice and high as mountains. But I won't die, I'll come back for you. See! The water has softened the rope and my paws are free. Driftwood—I'm clinging to it. Father, don't let me drown. . . . Oh, it's so cold, so dark, and the sea is like a huge wild animal. Father . . . Father . . . I'll come back.

"Enough!" The sight of one so young writhing in mental torment was pitiful. Mother Mellus could stand it no longer. Sweeping the mousemaid up in her paws, she carried her off, calling back to those in the sickbay room, "This little one has had enough—me too! I can't listen anymore to the sufferings of the poor child. We will sleep out in the orchard, beneath the trees, where it is cool and shadowed from the dawn; just Mariel and me."

The door slammed and they were left looking at each other, all save blind Simeon, who summed it up in a few phrases.

"She's right, y'know. I think we all got carried away

listening to the tale of Sto—er, Mariel. The poor maid needs rest, but at least we know who she is now."

Abbot Bernard stuffed his paws into wide habit sleeves and yawned. "Right you are, Simeon. I think we all need some rest. Aahhh, bed beckons."

Tarquin threw a dramatic paw to his brow. "Gads! How you can think of sleep at a time like this horrifies me, particularly when there's so much food left. Any of you chaps fancy sharing a bite with me? I'll tell you about the sweetest gel in the entire territory. Hon Rosie's her name, an absolute whackeroony of a filly, an' Tarquin L. Woodsorrel's the first to say it."

Dandin chuckled. "Sounds like a tale for a long winter's night. I'm off to the dormitories. G' night, or is it good day?"

Down in the orchard Tarquin sat stuffing dewberry and sugared apple cake, strumming his harolina mournfully.

"O Rosie, why did you leave me?
You're enough to give a bally chap the pip,
Laughin' in my face, ha ha ha ha ha,
An' leavin' me in tears as off you trip. . . . Yowch!"

A hard green apple bounced off Tarquin's head as Mother Mellus's voice called out from the trees, "I'll leave you in tears if you don't quit your caterwauling and let us get some rest. I'll wrap that harolina round your head, see if I don't!"

13

A stiff southerly breeze had sprung up, chasing the mist before it. The *Darkqueen* under full sail dipped her head as she cut the night sea. Bow waves scudded spray to fleck her wake, ragged clouds swirled overhead with no moon to light them on their way, timbers creaked and ropes hummed as the burgeoning canvas pulled the sleek craft across the main.

Graypatch knew it was dangerous to sail the *Darkqueen* in any northerly direction, but northeast was better than northwest, and he was a bit more familiar with the coastline in the northeast area. It was still some time until dawn.

"Keep her head in to the shore, Fishgill," Graypatch called to his steersrat. "Deadglim, sound the water for reefs as y'go. Frink, stay up that topmast and keep yer eyes peeled north and westward. Any sign of a sail, give me a shout. I'm goin' below to look at the charts. Stay on duty, now. Anybeast I catch nappin'll be dead afore he wakes up."

The charts in Saltar's former cabin were few and

sketchy. Searats were notorious for sailing by instinct and rule of paw. Graypatch found a scrap of parchment and began drawing his own map of the coast from memory.

"Hmm, if I recall right, the badgers' mountain is further south'ard, then there's the seamarshes, and I remember some outlyin' cliffs boundin' 'em t' the north. Then dunes is next, an' the toadlands. I reckon we're a full night's sailin' with the wind behind us. . . . Got it! Haha, I knew me old brain wasn't rustin'. Somewheres up this coast is a river that runs into the sea. Eye, it comes out of the forestlands and across the shore. All's we do is keep a lookout fer the trees a-growin' inland to the starboard side. I know the river's somewheres there, I can feel it in me bones."

Daybreak found the *Darkqueen* still beating north up the coast. The morning was heavy with rolling seamist, promising to clear into hot sunshine. Promises were not much good to the Captain of *Darkqueen*, however. With Frink peering to port and Fishgill to starboard, it turned into a guessing game as to what would show first, the trees to landward, or the enemy to seaward. Graypatch paced the deck anxiously.

A grizzled searat called Kybo came scurrying up with bad news.

"Just been checkin' provisions, Cap'n. Nought but a few breaktooth biscuits left, an' we're out of fresh water!"

Graypatch slammed the rail with his claw. "Stow the gab, Kybo. There'll be fresh water an' vittles aplenty where we're bound. Somewheres along this coast there's—"

"Land ho!"

Graypatch dashed to the starboard rail. "Where away, Fishgill?"

"Straight as y' look, Cap'n. The mist's a-clearin'; I can see the trees growin' green an' some atop of some dunes inland."

Graypatch clapped Kybo on the back and winked with his good eye. "See! I told yer, matey. Hoho, let's see if they can find us now. Fishgill, Deadglim! Keep yer eyes skinned for a river runnin' out o' those trees across the shore. Ahoy there, Frink. Any sign of Gabool or his ships on your side?"

"Nary a sail, Cap'n. The mist's liftin' an' all I see is a bright day an' some seabirds!"

The news cheered Graypatch immensely. Helm down, the *Darkqueen* raced along the shoreline as a stiffening breeze sprang up from the south. Graypatch called all claws on deck, where they could watch for the river.

It was early noontide before the river was sighted, flowing through a deep defile in the dunes and bubbling out to meet the sea. The strain and tension was showing in Graypatch's face. Though his search had been rewarded, he knew precious time had been wasted. Gabool's ships would not be meandering about at half-sail, they would be hunting at full speed and bound to turn up sooner than later. Moreover, conditions for navigating the river were not favorable. It was ebb tide.

Graypatch would have liked to approach the river at high water, sailing his ship straight into the forest. He cursed aloud, knowing the decision he was making would leave them totally vulnerable to attack. Dropping anchor bow onto the river, he addressed the *Darkqueen*'s crew.

"Hark t' me, lads. There'll be no flood tide until late tonight, so here's the plan. We're goin' to haul the ship through that river which runs across the shore an' into the forestlands. Once we're among the trees we're safe. No one'll find us up there. It's a snug berth—lots of fresh water, fruits, an' good meat t' be had. Trust old Graypatch, me lucky buckos . . ."

"Hah! Tell that t' the frogs, Graypatch. We'll never drag *Darkqueen* o'er that long shore. Any rat with half an eye can see that river's too shallow!"

Graypatch's good eye glared down at the objector, a burly searat. "Stow that kind o' talk, Bigfang! Either we haul her up into the trees or we sit here like ducks at a weddin', waitin' fer the tide tonight, and get ourselves caught by Gabool's ships. Now which is it?"

Bigfang and the searat crew grumbled and muttered,

but there was no real objection to Graypatch's plan, which they knew was their only hope. The master of the *Darkqueen* rapped out his orders.

"So be it! Everybeast aboard ship—I mean everyone, all of you and whatever slaves are in the galleys. I want you all ashore, split into two groups either side o' that river, pullin' on the ropes. Kybo, Frink! Get the anchor rope to port and another one as thick to starb'd. Now when I say pull, I want yer to put yer backs into it, buckos—hear me. Right? All ashore!"

Standing waist-deep in the shallow river, Graypatch eyed the lines of crew and oarslaves either side of the banks. He raised his sword, bringing it down with a splash into the water as he yelled, "Pull! Pull! Bend yer backs an' curse yer mothers! Pull, I say!"

Grunting and sweating, the crew heaved on the taut ropes across their shoulders, digging their claws into the sand for purchase.

"Pull, you 'orrible seascum, pull! You couldn't drag a worm out o' bed between the lot of yer. Pull!"

The ropes creaked and groaned as *Darkqueen* began to move forward, fraction by agonizing fraction. Graypatch waded from the river and took a place at the head of the port rope.

"Hoho! She's movin', me lazy lads. Pull, pull as if you were pullin' buckets o' dark wine from a barrel. Pull!"

Darkqueen had moved twice her own considerable length when the river shallowed out drastically, and she buried her nose in a sandbank.

Bigfang threw down the rope. Followed by many others, he waded into the river and began drinking the fresh running water.

Graypatch drew his sword in high bad temper and began bellowing hoarsely, "Get out of there, you worthless idlers! Get back on your ropes, you frog-hearted, backbitin', jelly-clawed slackers. I'll carve the hide from your bones. I'll strangle every jackrat of yer. I'll . . ."

Across the open sea, just beyond the tideline, Garrtail's

ship *Greenfang* was bearing down on them under full sail!

"Mariel, your name is Mariel, daughter of Joseph the Bellmaker."

The mousemaid hauled her Gullwhacker in from the infirmary window, where it had hung to dry. She swung it experimentally, nodding with satisfaction at the clean knotted hemp.

"I know my name, Dandin. And I know my father's name. I can remember everything now. Stand aside."

Dandin and Saxtus followed her down the stairs, across Great Hall, into the Abbey kitchens. Mariel picked up an empty floursack and shook it out. She started packing it with any food to paw. Saxtus nibbled his paw agitatedly. "What are you doing, Mariel?"

The mousemaid continued filling the sack. "Packing rations, Saxtus."

Friar Alder and his young assistant Cockleburr came bustling up.

"Hi there, young missy. What do you think you're up to?"

Mariel tested the weight of the sack and threw it across her shoulder. "Borrowing some supplies, Friar. Don't worry, I'll repay them."

Friar Alder held out a restraining paw. "Now, hold on a moment, please."

Mariel grasped Gullwhacker tightly. "Stay out of my way, Friar, please. You have all been very kind to me at Redwall and I would hate to harm any Abbey creature, but there's something I've got to do—and nobeast will stop me."

Cockleburr hopped up and down, stumbling on his apron. "Walloping winters, Friar. Get out the way. I've seen her use that Gullywhacker thing!"

Dandin jumped between the Friar and Mariel. "Violence is no answer, Mariel. We are creatures of peace. It's wrong to offer harm to a Redwaller."

The mousemaid shook her head. "Don't you understand, Dandin? I don't wish to harm any creature in this

Abbey, but I have scores to settle with my enemies. Look, just let me go and leave me alone, will you."

"Oh, and what do you plan to do then, Storm Gullwhacker?"

Mariel turned. Standing in front of the great oven was Mother Mellus, accompanied by the Abbot, Simeon and Tarquin.

"My name's not Storm Gullwhacker, it's Mariel," she said defiantly.

Blind Simeon tapped his way forward until he touched her sleeve. "Then start acting like Mariel and not behaving like the old Storm Gullwhacker. We are trying to help you, child."

Mariel looked at the floor. "Don't need any help."

"Not true, Mariel." There was a touch of firmness in Mellus's voice as she interrupted. "Every creature needs help. How do you suppose we live here in harmony together? By helping each other. This Abbey was not built by one creature; it needed cooperation and help. Tell me, where do you think you are going with a knotted rope in a borrowed habit carrying a sack of stolen food?"

Suddenly Mariel felt helpless in the face of all this peaceful opposition. The sack slipped from her paw as she brushed away a threatening teardrop.

Tarquin saved the situation by throwing a rangy paw about her shoulders. "Come on, old gel. Chin up an' never say boo to a goose, wot? Tell you what we'll do—let's tootle over to that dusty old gatehouse place an' hold a council o' war. Get the stew sorted from the dumplin's, eh?"

Abbot Hubert slipped Mariel a clean kerchief and stood in front of her as she scrubbed at her eyes.

"Splendid idea, Tarquin. A good sensible talk never hurt any creature. Come on, we'll all go together. Many heads are better than one."

The gatehouse proved far too dusty and cramped, so they sat on the low steps in the shade of the west rampart. The Abbot ordered lunch to be sent out to them, with cold mint and rose cordial.

Mother Mellus folded her paws. "Now, where exactly do you plan on going?"

"Terramort Isle." Mariel's answer was loud and clear.

"Do you know how to get there, or where it is?"

"No, but don't worry, I'll find it myself."

Simeon chuckled. "As the blind squirrel said, reaching for a cloud."

Mariel bristled. "What does that mean, that I'm stupid!"

"Don't be silly," Tarquin interrupted. "Oh, haha, I say, 'scuse me. Lunch, chaps. Here comes lunch!"

As they sat eating, the Abbot gave Mariel a friendly wink. "Simeon didn't mean anything. All he said really was that you need help. I think the first thing to do is to find out where Terramort Isle is; at least that will be a start. Has anyone ever heard of Terramort in the past, any mention from travelers, scrolls, books, old rhymes—anything at all?"

"I think I may be of some help there." Brother Hubert had been eavesdropping on the conference from the door of the gatehouse. He wandered over cleaning dust from his spectacles. "Hmm, is that food I see? I think I'll join you."

Seating himself comfortably, he began helping himself to cheese, bread and cold cider.

Simeon coughed politely. "Ahem! I don't suppose that you've ever heard of Terramort, Hubert?"

Brother Hubert blinked over the top of his spectacles. "On the contrary, as soon as I heard the name it brought to mind a young mouse who should have been learning the precepts of Redwall Abbots in bygone days. Yes, he thought I was dozing and he began leafing through the scrolls of Fieldroan the Traveler . . ."

Tarquin hastily swallowed a redcurrant muffin. "Fieldroan! Well, there's a thing! My Father Lorquin knew him, of course. Old Fieldroan had more seasons to gray his hairs than a hedgehog has spikes when he and the jolly old pater were chums. D'y'know, I thought I recognized that poem young Saxtus recited at the feast—

know bits of it m'self. Blow me if it isn't one of Fieldroan's very own rhymes!"

Brother Hubert sniffed severely. "Indeed. Well, as I was saying, before I was so rudely interrupted, Fieldroan was a compulsive traveler. I met him one winter and sheltered him in the gatehouse through half a season of deep snow. He left some of his scrolls with me because they were becoming too bulky to carry about on his journeys."

This time it was Dandin's turn to interrupt. "Where are they, Brother Hubert? Do you have them?"

"Patience, young mouse, patience. I'll have to search them out. Unfortunately my gatehouse has become a little, ahem, untidy of late."

Leaving the meal half finished, everybody hurried to the gatehouse, intent on being the first to discover the scrolls. Brother Hubert scurried about in alarm.

"Don't touch anything. You don't know my storage system, any of you. Valuable writings could be lost, my collating disturbed . . ."

"You old fraud, Hubert," Simeon chuckled. "Your system is nothing but layers of dust. Even I can feel that at a single touch. Don't worry, friend. By the time we're finished we'll free the gatehouse of rubbish and dust and provide you with a proper tidy system. I think everything will have to be moved out here onto the lawn. It's the only way we'll find anything from that jumble."

Midafternoon saw the sunlit lawn dotted with piles of manuscripts, books, scrolls, parchments and pamphlets. Covered in dust, the friends sat by the wall, sipping cold mint and rose cordial.

Saxtus shook his head for the umpteenth time. "No, it wasn't any of that lot. I'd know them the moment I saw them."

Bagg and Runn sat on top of the wallstairs, laughing and giggling. "Hoheeheehee. . . . Whoohahaha. What a bunch of dustbags!"

Brother Hubert tried to ignore them. "Yes, I'd recognize those scrolls instantly myself . . ."

"Teeheeheehee! Rec'nize them himself. . . . Yaha hahaha!" They rolled about on the ramparts, kicking their legs in the air and wiping tears of merriment from their eyes as they went into fresh gales of laughter.

Mariel liked the fun-loving otter twins, but this was neither the time nor the place for fun and games. "Hi, you two," she called up to them. "Are you both sitting on a feather, or is it just a mad fit of the giggles?"

Bagg and Runn were laughing too much to answer. They fell about, slapping their paws down against the walltop and shaking their heads from side to side. The laughter was so infectious that Mariel and Saxtus began chuckling, and even Brother Hubert could not suppress a dry smile.

Simeon turned his sightless eyes toward the walltop. "Now then, you young villains. What's so funny? Let us in on the joke, please."

Bit by bit the story came out from the laughing twins.

"Woohoohoo! You're all lookin' for scrolls. . . . Hohoho!"

"And you've. . . . Teeheehee! Shifted everythin' out of the gatehouse. Haha!"

"Yahahaha! But when you started carryin' all that stuff out. Ohohoho!"

"Br-Br-. Brother Hubert. . . . He-he. . . . Heeheehee! Gave old scrolls to Simeon t' stick under the gatehouse door an' keep it open. Hawhawhawhaw!"

"An' I said to Bagg. . . . Ohoohoohoo! S'pose they're the scrolls that everyone's lookin' for. Ahaahaahohohoheehee!"

Simeon turned his face to Brother Hubert, who looked guiltily toward the Abbot, who shook his head in disbelief. He was about to say something to Mariel, but the mousemaid was already at the gatehouse door, easing the flattened bundle of scrolls from under it.

"It's them, all right—the scrolls of Fieldroan the Traveler."

Rubbing dust and sweat from his brow, Dandin nudged Hubert. "Well, at least your gatehouse got a good free tidy-out, Brother!"

Smiles broke into chuckles, which gave way to open laughter all around.

Sister Sage shook a quilt out at the infirmary window and began folding it neatly as she reached for her feather duster.

"Well, it's nice to know that all some creatures have to do is sit out on the Abbey lawn in the sunshine and laugh all afternoon, I must say!"

14

Graypatch drew his sword, waving it and roaring as he waded from the stream. "Now we'll see what yer made of, you sons of searats! Catch 'em in the shallows afore they're ashore an' massacre every rat of 'em. Sharp now. It's our necks or theirs. Charge, me buckos. Charge!"

The *Greenfang* had sailed into shore as close as Garrtail could take her. She listed slightly in the shallows then settled askew. Garrtail had his crew ready. Lining the rails, they gripped weapons between their teeth and waited his order as Graypatch's rats thundered across the sands.

Garrtail vaulted over the side, landing chest deep in the sea. "Follow me, lucky lads. It's booty for all aplenty when we've slain that load o' turncoats an' traitors. Over the side, all of yer!"

Quick thinking and speed had given the advantage to Graypatch. His searats were at the water's edge as Garrtail's crew came over the rails of the *Greenfang*.

Wading out, Graypatch called over his shoulder, "Keep to the shallows. Don't go too deep, lads, but hold Garrtail's scum in the deeper waters where they can't fight so good. Bigfang, get back to the *Darkqueen*. Kybo, you go with him. Get hold of any long boathooks or pikes you can find. Look lively now—I'm not goin' back to Terramort with me head in the bows an' me body in the stern for Gabool to gloat over!"

Garrtail was out ahead of his crew. Realizing the urgency of the situation, he waded and cursed as he made his way toward Graypatch.

"Come an' fight, you frog-livered schemer. I'll carve you to fishbait!"

Graypatch balanced an iron marlinspike in his claw. Taking careful aim, he flung it. The pointed missile hissed out across the rippling waves. Standing almost chest-deep in the water, Garrtail had little chance to dodge or leap out of the way; it caught him between the eyes. The Captain of the *Greenfang* fell backward into the sea, slain instantly. His crew, on seeing their leader dead, milled about in the water betwixt ship and shore. All heart for the fight had deserted them now they were without a Captain.

"Ahoy, Graypatch. Lookit what we found!"

Bigfang and Kybo came splashing into the shallows with two galley slaves, all four laden with pikes, long boathooks and bows and arrows. Graypatch snapped out swift orders, his clever brain working fast.

"Kybo, you stay here with half the crew as archers. Keep pouring arrows at 'em, hard as you can—fire high over the pikers. Bigfang, take the other half of the crew and wade a bit deeper. Stick any of the *Greenfang* crew who try to get ashore an' circle behind us. Deadglim, give me yer burnin' glass an' a bow 'n' arrows."

With its unanchored keel scraping gently off the sea bottom, the *Greenfang* began a slow drift away from shore with the outgoing tide. The crew split two ways, some trying to swim back to ship, the other, bolder spirits wading toward shore, yelling as they thrust their swords at the pikerats.

Kybo and the archers had easy targets, arching their arrows over the top of the pikers into the unprotected backs of those who were swimming to the ship. Their screams mingled with the angry yells of those with pitifully short swords, trying to do battle with long pikes and boathooks.

On shore, Graypatch had soaked rags in lamp oil and bound them around arrowpoints. In the hot sun it was the work of a moment with a burning glass to concentrate the sunrays into flame upon oil-soaked rags. Kybo followed behind, carrying the fire arrows as Graypatch waded out, testing the wind to make sure it was with him. The first arrow blurred high over the heads of the searats like a red comet, arcing into the big mainsail of *Greenfang*. Two others followed swiftly. One stood quivering in the stern, the other burying itself deep into the mast.

Graypatch amused himself by firing the remaining fire arrows at the helpless rats who were still trying to swim for the ship. He laughed aloud as one wretched creature sank with a sizzle and a scream. All around, the water ran red with blood as the breeze stirred the flames to a roaring inferno. Bodies of the wounded and the slain followed the blazing *Greenfang* out on the ebbing tide. Graypatch, his single eye illuminated red in the glare, called out, "Make sure there's none left alive to tell the tale, mates. Haharr, Gabool will never know what happened to us an' the *Darkqueen*, or Garrtail an' the *Greenfang*. D'ye hear me, Gabool! Blast yer eyes, lungs 'n' liver, wherever ye are!"

As the searats waded ashore, Bigfang muttered to Kybo, "Graypatch is gettin' too big fer his seaboots, matey. There'd be no victory today if I hadn't found those bows an' arrows, mark my words."

Kybo agreed wholeheartedly, though under his breath. "Aye, did y'see him there, yellin' an a screamin' to kill *Greenfang*'s screw down t' the last rat? I'll bet some o' those buckos would've joined us. We all had mateys among that crew, but they're gone to Hellgates now."

Bigfang flung his pike upon the sands. "Right you are, shipmate. I think we've a come out o' the frypan into the fire here. Graypatch is startin' to act up as wild as Gabool. Did ye hear the way he was yellin' at me fer drinkin' water earlier? I take that from no searat, Captain or not. Still, we'll bide our time, eh, matey."

Graypatch wandered over and slapped Kybo with the flat of his swordblade. "C'mon, gullywhumper. Back aboard the *Darkqueen*. We can afford to wait the night floodtide to send us across the shore now. No more pullin' her on towropes."

Kybo turned to look at the last of the *Greenfang*, wiping smoke from his smarting eyes as the blazing hulk drifted seaward.

Gabool was in a foul temper. Most of his servant slaves had gone to the galleys of the three ships under repair, and he was left with only four. Blinking his red-rimmed eyes, he watched them polishing his bell. The Warlord was afraid of the night; sleep brought with it only nightmares of avenging mice, fearsome badger figures and the angry boom of the bell, tolling around his brain like a harbinger of doom. Virtually alone now in Fort Bladegirt, he did not have the satisfaction of asserting his power as King of all Searats. There was nobeast to plot against, to bend to his will, only sitting around waiting and festering with hate for his one-time ally Graypatch. He aimed a kick at a dormouse who was down on all fours furiously rubbing away at the great bell.

"You there, scabpaws. Where's my food?"

The slave continued polishing, not daring to stop as he replied, "Master, I am not a cook. You sent the cooks away to your ships. All I do is polish your bell as you have told me to."

"Get me something to eat and drink," Gabool snarled. "You're a cook now."

The dormouse dropped his rag and bowed, trembling. "Master, I cannot cook. I am only a bell polisher . . ."

Gabool's cruel claws dug into the slave's body as he drew him upright, glaring at him through sleepless sore eyes.

"Get down to the kitchens, and light a fire. You'll find

dead seabirds there—roast me a few, bring wine too. Get out of my sight!"

As the dormouse picked himself up and scurried off, Gabool vented his spleen on the remaining three slaves.

"Out! Get out, all of you! Leave me, I want to be alone."

Gabool flung a knife at the last dormouse to disappear around the door. It clattered harmlessly off the wall, and he slumped dejectedly in his chair. "Must be losin' me touch. Should've pinned him easily."

The afternoon sun slanting through the window cast its warmth over him. Gabool's tired eyes began to droop. He sighed as his chin slowly sank onto his chest. Outside, the sounds of the restless sea grew distant. Finally sleep overcame the King of Searats; his eyes closed and his head slumped gently forward in the quiet summer noontide.

A badger was advancing upon him, a huge warlike badger brandishing a broadsword that made a searat blade look like a toy. He turned in fear. A mouse had crept up behind him—it was the one he called Skiv—she was carrying a heavy knotted rope and the light of battle was in her eyes. Somewhere he could hear Graypatch laughing, a contemptuous mocking sound . . .

Bong!!!

Gabool sat bolt upright, wide awake. There was no creature in the room save himself . . . And the bell.

"Well, what a riddle t'be sure. I'll bet even Hon Rosie couldn't make head nor tail of this jolly old thing. Wot, wot?"

Mariel aimed a candied chestnut at Tarquin and threw it. He merely caught it in his mouth and munched reflectively. "Course, y'know, I've never seen her solvin' riddles and whatnot. Bet she's bally clever at it, though. Hon Rosie's pretty good at most things."

Mellus stuck a huge paw under Tarquin's nose. "Listen, doodlehead, if I hear you mention Hon Rosie one more time . . ."

The friends sat at table in Cavern Hole. They were not

to be disturbed, on the Abbot's orders. Outside in Great Hall the rest of the Redwallers took supper and chased reluctant Dibbuns around in an effort to get them washed and up to their beds. Mariel picked up the scrolls from amid the supper-laden table.

"There's no puzzle or mystery about it, the whole thing's a straightforward map in rhyme. Maybe we don't know what certain things are—Fieldroan the Traveler had an odd way of expressing himself—but don't worry, I'll find out what it all means as I go along."

Saxtus helped himself to more mushroom-and-cress soup. "Read it again, Mariel. Perhaps it may sound clearer if you do."

Mariel drew a deep breath. "Right, here goes for the tenth time . . .

If I were fool of any sort,
I'd leave Redwall and travel forth,
For only fools seek Terramort
Upon the pathway leading north.
This trail brings death with every pace;
Beware of dangers lurking there,
Sticklegs of the feathered race
And fins that in the ford do stir.
After the ford, one night one day,
Seek out the otter and his wife.
Forsake the path, go westlands way,
Find the trail and lose your life.
When in the woods this promise keep,
With senses sharp and open eyes,
'My nose shall not send me to sleep'
For buried ones will surely rise.
Beat the hollow oak and shout,
'We are creatures of Redwall!'
If a brave one is about,
He'll save any fool at all.
Beware the light that shows the way,
Trust not the wart-skinned toad,
In his realm no night no day.
Fool, stay to the road.

Where the sea meets with the shore,
There the final clue is hid;
Rock stands sentinel evermore,
Find it as I did.
The swallow who cannot fly south,
The bird that only flies one way,
Lies deep beneath the monster's mouth,
Keep him with you night and day.
His flight is straight, norwest is true,
Your fool's desire he'll show to you."

Brother Hubert made a show of polishing his spectacles busily. "Complete balderdash and nonsense, of course. Fieldroan was, like most old travelers, given to tall stories and half-truths. The very idea of it! Sticklegs and fins, otters' wives, sleeping noses and buried ones rising. Huh! Truth was a cuckoo's egg to that fellow."

Tarquin left off chewing an enormous turnip 'n' leek pastie. "I say, that's a bit strong, old boy. What reason would old Fieldroan have to tell a pile of fibs? Personally I'm inclined to believe the bally poem, even though I can't make head nor tail of it."

Simeon touched Mariel's paw. "What do you think, young one? After all, the decision to travel upon this information is yours."

Mariel patted the blind herbalist's shoulder. "Thank you, Simeon. I will tell you what I think. I never knew Fieldroan so I cannot say if his poem is totally correct, but it is all I have to go on if I am to reach Terramort, so I will do what the rhyme says to rescue my father and return the great bell to Lord Rawnblade."

The Abbot pursed his lips. "But that is not all you intend to do, Mariel."

The mousemaid's voice had a ring of determination which no creature could deny.

"I have only one other thing to do—I must slay Gabool the Wild. None of you can know the hatred I bear toward this barbarian. He must be sent to Hellgates so that decent creatures can live in peace; only then will I rest. I must do this alone. I thank you my friends for all the kindness and hospitality you have shown to me, a stranger in your midst. Continue to live, prosper and be happy in your wonderful Abbey, but do not try to follow me. The responsibility is mine alone, and I cannot allow any Redwaller to risk life and limb on my behalf. Now I must sleep. Tomorrow my journey begins."

When the mousemaid had retired to the dormitories, Dandin looked at the friends around the table in Cavern Hole.

"I am going with her. She cannot achieve her aims alone."

Mother Mellus rapped the table. "You'll stay right here at Redwall, Dandin."

The young mouse turned to the Abbot. There was no change of verdict.

"Dandin, we are creatures of peace, and also duty. You must obey Mother Mellus. You are still a very young mouse in our care."

"But . . ."

The Abbot held up a paw in a gesture of finality. "No more arguments, please. The hour is late and sleep beckons." Shadows of drifting nightcloud meandered past the moon. A light breeze made the hot night more tolerable, and trees rustled and sighed in Mossflower Woods, sending their whisperings echoing around the stones of Redwall. Simeon sat propped up by cushions in his armchair near the open window—he seldom slept in bed. It was sometime after midnight. Unsure of whether he was half awake or half asleep, the blind herbalist felt a presence in the room.

"Is that you, Bernard, old friend?" he said softly into the darkness.

The voice that replied was not that of the Abbot; it was strong, firm and reassuring, a voice that Simeon instinctively felt he could trust.

"Simeon, friend, Dandin must go. Mariel needs him."

The blind mouse felt a light touch against his paw. All around was the scent of woodland flowers, columbine, wood anemones, bryony, honeysuckle and dog rose. The voice spoke again.

"The blood of Gonff flows in Dandin. Mariel needs a friend as I once did. Do not be afraid, come with me."

Simeon arose from the chair and left the room, guided by his strange visitor, though somehow with the odd feeling that none of this was real and he was still sitting in his chair. Convinced that he was asleep, Simeon decided to settle back and enjoy the dream.

Down stairs and down more stairs, along winding and twisting corridors, never touching the walls as he usually would, yet not putting a paw wrong, as he was guided by the friendly presence, the blind herbalist practically floated. He heard a door creak softly as it opened. Gliding through, Simeon sensed that he was in a rock chamber somewhere deep beneath the Abbey. It was so peaceful and quiet here, yet wistful, with a breath of summers long gone, and autumn mists hanging like dried tears. Simeon could not suppress a long sigh in the silent calm of the chamber. Something was pressed into his paws; he felt it as the voice spoke again.

"Leave this with Dandin. Do not wake him—he will understand."

Drawing the thing from its long case, the blind herbalist felt it. From the smooth pommel stone, across the curving hilt and down the perilous blade to the winter-keen tip, Simeon touched it. He had never felt a sword before, but the blind mouse knew that had he felt ten thousand swords, none would have been fit to compare with this one. The balance was perfect—wieldy, yet light as a feather; dangerous, but safe as a rock to the paw that held it; a blade of death, yet of destiny and justice.

Simeon hardly remembered the journey back. He dimly recalled leaving the sheathed sword alongside Dandin as he lay sleeping. Then he was back in his armchair, wide awake, with the cool night breeze wafting on him through the open window, the woodland flower scent, and a fading voice calling from far off: "Goodbye, Simeon. May the seasons rest easily upon you . . ."

Simeon smiled and settled back in his chair as sleep closed in on him.

"And may the peace of Redwall Abbey be upon you, Martin the Warrior."

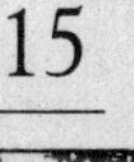

15

The sails of the *Darkqueen* had to be tight furled to avoid overhanging trees. Oarslaves had been brought up from the galleys, pitiful wretches; they stood on deck, using the long oars to punt the massive vessel upriver. Graypatch stood at the helm, supervising the movements, moonlight patching down through the night foliage upon his lean figure. Floodtide had lifted the *Darkqueen*'s nose from the sandbank, and then with a favorable night breeze she had spread sails and glided across the shore toward the forest-fringed dunes.

Pakatugg had been following the progress of the ship since he first spotted it offshore from the dunes. The recluse squirrel had followed along the shoreline and seen everything, from the near mutiny of Graypatch's crew as they hauled the *Darkqueen*, to the murderous encounter with Garrtail and the burning of *Greenfang*. Pakatugg was on the scavenge; anything he could steal from the searats he considered would be his by right. When he saw the ship sailing across the beach toward the forest, his respect for Graypatch grew—he would have to treat this searat with some respect. A ship in full sail, gliding over a beach in the night, what a strange sight!

Dawn was peeping over the treetops to a loud chorus of birdsong when Graypatch chose an inlet far upriver. With no proper anchorage on the pebbly riverbed, he ordered *Darkqueen* made fast by stem, stern and midship ropes to a sycamore and two elms. Graypatch felt a real sense of triumph as he gave orders.

"Frink, Deadglim, take Ringtail, Lardgutt, Ranzo an' Dripnose. Patrol this forest awhile, see what y'can see. There must be life hereabouts—we crossed a path that was forded by the river durin' the night. There's always somebeast around to tread that path—might be a settlement of some sort. Anyhow, get your carcasses movin' an' report back to me at noon. Kybo, Bigfang, Fishgill, you stay on deck an' keep a weather eye out hereabouts. I'm off t' me bunk for some rest after steerin' all night. The rest of you, keep your heads down below decks until we know what sort of country this is."

Pakatugg tracked the six searats as they patrolled northward through far Mossflower Woods. He could tell they were raw and inexperienced in woodland matters. Frink, who was leading the party, walked straight into a bed of stinging nettles, tripping on an exposed treeroot and falling headlong.

"Yaagh! Owouch, help me, mates. Ow, oo! These things are alive!"

Lardgutt and Ranzo pulled him out. He sat nursing a rapidly swelling face and cursing.

"Chahah! Me nose—look, it's blowin' up like a balloon. Garr! I hate this place—trees everywhere. A rat can't even take a decent breath. Give me the open sea anytime."

"Ahoy, Frink. Over here! Ringtail's been stung by one o' those wasp things."

Deadglim pulled the dart from Ringtail's paw, catching a glimpse of Pakatugg dodging behind a tree with his blowpipe as he did. Deadglim inspected the dart and flung it away.

"So that's what a wasp looks like, huh. We've got some learnin' t' do before we're proper landlubbers. I'm goin' back to the *Darkqueen.* You lot carry on with your patrollin'."

Pakatugg missed the wink which passed between Deadglim and the other five. The squirrel followed the remainder of the patrol, sniggering quietly at their ignorance of woodland lore.

"Hey, Frink, what d'you suppose these are—strawberries?"

"No, they're blackberries or raspberries or somethin'. Anyhow, why ask me? I don't know—don't wanna know either."

"Haha, why don't you try eatin' one, Lardgutt? Are yer scared mate?"

"Who, me? 'Course I'm not. Here, watch this."

"How does it taste, Lardy, me old shipmate?"

"Mmmm, tastes nice. Wonder what they're called?"

"Deadly nightshade or somethin'—they're probably poison."

"Yarghphutt!"

"Garn, what'd you spit 'em out for? If you ate some an' didn't die, then we'd know they'd be all right to eat. Proper mean to your mates you are, Lardgutt. Betcher Kybo wouldn't 'ave spat 'em out."

Pakatugg decided it was time for a wasp sting again. He was chuckling silently to himself and loading his blowpipe when a tattooed arm circled his neck and a swordblade pressed against his throat.

"One move an' yer fishbait, squirrel. We might not know much about forests, but a searat can sniff the enemy a mile away. Ahoy, lads, lookit what I got!"

They flocked around; Deadglim, licking his knifeblade and smiling evilly at Pakatugg. Frink snapped the blowpipe and threw it aside.

"So it's our wasp, eh. What's yer name, wasp?"

Pakatugg swallowed hard and tried to stop trembling. "Pakatugg's my name."

Frink twitched his tender nose. "Pakatugg, eh. What'd you call 'im, Ranzo?"

"Hah! I'd call him Deadsquirrel, or maybe Nopaws. Then again, Slittongue might be an 'andsome title fer a squirrel who follers searats round a-firin' darts at 'em."

They bound Pakatugg's paws tightly. Dripnose threw a noose about his neck and gave it a sharp tug.

"Move lively, matey. We'll see what name Cap'n Graypatch can think up for yeh."

Clary, Thyme and Hon Rosie stood to attention in the armory at Salamandastron. Lord Rawnblade paced up and down, a worried frown creasing his broad brow.

"Longeyes has reported a smoldering wreck of a ship—*Greenfang*, it's one of Gabool's. There may have been trouble farther north up the coast. Clary, I want you to take your patrol up there, fully provisioned and well armed. Find out what'd been going on and report back to me. But if you are needed up there by any good creatures, then stay and help out as best you can. Understood?"

Clary made an elegant salute with his lance. "Leave it to us, sah!"

Rawnblade allowed himself a fleeting smile. "Thank you, Clary. Move your patrol out whenever you wish."

The badger Lord watched them go from his high window. The three hares swiftly bounded across the beach, sometimes skipping in and out of the small wavelets at the water's edge. Rawnblade turned back to his forge and quenched a red-hot spearhead in water. He remembered, long seasons back, three similar hares, young carefree fighters, their bodies washed up on the tideline after Gabool's searats had finished with them.

Rawnblade set the spearhead on the anvil and began beating it with mighty blows. His heavy hammer rose and fell; sweat mixed with tears and sizzled into the embers of the forges as the ruler of the fire mountain renewed his vow.

"I cannot leave my mountain and these shores undefended, but one day, Gabool, one day you will sail back to here and I will be waiting. Oho, Gabool, all the seas of the world cannot keep us apart—it is written that we will meet again. We will meet! We will meet! We will meet!"

Rawnblade repeated the phrase over and over with each hammer blow upon the spearhead, releasing his pent-up frustrations. When he finally stopped, the spear-blade had been battered to four times its size and was thin as a leaf!

From the western flatlands fronting the Abbey, a chorus of larks wakened Mariel. She stood stretching and rubbing her eyes for a brief moment until realization hit her—it was almost an hour after dawn. The mousemaid slung Gullwhacker around her neck and opened the door carefully, listening for familiar sounds of Abbey bustle. Thankfully she noted silence from outside and inside the building. Stealing quietly down the corridor, Mariel could not help a slight sense of bewilderment. Usually Redwall was alive and humming by this time. Tip-pawing through Great Hall, she retrieved the knapsack of supplies she had hidden behind a column before supper. Thanking her lucky stars, she dashed across the lawn toward a small wicker gate in the north wall and unbolted it. Taking one last backward look at the sleeping Abbey, the mousemaid sniffed, wiped her eyes, took a deep breath and left Redwall with its happy memories behind her.

Flatlands to the left, woodlands to the right, Mariel strode the brown dusty path that wound northward. Early dew was drying from the lea already; it was going to be a hot day. She stayed on the side of the path where Mossflower provided treeshade. Strange that the Redwallers should sleep so late, she thought. Still, it was far better, in a way. Mariel had been dreading any long tearful farewells; it would be far easier this way, even though she felt rather guilty, stealing off like a thief in the early dawn. "I, Mariel," the mousemaid called aloud to Mossflower country, "swear by this honorable weapon known as the Gullwhacker that one day I will return to Redwall

Abbey and all my true friends and dear companions I leave there. Always providing that I live through the dangers of the task ahead of me, that is. Oh, and providing of course that I can find the way back. No, that's nonsense—I'd find my way back if I had only one leg and the snows were as high as the treetops. But what if I'm slain or I fail in my quest? Well, in that case I solemnly swear that my spirit will find its way back to Redwall Abbey. There! That's that. I feel much better now, even hungry enough for a spot of breakfast."

Without stopping her march, she munched bread and cheese from the knapsack. A stroke of luck provided a gnarled apple tree hanging its boughs low over the path, so she plucked an early russet apple and bit into it, noting her find as a lucky omen for the journey ahead.

Woodpigeons cooed within the dimness of woodland depths, bees hummed and grasshoppers chafed out on the sunlit flatlands. Mariel began skipping, twirling Gullwhacker at her side, suddenly filled with a sense of freedom and adventure. What better than to travel alone, eat when you please, rest when you feel the need, camp by your own little fire at night and sleep snug in some forest glade! The feeling flooded through her with such force that it made her light-headed, and she began singing aloud an old playsong, known to mice everywhere.

"The winter O, the winter O,
With cold and dark and driving snow,
O not for me the winter O,
My friend I tell you so.
In spring the winds do sport and play,
And rain can teem down anyday,
While autumn oft is misty gray,
My friend hear what I say.
When summer sunlight comes each morn,
The birds sing sweet each golden dawn,
And flow'rs get kissed by every bee,
While shady stands the tree.
The summer O, the summer O,
Amid its golden peace I go,

From noon to lazy evening glow.
My friend I told you so."

Mariel held the final note, leaping high in the air and twirling. She came down on the far side of the path, stumbled and fell. Rolling over, the mousemaid slipped down the side of the ditch bordering the flatlands.

"Tut tut, dearie me—leapin' mice, what next? Though I must say, old gel, you held that last note gracefully. Hon Rosie couldn't have done better. Bear in mind, though, she wouldn't have dived nose first into the ditch. Not the done sort o' thing for young fillies. Wot?"

Tarquin lent a paw to pull Mariel from the ditch. She was completely taken aback at the appearance of the hare.

"Where did you come from, Tarquin? I never even heard you following me."

Tarquin L. Woodsorrel adopted a pose of comical outrage. "Following? Did I hear you say following, marm? Boggle me ears, I wasn't followin' you, snubnose, I was right alongside you, mousy miss. Oh yes, seasons of trainin' y'know. Camouflage an' all that—dodge an' bob, duck an' weave, disguises too. D'you want to see me become a daisy or a bally buttercup?"

Mariel was smiling as she dusted herself off on the pathside, but she chided the garrulous hare.

"Very clever, Tarquin, but you can't come with me—it's far too dangerous."

Tarquin adjusted the fastenings of an oversized haversack filled to bursting with food. "Balderdash, young 'un. Absolute piffle and gillyswoggle! I'm goin' my own way, just keepin' you company on the road to see you don't practice any more ditch divin'. Come on, step out lively now, leftrightleftrightleftright an' all that."

Mariel kept pace with him, jogging to match his lanky stride. "Well, as long as you know you can't come all the way with me . . . but why are we walking so fast?"

Tarquin kept on, pawing it out at the double. "Goin' to be late for lunch if we don't move smartly. Come on now, keep up."

• • •

It was about lunchtime that they rounded a bend in the path to find Dandin awaiting them with a wild summer salad he had gathered to garnish the bread and cheese, together with a flask of elderberry cordial he was cooling beneath an overhanging willow. The young mouse waved to them.

"Hi there. Good job you made it—another moment or two and I was going to start without you."

Mariel placed her paws on her hips, chin jutting out angrily. "What in the name of fur are you doing here?"

Dandin smiled disarmingly. "Oh, it's all a bit of a mystery really."

The mousemaid turned on Tarquin. "And you, how did you know he was here, you great lolloping flopear? It's a plot, that's what it is. You set this up between you!"

Tarquin sprawled on the grass and began constructing a giant cheese and salad sandwich. "Steady on there, missy, I was waitin' outside the north wicker gate for you to appear right through the bally night. Then about an hour before dawn young Dandin here pops out, so I merely told him to get a move on an' we'd meet him further up the road for a spot of lunch. Rather civilized, don't y'think?"

Mariel was fuming with temper, but she plumped herself down and began eating because the walk had given her an appetite. Through mouthfuls of food she berated the smiling duo.

"You can wipe those silly smiles off your whiskers. You are not coming with me, either of you. Is that crystal clear?"

They both munched away, smiling and winking at each other as they nodded agreement with the furious mousemaid.

When lunch was finished Dandin repacked his knapsack and thrust the marvelous scabbarded sword into his cord girdle.

"Rightyo, Tarkers. Let's get moving. I wonder if this pretty mousemaid is going our way. D'you think she'd like to walk with us?"

"Doubtless, old lad. We'll string along with her a

piece. D'y'know, she's an excellent ditch diver—you should've seen her this mornin', looped the loop graceful as y'please, straight into the jolly old ditch on her snout."

Stone-faced and in high dudgeon, Mariel marched on between them.

Tarquin and Dandin made perilously light of the situation.

"I say, Mr. Woodsorrel, that's a strange noise those grasshoppers are making."

"Not the confounded grasshoppers, laddie buck. Sounds like some wild creature nearby grindin' their teeth."

"Hmm, not very good for the old molars, that. Temper, temper! . . . Look out, she's swinging that knotty rope thing."

By midafternoon Mariel had simmered down somewhat. She even let slip the odd smile or giggle at the antics of her comical traveling companions, and at one point designed to talk to them.

"It's getting very hot. What do you say we take a rest in the shade, have a snack and then push on until dark?"

The suggestion was well received. They flopped down gratefully with their backs against a tree-topped oak. When they had eaten, all three napped for a while, but the long summer day took its toll; what was meant to be a short rest for hot dusty eyes turned into quite a lengthy sleep.

Dandin was wakened by a paw across his mouth. He gave a muffled cry as Tarquin hissed a warning. "Ssshh, not a sound!"

The young mouse sat up carefully and looked around. Mariel was standing still as a statue, her Gullwhacker at the ready. The hare bent an ear in the direction of the woodlands opposite.

"Somebeast is stalking us," he breathed to them both. "Over there, behind that yew thicket, I'm sure. Dandin, go with Mariel to the left. I'll take the right. We'll jump the blighter an' turn the tables in our favor. Go!"

Paw by paw they crept forward, listening to the rustle

of the thicket, where it was plain some creature was moving about. Skirting to the left, they made out a dark shape in the shadows. Tarquin yelled out the signal.

"Up an' at him!"

Throwing themselves headlong, the three friends pounced upon the miscreant.

"Yow! Ouch! Whoo! Eeek! Yarrgh! Lerrimgo! Gerroff!"

Young Durry Quill watched them as they hopped and leaped about like boiled frogs, yelling in pain at the spikes, embedded in paws and bodies, that they had collected from him in their mad plunge. He twitched his nose.

"Serves 'ee right fer jumpin' on a young lad like that. Ain't you beast got no manners at all?"

Mariel hopped about in agony and frustration. "Ah ah! You sure you haven't brought the rest along with you? Ooh ooh! I wouldn't be surprised to see Mellus, Simeon and the Abbot leap out from behind that hornbeam yonder. How many more of you are there? Am I taking the whole population of Redwall along with me? Ow ooch!"

Durry was quite amused at the idea. "Heehee!" he snickered aloud. "No no, 'tis only me alone. Now do you stop a leapin' round an' let me get those spikes out. I'll fix 'ee up, never fear."

They waited in painful silence as Durry Quill nipped the spikes out with his teeth. Working smoothly and easily, he made a large wad of dockleaf, wild cloves and rowan berries.

" 'Ere, rub this on where you be stickled—'twill ease all pains."

Dandin was surprised and delighted. It worked like a charm. A short space of time and it felt as if he had never encountered a hedgehog spike.

Early evening found them back on the north path, with Durry explaining himself to the other three travelers.

"My ol' nuncle Gabe, 'ee wants me to be a cellar 'og. It's a good job, mind, but a young 'un wants to see summat afore he settles hisself down to a life of cordial, wine an' ales, ho yes. I 'eard all about it 'ee, Miz Mariel, an' I couldn't sleep for thinkin' about it. Durry, I says to myself, Durry, a young 'og would be right honnered to tread the roads wi' such a fearless mousemaid. So I packs me sack, gives you a liddle start—there I tells a whopper, I overslep' really. Anywise, I follered 'ee, an' 'ere I be, fit as a flea, fat as a beetle, an' ready fer ought."

They laughed heartily at the honest and earnest hedgehog.

Dandin pointed up the road. "Look, there's a ford coming up. I can see the sun glinting off the waters. Hope it's not too deep for us to cross."

Quick as a flash a big heron flapped down on the path in front of them. His sticklike legs bent as the long snaking neck curved itself ready for a strike, the fierce circular eyes contracted and dilated angrily, a dangerous pale yellow beak pointed down at them.

"Irrrrrraktaan, this is my waterrrrrr! Rrrrrrun for yourrrrr lives . . . Back! Come near Irrrrrraktaan's waterrrrr and you die! I am Irrrraktaan, mighty killerrrrrr!"

16

Graypatch's eye came close to Pakatugg, and the searat's tone was wheedling, almost friendly.

"Now then, matey. You know the lay o' the land 'ereabouts. Don't be afeared of old Graypatch or none of this riffraff aboard the *Darkqueen*, you just tell me about all the snug little berths an' cosy coves in this neck o' the woods."

Pakatugg felt a little bolder now that the searat Captain had untied his paws and taken the noose from about his neck, but he was quite nervous about the horde of grinning searats who lounged on the deck around him. This one called Graypatch, though, he sounded different—maybe they could talk reasonably. Feeling naked without his blowpipe and darts, Pakatugg did his best to muster up a commanding tone.

"There's not much at all in this region. You've come to the wrong place. Far north's where you want to be, that's where all you types usually land."

Graypatch bent his head to one side and winked at the squirrel. "Aharr, is that so? What scurvy luck fer us, eh?

Still, never you mind, we've landed up here, an' here we'll stay. Now I'll ask you again, messmate, nice an' polite as you please. I want somewhere with peace an' plenty to settle down. Now where d'you suppose that'd be?"

Pakatugg mistook Graypatch's reassuring manner for weakness, and he decided to take a firm line with this ragamuffin rat and his tawdry bunch. After all, the hares always did it and creatures took notice of them.

"Look, I've told you once, you're wasting your time around here. Up north is much better for vermin like you!"

Still smiling, Graypatch kicked him in the stomach, knocking him to the deck. Looping a rope around Pakatugg's footpaws, he rasped out an order:

"Haul away, buckos!"

Pakatugg swung upside-down in midair, suspended above the deck as a gang of searats yanked him higher and higher on the rope.

Graypatch shook his head sadly. "Did y'hear that, mates? He called us vermin!"

Pakatugg swallowed hard and closed his eyes as he heard weapons being drawn.

The searat Captain squinted his good eye at the hanging squirrel. "Have ye ever fed the fishes, squirrel?"

"N-No. What d-do you f-feed 'em on?"

A harsh roar of laughter went up from the crew. Graypatch drew his sword.

"What do we feed 'em on? Why, you of course. Those liddle fishes'd be right partial to squirrel carved up into tasty strips."

He slashed at the end of the rope, which was secured to the mast. Pakatugg came down on the deck with a bump. Graypatch drew a curved dagger from his belt. Using his sword blade like a butcher's steel, he rubbed them together, putting a fine edge to the dagger blade. He grabbed the squirrel by the ear and brandished the dagger with a fearsome yell.

"Start from the top and work down to the tail—that's the best way!"

"No, wait! There's an Abbey not far from here. They've got it all. Food, shelter, plunder—the lot! Spare me, please!"

Graypatch put up his weapons and aimed a kick at the blubbering squirrel. " 'Ere Ringtail, Dripnose, take 'im below an' put 'im in chains. Don't be too gentle now, and don't feed the slug too well. When I'm ready he'll take us to this Abbey place. Ain't that right, squirrel?"

Pakatugg nodded vigorously, his tears staining the deck.

Colonel Clary, Brigadier Thyme and Hon Rosie had stopped near the sand dunes to take refreshment and a short rest. Clary was lying back, voicing his thoughts to the other two.

"No trouble so far, wot? Longeyes must have spotted the burnt-out ship a bit further up the coast. We'll patrol further up and camp on the jolly old seashore tonight—might even try a shellfish stew, eh, Rosie? Long time since you've cooked one. If we don't catch sight of any bother by tomorrow afternoon late, we'll head back to Salamandastron."

There was a whooshing noise and a trident buried itself in the sand not a paw's-length from Thyme.

"Ears down, chaps! Attack!"

Throwing themselves flat facing three directions, the long patrol started instinctively pushing the sand around them into a barrier. The croaking of countless natterjacks filled the dunes.

"Dig your slings and stones out, too many for lances," Clary called to his companions. "By the left! This is all we need, that villain Oykamon and his slimy mob attackin' us when we're out on a mission. By the right, center and by the cringe, I'll show 'em!"

Hon Rosie slung a flat pebble at a toad charging over the hill. It connected with a splat, knocking the toad out like a light. "Whoohahahahoohah!" she whooped. "That bagged the blighter. I'm pretty fair at slingin'. I'll get that big fat rogue, you watch. Whoohahahahoohah! Good shot, Rosie!"

Thyme waggled a paw in his ear between launching off missiles. "Stone me, Rosie. You could scare 'em all off with that pesky laughin' of yours."

"Whoohahahaoohah! You are a card, Thyme, no mistake. Watch that feller to your left! Oh, never mind, I'll lay him out. Howzat, middle an' stump!"

Clary got two toads with one of his special bouncing shots. "Corks! I say, there must be squillions of the reptiles. We're goin' to run out of stones before they run out of soldiers, I suspect."

Thyme banged the heads of two venturesome toads who had climbed the barricade, and they both fell back senseless.

"One thing you can say about big chief Oykamon—he keeps his word. He said he'd be back with a full complement. We're on a sticky wicket, Clary old lad. Any ideas?"

Colonel Clary glanced up at the sky before launching off another stone. "Funny you should say that, Thyme. Matter of fact, I've come up with a pretty good wheeze, actually. It'll soon be evenin'. Now the minute it starts gettin' darkish, keep your eyes peeled for a sight of the old arch baddie himself, Oykamon. Rosie, you're the best shot—choose yourself a jolly good big pebble. I want him knocked out cold. That'll upset the lads of the sandhills, and they'll prob'ly crowd round to see if he's dead. Then we'll make a run for it, go straight for the sea, just about paw-deep, and keep goin' north. Toads aren't too fussy on salt water, so they'll give up following us if we sprint fast enough. How's your throwin' paw, Rosie old gel?"

"Top-hole. Don't fret, Clary. I'll put the old bandit asleep until this time next season. Now let's see, which is m' biggest stone? Oh, this one's rather pretty, nice little sticky-out bits. Whoohahahahoohah!"

Luck was on the side of the long patrol that evening, and Clary's plan ran true to form. Illuminated by two lanterns, Oykamon appeared atop a nearby dune, his bulging throat pulsating in and out as he bellowed.

"Krroikl! You were warned, longears. Now you will

die knowing the power and might of Oykamon. Krrrikk!"

Hon Rosie popped up, twirling the large rock in her slingshot. "Shall I bowl him a googly, Clary?"

"Certainly, Rosie old gel. Shut the fat blighter up."

The rock flew straight and hard, whacking Oykamon with a force that sent him head over webs. Clary and Thyme's slings took the lantern holders out. Immediately, the dunes and shore became a mass of natterjacks. Croaking and clicking with dismay, they hopped speedily over to their fallen leader. The hares of the long patrol were up and gone with a turn of speed that would have left a hunting hawk flabbergasted.

They splashed along the shoreline in the failing light, a red bronze sun turning the wavelets to liquid gold as they skimmed and bounced.

"Excellent shot, Rosie. An absolute bull's-eye, wot!"

"Rather. He did a full double backflip when that rock beezed him."

"Oh, d'you think so? Thanks awfully, chaps. Whoohahahahoohah!"

Dandin spread his paws wide. "Back off. This bird means business!"

Mariel sprang forward. The heron struck, and she dodged sideways, narrowly getting clear of the huge pointed beak, which left a deep dent in the path.

"Mariel get back, he'll kill you," Dandin yelled.

The heron hopped in on spindly legs, flapping his wide wings and screeching, "Irrrraktaan will spearrrrr your hearrrrrt! Irrrrraktaan knows no fearrrr!"

Mariel rolled over and over, keeping a fraction ahead of the murderous stabbing beak. A movement caught Iraktaan's quick eye, and he glanced to one side. There was Durry Quill, rolling past him in a tight ball. The heron struck at the hedgehog, but his beakpoint encountered a hard spike and bounced back with a pinging noise.

The moment's breathing space was all Mariel needed. She whirled Gullwhacker and struck Iraktaan across the legs, right on the narrow knee joints. The knotted rope wrapped round the heron's legs several times. He tried to move but crashed to the ground. Immediately, Tarquin was there. He sat across the middle of Iraktaan's neck. Before the great bird could start flapping its wings, Dandin passed the remainder of the rope across them and stood on the rope's end. Durry Quill tugged and chewed at some bindweed, snapping several lengths off.

" 'Ere, tie that burd up wi' some o' this."

Tarquin grabbed a strand and wound it round and round the clacking beak. Dandin took the rest and hobbled Iraktaan's legs securely, passing it through the joint of one wing and knotting it off. Breathing heavily, they stood up. Mariel disengaged Gullwhacker from the heron's legs and whirled it close to the bird's head.

"Be still! Be still, I say, or I'll scramble your silly brains!"

The heron's eyes rolled madly, but he lay still, feathers in disarray, hissing and blowing through his fearsome beak. Dandin unsheathed the sword of Martin and placed the point at Iraktaan's crop.

"When we are gone, you will be able to free yourself. But hear what I say, Iraktaan. Follow us, and I will slay you with this sword. It has taken more lives than there are feathers on your body. I am Dandin the Sword Carrier, and you can believe my word. We wish only to cross the ford in peace. Stay where you are, wait until we are gone, then loose yourself."

Iraktaan wriggled a bit and made stifled noises but they ignored him. The ford appeared neither too wide or deep, but with masses of long trailing weeds waving beneath the surface. Tarquin took a few paces back as if he were going to rush at it with a hop, leap and jump. "Wish me luck, chaps. Here goes!"

Dandin stood barring his path. "Wait, Tarquin. Remember the old saying, look before you leap?"

"Of course, old lad. Well, I've bally well looked, and now I'm goin' to jolly well leap . . ."

"Oh no you're not!"

"I say, Dandin, you've become rather bossy since you started wearin' that blinkin' sword. 'My name is Dandin the Sword Carrier,' eh? Righto, give me one good reason why I shouldn't leap, and I shan't."

Dandin recited the words of the poem which he had memorized.

"This trail brings death with every pace;
Beware of dangers lurking there,
Sticklegs of the feathered race
And fins that in the ford do stir.

Well, as you can see, we've already met the sticklegs—Iraktaan took care of that. Our next hazard is fins that in the ford do stir. Let's try out an idea before we attempt crossing."

Together they went to the water's edge. Dandin took a crust of bread from his knapsack and tossed it into the ford. It drifted on the surface of the water. They stood watching the bread. Like a small golden-crusted boat, it moved slowly downstream on the calm river.

Durrey did not seem too impressed. "My old nuncle'd say that there's a waste o' good food."

Quick as a lightning flash, a mighty silver black-banded body whooshed out of the weeds. There was an explosion of water, a gleam of needlelike teeth, a huge splash, and the ford returned to its former calm.

Durry Quill grabbed hold of Mariel's sleeve tightly. "Sufferin' spikes, what were that?"

Tarquin sat down in the dust looking decidedly shaky. "Pike, old lad. An absolute whopper. A fish like that'd rip you up as soon as look at you. Dandin, I'm never backward in comin' forward—you were right."

Dandin was pacing the ford edge. "Look, there's more than one, much more."

Peering carefully into the reeds, they were able to make out at least eight of the long, sleek bodies. Nose-on to the current, they backed water, fully grown, hook-jawed and totally dangerous.

Mariel sat down with Tarquin. "Time for thinking caps. Glad you came with me, after all!"

They sat in silence, watching the setting sun sink beneath the trees. Durry Quill drew patterns in the dust. "Mayhap we need a bridge."

Tarquin snorted. "Right you are, let's start buildin' one right away. Shouldn't take us long—middle of next season, with a bit of luck."

Durry snorted back at him. "If brains was bees, there'd be no honey between your ears. Why, from where I'm a sittin' I can see a great dead tree limb among yon bushes. What's to stop us usin' it as a bridge?"

The hare stood up, bowing gracefully to the young hedgehog. "Profuse apologies an' all that, young master Quill. Forgive me. The excellence of your suggestion is only surpassed by your good looks and keen intelligence."

Placed across the ford, the thick, dead tree limb looked wobbly and unsafe. As Mariel tested it she noted the position of the voracious pike.

"See, the fish have come out of the weeds. They're all waiting both sides of our bridge, just beneath the surface. We'd better not put a paw wrong crossing that thing."

Mariel decided that she would go first. Stepping onto the branch, she wound Gullwhacker about her neck and held her paws wide to give herself a bit of stability. The mousemaid paced forward carefully, the branch shaking slightly beneath her tread. Hungry pike nosed closer, their underslung jaws agape as they watched her.

"Don't look down, Mariel," Dandin called out. "Keep your eyes straight ahead on the other side. You're doing fine!"

Now she had reached the center, the branch dipped slightly, its underside touching the water. A pike butted the branch with its curving mouth, causing it to wobble dangerously. Mariel went down on all fours, gripping the bridge firmly. She waited until it ceased moving then scampered across swiftly, leaping the final part and landing safe on the other side of the ford.

"Well crossed, young mouse, well crossed, I say. Who's next?"

Dandin elected to try, with Mariel sitting on one end

of the makeshift bridge and Tarquin holding the other end down. Dandin held the sword in both paws, straight out in front; it helped to balance him. The young mouse had a surprising natural agility. Despite the pike nosing against the branch, he made it across with ease, even leaping ashore with a fancy twirl of the sword.

Tarquin nudged Durry Quill. "Your turn, old chap."

The young hedgehog blinked his eyes and gulped. "If I turns out t' be a fish's supper, tell my old nuncle Gabriel that I love him dear an' I was a-thinkin' of him even as I was bein' ate. Ah well! C'mon, Durry. Brace up, Quill. If y'don't try now, y'never will."

With these few poetic lines, Durry scuttled out across the branch on all fours. It shook and wobbled furiously. The others held their breath, not wanting to call out advice lest they should upset him. The hedgehog was at the center of the bridge when a monstrous pike hurled itself clear of the water, arching its sinuous body as it slammed forcibly into the branch. Durry plopped off into the ford, yelling as the pike closed in on him, "I'm a-thinkin' of 'ee, Nuncle Gabe. Heeeeeelp!"

"Eulaliaaaaa!"

Tarquin L. Woodsorrel came tearing out along the branch, half in and half out of the water, the branch flopping up and down madly into the ford. Grabbing Durry by the snout, he swung him clear of the pike's jaws. Kicking one pike savagely and braining another with his harolina, the hare carried straight on with his mad dash. He sprinted out of the water with Durry held tight, a damaged harolina, and a big female pike latched onto him, its teeth sunk into his bobtail. Tarquin let go of Durry and performed a mad war dance on the bank.

"Yahwoo! Leggo, y'beast, leggo!"

Mariel twirled Gullwhacker and struck the pike, batting it with all her might. It separated from Tarquin's tail and shot through the air, landing in the ford with an awkward splosh.

"Hooray!" Durry cheered. "I ain't ate, and we're all safe 'n' dry."

"Hah, I'm glad you're pleased, young Quill. Look at

me! A chunk of m' bottom and half a tailbob missin'. What'll Hon Rosie say when she sees my handsome form disfigured?"

They made camp in a forest glade farther up the road as night fell. Mariel and Dandin setting out the supper, Tarquin repairing his harolina, whilst Durry Quill put together one of his sovereign poultices for the hare's nether end. Mariel conversed quietly with her friend as they sat eating.

"Dandin, where did you get that beautiful sword?"

"You'd never believe if I told you, Mariel, but it came to me in a dream."

"A dream? Surely you're not serious . . ."

"Oh, but I am. Strange, though. I dreamed I saw a mouse in full armor. He just stood there, watching me and smiling. I felt so peaceful and friendly and at ease with him, it was wonderful. He said to me, 'Dandin, go with Mariel.' Just those four words, then he took his sword and scabbard and laid them at my side. I knew it was only a dream, a dream which I wanted to last forever, but it didn't. When I woke before dawn, there were the sword and scabbard by my side. It must have been the spirit of Martin the Warrior—he founded our Abbey. Martin is guardian of Redwall. They say he comes whenever the Abbey or its creatures are in danger. I always thought it was just a nice story, until he visited me. I'll never forget it, Mariel."

The mousemaid crumbled a piece of bread and watched the ants bearing the fragments away, her face a strange picture of wonderment.

"As you were speaking, Dandin, I remembered. It all came back. I dreamed of your Martin last night. He was just as you described him, a wonderful brave figure. He said: 'Be brave, Mariel. Follow your heart's desire.' He was there in my dreams one moment and gone the next. I know what you mean when you say you'll never forget. I was so sad when he disappeared."

"Anybeast want more soup? If not, I'll just have what's left in the pot t' keep me goin' through the old night watches, wot? I say, Dandin, can you recall the next part of that rhyme thingummy?"

The young mouse thought of his friend Saxtus as he spoke the lines.

"After the ford, one night, one day,
Seek out the otter and his wife.
Forsake the path, go westlands way,
Find the trail and lose your life."

Durry sniffed as he beat Tarquin to the last of the soup. "Lackaday, that sounds cheerful, don't it? I wonder who the otter 'n' his wife be."

Night closed in on the few red embers of the campfire in the glade as the travelers lay to rest, Tarquin with his harolina, Durry with a well-licked soup bowl, Mariel with her Gullwhacker and Dandin with the strange ancient sword of Martin the Warrior.

17

Orgeye of the *Waveblade* had dropped anchor in Terramort cove earlier that same evening. Confining his crew to shipboard, he strode up to Fort Bladegirt, aware of the reception he would receive coming back empty-clawed. Gabool was in a murderous mood; even the slaves were hiding and dared not attend him. The King of the Searats had gone past sleeping. His eyes were completely blood-red, but he quivered with a furious nervous energy, roaming the banqueting hall, drinking wine straight from the flagon. Orgeye walked in without knocking. Gabool did not acknowledge him at first, but strode about shouting, "Look! . . . Look at this, half-cooked seabird still with the feathers hanging from it!"

He hurled the silver platter, splattering food across the walls.

"Not a slave to look after my needs. Me, the Ruler of all Seas! Wine? This tastes more like vinegar. They're tryin' to poison me. That's it! They can't get me while I'm asleep because I won't go to sleep . . . No sleep . . . No rest for Gabool . . ."

He appeared to notice Orgeye for the first time. "Saltar! No, it can't be—I slew him. Haharr, it's Orgeye, my old grogmate. Belay there, I knew you wouldn't let Gabool down. I knew out of all those slopbacks you'd be the one to bring me back the *Darkqueen* an' Greypatch's mangy skull!"

Orgeye moved away until the big table was between him and the Warlord. "Gabool, listen. I scoured the seas to the far west from here and past the horizon. I searched the bare rocks and small islands until I ran short of vittles an' water for the crew an' meself. There's no sign of Graypatch at all. Wherever he's taken the *Darkqueen* to, we'll never find him, on my oath!"

The flagon narrowly missed Orgeye. It smashed upon the door, cascading blood-red wine everywhere. Gabool looked madly about for something else to throw.

"Garrr! You lyin' traitor, you useless mud-suckin' scum. If you couldn't find him west'ard, you should have sailed south."

Orgeye was backing toward the door. He did not want to be in the same room with this mad creature.

"Hold fast there, Gabool. Take it easy. I only put in to Terramort for fresh provisions. You say go south—right, then I'll take the *Waveblade* on a southern course, soon as I've taken fresh vittles aboard."

Gabool drew his sword and advanced, foaming at the mouth. "Vittles, you bottlenosed trash. Vittles? I'll give ye vittles, bucko. I'll carve yer tripes out and feed 'em to your scurvy crew. Set course south an' gerrout o' me sight. You don't get a crust o' my bread or a drop of water until you bring me the *Darkqueen* an' Graypatch's head!"

Orgeye barely had time to slam the door and run. Gabool was tugging and pulling as he cursed, and his sword was buried deep in the heavy oak door. Behind him the bell tolled once. He heaved the sword blade from the door and came at the bell.

"Silence, d'ye hear me! Silence! Boomin' an' bongin' away night an' day so a body can't even sleep. I'll teach yer a lesson!"

Two dormouse slaves peering through a crack in the door watched fascinated as the King of Searats attacked a bell with his sword. The bell clashed and clanged as Gabool hammered at it, both claws gripping his curved blade. The one-sided fight could have only one possible outcome. The sword blade snapped against the great bell and Gabool lay facedown upon the stone floor, panting and sobbing as the metallic echoes of the bell swirled around the banqueting hall.

The dormouse slave turned to his companion. "Did you see that?"

"Aye, that I did. It looks like His Majesty is two waves short of a tide. Whoever saw a rat fight a bell?"

"Right, mate. And look, he lost. The great Gabool's cryin' on the floor like a baby squirrel who's lost his acorns. Hahahaha!"

The laughter rang through into the hall as the two slaves fled back into hiding.

Gabool gritted his teeth at the bell. "Go on, laugh, yer great brazen lump. Laugh away, but next time I'll get a bigger sword!"

Abbot Bernard sat at late supper with Simeon, Mellus and Gabriel Quill. Foremole wandered in and sat picking at the barely touched food on the table.

"Burr, maisters. No news of 'ee young 'uns, then?"

Simeon felt the round firmness of an apple as he polished it on his sleeve. "No news as yet, Foremole. But don't worry, they've got everything on their side—youth, health, strength and a sense of adventure. I wish that I were with them, old as I am."

Mother Mellus tapped the table fretfully. "I wish I were with them, too. I'd tan that Dandin's hide until he turned blue, the disobedient little wretch. That's all the thanks you get for looking after them, caring, worrying when they're ill. What about that scallywag nephew of yours, Gabe Quill?"

"Well, he fair shocked me, I can tell 'ee. Young Durry were always a quiet sort of 'og, good worker too. If you were to ask me I'd say as 'ee were led astray by that

Storm Gullywhacker. My word, she's a wild 'un fer a liddle mouse, that she is."

"If the three were gone together then I think it is for the best."

Mother Mellus pushed aside her plate. "How can you say that, Simeon?"

"Because either Dandin or Mariel has the spirit of Martin the Warrior walking alongside them, though I am not sure which one it is."

Abbot Bernard looked thankfully toward his friend. "Well, bless the seasons! Tell me more of this, friend Simeon."

Mellus, ever the big practical badger mother, stood up from the table. "I'm off to my bed, can't stop around here all night with young 'uns missing and you lot yarning away bout long-dead warriors. Martin or no Martin, first thing tomorrow I'm putting that big otter, wotsisname, Flagg, out on their trail. He'll bring the rascals back!"

When she had gone, blind Simeon began recounting his strange but wondrous experience.

"It happened last night as I sat dozing in my chair by the window. Oh, pour me some October ale, will you, Gabe—my throat's a bit dry."

Somewhere out in the darkness a young blackbird chirruped as its mother drew it under her wing against the all-enveloping night.

Dawn broke gray with an unexpected shroud of drizzling rain. The four travelers were abroad early, continuing their northward trek upon the path. The flatlands to the west had been left behind after the ford, now the forest closed in either side of the path.

"Pretty good this, wot? The jolly old trees leaning over are like an umbrella, dontcha think?"

Durry shook himself. "No I don't, if tain't churnin' up the path into mud this rain is a drippin' off those trees onto the back of 'ee neck. Still, as my old nuncle allus says, if it be rainin' then there do be water pourin' from the sky."

Mariel smiled and winked at Tarquin. "A wise fellow, your old uncle."

Durry nodded in innocent agreement. "Oh aye, Nuncle Gabe's never short of wise sayin's. There do be no better way o' eatin' than with 'ee mouth, a full barrel's not an empty 'un, an' 'ee can allus tell a squirrel by his tail."

Tarquin chuckled as he tuned his harolina. "Hmm, that makes sense."

Durry sniffed. "A course it do. Bet you never see'd a squirrel wi'out one o' those lollopin' great bushy tails, did you?"

"Er, ah, no, don't s'pose I did, really."

"There, that goes to show 'ee then. You can allus tell a squirrel by his tail, jus' like my nuncle says."

Dandin kept in close to the pathside. "The rain's getting heavier."

There was a distant roll of thunder, lightning illuminated the sky. As they trudged on Durry whispered to Dandin, "Lookit, Mariel's dropped back. 'Pears to me she's shiverin' an' un'appy about summat."

They hurried back to Mariel. She was clutching herself, rain dripping from her face and paws, shivering as she faltered along the path.

Dandin looked worried. "Mariel, what's the matter with you?"

The mousemaid leaned against a spruce tree. "Thunder, the rain and the lightning . . . Reminded me of being thrown in the sea by Gabool . . . Terramort, my father . . ."

Tarquin took charge. "Golly, you look like a whitewashed duck, old thing. Here, Dandin, lend a paw. We'll get her under some dry trees and light a fire, she'd better rest up until this lot clears."

Slightly off the path on the east side they found a fir grove. Durry dug a shallow pit and kindled a small fire with dead branches and dry pine needles. With her back against a fir, Mariel sat dozing, soaking in the warmth of the fragrant dry atmosphere. Beyond the trees the rain pounded hard against the path, sending up brown splotches as it churned the dust to mud. Durry brewed some sage and mint tea, and they sipped the steaming liquid gratefully.

About halfway through the morning Dandin became aware that they were being watched by something crouching in the grass on their left. Slowly he unsheathed the sword, signaling with his eyes to Tarquin and Durry. All three rose quietly and moved toward the long grass until they could see the watcher.

It was a large snake!

Dandin had never seen a snake before, though he had heard many stories at Redwall of the dangerous poison-teeth. He felt a shiver convulse his whole body at the sight of the slithering coils, the flickering tongue and the twin beads of cold ruthlessness of the reptile's eyes. It came clear of the long grass, hissing and weaving its head from side to side as it menaced them. Dandin unsheathed his sword, whispering to Tarquin, "What do we do now? It looks very dangerous."

The hare took the nearest weapon to paw, his haversack of food. He stood at ease, swinging it experimentally as he replied, "Nothing to worry about really, old bean. See those black markings on the thing's back? Well, that's supposed to be an adder. Camouflage, I think—the bally creature's a bit small for an adder, take my word, laddie. There's lots of harmless grass snakes who mark themselves up with plant dyes an' whatnot, just so travelers like you an' I will think they're adders an' become frightened of 'em."

Dandin kept his sword pointed at the serpent's head. "D'you think so, Tarquin?"

" 'Course I do, old son," the confident hare snorted. "The blighter's a fraud, a blinkin' charlatan. Right then, you dreadful snake thingy. Move out or I'll brain you on the bonce with this havvysack, d'you hear?"

The snake, however, had other ideas. It had fixed its reptilian stare on Durry Quill and was gliding slowly toward him. Durry stood rooted to the spot, trembling and unable to move under the hypnotic spell of the reptile's evil eyes.

• • •

Sitting in a half-slumber, Mariel gradually noticed that some creature was talking to her. She opened her eyes partially and saw the armor-clad figure of the dream mouse warrior whom Dandin had called Martin. His voice was strong and stern.

"Mariel, rise up, your friends are in danger. Rise up, Mariel!"

The mousemaid's eyes snapped open. She took in the situation at a single glance. Throwing caution to the winds, she acted swiftly.

The snake's eyes were fixed on Durry as Mariel grabbed her Gullwhacker. With a mad, silent dash and a mighty leap the mousemaid jumped clear over the snake's head, bringing the knotted rope down with a mighty crack on the reptile's flat head as she traveled through the air. The snake instantly dropped like a limp piece of cord, stunned by the sudden impact of the blow.

"Durry, are you all right? Durry, speak to me!"

The young hedgehog blinked and rubbed his eyes as Dandin flung a beaker of cold sage and mint tea into his friend's face.

"Phwaaw! I'd sooner be in yon ford wi' pikes than lookin' at that bad thing. I don't reckon that were no grass snake."

Tarquin took a quick close look at the snake, which was beginning to recover speedily.

"Nor do I, old fellah. Still, a chap's allowed a mistake or two, wot? The bally thing's a real adder! Oh, not a fully grown one, I'll grant you, but nevertheless . . ."

Dandin grabbed the hare, shoving him out upon the rain-spattered path. "Quick, let's get out of here. We're not stopping to argue with an adder. Come on, the rain'll put those fire embers out."

Grabbing their packs, they dashed out of the grove onto the path, stumbling and squelching as the snake's angry hiss sounded behind them.

Mariel felt much better as she ran alongside her companions. Pounding along the muddy path with the rain bouncing off them, they kept up a breakneck pace until they were certain the adder was far behind them. Farther along the road they halted, heads bowed, panting and blowing as they fought to regain their breath. Dandin glared at Tarquin. "Don't ever do that again, friend."

Tarquin shrugged nonchalantly. "Sorry, old bean. How was I t' know?"

Durry shuddered. "You should've chopped often its head wi' that sword when you 'ad the chance, Dandin."

Mariel shook her head. "No, we do not need unnecessary killing, Durry. As long as we are safe and in one piece, the adder has a right to life, the same as any creature."

By early afternoon the black cloud had shifted. The rain halted abruptly and a warm wind chased broken white clouds across a blue sky considerably brightened by the sun. The companions took food upon the path, walking as they ate. Steam and vapor rose from their wet fur and clothing as they tramped northward. Durry's spirits rose, even to performing a passable imitation of Tarquin's flippant attitude.

"Ho, I say, old bean, be that a wood pigeon or a great eagle? Blow me, I do believe it's carryin' me off over the jolly ol' treetops to eat me all up. Ho dearie me, I don't s'pose it's a wood pigeon. Must've made a jolly ol' mistake, wot wot?"

Tarquin took the ragging in his carefree stride.

"Well, roast my aunt's chestnuts, was that a hedgehog or a noisy pincushion? No, it couldn't be. I s'pose it was a jolly old talkin' gooseberry, bit too spiky to bake in a pie, so somebeast slung it out onto the path and it's followin' us."

Mariel looped Gullwhacker swiftly about Tarquin's shoulders. "Look out, it's an adder just dropped out of a tree!"

"Yaaagh! Whoohooh! Don't do that, miss. You frightened me half t' death."

Dandin had been watching the way ahead. He pointed forward. "Look, there's the otter and his wife!"

Durry kept up his banter. "No tain't, it's the frog an' his gran'father."

But Dandin was sure of what he could see. "Stop fooling around, Durry. Can't you see? Look on the left side of the path further on—it is the otter and his wife."

Mariel smiled. "Yes, you're right, Dandin, though I never thought the otter and his wife would look like that!"

18

It was an ill-tempered and pawsore crew that blundered their way through Mossflower led by Pakatugg, whom Graypatch prodded ahead of them by swordpoint. Far behind them the *Darkqueen* lay hidden in the creek.

Bigfang as usual was voicing his thoughts aloud. "We could be traipsin' anywheres, mates. I reckon we're lost. Leavin' *Darkqueen* deserted like that. Me an' Kybo or any couple of us could have stayed back as sentries. I tell yer, mates, it's a bad omen, us lost out 'ere in the forest an' *Darkqueen* wi'out a guard to watch her."

Graypatch gritted his teeth. Pushing the reluctant hedgehog pathfinder forward, he called back, "That loudmouth sounds like Bigfang again. Don't worry, matey, I can hear ye. If you like to go back an' mount sentry on *Darkqueen*, don't let me stop yer. Take Kybo too, if ye've a mind. Aye, y'can laze about on the ship's deck while yer messmates do all the marchin' an' fightin' for you. Is that what ye want?"

Bigfang knew he was trying Graypatch's patience, but he continued, hoping for some support from the rest of the searats.

"It's not like the open sea, messmates. This filthy jungle's so thick you can't tell thither from yon. Aye, I still reckons we're lost. An' it ain't right leavin' our only ship undefended . . ."

Graypatch tugged on the halter around Pakatugg's neck, bringing him up sharp. His single eye glared so hard at Bigfang that the complaining searat took a step back.

Graypatch's tone was dangerously level. "Right, bucko, get back to the ship. Go on, take two more with yeh. If one o' Gabool's craft sailed up that creek fully crewed, what d'yer think three, or even four, could do against it, eh? Nothin'! Not a thing, addlebrain. The ship's safe layin' hidden in that backwater; nobeast is goin' to find her. I need every fightin' rat I've got for what lays ahead. Now get marchin', afore I cuts yer adrift an' leaves you for lost in these woods. One more word from ye, Bigfang, that's all. Just one peep!"

Unaccustomed to the foreign woodland, the crew stumbled on for the remainder of the day, insect-bitten and nettlestung, thrashing at the undergrowth with dagger and cutlass. Graypatch led his sullen band, whilst muttering dire threats to Pakatugg on the consequences of leading them astray.

Evening shades were drawing close as Graypatch and his crew sighted Redwall Abbey. The searat Captain tugged sharply on the rope halter, dragging the miserable Pakatugg back from the path into the cover of Mossflower Woods. Graypatch pricked the squirrel's chin with his dagger tip.

"So that's Redwall Abbey, eh, mate. You did well. I don't reckon there'd be as cozy a berth within a season's march of here."

Bigfang hefted a spear. "Come on, let's rip 'em apart an' take the place."

Kybo and the others moved forward, weapons at the ready. As Bigfang took up the lead position, Greypatch tripped him. He fell heavily, half rising to find Greypatch's sword edge at his throat.

"Didn't take yer long to vote yerself in as Captain round 'ere, did it, Bigfang?"

"You said it was a cozy berth. Let's take it, less'n you're scared."

Graypatch kicked Bigfang flat on his back, his single eye watching the rebellious crewrat scornfully.

"Careful isn't scared, mate. I'm careful. Who knows how many are behind those walls, or what manner of creatures they are. All that's got to be found out, then we'll have the measure o' them. Now take you, Bigfang. You're not scared, are yer, bucko? No, you're stupid! Thick'eaded an' dimwitted, that's you. Harken, you scum. Anyone wants to challenge me as Cap'n, let that rat do it now an' we'll settle it right 'ere."

There was a murmur and a shuffle from among the large rough contingent, but no rat took up the challenge. Graypatch nodded with satisfaction, he swung his sword and cut through a tuft of Bigfang's whiskers before turning confidently away from his former adversary.

"Good, that's as it should be. I'm Cap'n 'ere—me, Graypatch. 'Twas me that brought you 'ere; without me you'd still be servin' crazy Gabool, wonderin' who'd be next to feed the fishes, worryin' whether you'd looked at him the wrong way an' were due to wake up with a dagger in yer back. Trust me, lads, an' we'll live off the fat o'the land."

Ranzo stood alongside Graypatch, brandishing a cutlass. "We're with you, Cap'n. You just issue orders an' we'll be there."

Graypatch lounged against a tree and plucked a low-hanging pear. "Lookit that, will yer! Vittles a-growin' on trees, by thunder! What we'll do is this. We'll drop anchor 'ere for the night, then at the crack o' dawn tomorrow when they're all nice an' peaceful, we'll drop over an' pay 'em a visit."

He threw the halter over a limb of the tree, tugging it slightly so that the miserable Pakatugg had to stand on tip-paws.

"As fer you, matey, you stand by 'ere. I'll need you

on the morrow. Don't try any funny moves now, or there won't be only pears hangin' from this tree!"

Simeon stood upon the west wall ramparts with his friend the Abbot, as they did most evenings before turning in.

"More rain tomorrow, do you think, Simeon?"

"No, Bernard. It will be a fine hot summerday with hardly a cloud in the sky. The weather should stay fine for Mariel and her party. I wonder where they are now."

"Who can say? Rushing and dashing off on quests and adventures—it must be nice to be young and have all that energy."

Simeon smiled. "Talking about energy and youthfulness, I think I hear Mellus coming from the woods with her party of Dibbuns. I hope their wildberry-gathering expedition was a success."

Abbot Bernard folded his paws into the wide habit sleeves. "Success or not, maybe it has tired them out and they'll sleep soundly tonight. Where are they now, Simeon?"

The blind herbalist inclined his head to one side, listening carefully. "Just coming out of the woodlands slightly northeast of here. Can you see them yet, Bernard?"

"Ah yes. Poor Mellus looks as if she's had a full day of it. Rather her than me. I used to take them out when I was younger, but we never had a pair like those little otter twins Bagg and Runn then. Don't think I could put up with a full day's wildberry gathering in Mossflower with that pair. Mellus has seen us, she's waving."

Simeon turned in the direction of the badger and waved back. "Mother Mellus, how did the berry gathering go today?"

Mellus's gruff boom rang up from the path below. "It was good, Simeon. I got some herbs that you may need too; arrowhead, motherwort, pennybright, oh, and some slippery elm bark."

"Thank you, friend. I hope Bagg and Runn behaved themselves."

"Surprisingly, they did. Those two collected more berries than the rest put together. That little mole Grubb was the naughty one today. The wretch covered me in sticky-buds while I took my lunchtime nap, then he began eating the berries the other Dibbuns had collected and he tied three little mice's tails together with vines. Next time he can stay behind in the kitchens and help Friar Alder to peel vegetables. Where is he now? Hey, come back here, you little rip!"

Baby Grubb had run off in the opposite direction from the Abbey and was scuttling along at a fair rate. Away he went up the north path, chattering to himself.

"Burr, oim agoen' to foind a'ventures wi' Gully-whacker an' 'ee others."

Mother Mellus broke into a shambling run. "Come back this instant, you little rogue. You're going to bed!"

Grubb trotted off the path, into the woodlands. Graypatch and Frink, hiding behind a broad oak, watched the infant mole unsuspectingly coming toward them. The searat Captain held a noosed rope ready.

"There ain't nothin' like a baby 'ostage to make things easy," he whispered to his crewrat.

Grubb trundled along, oblivious to all about him. He needed a weapon if he was going to join the travelers on their adventure. Right next to the broad oak was a sycamore sprout, little more than a thin stick. Grubb began heaving and tugging upon it.

"Hurr, this'll do oi, 'ee'll make a gurt spearer, ho urr!"

As Graypatch opened the noose to cast it over Grubb's head, Mother Mellus swept the tiny mole up with one huge paw, unaware of the searats.

"Got you, mischiefskin! Right, m'laddo, bed for you with no supper. What have you been told about pulling young trees up by the roots? Just wait until Abbot Bernard hears about this, you wretch!"

Graypatch had pulled back behind the oak. He and Frink held their breath as Mellus strode off with a loudly protesting Grubb under her arm.

"Boohurr, let oi go, missus. Oi wants a'ventures."

"I'll give you adventures, you rip. Adventures in bed!"

"Gurr, when oi get ter be a biggun, oi'll spank 'ee fur thiz!"

Frink wiped his brow and sat down heavily. "Shiver me sails, Cap'n. Did you see the size of that ol'badger?"

"Did I? Now y'see what I said earlier is true, Frink. Careful is best. If we'd roped the liddle mole, that ol' badger would've done fer the pair of us with one swipe, you mark my words!"

At the open gate, Abbot Bernard carried Grubb inside. "Come on, Dibbun, Grubb, berry pie and custard for supper."

"Burry poi an' cuskit, oh joy! But zurr, Ma Mellus says oi ain't a-getten none fer bein' pesky."

The Father Abbot set Grubb down upon the lawn. "Hmmm, did she? Tell you what, little Grubb. You can have some this time, but next time you're pesky it's straight off to bed without any. Go on, hurry and get washed up or it'll all be gone."

Grubb smiled one of his most winning smiles at his benefactor. "Oi knowed you wudden let a hinfant starve. You'm a gudd beast, zurr!"

Simeon joined the Abbot to follow up Mellus and her herd of Dibbuns.

"Ah, Simeon, smell that. Young Cockleburr makes the finest cornflower custard I've ever tasted. Can you smell it?"

Simeon looked pensive. "Hmmm, I think my senses are trying to tell me something and it's not the smell of custard, Bernard. It's. . . . It's. . . . Oh, it's probably nothing, friend. Let's go inside. You're right, that custard does smell delicious."

The four travelers stood facing the rock which reared up from the earth on the west side of the path. Mariel looked up at it.

"So that's the otter and his wife. I expected real otters, not a great lump of stone. Still, it does look very lifelike. I wonder who carved it."

Tarquin rubbed his paw up and down the smooth

brown rock. "Somebeast must've done this when the land was young, more seasons ago than we could ever imagine. Jolly fine work, wot? I think the rock once looked naturally like an otter and his wife. Whoever did it only had to improve on what mother nature had already started, eh?"

Dandin nodded agreement. The rock was a sort of double lump, looking not unlike a male otter standing on his hindpaws with a female otter sitting at his side. Long ago some clever creature had carved the details of the otters' faces into the stone, giving them a very lifelike appearance.

The four friends made night camp at the base of the figures on the woodland side. Tinder and flint kindled a small fire. Tarquin, taking his turn as cook, decided on candied dried plums, sweet chestnut scones and dandelion cordial. They sat around the bright flames, which provided an island of golden light against the gloomy vault of the forest in front of them. Dandin recited the next stanza of the rhyme which provided guide rules for their quest.

"Seek out the otter and his wife.
Forsake the path, go westlands way,
Find the trail and lose your life.
When in the woods this promise keep,
With senses sharp and open eyes,
'My nose shall not send me to sleep'
For buried ones will surely rise."

Durry Quill's eyes were drooping. He was beginning to nod.

"And frogs will fly on mayday morn,
While fishes sing aloud at dawn.

Huh, I can't make top nor tail of it. It all sounds like nonsense to a pore lad who's been hippotized by a serpent."

Mariel stirred the fire with a green twig. "It may sound

like gobbledygook but it's proved true so far, Durry. We'll just have to wait until it's light and find out for ourselves, I suppose. What d' you say, Tarquin?"

The hare nibbled on a candied plum reflectively. "Don't know really, old gel. Y'see I've never patrolled this far up north. Strange country, very strange. Take these woodlands west of the path; they're not even mapped, y'know, I'm not sure they're even part of Mossflower."

Dandin hunched closer to the fire. "I'm certain they're not. They don't have that comfortable homey feeling you always get in Mossflower Woods. This area looks wilder, more grim, hostile somehow. But as you say, Mariel, we'll find out for ourselves tomorrow. I take it we have this statue of the otter and his wife to use as a bearing point and strike out west from it."

"Sssnnnngggghhhhrrrrr!"

Durry Quill was not listening, he was lying on his back with all four paws in the air, making the most uproarious noise.

Tarquin sniffed. "Listen to the beast, snorin' like a flippin' hog, just as I was going to play a few tunes on me harolina to cheer us up."

Mariel lay down, using her haversack as a pillow. "Oh please, it's bad enough having a snoring hedgehog without the addition of a caterwauling hare singing lovelorn ditties. Let's all go to sleep while we have the chance of a full night's rest."

Dandin and Mariel soon joined Durry in slumber. Tarquin still sat up, a little sulky as he fondled his unplayed harolina.

"Caterwaulin' indeed. Shows how much mice know about music. Now if Hon Rosie were here I'll bet she wouldn't object to a chap havin' the odd plunk on the jolly old harolina. Ah well!"

He fell asleep humming and serenading himself quietly.

"A hare beyond compare, so spiffin' and so fair,
Oh, Rosie, Rosie, dear my honey Hon,

I wouldn't swap your affections for a heap of
confections,
Not for . . . blackb'rry pie, oh my oh my.
October Ale would surely fail,
Summer salad couldn't stop my ballad,
Hazelnut pudden'd just taste wooden,
As for cheese on toast it'd make me weep.
Feel so hungry, Rosie, I'd better go . . . to . . .
sleep . . ."

Overcome by weariness, the travelers slept at the fringe of the darkened forest, whilst on the path the stone figures of the otter and his wife stood like eternal sentinels in the silent watches of the night.

Out at sea a shroud-like fog had dropped. Completely lost, without bearings by the stars or the sight of landmarks, Orgeye abandoned the helm of the *Waveblade*, which had been sailing a southern course until the fog descended. He posted two searats with weighted ropes to test overboard for shallows and reefs. Cursing Gabool for his uncontrollable mad temper which had driven them into this unknown position, Orgeye went below to his bunk to await the coming of dawn.

Hidden in Mossflower Woods a mere stone's throw from Redwall Abbey, Graypatch and his crew also awaited the arrival of dawn.

Pacing his bedchamber in Salamandastron's mountain, Lord Rawnblade Widestripe awaited yet another dawn, knowing that each fresh day brought his time of encounter with the searats a little closer.

Wandering the empty halls of Fort Bladegirt on Terramort Isle, Gabool the Wild awaited a dawn that would dispel his nightmares of ringing bells, badgers and avenging mice.

In fact there were many different creatures in diverse parts, each waiting to see what the new day might bring: adventure, danger, victory, defeat, peace of mind, or death.

BOOK TWO

The Strange Forest

19

Light tendrils of mist clung to the burgeoning greenery of Mossflower Woods, and the rising sun tinged buttermilk hues across a sky of powder blue in the shimmering peace of dawn. Graypatch shook dew from his claws as he stamped about, restoring circulation around limbs unused to sleeping out in the woodlands. Deadglim sat gloomily chewing on young dandelion stems, sulking because his Captain would not allow a fire, lest the telltale wisps of smoke betray their position.

Graypatch wiped his sword blade dry as the other searats awoke, rubbing sleep from their eyes.

"Come on, hearties," the searat Captain chuckled. "You're like a pack of dormice staggerin' about after a hard winter. Rouse yer carcasses, the sun's gettin' up an' it's going to be a good day to inspect our new home. Thank yer lucky stars we're not out on the seas. There'll be a fine old fog there that'll last until noon. If you was aboard ship now in blue waters, you wouldn't be able to see the tail behind your back, hahaha! Gather round now an' listen to me. I'll tell you about the plan I've got charted for us. Leave it to ol' Graypatch—we'll soon be livin' like kings!"

Flagg the otter was always ready and willing to oblige. Mother Mellus had asked that he track down Dandin and Durry Quill. She was sure that a fellow as big and capable as Flagg would have them back home at Redwall in no time at all. Determined to start his journey bright and early, Flagg shouldered supplies, checked his slingshot and stone pouch, then slipped out by a wicker gate in the Abbey's north wall. Scarcely had he let himself out into the woodlands when he became alert. Watching from the shelter of an ash grove, Flagg witnessed a curious sight.

Graypatch had assembled his oarslaves, mostly dormice and shrews. They grouped on the path in a ragged bunch, thin and underfed. The five score searats who comprised the crew of the *Darkqueen* lurked in the pathside ditch, fully armed. Graypatch issued his orders.

"Lissen now, mates. You lot stay in the ditch an' keep yer heads down. As for you scurvy oarpullers, you don't breathe a word, just follow me an' try to look hard done by, haharr, though that shouldn't be too hard. Mind though, if one of you steps out o' line the crew in the ditch'll deal with ye. Ringtail, you're in charge down there; wait my signal. As soon as these country buffers open the big gate to bring us food out, I'll tip yer the sign an' you rush in. Slay any that look like trouble right off. The rest we'll let live to serve us."

Flagg had heard enough. Luckily he had asked Mellus to leave the gate open until morning. The big otter scuttled back through the woods, across the fields and slipped inside, bolting the gate securely behind him.

Mellus was strolling toward him from the direction of the unfinished bell tower.

"Flagg, I thought you'd be gone by now . . ."

The otter held a paw to his lips. "Sssshhh! Not so loud. We've got trouble—no time to explain now. Check all the wallgates are tight shut and bolted. I'm going to rouse the others. Please, marm, don't stop to ask questions, just do as I say like your life depended on it. This is urgent!"

The badger caught the tone and look in her friend's eyes. She nodded wisely and hurried to do his bidding.

The sun was nearly up. Mist hung low on the path and flatlands as Graypatch halted his bedraggled column of oarslaves at the main gate of Redwall Abbey. Glancing up, he was slightly taken aback to see a line of grim-looking Abbey dwellers staring down at him from the threshold of the high walls. Fixing a friendly smile on his face, the searat Captain called out a greeting.

"Good mornin' to yer, sirs. Whew! It's goin' to be another scorchin' summer's day again. I wonder, could I have a word with whoever's in charge of this marvelous place?"

Abbot Bernard kept his tone polite. "I am the Father Abbot of Redwall Abbey. What can I do for you, my son?"

Down in the ditch, Kybo jostled Ringtail and sniggered. "Did ye hear that, matey—his son! Now we know what Graypatch's daddy looks like. Heehee!"

Ringtail silenced him with a smart slap. "Stow yer noise, fool. Be quiet an' listen."

Graypatch touched the dagger hidden behind on his belt. "Ah well, what better creature to ask for help than the Father Abbot himself. As y'can see, sir, we're poor wretched seafarers who lost our ship in a great storm. We've been adrift fer nigh on half a season now, wanderin' round woodland an' plain like birds without wings, an' we're sore in need of a bit o' food an' water. Have ye any vittles to spare?"

The Abbot nodded. "Tell my friends what you need." He stepped back, letting Flagg and Rufe Brush come forward.

Graypatch allowed himself a smile; they were halfway home. "Good day to you, sirs. We need water an' bread, nothin' more. Oh, I know we look rough an' dirty, but we're all honest creatures. You've nothin' t' fear from us . . ."

Flagg smiled back. "How many d'you have with you, cully?"

The searat Captain shrugged. "Only what y'see here, matey. If you was to open yer doors we could come in an' rest awhile, save you the trouble of bringin' supplies out to us. I've never been inside an Abbey."

Rufe Brush gripped his javelin tight as he murmured, "No, and you're not likely to get inside this one."

Flagg continued smiling. "What about that gang hidden in the ditch?"

Graypatch waved toward the mist-shrouded ditch, a look of injured innocence on his villainous face. "Ditch? Gang? What d'yer mean, shipmate?"

Flagg fitted a pebble to his sling. "I'll show you . . . shipmate!"

The stone zinged down, plowing a furrow through the ground mist.

"Yowhoooo!"

Bigfang's head appeared out of the white shroud. He was clutching his nose, which was bleeding like a tap.

Ringtail's voice rang out. "Get down an' shuttup, yer big oaf!"

Rufe Brush leaped to the battlements, his javelin poised. "This is for you if you don't shift yourself fast, searat!"

Graypatch took the warning seriously. He dashed across the path and leaped over the ditch, landing on the flatlands beyond.

"Come on, mates. Out o' that ditch an' show 'em who we are!"

The crew scrabbled out of the ditch to stand on the flatlands at their Captain's side. He took his sword from Frink and waved it.

"I'm Graypatch, Master of the *Darkqueen*, and this is my crew. Haharr, bet you country bumpkins never clapped eyes on the likes of us. We can fight an' slay just like we do all over the high seas, so listen to me now, you woodland clods. Surrender, or I'll bring this place down round your ears. You know nothin' of warfare an' we're all covered with the scars of many a battle, d'ye hear me?"

Young Cockleburr, Friar Alder's kitchen assistant, could stand no more. His fighting spirit was roused. Using his apron strings as a sling, he launched a small rock-hard turnip at Graypatch.

"Bubbling brothpans! Take that, you simmering sea-scum!"

It struck Graypatch hard in his one good eye. The searat Captain fell back, completely blinded, blackness interspersed with bursting colored stars filling his vision.

Ringtail quickly picked him up, supporting him as he shouted at the woodlanders on the walls, "That's it, you've done it now. This is war!"

Driving the oarslaves in front of them, the searats retreated back up the path to the shelter of Mossflower. The Redwallers laughed and cheered, congratulating each other on their brave stand.

Cockleburr was delirious, he patted Flagg heartily. "Galloping gravyjugs, we showed them, didn't we!"

Foremole waddled up, his normally merry face creased with worry. "Hurr, may'aps' ee did, but 'twere only luck, maisters. Them'ns is searat spawn, gurt warriors an' wicked cruel slayers. Ho urr, you marken moi words, they vermints'll be back, doant doubt et."

The cheering died away.

Simeon spoke up. "Foremole is right. We're not warriors, though we have the might and safety of these walls in our favor. We must take extra care in the coming days, post lookouts, stay within the Abbey and its grounds, and be constantly on guard against tricks. From what I could hear, this Graypatch sounds to me like a very cunning beast."

The Abbot turned to Flagg and Rufe Brush. "I leave you in charge of all arrangements. Unfortunately I am no use at all when it comes to matters of war. Both of you have my complete confidence. You are brave beasts, and I trust your judgment. What do you say, Mellus?"

The badger shook her great head, halfway between maternal instincts and righteous rage. "Did you see those poor slaves? Some of them weren't much more than Dibbuns. Can't we do anything about them? They looked so thin and wretched; we must help them somehow."

Flagg placed a gentle paw on Mellus. "I know how y'feel, marm. I think every creature here would love to give the sorry little things some aid. But you must understand we have to defend the Abbey, we're all needed here. What good would it do those slaves if Redwall fell into the claws of Graypatch and his crew?"

Saxtus had stayed silent in the background throughout the whole incident, but now he felt the time had come for him to speak.

"Mother Mellus, I have never experienced war in my life. I do not think I will like it. However, if it is war, then Redwall Abbey comes first, before slaves, or even ourselves. Perhaps if we defeat these searats then we can think of rescuing others. Meanwhile our Abbey is our main concern."

Flagg shrugged. "Hard words, Saxtus mate. But you're right, of course."

Inland the mist had vanished with the advent of a hot summer morn. Tempers were also running hot in the woodland camp of the *Darkqueen*'s crew. Graypatch sat back in the shade with a leaf poultice held against his throbbing eye. The injury had resulted in temporary blindness with his eyes swelled shut. The searat Captain dearly wished he could lay claws upon Bigfang for yelping out aloud and giving the game away, but knowing he was at the mercy of his own savage crew, he had to walk a diplomatic tightrope. Graypatch tried to make light of the encounter.

"Yah, what are they, eh? A bunch of root crunchers. We could take 'em with one claw. Stupid mob of strawsuckers, what do they know of fightin' an' killin', eh?"

Kybo tried disguising his voice so the Captain could not identify him. "Strawsuckers, matey? Huh, they still sent us packin'. We should've did like Bigfang said and rushed the place soon as we arrived here."

Graypatch knew the voice. He made a mental note to see Kybo as soon as he regained his sight.

"Rushed 'em? What good would that've done? I don't think things would have turned out any different."

Bigfang picked dried blood from his top lip. "Hoho, don't you, then? Listen, rat, if we'd rushed 'em, I could have taken that place."

Graypatch tried to control his temper. "Tcha! But instead you got a stone on the nose and yelped like a fieldmouse at a funeral. Go on then, bucko—tell us what you would have done!"

Bigfang was a large, barrel-chested searat. He picked up a dead branch and snapped it in two pieces.

"I'd have broken 'em with the element of surprise—charge and kill! An hour before dawn I would have set light to those big gates. When they burned down, the crew would have been in there a slayin' an' rippin'. But you know better, don't you, Graypatch. What did we do? Hid in a ditch, playin' peekaboo like frogs hidin' from a hawk. And you, matey, you, the great Graypatch, terror of the waves, put out of commission with a turnip by a little cook, hahahaha! Wheedlin' round the road like a lame beetle. Please, sir, give us bread an' water, kind sir. . . . Hah! Bilgewater! Some searat invasion that was, mates, I'll tell yer!"

There was a murmur of agreement from the crew.

Tied in a line with the oarslaves, Pakatugg trembled nervously. Bigfang had wanted to kill him. If there was a power shift among the searats and Bigfang became their leader, the squirrel's life would be worthless.

On an impulse he yelled out over the rumblings of disagreement, "Graypatch is right. There's more sense in tricking your way into the Abbey than just burning and slaying!"

Ranzo leaped up and knocked Pakatugg flat with a spear butt. "Slaves an' prisoners tellin' us what t' do, eh, shipmates! I think we're all goin' soft in this forest!"

Bigfang threw a claw about his shoulders. "Aye, Ranzo's right. We were better off with the deck of the *Darkqueen* under us. That craft'd outrun any vessel on the seas. I say we set sail for the open waters in *Darkqueen*. Who's with me, mates?"

A roar of approval went up from the crew. They seized their weapons and any supplies lying about, forming in a mob with Bigfang at their head. As they marched off into the woodlands, dragging the oarslaves with them, Bigfang called out to his disabled adversary:

"Don't worry, Graypatch, I'm not goin' to kill yer. I'll leave that to this country—see how long you'll last in the woods without yer good lamp to see through. Hoho, you'll die with the flies crawlin' over yer, cursin' my name an' the day you tried to do me down. I'm Cap'n now."

The crew marched off through the woodlands, laughing and jostling each other, happy to be going back to the life they knew aboard the best craft of all Gabool's fleet, the good ship *Darkqueen*.

One searat remained, however. Fishgill the steersrat strode across Graypatch and sat beside him.

"Let 'em go, Cap'n. They'll either end up in Gabool's clutches or come back to you after gettin' sick of that bigmouth Bigfang. He's a fool an' a hothead—he'll either get himself or the crew killed."

Graypatch breathed a sigh of relief. "Fishgrill, matey, I knew you wouldn't let me down. Stay with me now. This eye'll be better in a day or two, then we'll see who's the real Cap'n of *Darkqueen*, and the best steersrat too."

Clary and the long patrol had become alerted when they found Pakatugg's secret den empty. Using their considerable skills as trackers, they had trailed the squirrel across the dunes. The hares found the river crossing the beach at midmorning. Checking the aftermath of the battle with *Greenfang*'s crew, they traced the river course inland.

At middday they sighted the *Darkqueen* tied up alongside the tree-fringed creek.

"Whoohahahooh!" Hon Rosie whooped with delight. "Who's for a trip aboard the *Skylark*?"

Brigadier Thyme jumped aboard. "Deserted, eh. Where

d'you s'pose the scurvy blaggards are now, Clary?"

"Haven't the foggiest, old fellah. Still an' all, I'll tell you where they won't be goin': to sea in this bally tub again. We'll make sure of that. Come on, chaps!"

In a short time the rudder was detached and hidden in the woods, the oars were weighted and sunk in the creek, the steering wheel was dismantled and flung widespread into the bushes, and the mooring ropes were hacked through so that *Darkqueen* drifted in and heeled at a crazy angle in the shallows. They jettisoned the worst of the provisions and made a leisurely meal off the choicest bits of the remainder.

Clary found some of the bows and arrows in the weapon locker. "Righto, chaps, settle down now. You take first watch, Rosie. Shout out at the first sign of a scurvy whisker and we'll give 'em billyo."

"Oh, I say, super! I'm rather good at the old archery game, y'know, I could score a bull's-eye on a rat's eye with no bother. Whoohahahahoo!"

Clary nibbled a ship's biscuit until a weevil poked its head out at him; he spat out quickly and tossed the offending morsel overboard.

"Phwaw! I think I'd turn to a life of crime if I had to eat tucker like that. No wonder they look mean an' ugly!"

20

The mist was heavy in the forest as Mariel and her friends struck westward into the strange new territory. Durry Quill kept repeating the lines of the poem aloud.

"Find the trail and lose your life.
When in the woods this promise keep,
with senses sharp and open eyes,
'My nose shall not send me to sleep.' "

"Your nose doesn't have to, your bally voice would send anybeast to sleep, Durry," Tarquin snorted.

"Didn't they teach you singin' at Redwall?"

"Floppyears, I weren't singin,' I were recititatin'. So there."

"Can't you two stop arguing and keep quiet?"

"Oops! Sorry, old gel, m'lips are sealed from now on, promise."

Dandin had to hack away at hanging vegetation and thick fern to keep the path clear. He did not like this forest at all. It was dank and steamy; with little sunlight showing through the matted treetops, the ground was squelchy underpaw and the going slow.

The travelers were not inclined to stop in the gloomy atmosphere. They snatched bites of food as they pressed onward, each with their separate thoughts.

Dandin thought of Redwall and Mother Mellus, the good badger who had reared him: Despite her scolding and reprimands, he missed her. He wondered how Saxtus was faring, now that he was the only one of the terrible duo left for Mellus to watch over.

Durry thought of his uncle Gabriel, his friends Bagg and Runn and the moles whom he felt a great kinship to. He imagined summer afternoons in the orchard with cool cider and cakes beneath the shady trees.

Mariel thought of her father, wondering where he could be and how his health was. She remembered the quiet strength of her father the bellmaker, his ready smile and gentleness, the care he had taken of her and the pride he took in his little daughter, whose name he likened to a bell ringing over meadows on a summer evening. She blinked away a silent tear and gritted her teeth as she thought of cruel Gabool and the retribution she would mete out one day when she faced him.

Tarquin thought of sitting alongside Hon Rosie at the annual haredance and banquet in Salamandastron. Rosie always treated him mockingly, but that was just her way. Secretly he imagined she longed for him. The words of a new song came bubbling out of the irrepressible hare.

"If I were a cake upon the table,
You would take a bite from me
and I would shout if I were able,
Rosie, you're a sight to see.
Dolly ting bang clang, diddly ding . . ."

"Mr. Woodsorrel, I've told you once politely, now clamp a lid on it!"

"What? Oh, er, right you are, m'lady. It's just that lovely smell reminds me of Rosie's perfume that she wore to the banquet."

Durry Quill sniffed. "My spikes, so that's what perfume smells like. A lad like me never smelt it afore. Whaaaawwwhhooommmm! 'Scuse I."

Mariel was about to silence Durry when she yawned aloud also.

Dandin stopped swinging his sword into the tangled creepers. He leaned against a willow and yawned aloud, rubbing his eyes. "Hoooommmmm! Funny sort of smell, not like I'd imagined perfume to be. Bit sickly sweet, if you ask me . . ."

Tarquin sat down on the trail. His harolina slipped from his paws and he blinked owlishly. "Hooooooah! Take m' word for it, laddie, that's what perfume smells like. Whooohaaaw! Corks . . . can't keep . . . the ol' eyes ooooooh . . . pen."

Mariel lay down slowly, clutching the Gullwhacker to her like a baby mouse going to bed with her dolly. Through half-closed eyes she watched shadowy figures rising from the earth around them. The last thing she heard before sleep rode in on the cloying waves of heavy scent was Durry Quill's voice.

"My nose shall no—Whoooaw!"

Mariel's head ached furiously and a dark mist swam before her eyes, changing to brown then dull green. She caught a whiff of the fetid scent as a face swathed in barkcloth came close to hers.

"Heehee, dis'n wak'nin' up, athink!"

"Dese'n's near wak'n too abit."

"Eer's Snidjer, lookitout!"

The realization that she was bound to a tree woke Mariel completely. She tugged and strained at her bonds as a creature hobbled toward her. It was covered in trailing weeds and wore a barkcloth wrapper around its face, as did many others she could see crouching in the background. The creature carried with it the whiff of heavy scent. It stood in front of the mousemaid and spoke in a high, squeaky voice.

"Yerrherr, Snidjer gotcher—anyerr fren's!"

Tarquin had awakened. They were all tied tightly to

the same big tree. "Oh, great golly, m'poor head, it's burstin'. Who the devil are you, sir?"

The creature prodded Tarquin with a long thorny branch. "You sh'rupp. Snidjer's talkin' nochoo. Ennyow, werryerfrom?"

Dandin was awake. He lay with his eyes closed as he interpreted. "I think his name is Snidjer and he wants to know where we're from."

Snidjer giggled. "Heehee, smarteemouse dis'n—a smarteemouse!"

Durry was last to wake. He strained forward, trying to reach his head with bound paws. "Gwaw! My poor skull. This shouldn't happen to a good young lad like me. I think it was that scent which knocked us out. Oh, nunky, help! Send those 'orrible beasts away!"

Snidjer and his tribe giggled as they danced around the tree in front of their victims. Dandin watched them closely, trying to figure out what sort of creatures they were under the barkcloth facewraps and body hangings of thick weed.

"Tarquin, who are they? Have you ever seen anything like them before?"

"I should jolly well hope not, old boy. What a dreadful load of idiots—can't even talk properly. Rosie'd have a word or two to say to 'em about their sad lack of elocution, believe me!"

Snidjer pranced up to Tarquin, waving a torch made of smoldering herbs under his nose. The hare was not well-pleased.

"Pooh, take it away, you rascal. It's that beastly scent again."

Snidjer giggled. "Sleepasleep, sleepasleep, yerrherrah-errherr!"

Mariel groaned aloud. "So that was what the poem meant about my nose sending me to sleep. It's those smoldering herbs; they must be full of a sort of sleep drug. 'Buried ones will surely rise . . .' Ha! I remember that bit. Just before I was knocked out by that smell, I dimly remember seeing those creatures coming out of the ground, though how they did it I don't know. Wh-

where's my Gullwhacker? Oh, I wish my head would stop aching."

Snidjer wriggled with delight, the loose weeds quivering all over him. "Wannasee how we do it, clevermouse? Wannasee 'ey? D'Flitchaye cleverer than you a bigbit, yousee."

The weird creature stamped his paw several times upon the ground. Mariel watched, her eyes wide with amazement. All around the earth, clumps of weed and grass lifted like rough lids as more of the peculiar creatures came out of hiding from their subterranean pits. In a short time the area was thick with bark-masked, weed-clad beasts. They shuffled about, chanting in their high-pitched voices:

"We d'Flitchaye Flitchaye Flitchaye!"

Dandin struggled against his bonds as he roared aloud, "Hey, come away from that stuff. It's ours!"

Snidjer was waving Martin's sword about as his tribe emptied the contents of the travelers' packs onto the ground, fighting and grabbing for the food and drink. One of them swung Gullwhacker close to Dandin's head.

"Nahh sh'rup, you'n's Flitchaye pris'ners!"

Tarquin gulped against the rope that circled his neck. " 'S'no use, old lad. Stiff upper lip an' ignore the blighters—we're outnumbered at least ten to one. I say, what's the next bit of the jolly old rhyme? Maybe that'll help us, wot?"

Dandin promptly reeled off the required stanza.

"Beat the hollow oak and shout,
'We are the creatures of Redwall!'
If a brave one is about,
he'll save any fool at all.

That's it as best as I recall. Let's look about for this hollow oak to beat, then we can start shouting."

Durry blinked painfully as he tried to focus his eyes. "Phwaw! I'm lookin', though outside o' this clearin' I can't see nothin' but trees. My ol' nuncle Gabe'd say it were like lookin' fer timber in a woodland."

By now the supplies had either been eaten or squashed into the ground, though one or two of the creatures were still squabbling over flasks of cider and cordial. Snidjer swung the sword at an overhanging bough. He missed and landed himself flat upon his back. The Flitchaye chief lay sniggering as three smaller ones thrummed roughly away at Tarquin's beloved harolina. The hare fought against his tight bonds, crying out against the outrage.

"I say, put that instrument down! You're an absolute bunch of yahoos, d'ye hear me? Yahoos and hooligans!"

Concealing her voice beneath the surrounding hubbub, Mariel whispered to Dandin, "I'm working my paws loose. It shouldn't take long. The moment I'm free we'll have to see if we can grab our weapons and hold this lot off until we find the hollow oak."

"Hollow oak, old gel," Tarquin chuckled. "No need to look any further, we're tied to the bally thing!"

Durry groaned aloud. "An' I could've saved my poor eyes all that lookin' an' searchin'. 'T'aint fair."

Dandin glanced upward. "Hmm, so we are," he whispered back. "Right, when Mariel's loose we'll untie each other quietly. If we can reach our weapons, all well and good; if we can't, then the best plan would be to surround Tarquin and keep him protected while he beats the oak. Those long legs of yours should come in very handy for that, Tarquin. Er, Durry, what is it that we all have to shout out?"

"We are creatures of Redwall, good an' loud!"

Snidjer and the Flitchaye who was holding Gullwhacker hurried across to the prisoners. Snidjer carried the sword and some smoldering herbs. He glanced at them suspiciously.

"Worrayou talkabout, 'ey?"

Tarquin sniffed. "Actually, old bean, we were just remarking on what a vile smelly load of old forest weeds you bods are."

Snidjer's eyes glinted angrily and he waved the smoking herbs under Tarquin's nose. "You sh'rup, y'hear, sh'rup or Flitchaye send you sleepasleep s'more."

The hare coughed violently, his eyes watering as the Flitchaye chief held the reeking herbs closer. Suddenly Tarquin shot out both his long legs. Bound together as they were, the powerful limbs caught Snidjer a mighty kick that sent him head over heels.

Mariel freed her paws and unknotted the rope that held them to the oak and unbound Dandin's paws. With their backs to the dead oak the four companions faced the howling mob of Flitchaye creatures. Mariel tugged Durry's paws loose as Dandin untied Tarquin. Snidjer leaped up, quivering with fury as he waved the sword menacingly.

"Hawhaw y'done it now, cleverbeasts. D'Flichaye killyer now, killyer good 'n' dead. Gerrem, Flitchaye, gerrem!"

Again the mousemaid remembered attacking Gabool with the sword when her life was threatened. This time it was not only her, but also three good friends who were in danger of being slain.

Mariel felt the old Storm rise within her. Grabbing the ropes that had bound them, she knotted the ends and passed them to Dandin and Durry.

"These will have to do as Gullwhackers. Get thumping, Tarquin!"

The hare needed no second bidding. He pounded his long hindlegs against the hollow trunk, raising his voice to join the others:

"We are creatures of Redwall! We are creatures of Redwaaaaalll!"

The first wave of the Flitchaye mob struck them, armed with sticks and small daggers. Mariel and her comrades thwacked away at them with their knotted ropes for all they were worth. Most of the Flitchaye were repulsed, some knocked senseless, whilst others, half-conscious, clung onto the bodies of their attackers.

Snidjer stayed well back, swinging the sword as he urged a fresh wave of attackers to the fray. "Gerremall, Flitchaye. Grabbem, holdem—I cut'm up wid dis sworder!"

Durry Quill went down, felled by a heavy blow. Dandin and Mariel stood shoulder to shoulder, swinging their knotted ropes. Tarquin lay on his back, pounding the oak with his hindpaws while he lashed out at the enemy with his front paws, joining voice with his companions:

"We are creatures of Redwall! We are creatures of Redwaaaaalll!"

They were struggling against the odds, more so when Snidjer gathered a fresh batch of Flitchaye about him and headed the charge at his weakened opponents.

"D'cleverbeasts fallin' now. Gerrem, Flitchaye!"

Mariel and Dandin went down beneath the masses of weedclad bodies, still shouting as they were submerged beneath the Flitchaye mob:

"We are creatures of Redwaaaalll!"

Thick white fog enveloped both sea and shore as if the very clouds had dropped out of the sky. Sound was muted and nowhere was there vision or sight for more than a paw's length. Rawnblade Widestripe chuckled grimly to himself as he donned the long spiked helmet he always wore with his battle armor. Salamandastron was deserted; he had sent out all his hares to patrol on one pretext or another, some to the south, others to the east. The great badger Lord pulled down the helmet visor, focusing happily through the twin slits. Rawnblade's eyes should have been tired, but they were not. He had lain awake most of the night, listening to the muffled silence fog brought in its wake, restless, turning. Rawnblade had finally left his beloved mountain to stroll on the tideline along the shore by Salamandastron.

That was when he had heard it.

The sickening crunch of ship's timbers upon rock was unmistakable.

The searat Captain Orgeye was below sleeping when he was thrown forcibly from his bunk onto the cabin floor. Shouts from the *Waveblade*'s two lookouts brought him scrambling up on deck.

"Belay, we've run aground in this cursed fog!"

"Hell's teeth! She's run bow-on to a reef!"

Rawnblade had strained his ears to catch the shouts from the *Waveblade*.

"Cap'n Orgeye, what'll we do?"

"Bilgescum! You've been sleepin' on watch. If she breaks her keel on these blasted rocks, I'll rip out yer livers. Get over the side onto the reef an' see how she looks. Move yerselves!"

"Cap'n, she's nose-up on the stones, holed near the waterline an' trapped tighter than meat between yer teeth. What do we do?"

"What can we do, slophead? There's naught for it but to wait till this fog clears. May'aps we can beach her for repairs then."

Rawnblade expanded his massive chest, letting out a great sigh of pure joy at the memory of his night stroll. It was not often the big badger got a shipload of searats delivered to his doorstep. That was why he had sent his hares away. The Lord of Salamandastron wanted this one all to himself. Picking up his formidable broad-sword, he swung it easily across his shoulders and strode silently back to the tideline. Standing with waves lapping his studded leg greaves, Rawnblade Widestripe resembled a great carved statue set at the edge of the sea. Fog swirled about his armored body as he listened to the sounds of the cursing searats, who were waiting for the fog to lift.

So was Rawnblade.

He remembered the dead bodies of his three hares swaying in the shallows of the tideline, the work of sea-rats. A huge rumble of satisfaction welled up in his throat as he anticipated loosing his wrathful battle sword upon Orgeye and the *Waveblade*'s crew.

Colonel Clary notched an arrow to his bow, and the other two members of the long patrol followed his example. The fog had thinned to a milky river mist in the creek where the *Darkqueen* lay crippled. Clary's ears stood straight up as he listened to the noise of the *Darkqueen*'s crew. They were crashing heedlessly through bush and shrub, careless and noisy, as they made their way back to the ship.

Ringtail was first to spot the *Darkqueen*'s masts amid the forest greenery. He dashed forward with the light mist swirling about him.

"Ahoy, mates. There she lies. The *Darkqueen*!"

Even as the rest of the crew dashed forward, they saw Ringtail fall with a gurgle, an arrow through his neck.

"Down! Get down. The ship's been boarded!" roared Bigfang.

The searats obeyed, dropping down instantly behind trees and bushes.

Ranzo lay alongside Bigfang, pale with fright. "Ringtail's been done for. Who killed him?"

Bigfang peered through the mist-shrouded trees. "I don't know, mate, but I'll soon find out. 'Ere, bring up them oarslaves."

Brigadier Thyme raised himself from the heeling deck to obtain a better shot at the foebeast. He groaned aloud and sat down again.

"Oh, dash it, look what they're up to now!"

Clary and Hon Rosie stood up in dismay. Bigfang was approaching with the rest of the searats, and they were using Pakatugg and the wretched oarslaves as a shield in front of them. They stood in a bunch at the woodland fringe on the creek bank.

Hon Rosie relaxed her bowstring. "Golly gosh, I say, that sort of thing's not on, you know. Hey there, you bunch of moldy old cowards. Come out an' fight, beast to beast."

Bigfang prodded Pakatugg with his cutlass. "Moldy ol' cowards is better than foolish dead heroes, rabbit. Now what d'ye say we parley a bit eh?"

Clary twitched his whiskers firmly. "We don't parley with the likes of you, bottlenose."

"Bottlenose yerself, rabbit!" Bigfang snatched a spear from Kybo and hurled it. The spear landed with a quivering thud, pinning Clary's paw to the *Darkqueen*'s side. Immediately, Rosie and Thyme took a chance; shooting slightly upward, they sent their arrows over the tops of the oarslaves' heads, wounding Frink and slaying a searat named Reekhide.

The searats broke and ran for the cover of the bushes, dragging the oarslaves with them. Hon Rosie acted swiftly. Tugging the spear free, she pulled Clary into the scuppers.

"Knew they couldn't kill you, you old piewalloper. Are you hurt?"

Clary gritted his teeth, trying hard with one paw to stanch the flow of blood from the other. "Ahem! That feller's not very good at givin' a manicure with a spear, though I think he meant it to be a haircut."

Rosie could see by the tight-drawn expression on Clary's face that he was suffering greatly. She searched her pack for bandages.

"Not to worry, you'll soon be right as rain again, old lad."

Thyme put aside his bow and arrows now the confrontation was over. "Well, chaps, it looks like we're stuck aboard this tub until Clary's able to use the old paw again, wot?"

Out of sight and earshot of the hares, Bigfang was having trouble with his new command. Kybo had elected himself spokesrat for the rest, and he and Bigfang argued fiercely.

"We should've charged them when I flung that spear!"

"Huh, an' get caught in the water by those two with the bows—not me, matey. Did you see the *Darkqueen*? They've crippled 'er."

"I could get her seaworthy an' sailin' again."

"You! All you've done so far, Bigfang, is to get Frink wounded an' Reekhide killed. It was foolish chuckin' that spear. We should've got closer to 'em, then we could've done some real damage."

"Oh aye, an' what would you have done, scumbags?"

Kybo flung himself on Bigfang. They rolled over and over, grunting and kicking at each other. Bigfang was gaining the upper paw when he tripped and became tangled with the oarslaves. Kybo quickly sat on his adversary's chest. Pulling out a wicked skinning knife, he pressed the blade across Bigfang's throat. The former leader lay still, knowing that Kybo had won.

Kybo retained his position, breathing heavily. "Now you listen to me, addlebrain. I'm speakin' fer all of us, see! The *Darkqueen*'s scuppered—oars, rudder an' steerin' wheel gone, didn't y' see—an' they've heeled her over. She'll sit on the bottom of that creek like a stone in mud. I'm takin' this crew back to Graypatch; that Abbey is the only place where we'll have it safe an' easy. He was right. Now you can come peaceable or die here. What's it t' be?"

Bigfang swallowed, feeling the blade scrape his throat. "You win."

Mother Mellus crept up on Bagg and Runn the otter twins, who were hanging perilously over the north ramparts. She seized each one by an ear and pulled them down as they squeaked piteously.

"Now then, you two young fiends, what are you up to out here, eh?"

"Owow, leggo! We were keeping guard, that's all!"

"Eeeek, me ear! Somebeast's got to watch out for searats."

Mellus released them, shooing the delinquent pair down the steps to the Abbey lawn. "Run along now. Searats would eat two Dibbuns like you for tea."

"Ha, bet they wouldn't. We'd make 'em into searat pudden an' eat 'em!"

"No you wouldn't, they'd have your tails on toast. Then what would I tell the Abbot?"

The two small otters shuffled off disgruntled. Flagg the big otter called along from the west wall to Mellus, "The only tails on toast those scurvy rats'll have is their own tails, marm. You leave it t' me an' young Saxtus."

The badger gave a worried frown. "I hope you're right, Flagg. They're certain to be back. Searats like that lot don't give in easily."

Saxtus, who was on the east wall and within hearing range, called back at the same time as Flagg, "And neither do we!"

21

Snidjer approached Mariel, brandishing the sword. Weighted down by Flitchaye, she was unable to move. Helplessly she watched him raise the glittering blade. . . . From nowhere a huge voice rang out:

"I was born on a dark night in a storm! I'm the roaring child of Heavywing McGurney! Shake in your fur, Flitchaye. Stonehead's arrived!"

A barn owl of awesome proportions swooped down and hurled Snidjer high in the air. With a noise somewhere between a hoot and a roar, he launched himself into the fray. Mariel had never seen anything like it. The weed-clad, bark-masked Flitchaye scattered everywhere like ninepins.

Stonehead was aptly named. He used his massive head like a battering ram, thudding and butting with the speed of a striking snake as he shouted aloud at the terrified Flitchaye tribe:

"Stand and fight, you forest weeds! Why, if I couldn't slay a dozen of you before breakfast I'd die of shame! I can drink a river dry and eat an orchard bare! I'm Stonehead McGurney, bravest of the brave!"

Mariel and her companions got the feeling they would offend the big barn owl by joining in the fight, so they stood to one side, watching as he enjoyed himself to the full. The Flitchaye who were not laid out flat took to their holes and closed the lids. As Mariel retrieved her Gullwhacker and Dandin picked up the sword, Tarquin tuned his harolina and nudged Durry.

"I don't think I'd like to meet that chap when he's cross, do you?"

Durry kicked Snidjer on the bottom as he tried to rise. "Dearie me, he do 'ave a right ol' temper an' no mistake."

Six Flitchaye were backing off toward the woods. Stonehead spotted them and yelled, "Get back here! Down your pits and shut the lids! Run away and I'll follow you to the ends of the earth! You know I never lie! We McGurneys aren't the wisest owls anywhere, but by thunder we're the bravest!" He turned to the four travelers aggressively. "So you're Redwall creatures, eh! Should never let yourselves get caught by this lot! Flitchaye! Hah! I'll show you what they are! Come here, you!"

Snidjer came, but not quickly enough. Stonehead grabbed him in one powerful talon and ripped away the barkcloth mask and trailing weeds.

"There's a Flitchaye for you! Skinny little weasels dressed up, that's all they are! Here, do you want me to butt him right over the top of that hollow oak? I can do it easily, you know!"

Dandin interceded on Snidjer's behalf. "I think he's had enough, sir. Thank you for rescuing us. I am Dandin of Redwall—these are my friends, Tarquin, Mariel and Durry."

The owl shook their paws with his talons until they ached, then he kicked open the lid of a Flitchaye hole and beckoned to Snidjer.

"In there, you, and look sharp about it!"

Snidjer obeyed with alacrity. Stonehead took a huge dead treelimb in his claws and tossed it on top of the lid, locking Snidjer inside.

"There, that's the way to treat them! Don't take any nonsense! You don't think I was too easy on them, do you? Sure you don't want me to throw a few over the treetops?"

"No no, old chap. You did splendidly. Do you live alone in these woods?"

Stonehead blinked his eyes at Tarquin and snorted. "Alone? I'll say not! We McGurneys have always lived here! Got the wife, Thunderbeak, and four little ones—two sons and two daughters! They're only chicks, but you should see them fight! Come home with me for supper, meet my family!"

The savage golden eyes glared at them. They did not refuse.

If at all possible, Stonehead's wife Thunderbeak was even fiercer than her belligerent husband. The four babies sat at the foot of a dead ash with them, fighting uproariously at every opportunity, much to the amusement of their parents. The food was surprisingly good. There was a white mushroom salad specially laid on for the travelers. The owls did not eat. Dandin decided that it would not be polite to ask them what their diet was, though the odd barkcloth and weeds in the bushes left him in little doubt.

After supper Tarquin sang and played his harolina, an impromptu song.

"If you're ever caught by the Flitchaye
And the situation looks grave,
Then call for a McGurney,
The bravest of the brave.
He'll fight all night
And battle all day
Until you hear those Flitchaye say,
'Have mercy, have mercy, have mercy on us all!' "

Mariel smiled fondly at the owlets. "Bless them, they've fallen asleep."

Thunderbeak cuffed them roughly awake. "Where's

your manners! Dozing off when the nice rabbit's singing you a song! Wake up this instant!"

Mariel wrapped her Gullwhacker into a pillow and lay down. "Oh, don't scold them, please. They need their sleep, the same as me. Actually, if that nice rabbit starts singing another song he'll feel the knot of my Gullwhacker between his big bunny ears."

Tarquin sat up late, remembering the next lines of the poem and discussing their future route with Stonehead, though the owl did not appear to be a great deal of help. Tarquin racked his memory, whilst pretending to be attentive to Stonehead's advice.

"Let me see now, something or other about saving any fool at all, I think the last bit was. Oh, but that was you, wasn't it?"

Stonehead blinked fiercely. "What's that you say? I'm any fool at all! I think you could do with a lesson in politeness, rabbit! It's true we McGurneys aren't wise owls, but we're the bravest of the brave! Now defend yourself, or get kicked right over that tree!"

Tarquin held up his paws placatingly. "Sorry, old chap, I wasn't alluding to you, not a bit of it. The fools I was talking about is us, me and my jolly old friends. Point of fact, you may be able to help us with our route. I've remembered the lines, goes somethin' like this:

> Beware the light that shows the way,
> Trust not the wart-skinned toad,
> In his realm no night or day.
> Fool, stay to the road.

That's it. Y'see it mentions us again—fool! I don't suppose you happen to know what place the rhyme means, wot?"

Stonehead got up and paced about a bit. One of the babies gave his leg a drowsy bite as he passed, and he cuffed the sleeping infant affectionately.

"Wouldn't like to be a Flitchaye when she grows up—wonderful little battler. Yes, of course I know the place your poem mentions! You and your friends want the swampdark! Never go there myself—rotten place! Take you there in the morning. Get some sleep now, rabbit! You're quite a good singer; never have time for such nonsense myself, sooner have a good clean fight! Must warn you, though, if you start warbling and wake my wife up she'll probably rip your leg clean off! She's not named Thunderbeak for nothing, you know! Sleep well. Good night!"

Tarquin put his harolina carefully aside and lay down, gazing around at the dark dripping forest and the six savage owls in slumber.

"Blow me! I'd never take Hon Rosie picnickin' to this place."

"What's that, rabbit? Did you say something?"

"Er, no, old bean. Just good night."

"Good night! Now shut up and sleep! Or else . . . !"

Gabool the Wild was not affected by sleep anymore. He was driven night and day by an insane nervous energy, roaming the rooms of Fort Bladegirt. The non-arrival of Graypatch was preying upon his mind, though he did not doubt that his traitorous Captain would show up sooner or later. The King of Searats now began hoping that Graypatch would be brought back alive. He descended a winding stairway, muttering and chuckling to himself.

"No, don't kill him, that's too quick for me old shipmate Graypatch. Gabool's got somethin' nice fer him, a surprise, aharrharrharr! Aye, Graypatch'll remember old Skrabblag. I was Cap'n of the *Ratwake* an' he was mate when we brought Skrabblag from the warm isles in the deep seas to the south. Haharr, good old Skrabblag. Let's see if you're still alive an' foul-tempered."

Still laughing to himself, the mad King reached the bottom of the steps. He entered a side room and took a spear from its wallhanger. At the center of the room was a circular stone with a thick iron ring attached. Gabool thrust the spear through the ring and levered the stone upward. Sliding it to one side, he took the spear and crouched over the hole in the floor.

"Skrabblag, matey, it's me, Gabool. Sing out—are y'there?"

There was no reply. Gabool jabbed down into the inky darkness with the long spear. There was a dry, rustling sound, accompanied by an odd clicking noise. The searat grinned.

"Aharr, you murderous villain, I can hear yeh. What's it like down there, livin' on rotten fishheads an' scraps o' dead seabird?"

The rustling and clicking increased. Something caught the spear blade, but Gabool pulled it back quickly.

"Hoho, not so fast, bucko. I know you'd like to drag me down there, but you bide your time and old Gabool will give yer a little gift. Remember Graypatch? Aye, he was the one that helped catch you an' take you from your nice warm island to this cold dark berth. Well, you stop down there an' think what you'd like to do to Graypatch. Pretty soon now I'll let him drop in an' pay you a call. You'd like that, wouldn't yer?"

The clicking and rustling increased. Gabool laughed heartily as he slid the stone back into place with the spear.

Outside, the wind moaned around the rocks of Terramort and the stones of Bladegirt. The restless sea pounded coves and inlets as seabirds deserted the skies for nests and perches. Gabool sat once more in his banqueting hall, chin in claws as he slouched across the table and spoke to his bell.

"Hah! Yer gettin' dirty now since there's no slaves to spit an' polish yer shiny hide. An' that's the way it should be, big an' dirty with a brassy voice. One day the bell tower will be built, then I'll string you up there an' make you sing every time I tug the rope. I'll make yer sing or be quiet, just as I please. What've y'got to say to that, eh?"

The great bell remained silent. Gabool sat watching it until his weighted eyelids began drooping over weary blood-scared eyes. A ship in flames passed his vision, followed by another lying on its side in a creek, overgrown by trees, and yet a third ship washed up and holed upon a reef. Bluddrig, Garrtail, Saltar and Orgeye floated lifeless in the waves sweeping across his fevered dream, dead rats all. Through the shifting gray mists a huge armored badger strode. Raising his sword, he struck.

Bongggg!

Gabool was awake once more, glaring his hatred across the table at the bell whose very presence haunted his every moment.

22

"Haharr, me old shipmates, how was your voyage?"

Graypatch had his sight back now, though his eye was still quite swelled. He sat on a fallen log with Fishgill, watching his sheepish crew. Bigfang kept noticeably out of the way. Kybo, still the unofficially elected spokesrat, unfolded the unfortunate encounter with the hares and reported on the sorry state of the vessel *Darkqueen*. Graypatch listened to the woeful narrative as he sat sketching on the ground with his sword-point. When Kybo had finished, the other searats gathered around to hear what Graypatch had to say. He kept them waiting awhile before he spoke.

"A sad an' mis'rable tale, mateys, but what ship can last forever? *Darkqueen* was a good craft, but she'd be a floatin' death warrant for us against the might of Gabool. Leave 'er to rot in the creek, I say. Redwall Abbey's worth a hundred *Darkqueens*, we'll be Lords of this land, country gentlerats if y'please, instead of floatin' bilgeslops at the mercy of wind 'n' water, tryin' to grab a livin' with one claw while usin' the other to fend off that madrat Gabool. No more of that fer us, messmates. This is the warm soft country, and it can be all ours if yer willin' to follow me. Well, what d'yer say?"

There was an immediate roar of approval. Many claws reached out to pat the searat Captain's back.

"We're with you, Skipper!"

"Aye, Graypatch always led us right!"

"You give the word, Cap'n, an' we'll follow yer to Hellgates an' back!"

Graypatch tapped his swordpoint at the drawing he had been working on. "Right then, buckos, here's me plan. This here's the Abbey. Now what we'll do is this: there's nigh on a hundred of us, closer to a hundred an' twenty countin' the oarslaves. Bigfang, here's yer chance, mate. Rush 'em an' burn the gates you said, as I recall. Well, that's exactly what you're goin' to do. Take Frink, Fishgill, 'ere, and five others. Keep the oarslaves so you'll look more like an army. Try burnin' those big Abbey gates down any way you can. Now then, I'll be in front on the flatland t' other side of the ditch with Ranzo, Dripnose an' a score or so others. We'll make a great show of firin' arrows an' slingin' stones; that way the attack will look like it's comin' from the front, but it won't. Kybo, you take the rest round the east side and sneak through the woodlands—they're good 'n' thick there. Use ropes an' grapnels, just as if you were takin' a tall fat merchant ship. Ropes an' grapnels, lads, that's the key. Nice an' quiet like, slide over those walls. There's a little wallgate I've noticed on the north side. Get that open an' we'll be with yer in a trice. Bigfang should have the gates well ablaze by then. Do as I say an' we'll be takin' supper in Redwall Abbey tonight!"

Everyone cheered aloud, with the exception of Bigfang. Somehow he felt as if he had been tricked by Graypatch, though being in disgrace and having the whole crew against him left him in no position to complain.

Hot summer vegetable soup was being served with large flat oatcakes, there was fourseason plumcake and elderberry cup to follow. The sentries on the Abbey walls took theirs as they watched the surrounding countryside for signs of movement. The food was being served in the orchard. Sister Sage and Mother Mellus dished it out to the little ones, and each carried their portion to a corner of the orchard where the Abbot, assisted by Simeon and Foremole, stood ready to give them a lecture. Seated in a group beneath a gnarled apple tree, the Dibbuns began eating. Abbot Bernard cast a kindly eye over them, shook back his habit sleeves and began.

"Righto, my little friends. Carry on eating while I talk to you. Er, Grubb, stop dipping your oatcake into Baby Turgle's soup and listen to me, please."

Grubb did as he was told but immediately started complaining. "Yurr zurr Habbit, 'ee squirrel Turgle's a-drinken moi drink!"

The infant squirrel grinned over the top of Grubb's beaker and sucked noisily at his stolen elderberry cup. The Abbot turned his eyes skyward as if looking for patience. Foremole went among the Dibbuns and took charge of the situation.

"Gurr, you liddle terror, give 'ee drink back ter Grubb, an' yew, maister Grubb, touch yon Turgle's soup agin an' oi'll bite 'ee tail offen."

The Abbot took a deep breath and continued. "Now, as you may know, there are some very naughty creatures who've been hanging about outside our Abbey, but there's no need for you to worry or be frightened—we'll take care of them. Meanwhile, I want all you Dibbuns to be very good little creatures. Do what you are told by those who look after you, Mother Mellus, Sister Sage, Sister Serena, Simeon, Brother Saxtus, myself . . ."

"An' Bruvver Hoobit, too?"

"Yes, and Brother Hubert too."

"An' Foremole as well, Habbit?"

"Yes, yes, Foremole as well."

"An Muvver Mell's too?"

"Yes, I've already said Mother Mellus. Now listen to me please . . ."

"An' the fishes inna pond?"

"Now don't be silly, I said listen to wha—"

"An' a big red strawberry too?"

"Big red strawberry? What big red strawberry? Oh dear, Simeon, help me, please!"

The blind herbalist spread his paws wide and cried out, "The Grockledeeboo eats noisy Dibbuns!"

Immediately a silence fell; the little ones sat wide-eyed in fright. Simeon took the opportunity to finish the lecture.

"But we'll chase the Grockledeeboo away if you're all very good, so listen to me. You must obey all the grown-up creatures—do as they say. If you are sent indoors, go straight in. Do not try to leave the Abbey; we don't want you going outside. Stay out of the way, eat all your food, keep yourselves clean and go to bed on time. Most important of all, stay away from the walltops. If there is fighting, you could be hurt, and we couldn't have that now, could we?"

"No, sir, Simeon, sir!" the chanted chorus came back at Simeon.

"Hurr, liddle goodbeasts, you'm eaten up all 'ee vittles naow an' run along ter play."

Foremole chuckled as he strolled off with Simeon and the Abbot. "Oi'm a-thinken they'm got the message, zurrs."

Leaning against a battlement, Flagg twirled his sling idly, scanning the northward path. "All quiet this side, young Saxtus."

Saxtus licked plumcake from his paws before shouldering his spear. "This side too, Flagg. But I'm wondering for how long."

"Hmm, can you feel it too, mate? It's as if there's a sort of calm before the storm. I don't like it."

Dandin and Mariel were anxious to be away, but half the morning was gone and still they had to wait about. Stonehead's wife, Thunderbeak, had insisted on reprovisioning their empty packs, and she was somewhere off in the woods. Stonehead and his four owlchicks put on several exhibitions of wrestling, butting and kicking. Tarquin and

Durry had to keep avoiding being used as demonstration examples. Finally Thunderbeak arrived back with the knapsacks.

"Not much, I'm afraid, but it'll have to do! Plenty of apples, some white mushrooms, wild damsons, not too ripe, bit of celery, some other bits and bobs. Oh, there's some woodland scones, though they've been lying about a bit—my own make, very nourishing."

They thanked her, allowed themselves to be pecked and kicked one last time by the owlchicks, then struck westward, led by Stonehead.

The strange forest grew dimmer and more gloomy until finally they were in a world of black shadow and green light. Trees were immensely tall, with long bare trunks crowded together like black columns, the foliage growing at their tops completely blocking daylight, turning it into sinister green shafts. Little or no shrubbery grew on the forest floor, which was composed of squishy dark leaf mold with massive tree roots crisscrossing like dark giant veins. Mariel noticed that the silence was total. Whenever they talked their voices echoed spectrally around the gaunt trees. To cheer things up a bit, Tarquin twanged his harolina and began a ditty.

"Old missus hedgehog, here's what she likes,
A little fat husband with lots of spikes,
And a quarrel with a squirrel
Who wears flowers round his middle,
And a chestnut for her supper on a winter's
night . . ."

He came to a faltering halt as Stonehead turned his great golden eyes upon him.

"Do you have to make that silly noise, rabbit? One more song out of you and I'll wrap that hare-liner thing round your skull! This is bad country; we don't want to attract attention to ourselves, do you hear me?"

Tarquin walked behind Durry and Dandin, muttering under his breath, "Sure sign of a savage, no appreciation of good music. Huh, bet the bally feller wouldn't complain if it was a piece of boiled Flitchaye instead of a piece of beautiful music."

"Aye," Durry whispered back, "an' what's a poor lad t' do, wanderin' round like an ant lost in a dark well bottom? What I wouldn't give fer a flagon of my ol' nuncle's giggly juice right now."

Mariel watched the back of Stonehead's enormous figure, sometimes hopping before them, other times winging low between the trees. How he knew the way westward was a mystery to her. She had lost all sense of time and distance, tramping through this eerie world.

Quite suddenly, after what seemed an endless trek, Stonehead fluttered onto a fallen tree and turned to them. "This is it, Swampdark land! Never go any further than here myself! Not afraid of it, just don't like the place! Right, you're on your own now. I won't say good luck, because you'll end up dead or devoured, I'm sure of it! Always remember, though, if you ever get back to my part of the forest give me a call! We McGurneys aren't the wisest owls anywhere, but it's an acorn to an appletree we're the bravest!"

With that he was gone, winging away through the trees before they had a chance to thank him or say goodbye.

Dandin sat on the fallen tree and undid his knapsack. "Well, goodbye, Stonehead McGurney. I'm starving. Let's sit here awhile and have lunch in peace for a change. Golly, look at this!"

They climbed up onto the fallen trunk, staring in the direction they would be taking. It was practically pitch-black. Low-hanging trees with heavy weed trailing from them held out knotted and gnarled branches like predatory claws waiting to seize the unwary traveler. The ground was a greeny brown with odd clumps of blue and white flowers sticking up. Through it all ran several raised paths, humps of solid rocky earth which meandered off in various directions. The whole scene was one of complete depression; it weighed on their spirits like a millstone.

"Oh, corks, you chaps. The place is enough t' give a bod the complete pip just lookin' at it, wot?"

Mariel busied herself collecting twigs and dry bark. "Doesn't it just! Well, I'll tell you what I'm going to do—light a fire and cook up something tasty. Who knows the next time we'll get a decent feed, roaming through that lot!"

The suggestion was wholeheartedly endorsed. With flint and tinder they soon had a merry blaze going. The gloom was dispelled temporarily as they delved through their packs.

"Let's toast some o' these liddle mushrooms an' wrap some apples in wet leaves to bake." Durry was toasting away even as he spoke. Dandin took a bite at one of Thunderbeak's scones. He winced and held the side of his jaw.

"Ouch! I wonder how many seasons ago these were baked!"

Tarquin chuckled. "We could always sling 'em at any enemies we meet."

Dandin rummaged farther down his knapsack. Suddenly he gave a cheer. "Look, it's my flute! I'd forgotten that I'd packed it—must've stuck in my pack lining. Thank goodness the Flitchaye never found it. Well well, can you beat that, eh—the flute of my ancestor Gonff the Thief. Let's see if it still sounds all right."

Trilling an old Abbey reel called "Otter in the Orchard," Dandin set his companions' paws to tapping as the music skirled and tootled around the lonely trees. Hot food, a glowing fire and merry music lifted the spirits of the travelers. Even the blinking eyes that watched them from the dark swamp stopped winking and stayed wide open with fascination as they awaited the travelers' next move into their miry world.

Fleetleg, Shorebuck and Longeyes returned from the south beaches patrol to Salamandastron. They were first back. The hares found little welcome; the mountain chambers were deserted. Longeyes saw something at the doorway of the badger Lord's forge room: deep-scored marks in the solid rock. He groaned in despair. "Lord Rawnblade did this with his bare claws, gouged the rockface like this. I knew it would happen someday."

Shorebuck ran his paws across the scars in the solid rock. "The Bloodwrath has come upon Rawnblade Widestripe!"

Fleetleg picked up his lance. "Come on. We must find him. No badger Lord has suffered the Bloodwrath since Boar the Fighter. But be careful. Rawnblade might kill anybeast foolish enough to stand in his way."

The fog had long dispersed. Beneath the high bright sun on the tideline the three hares found the results of their Lord's terrible madness. Fully a hundred searat corpses drifted and rolled in the shallows around the reef, hewn, hacked or cleaved through. Blood spattered the stones and swirled in the water, broken swords and shattered spears decorated the rocks. Shorebuck slumped against the reef, his eyes shut to blot out the awful carnage.

"So this is why he got rid of us, sent out all the patrols. I've seen battlefields before, but never anything like this!"

Fleetleg leaned upon his lance. "It is written that a badger Lord can slay many when the Bloodwrath is upon him, but how did these searats come here? Where is their ship?"

Longeyes had been wading around the west side of the reef. He called out, "Here, round here. There's one still alive!"

The searat was mortally wounded. With his life ebbing fast he gasped out what he had witnessed.

"Ship . . . *Waveblade,* ran onto the reef in fog, stuck and holed. Cap'n Orgeye . . . waited until fog went. We fixed ship up, here on reef . . . waitin' for tide to lift us off . . . Ohhhh . . . ohhhh . . . monster! Badger came rushing out of sea . . . Eulaliaaaaa!"

Longeye cradled the searat's head on his lap. "That was Rawnblade!"

"Rawn . . . blade . . . I don't know. Giant . . . water rushin' off his armor, spikes, studs, silver metal . . . Like some wild beast out of the sea. Aaaaahhhh! That sword, like a great jib boom. We didn't stand a chance! D'ye hear me, mates? . . . Fivescore searat fighters an' we didn't stand a chance! Roarin', shoutin', 'Gorsepaw! Crocus! Sergeant Learunner! Killin', slayin' . . . I tell yer, mates . . ."

Longeye looked at Fleetleg. "Sergeant Learunner, wasn't he your father?"

Fleetleg stared out to sea. "Aye, Gorsepaw and Crocus were brother and sister too—my brother and sister. I was only a newborn infant then. Our mother never lasted more than a season after they died. Rawnblade reared me and when I was old enough he told me that he had found them floating on the tideline, delivered there by Gabool and his searats."

The injured searat lifted his head and stared at Fleetleg. "Screamin', shriekin' an' a-wailin' . . . An' dyin' . . . Dyin'!"

The searat's head lolled to one side. He died with eyes wide open, horror frozen on his face as his spirit sailed for Hellgates. Somewhere out on the blue deeps of the crested sea, the ship *Waveblade* ran before whichever course the wind chanced to take her. Summer breezes sent spray skimming over the decks, washing them clean of blood and battlestain. Stretched out on the forecastle, oblivious to all about him, Rawnblade Widestripe slept deeply, still fully armored, his great sword hanging loosely from one paw, unmindful of the stinging salt water which dewed his fresh scars. The awful Bloodwrath had left him; he knew not when it would visit him again. He slept on, as peaceful as any infant at its mother's side.

23

Evening shadows began closing in on a cloudless sky as the sun reddened and began its descent into the west. The stones of Redwall took from it their dusky red brown hue; heat shimmer on the flatlands gave way to purplish twilight. Gabriel Quill had relieved Saxtus on the walltop. The fat cellarmaster yawned, looked north along the path, blinked and rubbed his eyes before calling across to the west ramparts:

"Sister Serena, marm. What d'you make of this 'ere?"

Serena hurried across. Shielding her eyes with a paw, she peered shortsightedly in the direction Gabe was pointing.

"Hmm, don't know, Mr. Quill. Very pretty, though. It looks like a lot of party lanterns bobbing along the path, little golden lights . . ."

Rufe Brush came bounding up the steps. He caught the last phrase. "Little golden lights? Where? Oh, by the fur of my fathers! Sister, those little golden lights are fire! Torches, being carried toward the Abbey. I'll sound the alarm!"

In a twinkling Rufe was down from the ramparts, across the lawn and up in the half-finished bell tower. Grabbing the wooden cudgels, he began pounding on the hollow log.

Thonkthonkathonkthonkathonkthonkathonk!

As soon as the sound reached his ears, Graypatch sent the rope and grapnel brigade dashing into the woods on the east side of the path. Jumping across the ditch onto the flatlands with his own contingent, he stood with a thin smile playing on his lips, watching Bigfang.

"Rush 'em an' burn the gates, eh, shipmate. Well, it was your idea in the first place, so go to it, matey, go to it!"

Desperation and fear showed in Bigfang's face as the flickering torchlights illuminated it. He knew the element of surprise had gone with the sounding of the Abbey alarm. Furthermore there were only seven proper searats with him. Graypatch had sent them more to keep the oarslaves in line and watch his performance than to fight alongside Bigfang. Oarslaves and a frightened squirrel—that was all he had with him. Graypatch was trying to get him killed—that much was obvious. Bigfang laughed, a half-hearty cackle that grated on his own ears. He tried to sound belligerent in his reply.

"I'll burn 'em out, matey, never fear. Just make sure you're there to back us up and rush in when we do!"

Saxtus and three young otters stood with Flagg over the threshold. Piles of stones were heaped by them, ready for slinging. Friar Alder, with a mixed group of moles and mice, ranged the east and west walls, carrying spears in bundles. They were little more than sharpened yew stakes, but in the right place they could wreak considerable damage. Foremole headed a group that was in charge of large baskets of rock and rubble placed around the east and west walls so they could be conveniently tipped onto foebeast heads below. Sister Sage, Rufe Brush and Gabe Quill led a small contingent of archers.

The Abbey was not a place of war; as a result the weapons were sadly piecemeal, ancient and few.

Mellus paced the walls slowly, her gruff homely voice reassuring the Redwallers, who were all first-time warriors. "Be calm now, don't panic. They're outside and we're safe within. Don't go firing or throwing anything. Let them make the first move. Besides, they may just want to parley."

Flagg could not help snorting a little. "Just like a fox parleys with a baby mouse, if you'll pardon me turn of phrase, marm."

Mellus nodded confidently. "They look more like a bunch of searats than hungry foxes, though I'm pretty sure they'll find we're not baby mice, by any means."

Graypatch walked the far side of the ditch edge until he and his cohort were directly facing the threshold above Redwall's main gate. Bigfang faltered just short of the gate, and stood undecided amid the bearers of the blazing torches. There was an audible silence, finally broken by Saxtus as he called down to Graypatch:

"What do you want this time, rat?"

Graypatch smiled as he looked from side to side at his searats. Savage, bloodthirsty and eager, each one a picture of barbarism, decked out in their tawdry finery, they displayed an array of the most fearsome-looking weapons.

"We want this Abbey. You might have known we'd come back. Why don't you just give up now while you're all still alive, save yourselves and us a great lot of trouble?"

Saxtus picked up a sharpened stake and held it ready to throw. "It's no trouble, rat. Why don't you turn your vermin round, go back the way you came and save *yourselves* the trouble."

The searat Captain decided the time for talking was over. He raised his sword, yelling at the top of his lungs:

"Attack! Kiiilll!"

Saxtus dropped to one side as an arrow sped by his

head. Straightening up, he hurled the spear hard at Graypatch.

The searat saw it coming and ducked. Unfortunately there was another rat standing directly behind him who took the hurtling spear straight through his middle. He fell with an earsplitting scream.

The battle was joined!

Mellus watched as Bigfang and his gang of torchbearers made a rush at the gates. Straightaway she countered the move.

"Foremole, rubble over here, quick! Aim it down onto them. Try not to kill the slaves!"

Foremole and his crew hurtled the baskets of mixed rock and rubble over the parapet wall. Bigfang was about to swing his torch at the gates when the first basket hit him, extinguishing the flames as it stunned him. He lay spread on the path. The oarslaves backed off, but Frink and Fishgill threw their torches. One hit the gates and bounced back, but the other fell just right, at the bottom of the woodwork. Flagg was about to see to it when he tripped over Saxtus. The young mouse was crouching down, head in paws, sobbing uncontrollably. The big otter grabbed hold of him.

"Saxtus, matey, are you all right? Have ye been wounded?"

Blinded by tears and hardly able to speak, Saxtus shook his head. "Oh, Flagg, I've just killed a living creature. It's horrible! One moment he was alive, and suddenly my spear hit him. Did you hear him scream? He's dead, Flagg. . . . Dead, and I killed him!"

Flagg turned to Mellus as she passed. "They've fired the gates. See what you can do, marm. I'll be with you in a moment."

Flagg raised Saxtus's tearstained face with a rough paw. "None of us wants to kill anybeast, matey, but this is a war! It's kill or be killed now. We're not just protectin' our own skins, there's the whole of Redwall an' what it stands for. What about that dormitory of Dibbuns—do you want t' see them slain by searats? Make no mistake about it, young 'un, those rats'll kill us all if they conquer our Abbey. Come on now, Saxtus, me old Cully. Let's see you up on your paws defendin' your home!"

Saxtus wiped away his tears. Grabbing his sling, he fitted a rock and sent it hurtling into the searats.

"Come on, fight, you dirty cowards. You won't conquer us!"

Rocks and spears, arrows and lances filled the air, zinging backwards and forwards between searat and Redwaller. Mother Mellus and three moles, Buxton, Drubber and Danty, rolled a barrel of water from the Abbey pond to damp down the back of the gates. Foremole and his crew hurled baskets of earth over the ramparts to smother the flames licking up the front of the gates.

Grubb the baby mole, together with the little twin otters Bagg and Runn, had escaped from the dormitory. Wakened by the noise and clangor of battle, they decided to take part and distinguish themselves as warriors. Wandering through the deserted kitchens inside the Abbey, they searched for suitable armament. Bagg gave a shout. "Whohoa! Looka these!"

Friar Alder's large vegetable chopping knives lay sharp and gleaming upon the worn worktable. They selected one each, dancing about and waving the dangerous blades.

"Heehee, let's make searat pies!"

"I'm goin' to chop their chief's head right off. Choppo!"

"Burrhurr, this hinfant'll skin 'ee a few. Oi'll make they squeal!"

Creeping out onto the Abbey lawn, they ducked behind some bushes as Mellus and the moles hurried by, trundling another big barrelful of water toward the main gate. Runn held a paw to his lips.

"Ssshh! Come on, this way."

They mastered the steps to the top of the north wall near the east end, helping each other to scramble up the big roughhewn stone stairs, pushing the knives ahead of them as they went. At the top an argument broke out over which knife belonged to whom.

"Hey, that's my knife—this one's yours!"

"No, 't'aint't—I had the pointy one with the brown handle."

"Yurr, give yon Knoifer t' me—moin were the big 'un."

As they were sorting out the weaponry, a three-hooked grapnel narrowly missed Bagg's head. It caught a crack in the stones, and the rope attached to it was pulled taut. Grubb patted Bagg's head.

"Boi 'okey, that were near a gudd shot. It nurly went roight daown you'm ear!"

The whirring and clanking of grapnels increased as all along the east wall metal hooks clamped into stonework cracks and ropes pulled twangingly tight. Runn climbed up on Grubb's head and peered down into the forest darkness.

"It's searats, lads. Climbin' up the ropes to get in here!"

Bagg glanced over to the west wall, where the battle was concentrated. "Huh, no good a-shoutin' f'r that lot, they got enough t' do. 'Sides, Ma Mellus'd tan our hides an' make us go back t' bed an' not give us no breakfast tomorrow an' keep us in our room all day an—"

Grubb placed a grimy paw over Bagg's mouth. "Oh, tell oi no more 'orrible stories, otter. Usn's cut 'ee ropes wi' our gurt knoifs. Hoa hoa! 'Ee rats'll fall bump on they bottems when 'ee ropes do be cutted. Oi'll start in 'ee middle, you two come frum both ends, hurr hurr!"

Kybo was nearly at the top of the wall. Holding his sword between his teeth, he looked back at the others swarming up the ropes, their eyes glinting triumphantly through the darkness as they hauled themselves upward, claw over claw. It was a great distance from the walltop to the woodland floor, and Kybo was not too fond of heights. He partially closed his eyes and tried not to look down, staring at the wallface in front as he pulled himself ever higher. The searat's claw was about to stretch up and grab the battlement at the walltop, when there was an ominous chuckle, a sawing noise and a discordant twang as the rope parted company with the metal grapnel it had been lashed to.

"Oh noooooooooo!"

Kybo sailed outward from the walltop and dropped like a stone.

Several searats looked up in amazement, their eyes following Kybo as he plunged to the dark floor far below. In a very short time ropes were popping and cracking as they were sliced through by the Redwall Friar's keen vegetable knives. The thud of bodies and the terrified screams of searats filled the night air. One rat plunged earthward without a sound, staring in puzzlement at the loose rope still firmly clenched in his claws.

Bagg, Runn and Grubb were truly having fun. It took only three slices to cut through the toughest rope, stretched taut as they were.

"A wunn, a two, an' a three, an' away 'ee do go, vermint!" Grubb chanted happily.

And away the "vermint" did go, with a loud wail of despair!

Meanwhile, at the Abbey front Graypatch had drastically changed his opinion of the creatures he once called bumpkins; the accuracy of their stone-slinging had driven him and his searats off the flatlands and down into the ditch. Shaking with frustration, he ducked smartly as another salvo of rocks and homemade spears rattled overhead. The fire at the gates had been smothered under heaps of rubble. Bigfang was still lying senseless on the path; Frink, Fishgill and some others had their claws fully occupied trying to catch the little oarslaves, some of whom had crossed the ditch and were dodging about on the flatlands. Dripnose scrambled along the ditch bed to Graypatch. He was nursing a fractured limb, keeping his head well down as missiles rained in from above.

"Aagh! These creatures fight like mad things, Cap'n!"

"What did you expect them to do, weevilbrain—throw flowers at us?"

"Maybe not, but we're out of spears an' arrows. The crew are havin' to make do with throwin' back the stuff that's been flung at us. Huh, they don't seem t' be short of arms atop o' that wall."

Graypatch spat contemptuously. "Homemade rubbish! There's not a proper sword or cutlass between the lot of 'em. Just wait till Kybo an' his buckos come over their precious wall—we'll soon sort out the warriors from the wetnoses!"

Deadglim was nearby. He shook his head doubtfully.

"Well, where is Kybo an' the rest? They've been around there long enough to build a blasted wall, never mind climb one!"

A second later he regretted the outburst as Graypatch turned to him. "Avast there, smartmouth. Get yourself round to the back of the east wall an' see what's keepin' 'em. Look lively now. Dripnose, get Lardgutt an' see if you can drag that oaf Bigfang back down the ditch here. He's neither use nor ornament lyin' spark out on that path."

Mother Mellus seized a full basket of rubble and heaved it toward the ditch with a mighty effort. The screams and curses from below confirmed her accuracy. She winked at a group of enthusiastic slingthrowers. "That's the stuff to give 'em. Keep it up—we've got them pinned down tight. How are you doing, Saxtus?"

The young mouse dodged a flying rock and slung one smartly back. "Fine, marm, just fine. Though it's all a bit puzzling; I've noticed that we only seem to be fighting about thirty or so searats, and they had nearly a hundred by Flagg's count. Where's the rest of 'em?"

The badger weighed a large chunk of rock in both paws as she pondered the question. "I don't know, really. I wasn't counting. Maybe we'd better check around the walls to see they're not laying some sort of trap. You take the south wall and I'll cover the eas—Oh, thundering fur! The east wall, look, there's Dibbuns over there!"

The three small comrades in arms were looking for

more ropes to cut when Mellus, Saxtus and Flagg descended upon them.

"You naughty little rascals! What are you doing out of your beds, eh?"

"Burr, us'n's oanly a-cutt—"

"Give me those knives this instant! You could have cut the paws off yourselves, playing around with them. Oh, you scallywags!"

"But we was on'y savin' the Abbey!"

"Not another word, do you hear me! Wait until Friar Alder sees his best vegetable chopping knives. I wouldn't like to be in your fur!"

Flagg picked up a three-pronged grappling hook. "Hold on there, marm. Look at this—there's lots of 'em lyin' about. I wonder where they came from."

Grubb shook his paw severely at Mother Mellus. "That's what oi be tryin' a-tell 'ee, missus. 'Twere us'n's who chopped 'ee ropes off'n they 'ooks."

"But we won't nex' time if you start a-shoutin' an' a-scoldin'. So there!"

Saxtus was peering over the wall. "Golly! Look at this!"

Upward of half a dozen searats had been killed by the fall, impaled on broken branches or crushed by their falling comrades. The rest lay about in a pitiful state, moaning as they nursed broken and aching limbs. Flagg scratched his whiskers in disbelief.

"Well, give me fins an' call me a fish! So that's what the rest of the pesky vermin were up to . . ."

Grubb shook his furry head. "Not oop, maister. Only arfways oop!"

Saxtus laughed loud at the joke, but his merriment withered under Mellus's icy stare. Flagg, however, was shaking paws, hugging and patting the three Dibbuns.

"Well done, fellers. Strike me, you saved the Abbey an' no mistake!"

Bagg and Runn sat against the wall, rubbing their eyes and yawning. The badger swept them up, one in each big paw. She tried to look stern but could not help smiling.

"Come on, heroes. Bed for you three, and stay there this time."

Grubb rode down the wallsteps piggyback upon Flagg's broad back. "Oim not afeared of nobeast. Marthen 'ee Wurrier, that be oi!"

Graypatch stood out on the path, his sword tight at Pakatugg's neck as he called up to the ramparts, "Truce, or I kill the squirrel!"

Rufe Brush slackened off his sling. "Truce then. Speak your piece, rat."

All along the west and north walls the defenders put aside their missiles to listen. Graypatch stood in a pool of moonlight and delivered his message:

"Stop throwing and let us withdraw."

Rufe chuckled scornfully. "Had enough, mangy chops?"

Pakatugg squealed slightly as the sword pressed closer. Graypatch was in no mood to bandy insults.

"Aye, we've had enough . . . For one try. You may have won the battle but I'll win the war. Now let us walk away in peace, or this one dies."

Simeon appeared, leaning on his friend the Abbot. "Go then. You could have done that anytime without threatening the life of a helpless squirrel."

At a signal from Graypatch the defeated searats began their retreat north along the path. Graypatch could not resist a parting shot.

"Wait and wonder when we will return, mouse—then you will really see what a battle is like."

Simeon turned his head in the direction of Graypatch's voice. "Alas, I will never see anything for I am blind; but I can sense a lot. I can feel you are both evil and desperate. They say you have only one eye. I am surprised at you—even a fool with half an eye could see that you will never triumph against good if you are evil."

24

After their meal and a short rest, the four travelers struck off westward once more, into the gloomy dark swampland.

Mariel took the lead. Peering into the deceptive half-light, she chose a relatively straight path. The other three followed her in single file along the raised trail, avoiding smooth slippery rocks and testing each fraction of the way with hesitant paws. To both sides of them the overhanging trees grew out of stagnant-smelling smoothness, which occasionally threw up a liquid bubble, betraying the treacherous nature of its surface.

Durry sounded apprehensive. "Oh, nuncle, it wouldn't do a poor lad much good to fall in there."

Dandin brought up the rear of the file, his paw on Durry's shoulder. "Aye, be careful and take your time. I just wish it were a bit lighter in here—it's like trying to plow your way through pea soup, all muggy and dark green. What is it we have to beware in here? The wart-skinned toad?"

Second in line, Tarquin turned his head slightly as he spoke.

"Not a sign of the old wart-skinned blighter. I hope we're goin' the right way, trail leader old gel."

Mariel kept her eyes straight ahead. "As far as I can see, we are. I chose the longest and straightest of the paths. Aha! What's that up ahead? Stop a minute, please."

They halted. Directly ahead of them a light was shining in the gloom, a small flickering golden glow. It stopped, hovering farther up the path. When Mariel moved forward again, it moved also. Dandin recalled the rhyme.

"Beware the light that shows the way!"

"Right you are, Dandin old lad, wot? There's the very light we've jolly well got to watch out for."

Mariel halted once more. "Lie down and be still, you three."

They dropped down and lay perfectly still. Mariel flattened herself against the path and began inching forward. This time the light remained still, glowing a short way above the trail.

Durry lifted his head for a quick peep. "Where's she a-goin' to?"

Dandin stifled the hedgehog's mouth with his paw. "Ssshhh! Keep quiet and be still, Durry."

Mariel's crawling figure had now disappeared into the murky gloom. Ahead of them the light still glowed steadily. They waited with bated breath, pressing themselves flat to the earth. Suddenly from along the path a dismayed croak sounded, followed by a whoop from Mariel and the familiar thwack of Gullwhacker. Springing up, the three travelers made their way along the path as speedily as circumstances would allow.

The mousemaid stood over a stunned toad. It was an indescribably ugly specimen, completely covered in large wartlike growths. In one paw Mariel twirled her Gullwhacker, while in the other she held a curious contrivance. It was a lantern on a small carrying frame, wonderfully made from thin-cut rock crystal. Inside the lantern half a dozen fat fireflies buzzed, giving off a pale golden light.

Mariel prodded the toad lightly. "Two puzzles solved with one Gullwhacker: the wart-skinned toad and the light that shows the way. Three, in fact—take a look ahead."

By the light of the lantern, they saw that the path ended sharply a short distance from where they stood.

Durry shivered. "If we'd follered that 'orrible beast with his light we would've gone ploppo! Right into that swamp!"

Dandin prised a rock from the trail. "Aye, ploppo is the right word!" He threw the rock into the swamp. It disappeared, making a small hole which swiftly filled in, leaving the surface undisturbed.

The wart-skinned toad was beginning to recover, groaning pitifully and rubbing his head with slimy webbed paws. Mariel thumped the Gullwhacker down close to the repulsive creature.

"Want some more?" she inquired.

The toad recoiled in fear. "Muurraakk! No more. Rrrreb!"

Dandin unsheathed his sword and tickled the creature's nose. "Listen, I don't know what your game is but we want to get out of this place and you're going to lead us. Understood?"

Still rubbing its head, it nodded unhappily.

Dandin turned to Mariel. "Right, let's get going. Keep this creature in the lead."

"Kwirraawwwk!"

The wart skinned toad took off with a sideward leap at the swamp. Dandin reacted swiftly, but not fast enough. He barely grabbed the toad's back leg as it sailed through the air. The toad flopped into the swamp, pulling Dandin off balance. With a squeak of dismay he toppled from the raised path, slithering on its sloping side for an instant before plunging bodily into the treacherous ooze. Spreading its bulk flat and extending its webs, the wart-skinned toad slithered off across the swamp surface, leaving behind Dandin, who was rapidly disappearing into the bottomless waste.

"Help, do something, I'm being sucked under!"

Holding Tarquin's paw, Mariel stretched out, flicking her Gullwhacker toward Dandin. "Here, catch on to this!"

Dandin struggled to reach the rope, without avail. The swamp had pulled him in up to his neck now. Tarquin threw his harolina to Dandin. "Here, old, lad, put both y' paws on top of this. It might help to keep you up!"

Dandin did as he was told, but he could feel the tug of the swamp, and panic filled him completely.

"Help! Oh, help me, someone!"

An urgent voice was whispering to Mariel, "The tree! The tree!"

She looked up at the tree hanging low overhead and immediately understood. Clambering up into the tree, she edged out along a thick dipping bough. Below her she could see Dandin, ashen-faced as he hung on to the harolina, the swamp oozing around his chin and lips.

"Hold on, Dandin. Hold on!"

Knotting Gullwhacker tight to the end of the bough, she called out, "Tarquin, Durry, get up here and lean on this branch, belly down!"

Without questioning Mariel, they clambered up into the tree, scrambling out along the branch until they were close to her. Both Tarquin and Durry followed Mariel's example, straddling the bough stomachs down, jerking to exert more pressure on the limb.

The swamp had closed over Dandin's mouth. He took a final breath as it started to flood into his nostrils, fighting back the welling panic as it oozed around his eyes.

Mariel felt the branch bend lower. Grabbing Dandin's outstretched paws, she noosed the Gullwhacker tight around them, calling to her companions, "Back off now. Back along the branch. Quick!"

Following them with all speed, she managed to cry out as they hung over the path.

"Jump!"

The swamp had sucked Dandin under, his head disappeared from view.

Mariel, Durry and Tarquin jumped heavily from the tree to the path, falling in an awkward heap atop each other.

The bough straightened with a tremendous rush. Dandin was hauled clear of the swamp with a huge squelching *plop*!

He hung there, dangling above the swamp at the rope's end by both paws, covered from ears to tail in thick foul mud. Pulling the sword from where it stood quivering on the trailside where Dandin had dropped it, Tarquin leaned out, supported by Mariel and Durry. Holding the sword by its blade, he hooked the crosstree hilt into Dandin's belt and pulled him in. Mariel and Durry grabbed Dandin's limp body. Tarquin swung the sword upward with a mighty slash, severing the end of the bough that the Gullwhacker was tied to. All four fell back in a heap on the pathside.

While Tarquin undid the knots to free Dandin's paws, Mariel poured water from their flasks over his face, washing away the ooze that caked it. Durry forced his mouth open whilst Mariel poured water into it. Dandin struggled feebly and coughed. Mariel sighed her relief. Her voice choking with emotion for her friend, she tried to sound busy and practical.

"Thank goodness for that. I thought he was gone for a moment there."

Tears were flowing down Durry Quill's homely face as he joked. "Our Dandin a goner? Naw, he'll be a'right, I 'member Father Abbot sayin' he use to eat mudpies when he were a Dibbun. Hahahaboohoo!"

Laughing and crying at the same time, Durry hugged Dandin's paw.

A fire was lit, though only a small one with the limited supply of fuel in the swamp. Tarquin took a turn at making some mushroom and turnip broth while Mariel tended to Dandin. The young mouse had recovered sufficiently to sit up. He looked away from the darklands swamp and shuddered.

"Uuuuuuuhhhhh! It filled my nose and eyes and

sucked me under. Right under! It was horrible. I'll never forget it as long as I live!"

Mariel patted his back gently. "There, there, it's all right, you're safe now. Good job you thought of the tree, Durry."

The hedgehog looked at her oddly. "I didn't mention no tree, missy."

"Oh, it must have been Tarquin then. Thank you, Tarquin."

"Don't mention it, old thing, but y'don't mind me sayin', what tree?"

"You mean it wasn't you who said, 'the tree, the tree'?"

"Nope, sorry, must've bin some other beastie."

Dandin and Mariel looked at each other. Dandin smiled.

"Aye, the same one who told me to hold my paws up straight after I went under. Good old Martin the Warrior."

After a few hours they were able to resume their journey, backtracking until they found another path which looked fairly straight and safe. Mariel walked in front, holding the wart-skinned toad's lantern; it made the visibility slightly better. Tarquin followed at the rear, cleaning mud from his harolina.

"Supreme sacrifice, wot? Chap keepin' another chap afloat in a bally swamp with his harolina. Not many'd do that y'know. Bet Hon Rosie'd think it was a jolly noble effort on my part—fact I'm sure she would!" He turned to the big frilled lizard that was following him. "I mean to say, a chap's harolina is a very personal possession, wot? Omigosh! Eulaliaaa!"

Tarquin suddenly brained the lizard with the harolina, knocking it flying into the swamp. Other lizards sinuously scaled up from the sloping pathsides where they had been following the travelers. There were at least twenty or thirty, an assortment of newts and frilled lizards, their reptilian tongues flickering in and out as they watched the four travelers through cold basilisk eyes.

Durry threw up his paws in despair. "Lackaday, what

now? We've 'ad sticklegs, pikes, adders, Flitchaye, mad owls, a warty toad, an' now this, dragons! My nuncle Gabe wouldn't believe a word iffen I told him. More like he'd say that I'ad been a-drinkin' of his strong blackberry wine. Mariel, tell a poor lad who's far from home, what do we do now?"

It was a strange scene. They stood on the trail, holding a hasty conference, watched by the silent unblinking lizards.

"We have two choices, Durry: stand and fight, or make a run for it."

Dandin drew his sword. "I'm with you, Mariel. Just say the word!"

"Now steady in the ranks there, chaps," Tarquin interrupted. "I've already cracked a valuable harolina on one blinki' reptile's bonce. Hold fast a moment, will you. I could be mistaken, but just a moment ago I swear I felt a bit of a light zephyr."

Durry wrinkled his snout. "A what?"

"A light zephyr, me old scout. A vagrant breeze, a fortunate breath, a bally puff of wind, in fact. Just give me a moment, will you . . ."

Tarquin walked back down the trail to a tree, brushing aside a newt. "Beg pardon, old lizard, 'scuse me."

With an agility which belied his awkward figure, the hare climbed the tree. He stood on a high branch, paw to forehead, gazing out, nodded with apparent satisfaction, then descended the trunk swiftly, pushing through the lizards.

"D'you fellows mind not hoggin' the trail? Bad form, y'know, idlin' about an' stickin' your flippin' tongues in an' out like that."

Returning through the dumbfounded lizards to his companions, Tarquin murmured under his breath to Mariel, "Tarquin L. Woodsorrel reportin' back, marm. Don't show too much excitement, but I could see the sea from up in that tree, about a couple of hours' good hike from where we are. Does that alter the situation? Just thought you ought t' know, bein' expedition leader an' all that."

Dandin gave a wriggle of suppressed joy. "The sea!

Well, that does change things, but we've still got these lizards to contend with. Look, there's more coming out of the swamp."

The lizards from the mud joined their fellows upon the trail, waving long, prehensile tails and strutting about slowly with sinuous reptilian grace.

Mariel weighed the situation carefully. "Hmm, they haven't made any move to attack us yet. Maybe it's just a display of strength in numbers, though if we made a run for it they could easily stop us. This is their territory, they know it better than we do, and we're outnumbered at least ten to one. Right, one thing's clear—we can't stand here much longer or something's bound to happen. I've got an idea that might work. Hold my Gullwhacker and give me that sword, Dandin. Don't ask questions, just trust me."

Wordlessly Dandin gave her the sword. Turning from her companions, the mousemaid faced the gathering of reptiles crowding the path. "Which one of you is the leader?"

There was no reply. The lizards merely stood staring at her.

"Don't you have a chief, some creature in command?"

Further silence. Mariel brandished the sword of Martin. She gave a great leap and yelled, "Redwaaaalll! I am Mariel the Warrior. I'll fight you all together or one at a time! Come on, send your best killer out here and I'll meet him in combat! Lizards don't bother me, buckos. I've ate lizard stew before today."

Behind her she could hear Durry and the others snorting to suppress a fit of laughing giggles.

"Sounds like Mariel Stonehead to me!"

"Lizard stew? Oh I say, that's goin' it a bit!"

"D'you reckon they can understand her? Teeheehee!"

Mariel ignored them. She approached a large crested lizard who stood half a head above the rest.

"What about you, sliptongue? You're big and lazy enough to be a chief. Do you fancy your chance against Mariel the Warrior?"

The lizard blinked, turned slowly and walked majestically away, with Mariel shaking the sword at it.

"So, you're not only dumb, but cowardly with it! Well, let me tell you, slimenose, if any of your tribe try attacking my friends, you're the first one I'm coming after. I'll chop off your tail and stuff it up your nose! We're leaving now. I hope you'll heed my warning!"

Swaggering outrageously, the mousemaid joined her companions, telling them from the side of her mouth, "Right. Get moving. I'll stay at the back. Don't run, keep it to a brisk walk. Off we go!"

Tarquin led the way, almost helpless with laughter. "Good egg, Dandin. Did y'see that swagger? Hohoho, I thought she was going to wriggle clear out of her skin. Never seen anythin' so funny in all me life, young mouse."

"Haha, and did you see the way that big lizard looked at her when she called him slimenose? Cawhaw! His face was a picture."

"Chop off his tail 'n' stuff it up his nose!"

Mariel stifled a chuckle, picturing herself as the others saw her. "Don't laugh too much, pals—they're still following us."

And sure enough they were. Still silent, tongues flickering, eyes fixed staringly on the travelers' backs, the pack of lizards followed at an even pace.

"Not to worry, chums," Tarquin called back. "I can feel that breeze quite clearly now. Hey, d'you suppose the big chappie'd give me a ride on his back if I asked him nicely? After all, we are going the same way, aren't we!"

Two hours later the swamp thinned out, overhanging trees became few and far between, and the path petered off, giving way to firm ground and fragrant gorsebushes. But the greatest joy to the four travelers was the clear blue summer sky overhead. After days of dark forest and swamp, the fresh air tasted like springwater to them. They halted and looked back to the darkland swamp. The lizards were gathered on its fringes, still silent, flickering-tongued and beady-eyed, though some of them were preening and stretching in the sudden warmth of the sun, settling themselves down languorously to bask.

Free now of the reptilian threat, Mariel and her friends could not resist shouting their humorous goodbyes.

"Cheerio, you baggy-skinned blighters. Don't get your noses too muddy in the jolly old swamp, wot wot!"

"Bye-bye, tonguepullers. Give our regards to the old warty-skinned toad!"

"Yes, goodbye, you great bunch of dumbos. By the way, I've never tasted lizard stew before—it'd prob'ly make me sick. 'Bye now!"

"Ta-ta, vermints. D'you think you could make your way to our Abbey someday, just in case my nuncle Gabe don't believe me when I tell 'm about 'ee?"

Across the gorsefields they trekked, toward a range of high hills which fronted the westerly edge. Seabirds wheeled in the sky above while the irrepressible Tarquin strummed away on his cracked harolina.

"O, I wouldn't go through the swamps no more,
Not for an Abbot's feast.
Not even for a kiss from Rosie dear,
Though she's a lovely beast.
Give me the summer sunshine,
Don't mind a cloud or two,
Rather than that bally bog
And a pot of lizard stew!"

25

Graypatch and his searats were back sooner than any creature at Redwall Abbey expected. Smarting from the ignominious defeat and with the crew beginning to mutter behind his back again, the searat Captain decided to turn the tide in his favor with a shock attack.

He camped his crew farther up the path for the remainder of the night, waking them at dawn light to explain his scheme.

"Fire-swingers! That's the thing, buckos—the old fire-swingers!"

Bigfang was feeling a bit cocky now Graypatch's first attack had failed. "Fire-swingers me tail! I already tried fire, an' it didn't work. What's so good about your plan?"

Graypatch ridiculed Bigfang. "I'll tell you, matey. My plan'll work because I've got a brain an' you haven't. Rush the gate an' set fire to it—huh, I could think of a better plan than that in a storm at sea with both claws tied behind me back. So you either shut up an' listen, or I'll cut you loose in this country to fend for yerself, unnerstand?"

Bigfang subsided into sullen silence while Graypatch continued.

"Cut up all those lengths of rope we used for grapnels, tie rocks to the ends, all wrapped in dead grass an' soaked with lamp oil. That'll make good fire-swingers. Now, we sneaks along that there ditch so's those Redwallers don't see us a-comin'. Then we gets out on the flatland, lights up our fire-swingers an' twirls 'em an' hurls 'em. Think of it, mates—a good fire-swinger has more range than any weapon, so they won't be able to touch us with bows or lances or spears. We can stand around all season flingin' fire into their precious Abbey, an' they can't do a thing about it. Sooner or later some part of the buildin' will take flame. Haharr, then they'll be ready to talk terms, or be roasted alive. Well, what d'ye say, shipmates?"

The scheme was not greeted too enthusiastically, but Graypatch worked upon them, painting pictures of the good life to come when they would be masters of Redwall. His eloquence finally won, and they set about making large numbers of fire-swingers.

Midmorning at the Abbey found a repair crew clearing away the debris from the previous night's battle. The front gates had been made good and piles of green branches and rubble stacked in front to prevent them being set alight again. Because the normal Abbey routine had been disturbed, a large late breakfast was being served upon the southern wallsteps. Friar Alder and his young assistant, Cockleburr, had made crusty country pasties, and these were being served with melted yellow cheese and rough hazelnut bread. There was new cider, strawberry cordial and a number of latticed pear and redberry tarts to follow. Bagg, Runn and Grubb were the heroes of the hour, regaled with outsize portions of everything as they related their feats of derring-do, embroidering and expanding as they pleased.

"Hohurr, oi cloimed down 'ee roaps an' foighted with they'ns awhoil, then oi clambers back oop an' cuts a few more o' they roaps."

"That's true, I let some of 'em climb right over the top, 'cos I'm not afeared o' searats, then I jabbed 'em in their bottoms with my big sharp knife, so they screamed an' jumped back over the wall. Eek! they went. I'll bet there's a few sore be'inds 'mongst 'em today!"

"As fer me, I went choppo choppo with my sharp knife, though I let some of 'em climb right up on the battlements so I could stand on Grubb's shoulders an' punch 'em in the nose. Puncho! Ain't that right, Grubb, me old warrior pal?"

"Aye 't were so. They was a-cryen an' a-wailen. Oh mercy me, spare oi, they was moanen. Hurhurr, we'ns spared they aroight—more like splattered they all over t' woodlands. Burrhurr, us'n's the boys aroight."

Friar Alder squinted vindictively at the heroic trio. "Yes, and you used my best vegetable knives to do it with. I think you must have been chopping stones with those knives. I've been up since an hour before dawn, trying to sharpen new edges on them."

Ignoring the caustic remarks, Bagg and Runn propounded new ideas.

"We could have a Dibbuns army, y'know."

"Good idea, mate. An' we could fight lots of battles an' all that."

"Aye, that'd show some o'these old fogies."

"Haha, we'd send them all t' bed early."

"Burr, wi' no supper or brakkist on the morrow."

"Heehee, I'd scrub 'em all be'ind their ears, twice a day."

"Hoo urr, oi'd spank a few o' they, just fer nuthin' 't all!"

They froze at the sound of Sister Serena's voice behind them.

"Personally I've never spanked any creature for nothing at all. But I hear there were three of our Dibbuns missing from their beds in the dormitory last night. Sister Sage said that they were out on the east walltop, playing with Friar Alder's sharp knives. Now, if I found out who they were I'd give them a real good hide-tanning for being naughty little creatures. But I don't suppose you three would know who they were, would you?"

"Us, er, phwaw, er, oh no, not us, Sister!"

"We were in bed fast asleep, all night!"

"Burr aye, a-snoren like hinfant 'ogs, us'n's wuz, marm!"

Saxtus was coming from the dormitory with a scroll he had been studying. As he crossed the Abbey lawn he witnessed a strange incident. A whooshing noise in the air caused him to look up. He saw what looked like a small comet of fire with a rope tail. It soared upward, mounting high into the blue, then dropped toward earth, plummeting like a stone. The young mouse mentally charted its course and yelled aloud:

"Sister Serena, look out!"

Saxtus was rushing toward the south steps as he shouted. Serena, not knowing what the alarm was, immediately did the thing closest to her dutiful instinct: she flung herself upon the three Dibbuns sitting on the lower step, shielding them with her body. Hurtling through the air, the blazing rock, bound around with oil-soaked grass, shattered on the step where Serena had been sitting. Friar Alder gasped with shock as a sliver of rock cut his face and a heap of burning material landed on his spotless white apron. Creatures disturbed from their meal dived for cover, beating at smoldering garments and ducking the flying shards of rock that ricocheted from the stone wallstairs.

Saxtus beat at Sister Serena's habit. Luckily it was only scorched, and the Dibbuns she had protected were shocked but unharmed. Farther over to the center of the Abbey grounds, another fire-swinger shot out of the sky and burst on the winding gravel path, showering splintered rock and flame across the lawn. Saxtus, Flagg and the Abbot dashed about, roaring out warnings at the top of their lungs.

"Under cover, everybeast. Quick!"

"Inside the Abbey. Hurry!"

"Get those Dibbuns inside!"

Saxtus and Flagg ran upstairs. Rufe Brush was already

there. Notching an arrow to his bow, he aimed in the general direction of the grinning, jeering crew of searats standing on the flatlands around a fire. Rufe gritted his teeth, drawing the bowstring back to its limit.

"Scum, I'll wipe the smiles off your dirty faces!"

The arrow fell miserably short, causing further merriment among Graypatch and his crew. Saxtus, Flagg and Rufe stood watching as Deadglim dipped a fire-swinger into the fire; it flared up instantly. The searat began swinging it in clockwise circles alongside his body. Faster and faster it swung until it was like a blur of light. He let it go and off it sped like a rocket, out and upward.

Flagg could only stand and watch as it whooshed by overhead. He followed its course. Luckily it shot straight into the Abbey pond, extinguishing with a splash and a hiss. The big otter took the bow and arrows from Rufe.

"Here, matey. I'll put one across their bows!"

Flagg was a powerful fully grown male otter. He drew back the shaft to its point and let fly at Graypatch.

Again the arrow fell woefully short. Flagg grabbed a spear and hurled it with all his considerable strength. It did not even go as far as the arrow. Saxtus tried his slingshot. It went farther than either the spear or the arrow, but still not far enough. On the flatlands the searat crew howled their derision, dancing and jigging as they screamed out insults at the Redwallers.

"Yah country bumpkins, what's up? Can't y'throw?"

"Here, mousy, fire an arrow at me. Haharr!"

"Couldn't hit a crab in a pail. Hohoho!"

The three defenders watched helplessly as another fire-swinger came roaring over. This one had been thrown by Bigfang. It hit the partially finished bell tower, setting light to the wooden-frame scaffolding.

Saxtus hurried from the wall. "We'll have to organize fire-fighting crews!"

"Aye," Flagg agreed miserably. "Those things they're chuckin' have twice the range of any of our weaponry."

It was midafternoon. The Dibbuns would normally have been playing outside, racing around the orchard, paddling at the pond's edge, or frolicking on the lawns. Now they had to stay inside the Abbey building. It was a hot dusty afternoon and they were becoming fractious.

"Wanna go ou'side. Gonna play inna pond!"

"You come back here this instant, young squirrel!"

"Oi wants to sit in 'ee orchar'. 'Tis wurm in yurr!"

"You'd be a lot warmer if one of those flaming things hit you. Now lie down and take a nap. That'll cool you off if you lie still."

"I'm lyin' down, an' I'm still roastin'. When's tea-time?"

"Not for a while yet. Now be good!"

"Burr, oi wantser be naughty, oi loiks 'aven a liddle naughty now 'n' agin. 'Tis nice."

A fire-swinger hit the main Abbey door with a loud crash, and the Dibbuns broke into startled squeaking. Mellus distributed candied chestnuts as she reassured them.

"Hush now. It's nothing. Saxtus and Flagg will deal with it."

Graypatch tore at the roasted meat from the fire. Grinning wolfishly at Kybo, he winked.

"This is the life, eh, messmate! A whole Abbey at our mercy an' nobeast to stop us. Ahoy, Ranzo. Any more of these skylarks skylarkin' round?"

Ranzo fitted an arrow to his bow, squinting upward. "Leave it till evenin' Cap'n, they start to come down then."

The searat sprawled on the grass in the warm summer noon. "Aharr, this is a land of plenty, not like those cold northern isles." He stuck an apple on a stick and began toasting it.

Bigfang came to the fire to light another fire-swinger. Graypatch leaned close and whispered in his ear, "Brains, Bigfang. That's what it takes—brains. You leave the thinkin' to old Graypatch, matey. I'll guarantee they'll want to talk terms by this time tomorrow."

Bigfang held his silence, determined not to rise to Graypatch's bait. He would wait to settle their score.

• • •

Evening brought no change in the situation. The fire-swingers poured in with perilous regularity, each one coming from a different angle to land in an unexpected place, according to the mood of the searat that hurled it. Tired and red-eyed from fighting conflagrations which had sprung up all over the Abbey grounds, Saxtus and Flagg with their fire crews sat drinking cold mint tea, awaiting the next fire-swinger attack. Rufe Brush and his sentries on the west wall shouted warnings at the approach of each missile.

"Hiyo the grounds, fire coming in high and north!"

They dashed over as the incendiary missile appeared at the north end, Sister Sage calling out, "It's hit the north wall wicker gate. Quick!" Stumbling and tripping in the dark, they reached the blaze and began beating the flames down with wet sacking and green boughs. It took a while to defeat the blaze as they were bone-weary and dog-tired.

"Hiyo the grounds," Rufe Brush's voice called out once more. "One coming in dead center, right over me!"

The fire-fighters hitched up their habits and began dashing off in the direction of the main gateway. Saxtus tripped and fell flat. He rested a moment with his scorched face against the grass. A rapping sound caused the young mouse to look up. He gazed around in the darkness quizzically. There it was again. Saxtus stood up and investigated the noise further. It was coming from the wicker gate. Now there were voices.

"Y'don't suppose they've bally well gone to bed, wot?"

"Hardly, old chap. After all, they are under invasion, y'know."

"Imagine sleepin' through a fire-swinger attack. Whoo-hahahahooh!"

"Please, Rosie, don't laugh so close to me poor old ear, it's jolly well deafenin'. In fact, don't gurgle at all if y'can help it, old gel. Just think happy thoughts, eh."

"Oh come off it, Clary you old bodger. If I didn't have

a good hoot now and again I'd prob'ly swell up an' burst!"

"Hmm, no such blinkin' luck, wot?"

"Oh, whoohahahahooh! You are a card, Brig Thyme."

Saxtus unbolted the wicker door. Searats didn't laugh like that!

26

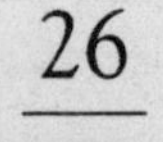

In the fading eventide light the four travelers breasted the big hills to find themselves confronted by a breathtaking sight. A long rocky beach lay beneath them. Lapping up to the shore, the rippling waves broke in a dark blue cascade, glittering red as the setting sun caught the sea, turning it to an iridescent green midway, which faded to purply black on the horizon. The huge crimson half-circle sank slowly in the west, throwing up gold and umber shadows on the undersides of long cloud layers with cream tops. Dandin and Durry had never seen the great waters before. They stared at the magnificent spectacle, awestruck by the immensity of sky and sea.

Durry sat down on the hilltop, spreading his arms wide. "I've seen the Abbey pond and that stream wi' the pikes a-swimmin' in it, but this . . .'tis too much fer one poor lad's eyes to take all in."

Dandin could add nothing to the truth in his friend's simple words.

They descended to the shore and found that what looked like a rocky beach from above was a mass of tall stone outcrops which gave them the sensation of wandering through a mazelike canyon.

Tarquin glanced up at the huge blockform monoliths. "We'll camp somewhere hereabouts for the night, wot?"

"Ye'll be washed away by the night tides if ye do!"

A fat old dormouse had appeared from nowhere. He stood smiling at them over the top of his quaint square eyeglasses. "My name's Bobbo."

Tarquin bowed with the old-fashioned elegance common to hares. "Pleasant evenin', Bobbo. Allow me to introduce us . . ."

As Tarquin went through the formalities, Mariel quietly assessed their new acquaintance. The dormouse was quite old and plump; he carried a knobbly stick which he leaned heavily upon; his garb consisted of a faded velveteen longcoat, tied about the middle with tough dried seaweed; all in all a curious character. His homely eyes twinkled behind the glasses as he wagged his stick up at a towering rock close by.

"Weary travelers all, come ye up to my abode. Follow Bobbo, if ye please."

He was such a friendly, harmless-looking old character that they followed, feeling instinctively that somehow they could trust him.

The dormouse's house was a sizable cave set high in the rock, and they made their way to it up natural ledges which formed a stairway in the stone.

A cheerful sea-coal fire illuminated Bobbo's home; the walls were hung with homemade fishnets and odd-shaped pieces of driftwood sculpted by sand and tide; rush mats scattered about served as seats, and delicious odors wafted from a black stockpot set on a tripod over the fire. Bobbo took a ladle and stirred the contents of the pot.

"It's only shrimp-and-sea-cabbage stew with a few turnips thrown in, but ye be welcome to share it."

He issued them with deep scallop shells and bade them help themselves.

Durry nearly sat on a small yellow-throated newt, which scampered fearfully away to a ledge at the back of the cave. It sat watching them, eyes blinking, throat pulsating. Bobbo strained some of the cooked shrimp from the pot and placed it on the ledge beside the newt.

"Take ye no heed to him, wayfarers. He fell from yon hilltops at high tide and was washed here by the sea waters. I named him Firl. Though he never speaks to me, he's a grand listener, aren't ye, Firl?"

The small newt blinked and began eating. Bobbo drew them each a drink of cloudy liquid from a gourd he kept hanging near the entrance, where night breezes kept it cool.

" 'Tis dandelion flower and wild-barley water. The plants grow plentiful on the hillside. Do ye like it?"

Durry took a long draught from his shell bowl. "By 'ecky! Most afreshin'. My old nuncle Gabe would dearly like t' know how you brew this, Mr. Bobbo. Would y'tell me how to make it?"

The dormouse added more sea-coal to his fire. "All in good time, Master Durry. 'Tis a long night and I've sat alone here many a season, longing for the sound of another voice. But first, let me tell you how I came to this place, then you can tell me all about yourselves and your long journeys from the good homes you left."

Outside, the tide washed in through the rock canyons, swishing and hissing as it threw spray against the walls of sea-scoured stone. The wind made a hollow moaning dirge of its night passage through the flooded maze. High in the safety of the dormouse's den the four travelers sat in comfort, listening to him. The high-toned singsong voice caused them to blink and nod around the fire as Bobbo's uncomplicated tale unfolded.

"Ah me, 'twas more seasons ago now than I do remember, a winter's night, and there was I, chained to a galley bench in a searat ship. They had taken me captive when I was very young, do you see. I had no memory of parents, home or even my name; the galley bench was all I knew. Well now, didn't an awful storm spring up, a fearful thing! Waves washed over the side and flooded the galleys where we poor wretches were chained to the oars, pulling until our backs were nigh broken, whipped, starved and ill-treated. Myself was chained next to a poor weak creature, a vole who just gave up life and died, right next to me, there on the galley bench. Listen now, for I tell you true, the master of this ship was a searat, the blackest-hearted scoundrel who ever stepped aboard ship—Gabool the Wild was his name!"

Mariel's eyes came wide open, but she did not interrupt Bobbo, who by now was in full flow.

"Ah well, there was I, chained to an oar and a dead creature, trying to pull my weight with the others as we battled against wave, storm and the slavedriver's lash. Gabool came down into the galleys.

" 'Why isn't that oar workin'?' says he. 'Because one of 'em's dead,' says the slavedriver. Then Gabool says; 'The way that oar isn't pullin', it looks like they're both dead. Throw 'em overboard an' get two more in their place!' Now before I could call out, the slavemaster bashes me over the head and I'm in the sea, chained to the poor dead vole. What took place next I cannot be telling you for I must have passed out. But the chains and the body of my dead oar partner saved my life, as I awoke next morning, high up on these rocks where the tide had thrown the two of us. The body of the vole was caught in a crevice. Without him I would have been washed back into the sea again, for I was hanging in my chains by both paws, high up on top of this very rock, with the shore far below me. When I could muster the strength, I climbed up to my dead partner. His paws were so thin and wasted that I found little difficulty slipping the manacles and chains from them. Do you know, I often wish that he had lived, for then I would have had some creature to talk with. Be that as it may, 'twas in climbing down these rocks that I found this cave.

"So here am I, Bobbo. The vole lies buried on the green hillside—I think he would have liked that. When I had freed myself of the chains, I threw them far into the sea from the high rocks. Here I have lived a solitary peaceful life, though not without its perils. I did try to make my way inland but was lost in the swamps for many days. Lucky I was to find my way back here. 'Tis best that here I stay. Maybe one day I will teach little Firl to speak, then we can talk together."

Bobbo left off, staring into the fire.

"So then, there you have it all. Look now, I can see you are for sleeping. Lie down and rest; you can tell me about yourselves in the morning. It is warm and safe here. You will sleep well."

Tarquin, Dandin and Durry needed no second bidding, but Mariel was not tired. The mousemaid sat up far into the night, questioning Bobbo about Gabool, though the dormouse had little information to impart. He was, however, eager to hear about the travelers, so in return for his kindness Mariel did not keep him in suspense until the morrow. She related all their adventures as Bobbo sat keenly drinking in every word, with Firl making tiny snoring sounds on the ledge behind them.

The squeal of sea gulls wakened Dandin as rosy dawn banished the coverlet of night. He lay still, only his eyes moving about, taking in their new surroundings. The other three were still fast asleep. Dandin rose and stretched as Bobbo stumped in, followed by Firl, his faithful newt. The dormouse bore twigs and a full sack.

"Dandin, it is a good morning I am bidding you. Look, dried applewood and sweet herbs to burn—it makes my abode smell fresh in the mornings. Now, you will find a small rockpool outside to wash in, and I will prepare wild oatcakes, small fish and gorseflower honey to break your fast."

The young mouse grinned. "That sounds excellent to me, Bobbo. Thank you."

He was back in a short while, splashing water over his sleeping friends. "Rise and shine! Wakey wakey! Oatcakes, honey and fish! Last one washed doesn't get any!"

Tarquin sprang up, shaking himself. "I say, you sly young cad, why didn't y'wake me earlier? By the pattern on me aunty's pinny, Bobbo, that smells good!"

Morning sunlight was beginning to flood the cavern as they sat eating.

Mariel had a surprise to reveal. "You'll never guess what I learned last night while I was talking to Bobbo."

Durry licked honey from his paws and juggled with a hot oatcake. "No, marm, you're right. We'll never guess, so hurry up an' tell us."

The mousemaid recited the appropriate lines of the poem:

"Where the sea meets with the shore,
There the final clue is hid;
Rock stands sentinel evermore,
Find it as I did.
The swallow who cannot fly south,
The bird that only flies one way,
Lies deep beneath the monster's mouth,
Keep him with you night and day.

Do you remember that part of the rhyme? Well, last night while you were all snoring, I sat up telling Bobbo of our quest, and guess what?"

Tarquin dipped his oatcake in the amber honey impatiently. "Whatwhatwhat?"

Mariel smiled intriguingly from one to the other. "Bobbo knows where the swallow is!"

"I say, good egg! What a spiffin' old Bobbo you are, wot!"

"Even more cleverer than my nuncle Gabe, an' that's a fact!"

"Do you really know, Bobbo? Oh, tell us, please!"

The dormouse stood up, brushing crumbs from his longcoat. "Do you come with me and I will show it to you."

Bobbo hobbled in front, with Firl at his heels. He led them on a southerly tack through the twisting winding canyons, keeping up a surprisingly lively pace, now disappearing into shadowed recesses and materializing into bright sunlight. Sometimes they crunched upon small pebbles, other times pattered across damp sand, occasionally splashing through sun-warmed shallow pools.

Finally they arrived at their destination. Bobbo leaned against a monumental edifice.

"Well now, friends, here is the very place!"

This rock was much larger than any they had previously encountered. It was almost a small mountain set in the sands, giving the impression of some vast primeval monster squatting upon the shore with its back to the sea. The dormouse led them to the east side of the rock, where a huge overhang projected over a pool that was both wide and deep.

Dandin looked about, expecting to see a swallow perched somewhere close.

Bobbo pointed to the pool. "See, right at the bottom, lodged between two rocks."

Gathering around the rim, they peered into the underwater grotto. Through the clear limpid water, aided by lancing rays of sunlight, it could be dimly seen. No bigger than the size of a mouse's paw, a swallow fashioned from metal, its outspread wings partially obscured by the rocks which held it captive amid the brightly hued sea anemones and corals on the bed of the pool.

Dandin shook his head in amazement. "How did you ever find it, Bobbo?"

"Fishing, young master. I was fishing for shrimp one day, sitting here staring down into the pool, when I saw it glint in the early sunlight."

"And didn't you try to get it out?"

"Ah well, I did try for nearly half a day with my hook and line, but it was too smooth and firmly lodged in the rocks. So I had to leave the little bird, do you see. Then after I found Firl I brought him along to this place to dive for it. Newts are excellent swimmers."

"Of course they are. Why didn't Firl get it?"

The small newt scampered down from the rock and cringed against Bobbo, eyes wide and throat palpitating madly.

"Ah well, do you see, it is not only the little bird who lives down at the bottom," the dormouse explained. "There is also a great shell creature, one with claws like vises, great eyes on stalks and long whiskers. Poor Firl lost his tail to the beast; it has only lately grown back. I would not let him go down there again, no not ever!"

Bobbo produced a piece of oatcake from his longcoat. Powdering it, he mixed it to a paste with some water and molded it around a small pebble.

"Watch now and see."

He dropped the coated pebble into the pool close by the edge. They gathered around and marked its progress as it sank rapidly to the bottom of the water. Near the part where the swallow lay, the pebble came to rest. It had no sooner landed than a gigantic blue-black lobster rushed out of a crevice, pounced on the stone and retreated swiftly with the object held tightly in its enormous pincered claws. It all happened so fast that the onlookers were stunned into momentary silence.

Bobbo shrugged. "So you see now, wayfarers. Is it not a dreadful monster?"

Durry blanched. "It's even too 'orrible to look at, Mr. Bobbo!"

Mariel's jaw was set, firm and resolute. "But I've got to go down there and rescue the swallow!"

"If you go down, then I do too!" There was determination in Dandin's eyes.

"Er, er, oh, dash it, count me in as well, you chaps!"

Mariel shook her head. "No, Tarquin. You and Durry stay up here with Bobbo. We'll need you two to lower us down and pull us out quick. Now let me think awhile. I'll have to figure out the best way to do this . . ."

Durry mopped his brow and blew out a sigh of relief. "Thank my stars! My old nuncle'd 'ave a fit if half a poor nephew walked back in on 'im one o' these days. Best we stay up 'ere, Mr. Woodsorrel. Just think what your Hon Rosie'd say if you turned up with no nose and on'y one ear. Bet she'd be rightly peeved."

"Peeved? Peeved ain't the word, young Durry. Rosie'd take a screamin' blue tizzy if she saw a magnificent specimen of harehood minus a hooter an' a lug. Good grief, I'd have to run off an' become a bally searat, or somethin' equally foul!"

• • •

It was noontide before Mariel and Dandin came up with a workable solution. They went back to Bobbo's cave, where they gathered together what rope they could find, plus all the cooked shrimp and small fish they could lay paws upon. Back at the pool, Mariel explained her strategy to the others.

"The idea is to throw as much food to the lobster as possible. Let's start right now. Durry, Tarquin, chuck the shrimp and fish in. I want you to keep your eyes on the lobster. Once it stops coming out to get the food, let me know. Dandin, you and I will search about for two rocks. We need something to weight us down and make us sink to the bottom of the pool. While we're down there, you keep watch, with the sword ready. I'll get the swallow, then Durry and Tarquin can haul us up out of it."

Soon the final preparations had been made. Mariel and Dandin sat on the rock lip of the pool with ropes tied about their waists. The mousemaid put aside her Gullwhacker; it would be useless underwater. Dandin took off his scabbard and held on to the sword. Durry and Tarquin were still dropping odd bits of food into the water.

"I think the old lobster villain's had enough. He's not botherin' to come out for any more tucker. The water's teemin' with jolly nice fish an' shrimp, but he seems to have had a tummyful—great glutton!"

Both mice picked up their rocks. Bobbo gave final instructions.

"Now then, do you go straight down and get the bird, tug on the ropes and we will haul you up fast. If we see the creature come out we will pull you up, whether you have the swallow or not. I wish you both luck and good fortune. Now take a slow deep breath."

Side by side Mariel and Dandin slid into the water, the coldness forcing them to take deep breaths, then the weight of the stones took over. With eyes wide open, the pool closed above their heads and they began their descent, into the silent aquamarine depths of the watery world.

BOOK THREE

The Sound of a Bell!

27

The hare shook paws with Mother Mellus inside Great Hall as the fire-swingers roared outside on the lawns and in the orchard.

"Long patrol from Salamandastron at y'service, marm. Colonel Clary, Brigadier Thyme and Hon Rosie."

Mellus inspected Clary's paw. "You've been hurt. I'll get a proper dressing for that wound. Sister Sage! Bring a clean dressing and some salve, will you."

Clary winced slightly as the dressing was applied.

"Much obliged, marm. Only a scratch, really. Good healin' fur us Meadowclarys have, wot? The young mouse chappie, wotsisname, Saxtus, he's told us what the position is. Not to worry, we'll have the vermin sorted out by dawn for you—dealt with their types before. Oh, by the way, marm, can I count on you to be on the west walltop in, say, two hours?"

Mellus nodded. "You can count on me for anything, as long as it gets those filthy searats away from Redwall Abbey, Colonel Clary."

Hon Rosie gawped around Great Hall in open admiration. "Oh, I say, what a super-dooper cottage y'have here. Whoohahahahooh!"

This time it was Mellus's turn to wince. "Colonel Clary, would it be possible for Hon Rosie to do her laughing outside? We have infants in the dormitories, trying to sleep."

Clary saluted. "Right you are, marm. Rosie! Put a lid on the giggles, old gel. Keepin' the babies awake, wot!"

"Oops! Silly old me, I'll go an' have a swift chortle in the shrubbery. Whooha—Sorry!"

Thyme went about his business efficiently. Mounting the west wall, he introduced himself to Rufe Brush and tested a bow and arrow.

"Hmm, this all the archery equipment you've got? Sadly lackin', old lad. Now let me see, range, trajectory, distance . . . Hmmm, yersss! Is there a wicker gate in your east wall leadin' out into the jolly old woodlands?"

Rufe nodded dumbly, slightly overawed by the militaristic hare.

"Good show! Next question: where'll I find your grub wallah—y'know the cook chappie, the chef?"

"In the kitchens, gettin' tomorrow's breakfast set up, I s'pose. Inside the Abbey, one floor down below Great Hall."

"Top-hole! See y'later. Face front now, don't turn y'back on the bally enemy, old chap. They'll shoot you in the behind, wot!"

Rufe was left so bewildered he nearly forgot to duck as a low-flying fire-swinger sped overhead.

"Hiyo the grounds, fire-swinger come in over main gate!"

"Hurr, maister Brush," a mole cried out from below. "You'm a bit late, baint 'ee? Durned foir-s'inger near burned moi nose offen."

Friar Alder reluctantly parted with his three best vegetable knives again. "Take care of them please, Mr. Thyme."

"It's Brigadier, sah, Brigadier—but you can call me Brig. Not to worry about the old frogstickers, we'll have 'em back good as new." Saxtus and Flagg sat with their backs to the Abbey building, taking a breather and a drink of cool dandelion and burdock cordial while Gabriel Quill and Friar Hubert took over the fire-fighting relief column. Flagg rubbed the cold stone beaker against his brow.

"Whew! I 'opes those hares c'n help us. Nice folk, though a little snooty in their manner o' talkin' like."

Saxtus took a long draught of his drink. "They're Salamandastron hares, Brother Hubert said, battle-trained and ready for anything. Leave it to them. They'll know what to do, Flagg."

Out in the woodlands beyond the east wallgate, Clary trimmed shoots from a thick yewpole with Friar Alder's knife.

"There, that should be just the ticket, wot? Six long staves, good solid yew. How's the oak comin' along, Rosie old gel?"

"Capital, Clary. We found a big old one, quite dead an' ready to topple, but loads of sound branches on it, just the right length too. Hahahahooh."

Thyme looked up from his labors. "I noted lots of fishin' line in the kitchens. We can plait it together; should be ideal."

Clary smiled grimly. "Well done, Thyme. Come on, let's go!"

An hour before daybreak Deadglim shook Graypatch awake. He went to the fire and warmed himself.

"How's it goin', mateys?"

Swinging his arm around ever faster, Frink suddenly let a fire-swinger go. It roared off into the lightening sky like a shooting star.

"Great, Cap'n, though we're usin' green vines instead o' rope now—there's loads of it growin' over yonder, plenty o' dead grass too. We could keep this up all season. It's bags o' fun."

Graypatch helped himself to roasted bird, tearing at it hungrily. "Haharr, so it is, shipmate. Get summat to eat now. I'll take over fer a while. Hoho, they must be run ragged inside those walls by now. Pretty soon they'll be too tired an' slow. Then a fire'll start that they won't be able to cope with. That's when we'll pay em a visit. Come on, me lucky bucks, keep a-slingin' those flames in!"

Bigfang stood up. Rubbing sleep from his eyes, he stared toward the Abbey walls in the gathering daylight. He ran across to Graypatch.

"Cap'n, look! It's those three big rabbits who were aboard the *Darkqueen*. See 'em, large as life on the walltop!"

Graypatch spat out some burnt feathers and picked at his fangs. "Noddletop! Those ain't rabbits. Don't y'know a hare when y'see one? Any'ow, what difference does it make to us who they are? They'll burn same as the rest of 'em. Wake yerself up, addlebrain, an' start throwin'."

They met on the walltop in front of the threshold, facing the plain from where Graypatch and his entire contingent could be seen around the large fire which provided ignition for the missiles—Colonel Clary, Brig Thyme, Hon Rosie, Mother Mellus and Flagg.

Saxtus stood to one side. He watched as Clary took command, all traces of jocularity and fun gone from the hare's normally quirky voice. There were six bows and a large stock of arrows on the threshold. Clary picked up a bow and a single shaft.

"I'm aware that you all know how to fire a bow, but I'll go over this once to refresh your memories. This bow, like the others we have made, is a longbow—solid yew and more than twice the size of the ones you are used to. It is strung with a cord plaited from fishing lines to give it extra power. The arrows, as you can see, are far longer than normal arrows; thicker too. They are oak, fire-hardened tips and leaf flights. Now, I have chosen you because you are the biggest, strongest creatures in the Abbey, the very ones to fire these long-bows. Let me demonstrate."

As Saxtus watched, Clary notched an arrow onto the bowstring.

"Stand side-on to the bow, keep it upright, draw back the string so that the shaft is fully occupied and the string taut. Bring the arrow up to the jawline, sight with one eye along the shaft, allowing for the arrow to take a curving course, mounting upwards and coming down right on the object aimed at. Right, now for a target."

Thyme pointed. "The rat dipping a swinger into the fire—get him!"

Clary adjusted his eyeline, drew the arrow back to its limit and let fly. The taut longbow string twanged as the heavy oak shaft hissed off into the dawn light. Saxtus held his breath.

Ranzo was about to start whirling his fire-swinger when the arrow struck him. It knocked him backward, dead before he could blink, the fire-swinger dropping from his nerveless claws.

Saxtus was still a novice in the art of war, and the sudden death shocked him. "Y-you k-killed him! He's dead!" he stammered to the grim-faced hare.

Clary issued longbows to the others. "Aye, young mouse, it was a clean shot. Keep your head down and issue us with arrows as we call for them. In case you're feeling sorry for that wretch, let me tell you something: fire is the most dangerous thing to any living woodlander. Once it takes a hold it means death and destruction to everyone and everything. Only a searat would use fire. Sometimes I think it is because they do not realize the danger, being creatures who live on the great waters. But most of the time I think it is because they are evil vermin. We at Salamandastron have battled against searats all our lives. I would not dare tell you some of the sights I have seen. Searats are complete enemies. They live only to kill and conquer; they are completely merciless."

Thyme notched an arrow to his bowstring. "Righty-ho, chaps. Give 'em vinegar, wot!"

Five more messengers of death hissed through the early morning.

It was then that Saxtus decided the hare's manner was merely a front, presented to others because they would forget the real purpose behind the guardians of the shores. The young mouse doled out arrows, knowing that he would never get used to warfare—and be a jolly fellow one moment, and a ruthless fighter the next.

Pandemonium reigned in the searat camp. Graypatch ran hither and thither, trying to stop his searats retreating out of the range of the deadly longbows, exhorting them to carry on with his plan, which had worked quite well until the appearance of the hares.

"Come on, shipmates. Don't let a few arrows scare yer off! Lardgutt, Kybo, get back here. We were beatin' 'em—we still can!"

Bigfang sat well out of range, a smug expression on his face. "I told yer about those rabbits, Graypatch, but you wouldn't listen, would yer? Oh no, you knew best."

The searat Captain's temper broke completely. "You lily-livered, worm-hearted, bilge-scrapin's! Mutineers, deserters, the whole pack of yer! We had the battle nearly won, an' now you've turned tail an' slunk off like a load of sea slugs! Look at me. Am I afraid? Am I scared? Haharr ha ha ha! I laugh at 'em!"

Graypatch grabbed a fire-swinger. Putting light to it, he began swinging it furiously.

"I'll show yer, Abbeyscum, I'll bring yer Redwall down in flames!" He dodged, ducking a flying arrow. The fire-swinger lost momentum right at its peak and the burning section fell onto his footclaws.

"Yaaheeeoooooh!"

Graypatch hopped about, beating at his burning limb, fur smoldering as he threw himself upon his back, screeching and thudding his scorched footclaws against the ground.

Hon Rosie fell back, whooping hysterically. "Whoohahahahooh! Oh, I say, chaps, that was a real old hotfoot!"

• • •

Down in the orchard, Gabriel Quill and Burgo Mole sat looking at each other.

"Yurr, they vermints baint chucken no more foir at us'n's?"

"Nor they aren't neither, Burgo. Hoho, your eyes are all red 'n' smoky!"

"Hurrhurr, talk about 'eeself, Gabe'l Quill. You'm gotten a sutty nose!"

Brother Hubert wandered wearily across. "Whew! Just look at the state of my paws—scorched, soiled and grubby. A fine state of affairs for an Abbey Recorder, I must say."

"Ho urr, scruffy old Hoobit. No more foirs now tho', zurr."

"Indeed. It's thanks to those hares—splendid creatures."

"I'll drink t' that, Hubert. What d'you say we go to my cellars and have a small drop to drive away the heat an' dust of our night's work?"

"Burr, oi'm with 'ee, Gabe'l. 'Tis a turrible thurst come on oi."

"Marvelous idea. Count me in, Mr. Quill!"

The three old friends trundled off paw in paw.

As Abbot Bernard watched them go, he felt Simeon pulling on his sleeve.

"I think there should be room for two more in Gabriel's cellar, Bernard."

"Yes, they'll manage to squeeze us in somehow, Simeon."

Inside the Abbey, young Cockleburr had been given charge of Dibbuns' breakfast time. He mopped his brow as he chased Grubb about with a bowl of corn pudding.

"Oh, wanderin' woodpigeons, will you come an' eat this breakfast, you dreadful scoundrel!"

Grubb hid beneath the table with Bagg and Runn. "Nay, oi baint eaten no brekkist. Us'n's a-goen out t' play."

"Sister Serena said there's no more fire an' we can go out."

"I don't like corn pudden, wanna play inna orchard!"

"Fidgetin' frogs, Mother Mellus told me nobeast goes out without eatin' breakfast first, 'specially Dibbuns."

"Ho well, do 'ee sling it unner yurr an' us'n's will force et daown."

28

Mariel and Dandin dropped silently to the bottom of the pool.

Dandin, with sword in one paw and weightstone in the other, immediately turned to face the lobster's den. He could see the big crustacean—it watched them as it lay unmoving, one great claw hanging in front, the other by its side. The lobster looked peaceful enough for the moment. Still, Dandin did not relax his vigilance for a single instant.

Mariel let go of her weightstone and tried to dislodge the tiny metal swallow, but it was lodged firmly between two slabs of rock. She chose the smaller of the two slabs and began wresting it out of the way. By this time both she and Dandin were longing for a breath of air. Struggling with the cumbersome rock, Mariel could feel the blood pounding round inside her head. She set her footpaws on the large rock and gave the smaller rock a mighty shove. Without warning it shifted, giving off an odd crumbling noise underwater. Clouds of silt and sand boiled up as it toppled to one side.

Disturbed by the noise and movement in its pool, the huge blue-black lobster came scurrying out. Dandin barely saw the monster come; he backed water, thrusting the swordpoint at its eyes. Mariel snatched at the swallow, but it slipped from her grasp and slid into the sand. In the confusion of disturbed cloudy water she realized that she had lost the precious object. Now the lobster had Dandin trapped up against the rock. Thinking quickly, he pushed forward, landing in between its claws. It was a clever move. He was stuck up against the hideous face of the creature, too close for it to use its cumbersome oversized nippers; they clacked across his back like giant shears, unable to bite him. But it was like being caught in a vise. Dandin was held fast in the embrace of the heavy-shelled joints. The sword was squeezed from his grip and fell to the bottom of the pool.

He shouted aloud in desperation, but the sound was only a boggle of noise, lost amid the air bubbles that escaped from his mouth. However, Mariel had heard it. Forgetting the swallow, she turned to the aid of her friend. Lungs bursting, she scrabbled about on the pool bed until her paw came in contact with the sword.

The lobster doubled up to rid itself of Dandin, and the hefty fanlike tail caught Mariel a swipe as she tried to get close. The air was now forcing itself out of the mousemaid's mouth in huge bubbles. She wondered why her friends on the surface were not attempting to haul them up. Her limbs felt like lead and her head was ringing. Blindly she struck out with the sword and pierced the lobster's back, down near its tail. Infuriated, the lobster turned, lashing out with one claw.

Instantly freed, Dandin felt himself being hauled quickly to the surface. The lobster locked on to the sword blade with its viselike pincer. Mariel felt herself being hauled up on the rope. She was now upside-down in the water, clinging grimly on to the sword, the lobster below her hanging on to the sword blade with one claw whilst trying to get at her with the other.

A large rock came splashing down onto the lobster, followed by another and another. It let go of the sword as it was battered to the pool bottom by yet more rocks. Mariel was pulled clear of the pool with a whoosh of spray and a rush of air, and she fell upon the sand, spitting out water and gasping for breath.

Tarquin sat her up, pushing her back and forward. Mariel's head was rising and falling as it nearly touched her footpaws, and the water gushed out as she coughed.

"Come on, old gel. Just like the village pump, wot!" Tarquin chuckled cheerfully.

Dandin was in slightly better shape, having been pulled out marginally sooner than Mariel. He sat with his back against the rocks in the sunlight as Durry fussed about him.

"Any more water t' come up, matey?"

"No, thank you, Durry. Just let me rest. I'll be all right."

They sat Mariel beside him. She wiggled a paw in her ear.

"Well, what about that little adventure, eh, and all for nothing!"

Bobbo squatted in front of her, smiling behind his glasses. "Well now, why do you say all for nothing, young mouse?"

Mariel scuffed the sand irritably. "Because we never got the swallow."

Bobbo pressed something into her paw. "Then tell me what this is!"

Mariel stared at the tiny metal bird she was holding. "But how . . . ?"

Bobbo chuckled and patted her paw. "It was Firl. I told you that the newts are very good at the swimming. He went in and got it while you and your friend Dandin battled with the creature. We could not risk pulling you up, you see. The water was too cloudy and disturbed, and we could not see what was happening. Then Firl dived in and I myself decided you needed air or you would both drown, so I said, 'Pull up, whatever is happening. Pull!' "

Durry swelled his chest out proudly. "The rocks were

my idea, missy. Me 'n' Tarquin hurtled 'em at the beastie as we pulled you out."

Mariel got slowly up and hugged them one by one. "What good friends you are, all of you."

Later, in the cave, they took a closer look at the little swallow. It was made of some shining blue metal which gave off strange glints in the sunlight, shaped like a fan-tailed swallow, wings spread wide as if it were flying. Dandin noticed a small hole bored through one of the wingtips.

"See this hole—what d'you suppose it's for?"

"I don't know, maybe for something to fit into it."

"Hmm, it'd have to be pretty thin to fit through that tiny hole."

Bobbo pulled a thread from the lining of his velveteen longcoat. "Something as thin as this, are you thinking, wayfarers?"

Dandin nodded. "Yes, that's thin enough. Let's try it."

The swallow hung by the piece of thread. It dangled there, turning slowly, then stopped, facing the right wall of the cave. They watched it; the little bird remained still.

Tarquin took hold of the thread. "Here, let's see the bally old bird." He spun it on the thread. Round and round it went, finally coming to rest facing the same way again, the right wall of the cave. No matter how many times it was spun it still ended facing the same direction.

The wall on the right side of Bobbo's cave!

Durry shook his head in amazement. "Just like the poem says, 'The swallow who cannot fly south.' "

Mariel smiled. "Aye, it flies the opposite way: north!"

Dandin recited the last lines of the poem.

"His flight is straight, norwest is true,
Your fool's desire he'll show to you."

Bobbo held up the swallow on its thread, watching as each time it stopped turning it pointed due north.

"This is a thing of great magic. You could be going anywhere, in dark or fog, yet it would guide you, see.

Northwest is at the point of the bird's neck, between its head and left wing. So you see, travelers, let the little swallow think he is flying north, but you take the northwest course. Truly a marvelous bird, my friends."

At supper they sat around the fire discussing their next move. Mariel knew well what it was.

"We need a boat."

Dandin left off polishing the sword. "How long would it take to build a boat? Where would we get the timber? We know nothing of boatbuilding."

A gloomy silence prevailed. The fire flickered warmly about the rock walls as they sat mentally wrestling with the problem. Bobbo looked from one to the other before speaking.

"Ah well now, it is sad and dreary your faces are. You are my friends, I would like you to stay here forever, but I know that your fate and search are elsewhere and you will leave sooner or later. So listen to what I must tell you. You want a boat; I do not have a boat, but I know where a ship lies . . ."

Mariel sprang up. "Where? Please tell us where the ship is, Bobbo."

The old dormouse sat back, stroking Firl's head gently.

"I saw her a few days ago; she was drifting north round the headland. A curious ship, with not a living creature aboard her. So then I followed her along the shore. She had neither masts nor rigging. The tide sent her up into the cove on the other side of the headland, and I boarded her in the shallows. 'Twas a terrible sight to see, a searat ship, *Greenfang* she was named, burnt out in some battle, though not anyone aboard of her. There was no supplies, or things I could be using myself. Ah well then. I anchored her fast to some rocks and left her there. Now I warn you, she has neither sail nor masts, the cabins are all gutted by fire, but the hull is sound and she has steering and a rudder. She will take you where you want to go. I will show you her on the morrow and you can decide for yourselves, though I see by your faces that your minds are already set on it. Go you to sleep now, 'tis probably the last good rest you will be taking in many a perilous day ahead. As for myself, I will bide here with my friend Firl. I am too old for such wild adventures. Peace is all I seek now."

By midmorning of the next day they were riding the charred hulk of *Greenfang* out upon the tide, with scant supplies, no proper accommodation and an outward wind. Mariel held the long tiller, the metal swallow constantly pointing north under cover of a makeshift awning. Tarquin wiped a paw bravely across his eyes, Dandin sniffed copiously, Durry wept unashamedly, but Mariel smiled fondly at the two small figures growing dim in the distance as they waved from the shoreline. She would never forget Bobbo the quaint little dormouse, or his silent friend Firl the newt and their peaceful existence in the cave amid the tall rocks. Now the mousemaid turned to the open sea, and the unknown dangers that lay before them.

29

Abbot Bernard realized the value of battle-trained hares. Accordingly he allowed the trio full rein in defending the Abbey, trusting to their military judgment.

Clary organized most things within Redwall whilst the threat of attack was still a possibility. He was very good at it. Sentries were posted upon the walls in a regular roster—with the exception of Simeon, no creature was excluded. At least one longbow archer was posted at all times, night and day, fully armed and ready to shoot. Apart from that, the day-to-day routine was not interfered with; creatures got on with the business of living at the Abbey, carrying out their chores and taking their ease and pleasure when permitted. Tonight was such a night.

The Abbot had ordered a special supper in honor of the hares, Flagg offering to take Thyme's watch with the longbow. Cavern Hole was the venue, tables were laid around the walls with a splendid running buffet spread upon them. One thing the hares did not lack was appetite. The splendid fare offered by the famous Redwallers made the Salamandastron food seem spartan in comparison. Colonel Clary found himself ushered around, plate in paw, by Sister Serena.

"Colonel, perhaps you would like to try some of this deeper 'n' ever pie?"

"Deeper 'n' wot, marm? Looks delicious, I must say. Jolly strange name."

"Yes, it's a great favorite of the moles, you know—full of turnip 'n' tater 'n' beetroot, to use the mole language."

"I say, I rather like this red gravy stuff, very spicy!"

"Oh, that's otters' hotroot sauce. You know what they say?"

"No, marm. What do they say?"

Serena chuckled and adopted her otter voice. "Ain't nothin' 'otter for an otter!"

Brigadier Thyme was being entertained by Gabriel Quill. The hedgehog was pointing out to him the finer nuances of food with drink.

"Now lookit this, Brig, a nice sparkly strawberry cordial. You might think it'd go well with yonder damson shortcrust an' cream."

"Well, what d'you think, Gabe old scout? Does it?"

"Not on your aunty's washtub, it don't. 'Ere, you try a beaker of my cowslip an' parsley comfort wi' that damson shortcrust. Go on."

"Mmm, absolutely top-hole, old thing. My, it does make a difference. I say, what's that jolly brown stuff in the tankards?"

"Good October ale. Redwall's famous fer it, an' I'm the beast as brews it. Now, you want to sample some o' that with cheese an' mushroom pastie—that'd make yer tail curl a bit."

"Rather. I've always fancied m'self with a curly tail. Hi, Rosie, how are you gettin' on with the jolly old nosebag, wot?"

Hon Rosie waved a ladleful of summercream dip. "Whoohahahahooh! Look at these Dibbuns chaps doin' an impression of us, Thyme. Very droll. They're an absolute hoot. Whoohahahahooh!"

Bagg, Runn and Grubb had decided to take on new

roles as hares carrying longbows. They strutted about with their bows and arrows, mimicking all the mannerisms of Clary and his long patrol.

"I say, ol' boy, ol' thing, ol' top, pip pip an' all that!"

"Hurrhurr, wotwotwot? Us'n's gotten gurt bows 'n' arrers, ol' bean. You'm jolly well watch owt iffen you'm one o' they searattens, boi okey!"

"Rather, ol' scout. Wot an 'oot. Whoohoohoohoo!"

Thyme twirled his whiskers in a very offpaw manner. "Hmm, exceedingly comical, I'm sure." He seated himself next to a mole who was munching away at a large crusty pie and nodded at the fellow. "Pie looks jolly nice. What's in it?"

The mole, who was named Burgo, turned full face to the hare. "Woild garleck, zurr!"

Brigadier Thyme nearly fell off the bench as the mole's breath hit him. "Good grief, what a dreadful pong!"

Burgo nodded. "Turrible, baint et. Oi dearly loiks the taste, but oi can't aboid the smell moiself, zurr."

Treerose, the pretty young squirrel, sidled up to Rufe Brush. "Oh, Rufe, I've baked you a special cake of nutbread and I've iced it too, with clover honey."

Rufe stood on one paw then the other, his voice a mumble. "Oh er, very nice er, thank you er, Treerose, er, er."

Treerose blushed and smiled winningly. At last she was getting through to the strong silent Rufe. "Shall we take it out into the orchard and share it, Rufey Woofy?"

Rufe straightened up and planked the cake back into her paws. "Take it where y'like with Rufey Woofy. My name's Rufe Brush an' I'm due back on the walls for sentry duty!"

He stalked off, leaving Treerose holding the cake. She stamped her paw petulantly, her lip beginning to quiver. Grubb slipped in and took the cake from her.

"Yurr, doant 'ee cry, missy. Iffen Rufe doant like they ol' cake, oi'll scoff et, ol' gel, wotwot, hurr hurr!"

• • •

Mother Mellus sat with Simeon and the Abbot. Clary had joined them and was reassuring the Abbot.

"Not to worry, Father. We're well able for searats. If they bother Redwall again, we'll be ready for 'em. Though I don't think we're in any immediate danger from the blaggards."

"Couldn't we go out after them, Colonel Clary?"

The hare turned to Mellus, his eyebrows raised. "Marm, go after them?"

"Actually it's not the searats I'm thinking of, it's the oarslaves. It's pitiful really—what sort of a life must those poor creatures lead as slaves of the filthy searats. Couldn't we, I mean you, arrange to sort of release them and bring them back here?"

"Now now, Mellus," Abbot Bernard interrupted the badger. "Colonel Clary and his patrol have been more than kind to us already, driving the searats off. I'm sure they have other business at Salamandastron."

"Not at all, Father. Lord Rawnblade sent us up to Mossflower to help in any way we can against searats. We'd be failin' in our duty if we refused you anything, especially a request from another badger."

Mellus smiled gratefully. "You'll do it then, Colonel?"

"Well, marm, can't promise anythin', you understand, but I'll have a word with my troops and let you know."

Mellus knew that Clary was going to grant her request; still, that did not stop her reinforcing her plea.

"Every time I think of those twenty very young slaves, the hunger, beatings and hardship they must be enduring—it's a wonder they're not lying out there in Mossflower dead from it all. Oh, there's your friend the squirrel too; the searats have taken him captive."

"Tcha! Old Pakatugg y'mean—that old reprobate prob'ly got himself captured through his own greed, doncha know. He's an unspeakable rogue really, sell his mother for two acorns and a loaf. Righty-ho, marm, you've made your point. Let me go and work out a plan with Thyme an' Rosie. We're pretty good at wheezes when we put our heads together."

Mellus sighed heavily and shook her great striped

head. "Let's hope you and your friends do come up with some good wheezes, Colonel. As for myself, my brain is too full of other things to think of wheezes. There's Mariel and Dandin, Tarquin, young Durry Quill too. They've gone off to face goodness knows what perils, questing for a bell, searching for a strange island, determined to slay Gabool the Searat. Where will it all end? I hope those youngsters are safe, wherever they are. Sometimes I wish that little mousemaid would have stayed as Storm Gullwhacker instead of finding out her real name was Mariel."

Clary halted his assault on a nearby vegetable flan. "Stap me, young Storm Gullwhacker, eh! So that's what became of her. Mariel, much nicer name for a pretty young gel, wot? Don't you fret, marm. That one's well able for anything. Three good comrades with her, y'say? Stap me! What more could she want? Makes a chap wish he was out there questin' with 'em."

Mellus was about to enlarge upon the dangers that faced Mariel and her friends when Clary moved on to make new friends and sample fresh delicacies.

Simeon turned in the badger's direction. "You really are a shameless coaxer at times, Mother Mellus."

She bristled slightly. "I was deliberately being shameless to help those little slaves who are in a *shameful* position, Simeon. What would you have me do? Sit safe here in Redwall Abbey and not bother about it at all?"

The blind herbalist spread his paws. "Apologies, apologies! I did not realize you felt so strongly about the slaves. Being blind, I cannot see them, but I suppose if I had my sight I'd shout for their rescue as loudly as you."

In the small hours between midnight and dawn the three hares stole silently through Mossflower toward the searat encampment, armed only with their lances. Clary stopped the other two a short distance from the glow of the enemy campfires.

"Righty-ho, got it all clear now. Me 'n' Rosie do the decoyin'; Thyme, you're the jolly old rescuer. When you've got a couple of slaves, make straight back to Redwall. The south wallgate is only bolted with a couple of dead twigs—one good shove an' it's open. We'll keep these villains chasin' their own tails for a while, then we'll get back to the Abbey just before dawn. Keep a lookout for us from the north walltop, be ready with a longbow in case we're followed an' it's nip an' tuck. Good luck, old scout. Come on, Rosie. Bob 'n' tack, duck 'n' weave. You know the drill, wot!"

Foul tempers predominated around the searat campfires. Graypatch sat apart, disgusted with the rest after their rout by five longbows on the flatlands, just as his fireswinger plan was beginning to look as if it might work. The searat Captain lashed out at any rat that came near him, giving vent to his contempt.

"Slimesloppin', mudsuckin' cowards! Haharr, 'tis a pity that those longbows never took care of more o' you mutinous deckscum, then I'd only have meself to think of, instead o' a pack of seascabbed poltroons!"

The crew lay about sulkily, not answering because they knew Graypatch was looking to pick a fight and slay somebeast to slake his spleen.

From over to Graypatch's left a voice called from the shadows, "Hoho, matey, you did a fine jig with your foot afire. Shove it in yonder flames an' do us another 'ornpipe. Go on!"

Graypatch whirled his sword, dashing toward the rats who were lounging in the area whence the insult had issued.

"Yer lily-livered maggot, stan' up an' say that to me face!"

Next instant a voice called from the other side of the camp, "Maggot yerself, stinkbreath. We're takin' no more orders from you!"

Graypatch veered, rushing in the direction of the second voice. "Belay, I'll rip the tongue out o' yer mouth. Show yerself!"

Another voice called from yet a third direction, "Flopnose! You couldn't rip yer mother's apron!"

Graypatch hurled himself on Deadglim and began throttling the unfortunate searat as he pleaded his innocence.

"Gwaaark! It wasn't me, Cap'n, I swear it. Gyuuurgh! I never said a wuuurgh!"

Frink was Deadglim's mate. He ran across to prevent Graypatch choking his friend to death, but Bigfang tripped him with a spear.

"Leave them be, rat. Deadglim might show a bit of fight back!"

Fishgill leaned across. "Who asked you to interfere, fatmouth!"

He slapped Bigfang across the head with the flat of his cutlass. As he did, someone else kicked Fishgill from behind.

"You leave Bigfang alone, fleahead!"

Fishgill turned and punched Lardgutt in the eye. "Kick me would you, weeviltail. Take that!"

Lardgutt drew his dagger, screaming furiously, "I never kicked yer! But you'll pay for that punch, snotface!"

Within a short time the entire camp was in uproar as fights broke out all over the place. Clary and Rosie flitted about like two fleeting moonshadows, belting heads and roaring out in imitation searat voices.

"Bigfang fer Cap'n, Graypatch is on'y a deckwalloper!"

"Avast, get stuck in, buckos. Poor Deadglim's bein' strangled!"

Rosie whacked a passing rat on the back of his head with her lancebutt. "Take that from Kybo, you scum. I never did like you!"

With a screech of rage the rat grabbed a corsair's hook and went after Kybo yelling, "An' all these seasons I thought you was my matey!"

The fight was going splendidly until Hon Rosie could no longer hold back her laughter.

"Haharr, you durty decksweepin', take that! Whoohahahahooh! Oh, I say, this is super fun, come on, chaps, scrag each other harder!"

Instantly the fighting ground to a halt.

"Corks, Rosie, you've torn it now, old gel. Y'need to gag that giggle," Clary could be heard muttering in the firelight shadows.

Graypatch left off throttling Deadglim. "We've been tricked, mates. It's those hares! Get 'em!"

But saying was far easier than doing. The hares were up and gone through the night-shaded woodlands before the searats could assemble themselves to give chase. Thyme had gone also, and with him two young shrews from the oarslave ranks, but this would not be discovered until daylight arrived.

30

Captain Flogga of the ship *Rathelm* was a hard and seasoned searat. He had served Gabool long and well, but the old Gabool was vastly different from the one he faced now. Flogga had taken no chances, keeping his crew fully armed and tight about him when he landed at Terramort. They had marched straight up to Fort Bladegirt and trooped into the banqueting hall—Flogga knew there was safety in numbers.

Now, sitting in front of the Searat King, he was shocked at the change that had come over the Warlord of the Waves. Gabool was gibbering mad! He was a truly terrifying sight, his fine silk gear all stained and torn, rings and bracelets tarnished and bent; the golden emerald-studded teeth still gleamed, though the eyes above them were blood-red, caked and running from many sleepless nights.

The searat Captain was frightened. Mad and disheveled as he was, Gabool looked doubly dangerous, and there was always the risk: was he really insane, or merely playing at it for some reason best known to himself?

Gabool's mood could switch from good humor to evil temper, from friendly camaraderie to murderous enmity, at the blink of an eye. Not for nothing was he feared by all searats, captains and crews alike.

Still, Flogga was completely taken aback at the way Gabool addressed him.

"Haharr, Graypatch, I knew you'd come back someday. Well well, me old shipmate Graypatch back at Bladegirt with a full crew about him!"

The searat Captain shook his head. "Gabool, don't ye know me? It's Flogga, Master of the *Rathelm*!"

Smiling craftily, Gabool waggled a claw at him. "Haharr, so you say, matey, so you say. But you can't fool me, Graypatch. I know who you are. Where's my ship *Darkqueen*, eh?"

"*Darkqueen*, don't mention that craft t' me. You've 'ad us chasin' our tails across the waves high 'n' low lookin' fer *Darkqueen*. I'm beginnin' to think it's all some kind o' game, like that treasure she's supposed to have stowed in 'er hold."

Gabool cocked his head to one side, both eyes roving up and down oddly. "Treasure y'say. Have you been talkin' to Saltar, matey?"

"Saltar! He's dead!"

"Dead? Saltar? Who killed him?"

"You did, right 'ere in your own banquetin' hall."

"Haharr, so I did, Graypatch, so I did. Listen matey, ferget *Darkqueen*. It'll be me 'n' you again, just like in the old days, eh?"

"But I keep tellin' ye, I'm Flogga, not Graypatch . . ."

Gabool winked slyly. "Nah, you can't fool me. Listen, about that treasure: it was never in the *Darkqueen*, I only said that to 'ave you brought back 'ere."

Flogga blew out a long sigh. He decided to humor the mad King. "All right, Gabool. So I'm back 'ere. Now what?"

Gabool leaned close, whispering confidentially. "Hearken t' me, Graypatch. The treasure is here, right here in Bladegirt. Only me knows where 'tis. D'ye want me to show it t' yer?"

Flogga suddenly became interested. "Aye, I'd like that, shipmate."

"Haharr. Well, tell this lot to stay here, an' come with me."

"Oh no, Gabool. What d'yer want to separate me from me crew for, eh?"

"Graypatch, I thought you was a brainy one, mate. We don't want t' share all that booty with this useless load of flotsam, now do we?"

Flogga stared at Gabool, uncertain of what he should do, suspecting the Searat King might be leading him into a trap, yet eager to get his claws upon the treasure. In the end greed won.

"All right, Gabool. It'll be just like the old days, fifty-fifty. Lead me t' the booty, mate, but 'earken—play me false an' my dagger'll find yer throat afore you're much older."

"Play ye false?" Gabool sounded indignant. "You're the one who played me false, Graypatch—but I'm givin' ye another chance, shipmate. Now get rid of these numbskulls an' follow me."

Flogga turned to his crew and gave them a "wait here" sign. He nodded and winked at them, outwardly confident, but inwardly apprehensive as he strode off after the Searat King.

Gabool fitted the spear through the iron ring and heaved. As the stone lifted he slid it to one side. Flogga stood in the doorway of the chamber, still wary of a trap. The Searat King pointed to the black hole in the center of the floor.

"Down there 'tis, me old matey. More booty than you could wink an eye at. Come an' get your half, Graypatch—or are you afeared?"

Flogga remained in the doorway. "I don't know . . ."

Gabool strode over and grasped his paw tightly. "Then we'll go down there together, eh? Tell you what, matey; we'll take a run an' jump in at the same time, both o' us. Haharr, just think, Gabool an' Graypatch, down there midst all that booty!"

Flogga gnawed at his lip. "Together at the same time, both of us?"

"Aye, matey. That's the way, come on. One t' be ready, two t' be steady, three t' be off!"

Clutching Flogga's claw, Gabool rushed him at the hole. Flogga, finding Gabool running eagerly alongside him, felt confident. They leaped together: Flogga down into the hole, Gabool right across it onto the other side, where he landed chuckling.

"Hoho, Skrabblag, I told yer I'd bring Graypatch 'ere for a visit!"

Flogga screamed with horror. Something was rustling and clicking in the darkness. As Gabool held a flaring walltorch over the pit, Flogga moaned in despair. A fully grown black scorpion was stalking him in the close confines of the pit. Claws clicking, armored hide rustling against the floor, it advanced upon him, the venomous needle-pointed sting in its tail held high, ready to strike. Gabool laughed insanely.

"You remember Skrabblag, don't yer, matey? Hahahaharr!"

Thick fog had dropped upon the sea, and the waters ran smooth, almost waveless. From her point at the tiller, Mariel could not make out the other end of the ship. One thing became apparent: they were becalmed, lying on the unrippled waters in the midst of the heavy dripping mist.

Tarquin brought food to her side. "Absolutely dreadful this bally fog, wot? Shouldn't bother us though, old gel. As soon as we move again at least it'll be in the right direction—the jolly little swallow feller'll see to that."

"Right, Tarquin. Where's Dandin and Durry? I haven't seen them for a while."

"For'ard—I think that's the right nautical jargon. They've found some line an' fancy their paws as fisherbeasts."

Mariel leaned on the tiller, gnawing at a cold oatcake as she stared about her into the blank whiteness. "Funny, isn't it—the fog seems to be ten times thicker at sea than on land. If you stare into it long enough you begin to see all sorts of odd shapes looming up on you."

"Hmm, quite eerie. I never liked it when I was at Salamandastron, y'know. Beastly stuff. It's like bein' surrounded by steam from a kettle, 'cept that it's all chilly an' clammy. Brrrr!"

"Hsst, Tarquin. Did you hear something?"

"No, unless it's those other two up at the front of the boat—beg pardon I mean the for'ard end."

"Yaaaaah look out!"

Crrrraaassshhh!!!

The burned-out hulk quivered as the high prow of the searat galley *Seatalon* rammed her amidships, heeling her high out of the water. The burnt timbers shattered under the impact as the hulk overturned and smashed completely in two pieces. Mariel grabbed the metal swallow before being hurled off into the fog. She hit the waters with a dull splash. All around she could hear shouting and confusion.

"Cap'n Catseyes, we've struck a vessel!"

"Then board 'er, you bilgeswillin's. See if there's any pickin's t' be had. Where away is she now?"

"We've rammed 'er in the fog, Cap'n. She's broke in two. Can't see a thing in this cursed fog!"

"Is *Seatalon* damaged, Fishtail?"

"No, Cap'n. We're all right. The other one broke right easy, though. Must've been some sort o' wreck, eh?"

"Aye, it'll be sunk by now."

"Cap'n Catseyes, there's two beasts in the sea!"

"Well, hook 'em out. Don't stand there dreamin'!"

"Look, it's a mouse an' a hedgepig!"

"Haul 'em aboard, pump the water outta them an' bring 'em t' my cabin."

Mariel trod water, holding the swallow between her teeth, the Gullwhacker about her neck weighing heavily in the sea. Cries from the searat ship died away into the fog, and now she was alone on the deep, shrouded by the all-enveloping mists and without her companions. Suddenly something grabbed her footpaws and pulled her under. Kicking madly she wriggled and fought underwater. The mousemaid lashed out, connecting hard with something. Whatever it was had let go of her. Mariel fought her way to the surface, and emerged next to Tarquin, who was spitting water and gurgling.

"Gwaawhg! I must've gone right t' the bottom then. I say, was that your paws I grabbed hold of?"

Mariel was overjoyed to see her friend. "Tarquin, it's you!"

"I'll say it is. Who did you expect, a fish with fur an' ears?"

"It was a searat ship that rammed us. They've got Dandin and Durry aboard. I heard them call it the *Seatalon.*"

"Oh, corks. Dandin 'n' Durry captured by searats! What'll we do?"

"What *can* we do?"

"Which way did this *Seatalon* go?"

"Over that way, I think—though it's hard to tell in this fog."

"Then there's only one thing for it, we'll have to swim after it and see if we can get our friends back. Come on."

They struck out into the fogged sea, swimming as hard and as fast as they could. After a while, Tarquin halted, treading water as he floated.

" 'Sno use, Mariel. Whew, I'm out of breath!"

"Me too. We could be going in circles in this fog."

"Then I vote we just float here until it clears. D'you want my harolina? It makes rather a good float."

"We'll both use it, then."

Together they rested their paws on the instrument. It buoyed them slightly, and they kicked their legs slowly to keep afloat.

"Well, this is a pretty mess we're in and no mistake."

"How far do you suppose we are from shore, Tarquin?"

"No idea, old scout. It's sink or swim from here on in. I say, I'm famished. You don't happen to have any tucker on you . . . ?"

"Sorry, all I had was that cold oatcake, and I lost that in the wreck."

"Ah well, at least we won't make a nice fat meal for

any fishes that are feelin' peckish. I suppose there *are* fishes around here."

"Could be, might be one or two big ones with huge mouths and sharp teeth . . ."

"Steady on, miss! You could scare a chap out of a season's growth, talkin' like that."

Mariel and Tarquin lost all reckoning of distance or position as they floated for what seemed like endless hours. Gradually the fog began to thin, giving way to slightly choppy water and mists, which were soon dispelled by a stiff breeze. There was not much to see—no sight of the searat galley, nor of land; they were completely surrounded by rising waves. Helping each other as best as they could, the two friends conserved their energy by floating, only swimming when the seas became too rough. Mariel looked up at the sky; evening was not far off.

"It gets cold on the sea at night."

"Hmm, y'don't say. It's blinkin' cold enough now. My paws have gone all dead an' shrivelled with the salt water."

"Mine too. Tarquin, I'm sorry I got you into this. I should have traveled alone. Now Dandin and Durry are the prisoners of searats and we're not going to last long out here."

"Oh, nonsense, old miss mousy. I wouldn't have had it any other bally way. None of it was your fault. We'd have come along whether you liked it or not. Now stop that kind o' talk an' save your breath."

"You're a good friend Tarquin L. Woodsorrel. I won't forget you."

"Should jolly well hope not. Rosie too. Hope she thinks of old Tarkers feedin' the fish now an' then. Oh, Rosie, you'll never find another as devil-may-care an' handsome as me, poor old thing!"

Mariel draped her Gullwhacker across the harolina. Her limbs were beginning to tire; seawater lapped into her mouth and she spluttered.

"I say, why don't you take the swallow out of your mouth an' tie it round your neck?"

"Good idea, Tarquin. Thank you."

"Oh dear, there's the jolly old sun beginnin' to set."

"I'm so tired, I could lie back in the water and go to sleep."

"Steady on there—don't start talkin' like that. Here, I'll hold you up for a bit."

"No, Tarquin, you need all your energy to stay afloat yourself."

"Fiddle-de-dee! I've got energy I haven't even used yet. There, how's that, Mariel Gullwhacker?"

"That's fine, Tarquin. But you won't be able to keep us both up for long."

"S'pose not, but when that time comes we'll sink together, wot?"

Clinging to each other, they bobbed on the open sea, oblivious of the glory of the setting sun and the many-hued sky which reflected in the waters all round. Night closed in on the hare and the mousemaid. Two massive paws shot down into the water and grabbed them both, hauling them effortlessly out of the night sea and onto a heaving deck.

"Woodsorrel, I might have known it would be you!"

Semiconscious and shivering uncontrollably, Tarquin peered up into the huge striped face of Rawnblade.

"I s-s-say, m'Lord, d-d-didn't know you'd taken t' b-b-boatin', wot?"

"You young rogue, I suppose you've brought this poor mousemaid along with you just to get her drowned!"

"Quite the c-c-contrary, s-s-sir."

"Hmm, we'll discuss that later, after you're both fixed up."

When Mariel regained consciousness she was in the cabin of the *Waveblade*. A charcoal fire burned in the small stove, and she was clad in cast-off searat garments. Lord Rawnblade made her drink some heavy dark wine and eat a little dried fruit.

Tarquin was fully recovered. Mariel could not suppress

a smile at the comical figure he cut, dressed in searat silks with a cloak of yellow chenille draped about him. Tarquin admired the daggers and swords he had stuffed into the wide-sashed belt of orange satin, and earrings and bangles jangled as he twirled about dramatically.

"Haharr, me booties, 'tis only I, Tarquin the Terrible!"

Rawnblade sniffed away a smile threatening to steal across his face. "I'd say awful was more appropriate than terrible."

The badger Lord turned to Mariel.

"So tell me, mousemaid, what were you doing bobbing about on the high seas in company with this addle-brained creature?"

Mariel sipped more of the wine, feeling its dark warmth comfort her. "Well, it's a long story, sir, but I'll start at the beginning."

Outside, wind keened the darkness, scouring the face of the sea as rain began to spatter the decks. *Waveblade* cut her course northward, her tiller lashed in position by the sodden Gullwhacker as the ship plowed on through the night, guided by a small metal swallow.

31

Abbot Bernard watched the two young shrews as they attacked the Abbey breakfast board like hungry wolves, swigging pear cordial, stuffing plum and greengage tart and grabbing hot elderberry muffins dripping with honey.

"My word, Mother Mellus, those two young ones can put it away!"

"Aye, bless them, you'd think we were facing a ten-season famine."

Simeon checked the paw of one from reaching for acorn and rhubarb crumble. "How many more of you do the searats have?"

"Seventeen, I s'pose, or eighteen—aye, eighteen countin' the squirrel."

Friar Alder turned his eyes upward, nudging young Cockleburr. "Dearie me, imagine another eighteen like that at breakfast!"

"Boilin' breadloaves, Friar. They'd eat us out o' kitchen an' Abbey!"

Clary sat in Gabe Quill's cellar, sampling the latest rose-hip squash with Foremole as they nibbled cheese and beechmast bake to counteract the sweetness of the drink.

"Ahurr, you'm say 'ee wants four of us'ns this comin' noight, zurr."

"Yes indeed, four stout mole chaps—all good diggers, mind you."

"Hurrhurr, baint no crittur better at diggen than us'n molers. Oi'd say Dan'l, Buxton, Groaby an moiself. Aye, we'n's the ones."

"Righty-ho, Foremole sir. Meet us at the gatehouse two hours after dark."

"Doan't 'ee wurry, zurr. Us'll be thurr, boi 'okey us will."

"Good chap, knew I could count on you. Have some more of this rosehip stuff. Quite nice, but a trifle sweet, wot?"

"No sweeter'n rose'ips orter be, zurr. Fill 'er up iffen 'ee please."

Gabe Quill filled a jug from a polished cask. He set it on the table, sniffing righteously over the remarks being made about the sweetness of his rosehip squash.

"Try some o' this elderflower an' larkspur cordial iffen you likes a less sweeter drink. But while you're adoin' that, tell me, Mr. Clary, why did you only free two slaves las' night?"

Clary sipped the new drink, raising his eyebrows appreciatively. "Well, Mr. Quill, it's quite simple really. More than two at a time would be rather awkward to cope with, seein' as how they've got to be helped every step of the way. After all, they are in chains, y'know; bein' oarslaves, they're still chained in twos, each creature to his galley bench partner. If we can manage more'n two, all well an' good. We'll see how many of the poor blighters we can bag tonight. Now, listen carefully, Foremole me old digger, here's the plan . . ."

Graypatch had been all day making the searats' woodland camp secure against intruders. He sat on a log, checking out the new setup with Fishgill.

"Tripwires hidden in the undergrowth all around the edges o' the camp, rope traps in the trees?"

"Aye, Cap'n. Me 'n' Frink an' Kybo rigged the rope traps. Anybeast sneakin' around out there at night'll find themselves suddenly hangin' upsidedown from a tree. The tripwires are all stretched tight an' well-hidden too."

"Good! Now these oarslaves—we'll hold 'em in the center of the camp, just to one side of the main fire. That way they'll be surrounded by the crew."

The evening fires had been lit. All around them, searats squatted, cooking whatever they had found during the day. Bigfang roasted dandelion roots and some small hard apples he and Lardgutt had come across, grumbling as he watched Kybo.

"Huh, what use is roots an' sour apples to me 'n' Lardgutt? We're searats; this woodland garbage wouldn't feed a sick maggot. Kybo, matey, how's about sharin' that great fat woodpigeon yer roastin', with a couple of old messmates?"

Kybo kept his eyes on the roasting meat, his claw straying to a long rusty dagger he kept nearby. "Get yer own rations, Bigfang. Me 'n' Fishgill an' Graypatch snared this one while we was layin' out tripwires an' you was lyin' round snorin' like a hog. You want meat, get out an' hunt it."

Lardgutt's eyes strayed to the roasting woodpigeon as he absently reached into the embers for a toasted apple, with the result that he scorched his claws. Bad-temperedly he flung the apple from him. "Yowch! That's it! I'll starve afore I eat that muck!"

Bigfang looked around at other searats who had not been fortunate enough to obtain meat. They were toasting, roasting and charring almost any kind of vegetation they could scavenge. Bigfang spat into the flames.

"Hah! Livin' off the fat o' the land, eh, buckos? Does this look like the berth we was promised? Landlords of Mossflower—look at us! Grubbin' fer roots an' berries, scrapin' about an' fightin' with yer own shipmates fer anythin' growin' outta the soil! Why don't we attack Redwall agin, that's what I want ter know. Sittin' round protectin' some oarslaves like they was precious booty, where's that a-goin' to get us, eh?"

Murmurs of agreement arose around the camp. Graypatch strode over, carrying a heavy limb of dead oak. He threw it onto the fire, causing a shower of sparks. Bigfang and Lardgutt were forced to jump back, beating off the fiery splinters which landed on them, their apples and roots completely squashed and ruined beneath the wood Graypatch had thrown on the fire. The searat Captain prodded Bigfang viciously in the ribs with his curved sword.

"Always the thickhead an' the rabble-rouser, eh, Bigfang. I don't know why I keep yer alive. It's not for your brains, I can tell ye. Anybeast with half a grain o' sense would tell yer what I'm about. Last night taught me a lesson: if those Redwallers want to free the slaves, they've got to come an' try, see? Look at it this ways, they're goin' to no end o' trouble to rescue slaves who they don't even know. I've seen their type afore. Now, imagine how they'd feel if we captured some of their own? Haharr, that'd be somethin' now, wouldn't it! Us havin' Redwallers as hostages. It'd be like ownin' a ticket fer free entrance to their Abbey."

Bigfang rubbed his ribs where the sword had scraped his hide. "How do we know they're goin' to come back?"

Graypatch shook his head as if despairing. "Short on brains an' long on mouth, that's you, matey. Of course they'll come back. They're noble creatures, they couldn't leave poor slaves in the claws of us cruel searats! But this time we've laid the traps, this time we'll catch them, an' I'll parade 'em in chains outside their Abbey. You mark my words, those Redwallers won't be so high 'n' mighty then. They'll be ready to listen to old Graypatch's terms, mates. Aye, short on brains, Bigfang, just like I said. You stick with me, matey. Let me do the thinkin', and one day we could be rulers of a whole slave army of Redwallers, hahah! Imagine that, they could be mercenaries, spearfodder—with an army that size we could build ourselves another fleet an' conquer Terramort for ourselves, kill Gabool an' seize his island. Then we'd be rulers of Redwall *an'* Terramort, mates!"

• • •

Hon Rosie lay on her back a short distance from the camp. She twanged upon a tripwire as she listened to Graypatch lecturing his crew. Clary and Thyme sat with the moles, holding a whispered conference.

"Super plan, y'know—tripwires, springropes an' hostages. I'd give the scurvy blaggard an 'A' for alertness, wot?"

Foremole extended his powerful digging claws. "Oi knows wot oi'd loik t' give 'im, pesky searatter!"

Clary was busy undoing a tripwire. "Good effort, all the same. Come on, hares, let's undo this little lot an' set it up in a new location. Thyme, can you manage those rope traps?"

"Certainly, Clary old chap. I say, these searats are rather good at tying knots and whatnot, must be with all that messin' about in boats."

"I 'spect so. How're you mole chaps feelin', fancy a spot of diggin'?"

"Hohurr zurr, we'm frisky as frogs an' fitter'n fleas. Whurr do 'ee want us a-start, gaffer?"

Foremole trundled about muttering calculations, glancing from certain spots on the ground toward the rat camp.

"Gurr'm, let oi see naow. Root crossens thurr, thurr an' yon. Stoans a-layen yurr an' thurr. Reckernin' fer a swift 'n' easy deep tunn'l, oi sez us'n's be hadvised to start diggen roight yurr!" He scratched a large X on the woodland floor with his digging claws.

Dan'l, Groaby and Buxton went to it with a will. Sentries were posted all around the fringes of the camp. Graypatch settled down close to the fire, his one good eye searching the woodland edge for signs of movement. Bigfang and Lardgutt fought briefly over possession of a ragged blanket before ripping it in half, then each lay down, trying to cover himself with the skimpy remnant. Gradually the searats' encampment quietened down for the night, the silence broken only by an odd crackle of burning branches on the fires. Sentries blinked their eyes to stay awake, heads drooping as they leaned heavily on pike and spear.

Brigadier Thyme watched the scene from the low

boughs of a sycamore some distance away. Finally satisfied that everything was ready, he climbed down and reported back to Clary.

"Operation Oarslave now feasible to commence. Sah!"

"Good scout, Thyme. Right, troops. Forward, the Buffs. Oh, and Rosie, try to remember, will you, one whoop an' we're in the soup!"

"Oh, I say, Clary, jolly poetic—one whoop an' we're in the soup. Not to worry, I've given up whoopin' for the movement."

A searat named Fleawirt lay asleep facing the main fire. It was difficult trying to sleep in open woodlands after a life of sprawling to rest in the swaying, rocking crew's accommodation of a ship. Fleawirt awoke. His face was scorched and burning with the fire, though his back was stiff and chilled to the bone by the night breezes. He turned grumpily over, placing his back toward the fire. As he did, a sharp twig stuck in his cheek. Fleawirt sat up, cursing silently as he rubbed his injured face. Then a very strange thing happened.

Sitting up, facing away from the fire, Fleawirt found himself looking at the oarslaves. They lay sleeping, chained in pairs, some whimpering in their dreams, others clutching each other tightly in slumber. Then there was a slight clink of chains and four oarslaves vanished into the ground!

Fleawirt rubbed his eyes and yawned, half turning to lie down once more. Then the oddness of what he had seen hit him. He stood bolt upright as another two slaves disappeared into the earth!

"Cap'n Graypatch! Look, the slaves!"

Fleawirt's cries aroused the entire camp. Graypatch sprang up and began shaking Fleawirt.

"What's goin' on? Tell me!"

"The slaves, the ground, four of 'em, then another two, the floor, I saw it!"

"Stop babblin' like a fool. Now tell me what happened, properly!"

"Well, I was sittin' up awake an' all of a sudden I saw

four of the oarslaves just vanish into the floor. I looked again an' another two went, right in front o' me eyes, Cap'n. I swear it!"

The oarslaves were wakening, yawning and rubbing at their eyes as the noise around them grew into a hubbub. Graypatch ran among them, scattering the thin bodies left and right, a flaring torch held high. Quickly he counted them—twelve, including the squirrel. Fleawirt was right—six oarslaves had vanished, somehow. He stumbled as he stepped into a small pothole, which on closer inspection proved to be a tunnel which had been backfilled after the slaves escaped. Graypatch sank his sword uselessly into the loose earth, stabbing at it wildly.

"It was a tunnel! They got six slaves out through a stinkin' tunnel!"

Bigfang strode about, nodding his head knowingly. "So, a tunnel, eh, mates—that's how they did it. Prob'ly got some of those squirrels to do their diggin' for them. I thought so!"

Graypatch grabbed Bigfang by the nose. Digging his claws in tightly, he twisted with cruel ferocity.

"Moles, muckhead, not squirrels! Moles, d'ye hear me?"

Bigfang pranced about, tears squirting from his eyes. Graypatch aimed a hard kick, which caught him in the rear and sent him sprawling.

"Now up on yer claws, the lot o' yer. Spread out an' get searchin'. They can't have gone far. I want 'em back, dead or alive!"

Clary, Thyme and Rosie appeared, just outside the clearing. "I say, slobberchops, you shouldn't've twisted the poor chap's hooter like that. He was right, we did use squirrels!"

"Get theeeeeemmm!" Graypatch's voice was somewhere between a roar and a screech.

The searats charged forward in a mob at the three hares. Then they hit the tripwires that had been carefully set anew. The hares melted into the woodland, being careful to travel in the opposite direction from Foremole and his crew, who were guiding the six slaves back to Redwall.

Graypatch and several others who had been at the back of the charge followed the hares, leaping over the sprawling heaps of rats who had fallen or tripped or been pushed onto the tripwires by the momentum of their dashing comrades. Graypatch looked back at them over his shoulder.

"Blunderin' idiots!"

There was an immense tug on his legs. Instantly he was swinging back and forth as he dangled upsidedown from a spring rope tied to a tree limb. His head cracked painfully against that of Frink, who was also suspended upside down by a rope.

Back at the camp, Bigfang had scrambled upright and was shouting, though his nose looked like a ripe plum ready to burst.

"See, I told you it was squirrels. I was right—the rabbit said so!" Chains clinked as hammers thudded, sending keen-tipped chisels biting through the chains and fetters of the oarslaves. Foremole patted each one fondly upon the head as they were freed.

"Hurr, guddbeasts, you'm go naow an' jump in 'ee barth, thurr be clean cloathen an' vittles aplenty when you'm warshed!"

Mother Mellus wiped her eyes on a spotted kerchief. "You can almost see their bones sticking out, poor little things!"

Flagg struck the last of the chains free. "Don't fret, marm. They've got mouths to eat with—they'll soon be fat as hogs."

Gabriel Quill sniffed. "Speak for yourself, streamdog!"

Before they went to the dormitories, Clary and his friends sat with Foremole and the crew around the fireplace in Cavern Hole, drinking a nightcap of mulled October ale.

"Excellent night's work, chaps. Eight down, twelve to go, wot?"

Thyme stared into the flames. "Right you are, old

sport, but it's goin' to get much harder each time, now that they know what we're really after. Much jolly well harder."

Hon Rosie emptied her tankard at a single gulp. "Clary, may I?"

"Oh, I s'pose so. Permission t' carry on, Rosie."

"I say, Clary, thanks. Whoohahahahahooh!"

Dan'I and Groaby banged their tankards down upon the hearth, wincing visibly at the ear-splitting sound.

"Gwaw! That's et, oi'm arf t' bed!"

"Hurr, an' oi too, afore oi'm deafened fer loif!"

32

Captain Catseyes of the *Seatalon* patted the new sword at his side proudly. Never had a searat set eyes upon such a sword as this. He watched the two new oarslaves bending their backs as they pulled in stroke with the others.

> "Up an' one, an' down an' two,
> Bend yer backs an' curse yer birth.
> Up an' one, an' down an' two,
> Pull those oars fer all your worth!"

The grating voice of the slavedriver echoed across the benches as he strode up and down, flicking his cruel whip, reciting the crude rowing poem as he laid out about him.

> "Up an' one, an' down an' two,
> Some have backs without no hide.
> Up an' one, an' down an' two,
> Those who couldn't row have died.
> Up an' one, an' down an' two,
> Here's a gift from me to you!"

He lashed out with the whip. An oarslave arched his back and screamed.

Catseyes nodded toward Dandin and Durry. "The two new 'uns, how are they shapin' up, Blodge?"

Blodge the slavedriver flicked his whip toward the pair. "No better or worse than the rest o' them, Cap'n. Though they're still fresh an' strong, a season or so eatin' slave slops an' the weight of that oar they're chained to should knock some o' the starch out of 'em."

Catseyes strode down the alleyway between the oars until he was facing Dandin. The searat Captain drew the sword, watching the lantern lights playing up and down the length of its wondrous blade.

"You don't look much like a warrior mouse. Where'd a liddle fish like you come by a blade such as this beauty?"

Dandin's eyes blazed fire at the Captain of the *Seatalon*. "I am Dandin of Redwall. That is the sword of Martin the Warrior. You are not fit to wear it, rat!"

Catseyes nodded to Blodge. The slavedriver flailed his whip hard against Dandin's back. The young mouse did not even flinch, he continued to glare his hatred at the searat Captain. Catseyes laughed.

"Feisty liddle brute, ain't you. Well, we'll see about that."

Fishtail the mate leaned across the rail, listening to his Captain's instructions as Terramort Isle appeared like a tiny pinpoint on the horizon.

"Cap'n Flogga should be there with the *Ruthelm*. It could be dangerous fer me, Fishtail—I'm no friend of Gabool or Flogga. When we drop anchor in Terramort cove, I want you to go up to Fort Bladegirt an' spy out the lay o' the land. Take most of the crew with yer, matey. I'll be all right aboard here with Blodge an' five others. Stay well armed an' careful, keep an eye peeled on that Gabool and learn if anybeast brought Graypatch back an' claimed the booty from the *Darkqueen's* hold.

Oh, an' you might have a chat with Flogga, see if he favors Gabool, an' listen out fer any talk of the other Cap'ns formin' an alliance against Gabool. But mind what I say, matey: be careful of Gabool—he's wild, an' crazy with it. I'll wait aboard this ship for yer return. Got that?"

"Aye aye, Cap'n. Leave it t' me."

The gruff voice of Blodge rang through the galley. "Ship oars, me lucky buckos. We'll ride in to Terramort on the swell."

All around Dandin and Durry the oarslaves leaned heavily on their oars, bringing the shafts down and locking them by wedging the ends beneath the benches, thus leaving the oarblades sloping high out of the sea to port and starboard, giving *Seatalon* the appearance of a bird with outspread wings as she drifted toward Terramort on billowing sails.

Durry licked his paws gently. "I feel powerful sorry for the pore child who owns these paws. What my o' nuncle'd say if he saw his fav'rite nephew a-chained up in some scurvy searats' galley I fears to think!"

Dandin wiped beading sweat from his brow. "I wonder where we are."

The little oarslave directly in front of him, a fieldmouse named Copsey, provided the answer.

"We're coasting into Terramort. Didn't you hear Blodge? It makes no difference where we drop anchor, us rowers stay right here, chained to our benches. That's the life of an oarslave, Dandin."

She bent her head against the oar and rested. Dandin patted her scarred back. "Not if I can help it, Copsey."

Wooden bowls were passed among the slaves. They leaned toward the alleyway, each holding the big bowl in their right paw, the smaller in the left. Blodge passed with his assistant, a small, evil-faced rodent named Clatt. They had with them two wooden buckets, one full of boiled barley meal, the other of water. Blodge filled the large bowls with water, Clatt the smaller ones with barley meal. Both rats thought it great fun to slop the water or meal carelessly at a bowl so that it missed and splashed upon the deck.

"Come on, scum. Lively now, an' hold those bowls out straight!"

"Aye, we're too kind to you idlers, treat you like a pair o' nursemaids, we do. Hee hee hee!"

Using their paws to eat the lukewarm mess, Dandin and Durry listened in to Blodge and Clatt's conversation.

"When I get to Bladegirt I'm gonna grab some roasted seabird an' sweet wine an' some o' those sugary dried fruits King Gabool keeps."

"Huh, you goin' to Fort Bladegirt? No such luck, Clatt. You're stayin' aboard with me'n Cap'n Catseyes an' four others."

"Gerrout, Blodge. Yer jokin' with me!"

"Cap'n's orders, matey. Do as yer told, or else!" Blodge drew a claw across his throat, indicating what would happen.

Clatt threw the bucket down, its contents slopping out onto the deck. "Hell's teeth! We may's well be oarslaves, stuck aboard this old tub all the time while others are havin' a good leave on Terramort. It's not right, mate, I tell ye. I'm sick an' fed up with it!"

"Nah, you stop 'ere with me, Clatt. I think there's goin' t' be trouble up at Bladegirt. Best we stay out of the way. Tell you what, shipmate—we'll go to the forecastle head cabin an' make skilly, you an' me."

Clatt brightened up at this suggestion. "An' some raisin duff. Can we make a pan o' raisin duff?"

"Aye, skilly an' duff. That'll gladden our 'earts. Ain't nothin' like skilly an' duff in a snug liddle cabin."

Clatt turned to the nearest oarslave, a very young shrew. "Avast, you bilgepup, d'you like skilly an' duff?"

The young shrew nodded vigorously. "Yes, sir!"

"Well, you won't be gettin' none, it's all fer me an' Blodge. Hee hee hee!"

Durry Quill gritted his teeth as they strode off laughing. "I'd like to meet that Clatt when I don't have no chains on one day!"

• • •

The *Seatalon* rode at anchor in Terramort cove as evening gave way to night. The wind had dropped, leaving the air still and warm. Captain Catseyes leaned over the rail, staring up to the lighted windows of Bladegirt. Blodge popped his head out of the forecastle cabin.

"Skilly an' duff, Cap'n. Me an' Clatt made enough fer all claws aboard."

Catseyes left the rail, adjusting the sword of Martin so it rode more comfortably at his side. "Thankee, Blodge. I think I will!"

The weary oarslaves were slumbering chained to their oars as the hooded mouse stole carefully into the galleydeck. He glanced around, shaking his head at the pitiful figures. The mouse was not young anymore, but he was well set up and strongly built. From his belt he drew several sharp three-cornered rasp files. Dandin had been watching him through half-closed eyes; now the young mouse sat upright as the other crept past him. Dandin caught hold of the stranger's dark cloak. "Who are you? What are you doing here?"

The hooded mouse held up a warning paw. "Ssshhh! I bring freedom!"

Dandin nodded, recognizing immediate friendliness in the stranger's voice. "What do you want me to do? Say the word and I'll help."

"Wake the others as quietly as you can. Here, take one of these and use it on those chains."

Dandin accepted the file. He shook Durry and Copsey gently. "Hush now, be quiet. Wake up the others, but do it softly."

All around Dandin oarslaves were being wakened as he worked away with the file. It was a good file. He freed himself then began on Durry's chains. The hedgehog smiled at him in the darkness.

"Wait'll I tells my o' nuncle 'bout this!"

The strange mouse gave a low whistle, and twenty other mice entered the galleydeck. They set about helping to release the slaves.

A small thin harvestmouse stood up. Unable to contain

himself, he laughed aloud and threw his broken chains noisily to the deck. One of the helpers muffled the harvest mouse in his cloak, but it was too late.

Pawsteps sounded above, then Captain Catseyes' high-pitched voice called out: "Who's that? Who's down there?"

The stranger took off his cloak. Beneath it he was a broad, fit-looking fellow, clad in a searat jerkin, though Dandin noticed that he was completely silvery gray. The mouse bundled the cloak up and passed it to Dandin. "Who's that calling out on deck?"

"Captain Catseyes, the Master of this ship. Why?"

"Everybeast back at their oars, hide the broken chains and leave this to me. Be quick now!"

The oarslaves seated themselves, whilst the other cloaked mice hid beneath the galley benches.

"Cap'n . . . Cap'n Catseyes," the strange mouse called up to the deck. "Gabool sent me down. His Majesty has news for you . . ."

Catseyes came bounding down the companionway. Anxiously he strode up to the strange mouse. "What news from King Gabool?"

The strange mouse stepped close in, drawing a dagger from the back of his belt. "Gabool doesn't know, but I brought you this!"

He slew Catseyes with one fierce thrust.

Dandin leaped forward. Unbuckling the dead searat's belt, he retrieved the sword and scabbard. More pawsteps sounded above on deck.

"Cap'n, can we get some wine from yer cabin?"

"Aye, skilly 'n' duff's better with a drop o' wine, Cap'n."

"That's Blodge and Clatt," Dandin whispered to the stranger. "Leave them to us when they come down."

"Right, how many more aboard?"

"Four besides them."

"We'll take care of them. Get that body out of sight and sit back down as you were. The rest of you hide."

Blodge and Clatt came stumbling down into the half-light of the galleydeck. Blodge peered around bad-temperedly.

"Cap'n, where are yer? Ain't we goin' t' get no wine tonight?"

"Not tonight or any other night, slavedriver!"

Clatt gave a squeak of dismay; blocking the stairway was the stranger, backed by twenty hooded mice. He whirled about to find himself facing Dandin. Blodge unwound the whip from about his shoulders and raised it threateningly. "Get back, or I'll have the hide off yer!"

Dandin chopped the flailing lash in two pieces with a sweep of his sword. "You'll never use that whip on another creature, rat!"

He hurled himself upon the slavedriver, who fell back yelling hoarsely as he grappled at his belt for his own sword.

Copsey and Durry gave Clatt a mighty shove in the back, and he shot from the alleyway straight into the arms of a bunch of oarslaves who were waiting, swinging lengths of broken chain. Clatt had time for just one short despairing scream. Just one, no more!

From above decks the sound of four bodies splashing in the sea told the oarslaves that the stranger and his companions had dealt finally with the remaining crew members. Dandin stood straight, distastefully wiping his sword upon the fallen body of Blodge.

"He died as he lived, a cringing coward who could only strike out at helpless creatures in chains!"

The freed slaves made their way up to the deck. The stranger and his band were loading up with any weapons that they could find. He nodded at Dandin. "All finished down there?"

The young mouse sheathed his sword. "As finished as it'll ever be. What next?"

"We take everything we can from this ship—weapons, food and clothing—then we get off and sink her. From there we go to the caves at the other side of the island. When the time is right we will attack Fort Bladegirt and put an end to Gabool the Wild. Are you with us?"

The freed slaves looked at Dandin. He grasped the stranger's outstretched paw.

"We're with you every step of the way and glad to be along! My name is Dandin of Redwall. What's yours?"

The stranger swirled his dark cloak about him, a broad, honest grin creeping across his strong features.

"They call me Joseph the Bellmaker!"

33

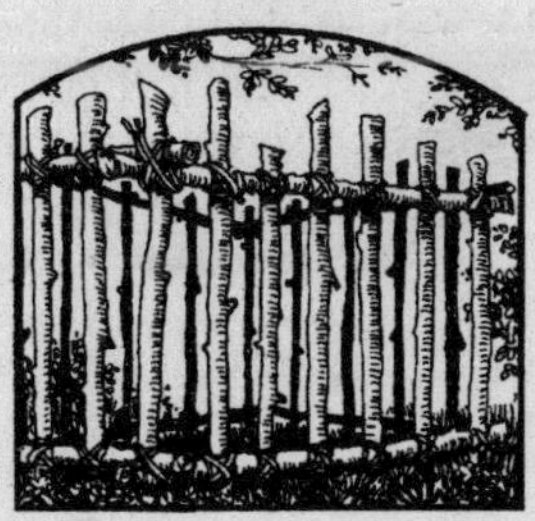

The morning was a fine one. Blue smoke from the searat campfires drifted through the high woodland trees, mingling with sloping shafts of sunbeam across leafy boughs of oak, ash, rowan, sycamore, elm and beech. Soft mosses, short grass and variegated flowers carpeted the ground, broken here and there by beds of fern and flowering nettles.

The beauty of it all was lost upon the searats; food was the more practical problem of the moment. Graypatch had argued, ranted and cajoled, but the faction led by Bigfang and Lardgutt won the day, appealing to greed rather than conquest. Hunger made Bigfang unexpectedly eloquent on the subject of food.

Graypatch listened, knowing he had no real answer to Bigfang's argument.

"Shipmates, we ain't woodland rats, we're searats. We always had plenty o' fish an' seabirds too, besides what stores we could plunder. But here we ain't got nothin', an' there's too many of us to be sharin' nothin'! Oh, leaves, berries, roots 'n' fruits are fine, if y'know which are the right ones an' which ones won't make a body sick or even kill yer. But we don't! So we're goin' to starve if we can't get proper vittles to eat!"

There was massive agreement with this statement. Graypatch shrugged.

"Well, fair enough, Bigfang. Tell us the answer—you're so smart!"

Bigfang had his answer ready this time. "I say we use our weapons to get food, not to fight some Abbey or guard a lot of useless oarslaves. Split up, go in gangs, fish the streams an' ponds, kill the birds with slingshots, arrows, anythin', but let's get some decent grub inside of us!"

Amid the roars of approval, Graypatch waved his sword for silence.

"All right, all right! That sounds sensible t' me. I never had no objections to a searat crew feedin' theirselves, mateys. But there's still these oarslaves. They're ours, and we can't let 'em be nabbed away by those Redwallers, so I suggest we build a cage for 'em, then we can go huntin'. Avast, what do ye say?"

Bigfang pointed his sword at Graypatch. "You do what you want, rat. We're goin' to get food!"

The entire crew stopped what they were doing and watched. Bigfang had finally laid down his challenge. Graypatch gripped his sword tight and confronted his enemy.

"So, it's come t' this, eh, matey!"

Bigfang circled, crouching low, sword at the ready. "I'm no matey o' yours, rat!"

"Haharr, I reckon you fancy yourself as Cap'n round here!"

"Couldn't make no worse a job of it than you, smartmouth!"

With a roar they clashed, blade striking upon blade. The searats formed a circle for them to fight in. Bigfang was strong; he used his sword like a club, hacking and bludgeoning at his opponent. Graypatch was vastly more experienced; he ducked and parried, dodging away from the main attacks, using the campfire as a barrier.

They fought in silence, none of the crew shouting encouragement to one or the other lest the shouter back the losing beast. Dust and ashes from the fire rose in billows as the pair battled savagely, Bigfang gaining the upper claw slightly with his size, strength and ferocity. Graypatch countered most of the moves, sometimes making Bigfang look awkward and ungainly, but as sword locked sword they gritted and sweated, their faces almost touching.

Graypatch began to realize that he was not as young and powerful as Bigfang. Fighting desperately to keep the foe from his blind side, he felt himself starting to tire and weaken. But experience was on his side; he kept his single eye on the main chance. Striving wildly, he turned Bigfang so that his back was to the fire and redoubled his attack. Bigfang was forced backward until one foot went into the fire. He yelped in pain. Graypatch dodged away, as if giving his adversary a chance to recover. Bigfang looked down at his scorched foot-claws for a vital second.

It cost him his life. Graypatch snatched the spear that Frink was holding and hurled it. He was too close to miss.

From the branches of a tall beech close by, a fat squirrel sat watching. He shook his head as he saw Bigfang fall. "Hmm, could've told him that'd happen. That old rat's no fool!"

Graypatch stood with his narrow chest heaving. He glared around the circle to reassert his authority as Captain.

"Come on, riffraff, anyone else wanna be Cap'n? Speak up!"

A deathly hush had settled over the crew. The only sound was the crackling of the campfire as they stood staring at the carcass of Bigfang, who only moments ago had been alive and arguing. Graypatch laid the flat of his sword against Lardgutt's throat.

"Come on, bagbelly. Do you fancy tryin' fer Cap'n?"

Lardgutt could not even gulp, the sword was so tight on his neck. "Not me, you're the Cap'n . . . Cap'n!"

Graypatch nodded approvingly, immediately changing his mood. "Right, matey. I'm the Cap'n an' I gives the orders. So let's see plenty o' stout wood bein' cut to make a cage fer our oarslaves. After that we'll head out into these woodlands an' plunder all the vittles a searat can lay claws on. Now, what've ye got t' say to that?"

Though the tone was subdued they all replied, "Aye-aye, Cap'n."

Rufe Brush gave a shout of delight as the fat squirrel came bounding in across the north wall with acrobatic skill.

"Oak Tom, you old bushrumbler! Well, curl my tail!"

They hugged and wrestled, as squirrels do, then the normally taciturn Rufe held his friend out at paw's-length.

"Let me look at you, treejumper. By the fur, you're twice as fat as a badger at a feast. What've you been doin' to yourself?"

Oak Tom patted his vast stomach and chortled. "Yuk-yukyuk! Rovin' and eatin', though mostly eatin'. Doesn't slow me down at all. I'm faster than I ever was, young Rufe!"

Again they fell to wrestling and hugging. Several Dibbuns had gathered to view the performance. They called encouragement, thinking it was some sort of fight.

"Bite his tail off, Rufe!"

"Kick 'im in 'ee gurt fat tummy, squirr'l!"

Mother Mellus and Abbot Bernard came hurrying over. Oak Tom released Rufe and performed several acrobatic pawsprings.

"Abbot Bernard, how are ye, Father? Oh, look out, it's old stripy top. Bet y' can't catch me for a bath now, Ma Mellus!"

The badger put on a mock-serious expression, wagging her paw at him. "Just let me catch you, Oak Tom. You were the worst Dibbun Redwall ever had to put up with.

I'll wager you've not had a bath since you left here last summer."

The fat, nimble Oak Tom bounded up on Mellus's broad back and whispered in her ear, " 'Course I have. Here, this is for you."

Pulling a small package from his traveling bag, he dropped it in Mellus's paw. The badger sniffed it appreciatively.

"Oh, jasmine and lavender soap! Where did you get it? No, don't tell me, I'd hate to think of one of my Dibbuns stealing."

Oak Tom pulled a long face. The Abbot patted his head fondly.

"She's only joking, Tom. Come and talk to me, tell me all the news of your travels. You're just in time for lunch—we're eating out in the orchard. Summer salad, leek and celery soup, hot rootbread and strawberry trifle to follow."

"You must've known I was comin' back. My favorite of all: strawberry trifle. Yahoooooo!"

Oak Tom went hurtling away toward the orchard in a series of blurring somersaults. Runn and Grubb watched him go.

"He must've been a terrible Dibbun, worser'n us!"

"Buhurr aye, oi weager'ee wurr a gurt fat hinfant!"

The news Oak Tom brought was extremely serious, particularly to Clary and his long patrol. They listened intently.

Mellus glanced anxiously at Clary when Oak Tom finished telling what he had witnessed at the searat camp. Clary paced about in the shade of a gnarled pear tree.

"A big cage, y'say. Just how big, Tom?"

"Big 'n' strong enough t' hold all twelve o' them. Well made too, with thick branches an' lashings. Very heavy, I'd say."

Clary struck the tree with his paw. "Darn! I knew it'd come t' this, somehow."

"What does it mean, Colonel?"

Clary coughed and brushed his whiskers with the back

of a paw. "Oh nothin', marm. At least, naught fer you to worry your head about. Leave it t' me. I'll have a word with my jolly old pals—we'll sort it out. Tickety-boo—that's the word, wot!"

Simeon groped about with his paw until he touched Mellus's cheek. "There was a lot of false bravado in what Clary said. I think he's worried."

Saxtus watched the lanky figure of the hare retreating toward the Abbey. "Yes, the more anxious hares get the lighter they seem to make of things, have you noticed?"

Mellus stared at the young mouse intently. "That's a shrewd observation for one so young, Saxtus!"

In the dormitory allotted to them, the three hares sat upon the rush-matted floor. Clary had laid out a plan of the searat encampment with various bedroom articles. He placed a lantern squarely in the middle. "That's where the bally cage is, chaps."

They studied it, Thyme stroking his waxed moustache whiskers.

"Hmmm, difficult, extremely awkward, wot! But y' say they've all gone out killin' birds an' the like. P'raps there's a chance we could pay the confounded camp a visit now and make a surprise sortie?"

Clary shook his head. "No chance, old lad. Oak Tom went an' scared off all the game in the blinkin' neighborhood. There won't be a bird or a fish for miles. They'll prob'ly be back by now, roastin' roots an' burnin' apples an' whatnot. It's a rotten ol' standoff."

Hon Rosie shrugged. "No way out—we're stumped!"

Clary sighed. "There is one way, the only sure way. I knew it'd come down t' this eventually, as soon as I saw those searats in Mossflower country I felt it in m' bones."

They sat looking at each other awhile, then Clary sniffed airily.

"Still an' all, Lord Rawnblade wouldn't have us do anythin' else."

Thyme chuckled. "Rather, old Rawney'd have a blue fit if we didn't!"

Hon Rosie picked up her lance and began polishing it. "I say, then let's do it, just for a lark. Whoohahahahooh!"

Gabool the Wild did not bother covering up the pit anymore. He cackled madly as he gazed in at the loathsome sight of the huge black scorpion perching on the carcass of Fishtail, former ship's mate of the *Seatalon*.

"Haharrharrharr! That'll teach Catseyes t' send scurvy traitors spyin' on me. What d'ye say, Skrabblag?"

The glistening arachnid clicked and rustled balefully. Gabool strode out gesturing into the air as he conversed with himself.

"No need for Cap'ns when there's a King! I'll show 'em, badgers 'n' bells, ships 'n' searats, Cap'ns 'n' Kings. Haharr, round an' round they run, a-chasin' each other through my head, but Gabool will win in the end!"

He swept into the banqueting hall, where the assembled searats watched in astonishment as he stood, claws on hips, talking to the great tarnished bell which dominated the center of the floor.

"Go on, ring yer way out o' that one, hearty! Oh, you'll sing fer me one day. Ring, ring, Gabool the King!"

He whirled upon the two crews. "An' what're you all gawpin' at, pray? Nothin' t' do, nothin' to report?

"The *Seatalon*'s been sunk in the cove!"

Not bothering to see which rat had spoken, Gabool dashed to the window. "Hellfires! That's two vessels in as many days, first *Darkqueen* an' now *Seatalon*!"

"That wasn't *Darkqueen*, Lord, it was *Rathelm*, Cap'n Flogga's ship."

Gabool stroked his long, unkempt beard. "*Darkqueen, Rathelm*, same thing. There's *Waveblade, Nightwake, Crabclaw*, an' *Blacksail*, all t' come in. Let me know the moment they anchor."

After he had left the hall the gossip ran rife.

"Gabool's crazier'n a scalded beetle!"

"Don't let him fool yer, matey. He could still recall what ships he's got out at sea—aye, an' their names, too."

"I tell yer he's bats, chattin' away to a bell, pretty as y' please."

"Well, crazy or not, this is the place where all his booty's hid. Cap'n Flogga told me that."

"Aye, an' where's Flogga now?"

"An' Fishtail as well. I've seen nary a sight o' him since we came here."

"I say let's wait'll the rest o' the fleet's in, then we'll see what the other Cap'ns have t' say about all this rigamarole."

"Wait—what else can we do but wait, shipmates? Both our vessels are sittin' on the bed o' the cove down there. Somebeast scuttled 'em; they're sunk!"

"Gabool's changed. See his eyes? They're red like blood. He's actin' strange, mates—runnin' round this place filthy as some ol' tramp. That was never his way. I don't mind tellin' yer, I'm scared."

"Anyrat who isn't is a fool, matey. But we're stuck 'ere, so we better make the best of it. Any vittles in the kitchens, I wonder?"

Tarquin kept for'ard lookout, Mariel took the stern, Rawnblade stood at the tiller, steering a course off-line with the little swallow's flight as it dangled on its thread beneath the awning.

Mariel left off scanning the horizon to stare at the impressive figure of Lord Rawnblade Widestripe. He resembled some giant stepped out of legend, clad partially now in helmet and breastplate, the sword Verminfate resting beneath one paw as he steered with the other. Spray glistened, dewing the shaggy fur, as his keen dark eyes gazed out across the seas, brows lowered as if he were pondering some mystery known only to badger Lords. This then was the creature for whom her father had cast and made the great bell; she could think of no nobler or worthier owner for her father's masterpiece. Her father, Joseph. The name meant everything to Mariel: security, love, guidance and a comradeship between parent and child that was more like having a best friend than a father at times . . . his humorous twinkling eyes and ready wit.

"I say, old gel, have y' gone asleep back there? Ships ahoy and astern!"

The sound of Tarquin's voice brought Mariel back to reality.

Three sets of sails had appeared on the horizon in their wake, and Lord Rawnblade gave swift instructions. Without questioning his authority, Mariel and Tarquin took up their positions whilst the badger Lord concealed himself in the cabin below.

The three vessels *Nightwake, Crabclaw* and *Blacksail* were traveling back to Terramort in loose convoy, though now they sensed Terramort was reasonably near they broke formation and began racing to see who could anchor first in the cove.

Captain Hookfin of the *Blacksail* held the tiller steady as they ran before the southwest wind, tacking occasionally to keep his craft on course. He cursed as the *Nightwake* drew level, with her master Riptung at the helm. "A cask of dark wine I beat ye back, Riptung!"

Riptung swung the tiller over recklessly, causing him to veer. "Haharr, not in that ol' tub y'won't, matey!"

With superb skill and daring, the corsair Grimtooth plied his craft between them both. "Hoho, I'll show ye how a real searat sails, mates, an' I'll drink that wine to teach ye both a lesson in searatship!"

The *Nightwake* was now closest to Mariel and the *Waveblade* as the three ships bore onward, all oars pulling and sails at full stretch.

Riptung wiped spray from his eyes and looked across. From the distance all he could see was a very small steersrat and an extra-lanky lookout, both decked out in the tattered finery of searats.

"Ahoy, *Waveblade*, where have ye come from?" Riptung called out.

The small steersrat indicated back across her left shoulder, but did not shout a reply. Riptung understood.

"South, eh? We wer down that way, must've missed yer. Are you on for a race back to Terramort, cask o' wine fer the prize?"

The small rat shook its head, jiggling the tiller and shrugging.

Riptung nodded. "Rudder trouble, matey? Where's Cap'n Orgeye?"

The lanky one on lookout pantomimed sleep, resting his head on the foredeck rail and pointing below.

Riptung laughed aloud. "Haharr, lazy ol' Orgeye, snorin' like a hog. Too much wine, eh?"

The lanky one did a stagger and held his stomach and forehead at the same time. Riptung smote the tiller, laughing uproariously.

"Scupper me, the drunken ol' blubberfish. Ahoy there, tell 'im when he wakes that he missed a chance o' winnin' a big cask o' wine."

The two searats waved back as the ships drew away, racing pell-mell for Terramort, Riptung shouting tidings of Orgeye to the other two Captains, who shook their heads with merriment.

Rawnblade's huge head poked out of the cabin doorway. "Have they gone?"

Tarquin blew out a long sigh of relief. "Aye, m'Lord, but it was a close thing. Any nearer to us and the game would've been up; they would have seen we weren't bally searats."

Mariel leaned back against the tiller, wiping her brow. "Whew! See that? It isn't seaspray, it's sweat. How they could ever have taken me and Tarquin for a couple of scurvy searats, I'll never know."

Rawnblade strode up on deck. "We'll furl in the sails and let them get in to Terramort well ahead of us. Up you go, Woodsorrel. I'm too heavy to be climbing masts, and Mariel's needed on deck."

Tarquin took a look at the swaying mainmast billowing with sail. He threw a paw across his eyes and staggered giddily.

"Oh, corks. Do I have to climb up that great swayin' thing an' fold all those windy old bedsheets? Do I really, sir?"

Rawnblade pointed a stern paw to the topmast. "Up, Woodsorrel, up!"

Tarquin spat on his paws but made a last-ditch plea to a passing gull. "I say, birdie old bean, just furl a jolly old sail or two as you're passin', there's a good chap."

The sea gull flew heedlessly on. Rawnblade stood with his hefty paw still pointed into the rigging. "Up!"

Tarquin nervously scaled the mast, calling out to the sea gull, who had decided to hover overhead and view the performance.

"Yah rotten ol' featherbag, bet your mum was a cuckoo. Oh golly, if Hon Rosie could see me now she'd split her fur laughin'."

34

At that precise moment Hon Rosie had never been more serious in her life. She stood in a small wooded area, just out of sight of the searat camp. With her were Clary, Thyme, Rufe Brush, Oak Tom and the pretty squirrel Treerose. The hares were armed to the teeth—lances, bows, arrows and a dagger apiece. Clary was talking to the squirrels.

"Now you know the drill, chaps. As soon as I shout out t' you then you come runnin', get the slaves away pretty darn quick an' head north, take a loop south an' straight back to the Abbey. I've left that big otter chappie Flagg a note—he'll know what t' do. Don't forget now—whatever happens, keep the bally slaves goin' full speed an' get 'em back to Redwall posthaste, wot!"

Rufe Brush clapped Clary on the back. "Got it. Keep the slaves goin' till we're safe back home, right? But what about you three?"

Thyme tested his bowstring. "Don't worry about us, laddie buck. We'll be right as rain, won't we, Rosie?"

"What, oh er, rather! Get the little thingummies back

to the wotsit and leave the rest to us. Tickety-boo an' all that!"

Clary glanced at the noon sky. "Time to go, troops!"

Rufe, Tom and Treerose shook paws with the three hares. Clary sent them off. "Get round the back of the camp an' wait for my signal."

"Righto. Goodbye an' good luck, Thyme."

"Toodle-pip, old scout. Chin up."

Treerose waved. "Goodbye, Rosie. See you back at the Abbey."

Rosie nodded. " 'Course you will, pretty one. On your way now."

When the squirrels had gone, Colonel Clary inspected his patrol.

"Very smart, top marks, good turnout, wot!"

Thyme brushed his moustache one last time. "No excuse for sloppiness, my old pa always said."

They nocked shafts onto their bowstrings and strode off toward the searat camp, talking softly to each other.

"Make me proud of you now, troops."

"Goes without sayin', Clary. We'll give Rawnblade somethin' to talk about while we're at it, wot!"

"I say, Clary. Is it all right if I laugh 'n' hoot a bit once the show gets under way?"

"Permission granted, Rosie old gel. You chuckle as much as y'like."

The searats were milling about the fires, shoving and pushing as they tried to get cooking space. There had been no fish or meat taken, as a result of Oak Tom's activities in the area. However, they had found a good supply of wild pears and apples, and plentiful dandelion roots. Now they cooked the fruits, telling each other that there would be good hunting tomorrow when the birds and fish returned.

The oarslaves sat miserably in their long wooden cage. It was exceptionally strong, being made from thick green branches lashed together with rope. The young creatures gazed longingly out at their captors, knowing the only food they would receive was the waste and scraps after the rats had glutted themselves.

Pakatugg pushed his face against the wooden bars. He had grown thin and gaunt in captivity, suffering the kicks and curses of searats. He bitterly regretted tracking the *Darkqueen* in quest of plunder. Now he sat staring through his prison at the woodlands beyond, thinking of his secret den far away, the cool green light from the shading trees, the mossy rocks and trickling stream . . .

Quite suddenly Pakatugg saw the three hares of the long patrol! They were striding grim-faced through the searat camp, making for the captives in the cage, fully armed with lance and dagger, each with a shaft drawn tautly on a longbow. The squirrel watched them silently, his eyes wide with disbelief. The hares ignored the noisy crew of searats as they marched purposefully forward.

The rat called Fleawirt was first to see them as he turned from the fire. "Hey! Where d'yer think yer go—"

Wordlessly Thyme turned and slew him, the heavy oak arrow knocking the startled searat back fully three paces. Pandemonium broke out. Before the rats could grasp what was going on, another two fell, pierced by shafts from Clary and Rosie. As swiftly as they loosed the arrows, the long patrol had fresh ones stretched upon their bowstrings.

"Get them!" Greypatch bellowed, drawing his sword. "Don't just stand there, kill 'em!"

Shaking the numbness of surprise from him, one called Shoreclaw plucked his spear from the ground and raised it. He was so close that Clary's arrow passed through him and wounded another standing behind. Rosie dodged a spear as the trio quickened their pace. She sent her arrow zinging into the snarling face of Kybo, cutting off the scream that issued from his mouth. Now the hares sent out the blood-chilling war cry of Salamandastron; it rang out above the clamor.

"Eulaliaaaaaaa!!!"

They arrived at the cage, still sending arrows from the

formidable longbows thudding into the horde of advancing foe rats.

Pakatugg shoved his paw through the bars. "Give me a dagger and I'll cut the ropes!"

Clary tossed him a freshly sharpened knife from Redwall's kitchen. "What ho, you old villain! Chop away at the back of the cage, would you."

A spear took Thyme in the right footpaw. Gritting his teeth, he wrenched it out and hurled it back, wounding its thrower. "Ah well, no more runnin' for me today, wot?"

Rosie stopped a charging rat with her lancepoint. "Hate to remind you, old thing, but we didn't come here to run."

Clary whacked out fiercely, breaking a leg with the heavy yew bow. "Famous last stand, wot? Go out in a blaze of glory an' all that. Right, chaps. Another quick volley, an' give 'em a shout t' let 'em know we've arrived. Fire!"

Three arrows flew from the longbows into the seething rat pack.

"Eulaliaaaa!!!"

Pakatugg slashed frenziedly at the remaining rope lashings in the back of the cage. The bindings parted and a section of the woodwork fell away. The oarslaves huddled dumbly in a group. He pushed through them, tugging at the back of Clary's belt through the front bars.

"I've done it, part of the back's fallen down!"

Colonel Clary winced as an arrow took him in the shoulder. "Wait'll the squirrels arrive, old thing, then follow 'em. Take all the slaves an' stick close to them, no matter what."

Clary threw back his head and yelled, "Rufe, Tom, Treerose! Now now now!"

Thyme was kneeling. Wounded in both footpaws, he bravely held his bow horizontally, firing as rapidly as his dwindling quiver of arrows permitted. Glancing back, he saw the three Redwall squirrels herding the timid oarslaves out through the broken cage into the woodlands. Rosie was throttling a struggling rat on her bowstring as

Clary held off the mob with a lance held in each paw.

"Mission accomplished, eh, Rosie old scout!"

"Rather! Whoohahahahahooh!"

Standing at the back of the crew, Graypatch ran around belaboring with the flat of his sword as he roared hoarsely, "Get into 'em! Come on, yer sluggards, rush 'em!"

Frink took aim and skillfully threw a long dagger. "Got 'im! I've wounded the big 'un in the ribs!"

The grin of triumph froze on his face as an oak arrow found him.

Thyme tugged at Clary's leg. "Out of arrows, old sport. Get me up on me pins an' give me a lance!"

Pakatugg assisted in getting Thyme upright. Clary glared at him.

"Where did you come from, mister? You were supposed to escape with the rest. I won't stand for insubordination, y'know!"

Armed with a searat cutlass and spear, the squirrel growled dangerously. "I'm stoppin' here, see. Don't like searats—dirty vermin beat me an' made sport o' me. Nobeast does that to Pakatugg. I'll teach 'em!"

Rosie flinched as a sword caught her high on the cheek. "Good for you, Paka, y'nasty old rogue, give 'em vinegar!"

Flinging their empty quivers and longbows into the faces of the rats, the long patrol brandished daggers and lances. Charging forward, they carried the battle straight into the ranks of the enemy, with Clary calling out aloud, "Nice day for it, wot!"

Thyme staggered forward. "Summer's my fav'rite season, old lad!"

Hon Rosie clapped Pakatugg on the back. "Let's give 'em one last shout, for Salamandastron an' the jolly old Abbey."

"Eulaliaaaa! Redwaaaaaaall!"

Accompanied by an old squirrel, the long patrol threw themselves into the howling mob of searats.

• • •

Not just Flagg, but every creature in Redwall Abbey stood out upon the north ramparts, scanning the path in the pale moonlight for signs of movement. Mellus and Flagg were armed with longbows; lanterns flickered all along the walltop in the hushed silence. Simeon the blind herbalist stood with the Abbot and the Dibbuns, their bedtime forgotten in the tense, waiting atmosphere. Simeon's voice was barely above a whisper, but it could be heard by many as he addressed the Abbot.

"What's happening out there, Bernard?"

"Nothing, old friend. It's very quiet and still down there."

"Hurr, be they a-cummen yet, maister Simmen?"

Simeon patted Grubb's velvety head. "Only if you're very good and stay quiet, little mole."

"Oi be vurry soilint naow. Hussshhher!"

"Whatever possessed them to go on such an insane venture?" Mellus murmured to Flagg. "Six of ours against all that rotten horde. And to think it was I who urged Colonel Clary to rescue the slaves in the first place."

Flagg shook his head. "No, marm, it weren't you. Clary had it in his mind to do the deed anyway. He left me a scroll tellin' all. I burned it in the kitchen stove as he wished me to. So don't blame yerself, marm. They were sworn to fight searats from birth; it was their destiny."

Minutes stretched into hours as the Redwallers waited, straining their eyes along the north path, sometimes expectant at a sign of movement, only to have their hopes dashed by the realization that it was merely a shadow as clouds scudded across the moon, or the rustle of breeze-stirred foliage.

The Dibbuns had finally fallen asleep. Sister Sage covered them with blankets from the gatehouse as they lay huddled together in the northwest corner of the walltop.

Saxtus and Sister Serena carried a caldron of leek and celery broth from the kitchens, followed by Friar Alder and Cockleburr, laden with wheat farls.

Gabriel Quill stared toward the eastern horizon over the treetops of Mossflower. "Be dawn in two hour, I reckons."

Foremole was slurping soup rather noisily from a wooden bowl when Simeon placed a restraining paw on him. "Hush, I think I can sense something."

The Abbot held up his paws for silence all around. "What is it, Simeon?"

The blind mouse leaned out across the battlements, his whiskers quivering slightly. "Metal, I thought I could hear metal . . . Yes, there it is! Any signs on the path?"

"None whatsoever."

"Sssh, there it is again, over there on the woodland edge—metal. Wait . . . it's chains, I can hear chains!"

Saxtus sprang up between the battlements with a whoop. "Hurrah! It's them, I can see Rufe Brush leading the slaves out of Mossflower onto the path. Hi, Rufe!"

Flagg acted speedily. "Marm, put an arrow to your bow and stand beside me here. We'll keep them covered. Saxtus, Foremole, Gabe, you'll find spears down by the main gate. Take twenty with you and escort them back in. Keep your wits about you an' your eyes open. Hurry now, they may be followed by searats!"

Without further event the last eleven slaves made it into the safety of Redwall Abbey. As the chains were being cut from their wasted limbs, the Abbot questioned the three squirrels who had taken part in the rescue. Treerose and Oak Tom were crying; even the normally tough Rufe Brush broke down and wept bitterly as they related what they had seen at the magnificent last stand of the long patrol.

"They didn't stand a chance, yet they came through the center of that searat camp laughing and joking. They were completely surrounded!"

Oak Tom was pale, his voice low and trembling. "I never thought that was what they meant to do, but it was the only thing they could have done to free the slaves. What makes it all so strange is that they knew what would happen, how it must end!"

Treerose accepted a spotted handkerchief from Foremole. "Oh, they were so brave! Rosie smiled at me and said she'd see me back here. Oh, Father Abbot, why did they do it?"

Abbot Bernard shook his head gently. "Who knows, child, who knows? Certainly none of us at Redwall. We are infants in the ways of war. Colonel Clary and his hares were complete warriors. Their seasons were numbered from birth—they knew this was the day their fates were sealed."

Saxtus hung his head. "Yet they knew they were helping Redwall and bringing liberty to the slaves, so they went to meet their destinies smiling and joking. I was wrong about the hares and I'll always remember that when I make judgments about other creatures."

Simeon and the Abbot went back to lock the main gates before turning in. Dawnlight was beginning to flush the skies.

"Triumph and tragedy in the one night, old friend."

The Abbot kicked away a stone which was hindering the closing gate. "Right, Simeon . . . Hey, you two, come in here. Right now!"

Bagg and Runn came strolling through the gateway in their nightshirts. Abbot Bernard wagged a stern paw at them.

"You two rascals should be fast asleep in bed. What are you doing out here on the path, may I ask?"

Bagg rubbed his eyes sleepily. "Wavin' g'bye to Flagg an' Mum Mell's."

Throwing the gate back open, the Abbot hurried out onto the path. "Flagg and Mother Mellus? I can't see them. Are you telling whoppers?"

Two heads shook vigorously.

"No, Father Habbit, sir. Honestly!"

"They went up that way an' into the woods." Runn pointed north.

"An' they was carryin' those big bows an' lots of arrers too!"

35

Gabool unsheathed his sword and glared suspiciously at the three Captains who had stridden into Fort Bladegirt at the head of their crews.

"What are you three doin' here? What d'yer want?"

"You told us to come back here, Gabool."

"King Gabool. You call me King, d'ye hear. Anyway, what news?"

"No news. Graypatch an' that dratted *Darkqueen* have vanished from the seas—no sign of 'em anywhere."

Gabool tugged absently at his matted beard. "That's no news. I've taken care of Graypatch an' *Darkqueen* long ago. Belay, have you three swabs been sinkin' ships in Terramort cove?"

"Ships, what ships?"

"Two of 'em, haharr, but never mind that. Have ye heard the bell? What about the great badger, did yer clap eyes on him?"

Riptung looked from Hookfin to Grimtooth. All three raised their eyebrows and shrugged. They watched as Gabool went across to the bell.

"See that! They don't hear ye, so why should I?"

"So it's right, he's mad as a gaffed fish," Riptung whispered to Grimtooth.

Gabool spun round. "Avast, don't you three start plottin' behind me back!"

Riptung took a cask from one of his crew. He banged it down upon the table, stoving its head in with the hilt of his sword. "Nobeast's talkin' about yer, King Gabool. Come an' share a beaker o' this wine that I won!"

Grimtooth strode to the window. He stood drinking his wine and looking out to sea, then turned, laughing, to the others.

"Hoho. Lookit, mates, 'ere comes the *Waveblade*, sailin' inter the cove like a stranded sardine. Haharr, I'll wager ol' Orgeye's still in his bunk snorin'."

They crowded to the windows to watch. Hookfin tugged Riptung's sleeve urgently. "Did you leave any watch aboard yer vessel, matey?"

Riptung swung a claw back over his shoulder. "No, they're all up 'ere with me. Why?"

Hookfin pointed down at the three ships. "Then who's movin' those vessels out ter sea?"

Riptung drew his sword and faced Gabool. "This is one o' your tricks. What's yer game?"

But Gabool did not hear the angry Captain, he was staring wild-eyed at the hulking figure that paced the deck of the *Waveblade*, distant but unmistakable.

"Aaaaah! It's him, it's the badger!"

Immediately the three searat Captains and their King started bellowing orders to the packed hall.

"Get down t' the cove, stop the *Blacksail* puttin' out t' sea!"

"Kill the badger. I'll make any rat a Cap'n who slays him!"

"Stop the *Nightwake*, some scurvy slob's tryin' to steal her!"

"The badger! Kill the badger, shipmates!"

"Get after the *Crabclaw*, buckos. Bring 'er back t' me!"

"Whoever kills the badger is a rich rat, you got Gabool's oath on that!"

Mariel stared at the three searat ships as *Waveblade* sailed into Terramort cove. Rawnblade swung the tiller, navigating between them.

"Strange, they've just arrived yet they're going out again."

Tarquin shaded his eyes and peered across. "Aye, an' those aren't searats who are sailin' them. What d' you think's goin' on?"

"Ahoy there, Mariel!"

The mousemaid gasped. There standing on the shore of the cove, waving at her, was Dandin. She jumped up and down, waving back.

"Dandin, Dandin! Stay there, we're coming ashore!"

They plunged over into the shallows and waded onto the beach.

Dandin hugged and patted Tarquin and Mariel, who in their turn squeezed him tightly, ruffling his whiskers and patting his paws as if they could not believe it was really him. Smiling happily (and sniffling a little), Dandin managed to extricate himself from the welcoming huddle.

"I thought you were dead, I was certain you'd been drowned, though there wasn't much time to think about that with the fix me and Durry found ourselves in. I tell you, don't ever become an oarslave, it's worse than being captured by the Flitchaye!"

When the reunion was finished and Lord Rawnblade had been introduced, Mariel looked about. "Where's Durry?"

No sooner had she spoken than, in company with two hooded shrews, Durry came pounding down the path to the cove. The young hedgehog looked very dashing, wearing a broad leather belt with several daggers bristling from it and a hood on his head.

"Oh, Durry, you do look a proper swashbuckler and no mistake!" Mariel laughed.

However, Durry Quill was in no mood for banter. Puffing and blowing, he waved back over his shoulder.

"Phew! Quick, 'urry up, there's about five 'undred searats 'ot on me trail. They're comin' after you, I think. Mikla, Flann, get that ship out to sea. I'll take these friends to the caves. Hurry!"

The two shrews Mikla and Flann waded out to the *Waveblade* to take her out of the searats' reach with the other three ships.

Mariel, Tarquin and Rawnblade followed Durry and Dandin as they raced off in the opposite direction to Bladegirt, toward the sheer rocky coast which veered up on the west side of the cove.

The searat frontrunners, with Riptung and Hookfin in the lead, came rushing down the path to the shore of the cove.

Riptung threw his sword down in frustration. "Hell's tail! They're too far out, we'll never get to 'em now!"

Hookfin raced down on the shoreline, searching for a dinghy to pursue his ship in. "Thunder 'n' blood! Ain't there nothin' we can give chase in?"

An enterprising rat called Felltooth stripped off his more cumbersome weapons, thrust a dagger in his headband and entered the water.

"*Waveblade*'s not too far out, Cap'n Riptung. May'aps we can swim to 'er an' use 'er to bring back the other three ships!"

Riptung retrieved his sword. "That's the way, matey. Some of yer go with 'im. Any good swimmers?"

Seven searats gripping daggers in their teeth waded into the sea.

Hookfin pointed in the direction of the crude trail which led up into the high rocks. "Look, it's the badger!"

Dandin glanced down to the yelling hordes racing across the shore to the rocks. "We've been spotted, here they come!"

Lord Rawnblade set his back against a rock, raising the sword Verminfate in both paws. "Get running, I'll stop them!"

Dandin stood in front of the upraised sword. Rawnblade was beginning to breathe heavily, his eyes glazing over as he watched the searats below. The young mouse took the badger's paw.

"There's no need for you to stay. Come with us. They'll never find us—you'll see!"

The badger Lord took considerable moving, all four tugging and pushing him farther up the trail and behind an overhanging outcrop of rocks, where they were out of sight of the rats. Durry went across to a big craggy boulder. He pushed it, moving it easily to one side. Tarquin gasped in astonishment at the tunnel that yawned before them.

"Golly! That's jolly clever, Durry—a secret tunnel. How did y' manage to move that whackin' great boulder with one single shove?"

Durry swelled his chest out. "I ate a good breakf'st."

Dandin laughed. "Take no notice of that little fibber. Come inside and I'll show you how easy it is."

They filed into the tunnel, Rawnblade stooping to get his great size through the opening. Dandin was last in. Quickly he set flint and tinder to a dry brush torch and passed it to Mariel. "Hold this and watch."

Leaning out of the cave entrance, Dandin gave the boulder a light push and sprang back. The massive rock tottered slightly and rolled back into its former position, blocking the tunnel entrance. He took a wedge of ship's timber and slammed it tight against the bottom of the boulder. "There, that'll stop anybeast moving it. The whole thing works on a fine balance, you see. Now stay quiet and listen!"

Hookfin and a bunch of searats rounded the rocky outcrop. Before them the winding trail ran upward into the high hills, completely devoid of signs of life. The searat Captain looked hither and thither without success. "This is the way they came. I'd stake me oath on it. Where've the scurvy blaggards got to?"

"They've vanished, Cap'n!"

"Stow yer gab, biscuitbrain. Nobeast just vanishes. They're round 'ere somewheres—I know it."

"Well, my old dad used ter say that badgers were

magic beasts. Maybe they 'ave vanished, Cap'n!"

Hookfin aimed a kick at the speaker. "Huh, your ole dad must've lived up a tree with a branch growin' through both ears. Don't talk such bilgerot. No, they're round 'ere, I can feel it."

"May'aps they're be'ind that big boulder, Cap'n."

This remark did not improve Hookfin's temper.

"Aye, an' mayhaps I'll beat your brains out agin that great boulder if yer make another stupid suggestion. Spread out an' look around."

As they searched, one searat close to the boulder nudged his mate. "Can you smell burnin', matey?"

"No, but it'll probably be Cap'n 'ookfin's old brainbox tryin' ter figger out where the badger went. Heeheeheehee!"

"You two over there, stop sniggerin' an' start searchin', or I'll lay me sword blade across yer backs!"

Rocking back and forth with silent mirth, the creatures in the cave listened to the searats outside. Even Rawnblade had to stifle a few chuckles. Finally Dandin took the torch and went off down the winding rocky tunnel.

"Come on, we can't stop here all day listening to those buffoons."

The tunnel sloped gently downward. Mariel stared at the rough rock walls in the flickering torchlight as she followed Durry Quill. "Where are we going, Durry?"

"Down to the main cave, missy. That's where us Trag warriors meet."

"Trag, what's that supposed to mean?"

Durry Quill flourished a fearsome dagger, muttering darkly, "Terramort Resistance Against Gabool. Trag see, first letter o' each word. You'll like our Chief though, he knows you very well."

Mariel was mystified. "Knows me? How?"

Durry smiled in the shadows as he answered, " 'Cos he's your daddy, Joseph the Bellmaker!"

Dandin felt the torch snatched from his grasp as Mariel dashed past. She disappeared down the winding tunnel, leaving them groping in the darkness as the mousemaid's voice echoed about them at a screaming pitch.

"Father! Fatheeeeerrr!"

It was an immense cavern, high above the tidemark on the sheer rock coast, facing the open sea and well lit by the summer sun. Free creatures, former oarslaves and Fort Bladegirt drudges, sat about on rocky ledges, cleaning and preparing weapons, cooking over fires and readying meals. All activity ground to an immediate halt as the mousemaid came hurtling down the tunnel into the cavern.

Heedlessly dropping the flaring torch, she threw herself into the paws of Joseph, hugging him fiercely as her tears flooded into the silver-gray fur of his broad shoulder.

"Father! Oh, Father! I always knew I'd find you again someday!"

Joseph the Bellmaker held his only child, the pain and anguish of many long days and nights turning to unbounded joy as a happy smile lit his strong face, banishing the glistening dew which threatened to spill from his proud eyes. "Mariel . . . Mariel my little maid, how you've grown! I never knew all this time whether you were alive, but in my heart I refused to believe that you were dead and I always knew you'd return somehow, my little Mariel!"

The others stumbled out of the tunnel, Durry Quill dabbing tenderly at his swelling snout, which he had banged against the rock walls in the darkness.

"Well, wait'll I tell my ol' nuncle, dashin' off an' leavin' a young 'og in the dark like that. Ain't you got no feelins, missy?"

That night the fires blazed merrily in the cavern of the Trag warriors, huge platters of shrimp and shellfish were served, with wild oat and barley bread, hot from the rocks it had been baked on, cakes of preserved fruits taken from searat ships were opened and a fine barrel of daisy and dandelion beer tapped. The friends sat around as Joseph related his story.

"Gabool pushed me from a high window of his banqueting room. Luckily for me I did not strike the rockface on the way down. I hit the water hard and was knocked senseless; I was weak and ill from being starved and imprisoned, otherwise I might have stayed conscious. The sea must have washed me around the headland, and I came to jammed against a reef on a small inlet somewhere up the coast of Terramort. That's where I was found by that fellow." Joseph pointed to a vole who was seated on a rock ledge sharpening a sword. The vole stood up and bowed to them, introducing himself by name, "Tan Loc." He sat down and resumed sharpening the sword.

"Tan Loc is a fellow of few words," Joseph continued. "He broods a lot. His whole family were slain by searats when he was taken captive. He lives for only one thing: to meet the murderer, Hookfin, Master of the *Blacksail*. But back to my story. Tan Loc and I helped each other stay alive. We could not afford to be seen—it would have meant certain death—so we stayed on this side of the island, surviving as best we could. One day we discovered this place and its tunnels—I will show them to you in due course. The tunnels were a new lease of life to us. They led to places all over the island, so we could travel anywhere and remain unseen. Some nights we would steal supplies from the ships, weapons too, and other items which would be of use to us. We soon came across others, house slaves from Fort Bladegirt who had managed to escape, sometimes oarslaves, thrown on the beach because they were too sick and weak to pull an oar anymore. In time our numbers began to swell. That was when we decided to form Trag, Terramort Resistance Against Gabool. Soon now we will be strong enough to attack Bladegirt in force, though our numbers would never equal the searat horde up there at the moment. Still, we will fight them and try to rid the earth of Gabool the Wild. We may not have the numbers, but we have the courage and determination."

Lord Rawnblade stood up, both paws resting on the

crosshilt of his destroyer Verminfate. "I am sworn to kill Gabool. He is mine!"

Joseph touched the long knife at the back of his belt. "Then you will have to be quick, Lord Widestripe. I made an oath to slay Gabool when the house slaves told me he had drowned my Mariel with a rock and a rope tied about her neck. That oath still holds!"

Mariel leaped up, the Gullwhacker swinging wide. "First there, first served! Gabool's life is mine to take. I am Mariel Gullwhacker, I claim the right!"

Tarquin leaned over to Dandin. "What about you, old feller?"

Dandin drew the sword slowly. "This is the blade of Martin the Warrior. No creature that is evil can stand against it, least of all Gabool!"

Tarquin and Durry held a hasty whispered conference, then they both jumped up, issuing their separate challenges.

"This 'ere is my scraggin' dagger, an' I'm goin' to scrag that scurvy Gabool good 'n' proper. I'm on'y a young lad, but I swear it by my ol' nuncle Gabe's best October ale!"

"Well, you'll have t' scrag away pretty fast, old chap, 'cos if Joseph has got the blighter with his long knife, Milord Rawnblade has paid the rotter a visit with that great log cleaver and our Mariel has been to see the scoundrel with her Gullwhacker, then along comes the bold Durry Quill with his scraggin' dagger, well, tell me this: what chance is an honest chap like meself goin' to get to brain the beggar with my jolly old harolina, wot? Listen, you lot, stop bein' so confounded greedy and let me be first to knock out a tune on the villain's noodle."

The sight of Tarquin striking a noble pose, harolina at the ready, caused the entire group to dissolve into helpless laughter.

Gabool was in no mood for laughter. The maddened Searat King dashed furiously around his barred and bolted room, slashing at phantom badgers as they stole out of the shadows to confront his bloodshot eyes, shrieking and thrusting wildly at the specters created by his tormented brain.

"Haharr, I'll finish ye all. I'm Gabool the King of all Seas!"

Bong! Bong! Bong! Bong! Bong!

He rent curtains and wallhangings; sparks showered from his sword as it clashed on the stone walls.

"Cursed noise, I'll send yer to Hellgates an' beyond!"

Down below in the banqueting hall, Riptung, Hookfin and Grimtooth laughed drunkenly as they flung hard apples across the tables at the great tarnished bell in the center of the floor.

"Haharr! Listen, Yer Majesty, it's yer old matey the bell a-speakin' to yer. It wants t' know where you've hid the booty. Haharrharrharr!"

The crews joined in the laughter as they pelted the bell with apples.

Boom! Bong! Boom! Bong! Boom! Bongggggg!

36

A pale dawn sun high above Mossflower Woods watched impassively as the otter and badger searched for the searat camp, longbows at the ready.

Flagg strained his ears for sounds of movement. "It's no good, marm. We should've asked the squirrels which way t' go."

Mother Mellus sat down upon a fallen limb and rubbed her eyes. "Perhaps you're right, Flagg. My old senses aren't what they used to be. If we don't find it soon we'll have to change direction."

The otter joined her on the limb. "Tell you what, marm. We'll take a liddle rest and then try a different path anyway. By the fur, I'm tired. Missin' a full night's sleep never did me much good, even when I was a cub. Aaaahhhh! Sit down on the grass 'ere an' put yer back against this limb awhile. There now, ain't that a little better?"

Mellus relaxed, settling her head back against the moss-covered limb. A big bumblebee droned lazily past on its quest for nectar, in the distance a songthrush warbled blithely its hymn to the coming summer day, somewhere close by a grasshopper that had strayed from the flatlands chirruped idly. The warmth of the rising sun beat steadily down upon the two weary friends. As sleep stole up and took their tired senses unawares, the longbows slipped from their paws, and their eyes drooped shut.

A small spider was starting to weave her web from the tip of a longbow to Flagg's nose. He twitched his snout, flicking at it drowsily with his paw as the voices intruded upon his dream.

"Somewheres around this way she was. I swear I saw 'er, matey!"

"Well, stow yer gab an' keep that spear ready. Y' can't take no chances with this scurvy rabbit. I could swear we've killed 'er three times a'ready. Tread easy now—is that 'er?"

"Where?"

"Layin' among those fern things, goggle eyes. Look, can't y'see?"

Flagg came awake, collecting his senses as he listened to the searats.

"Take no chances this time, mate. Sneak up, an' both of us in fast with the spears, hard as y'can, ten times apiece. See she doesn't jump away agin."

"Aye, did ye ever see anythin' like that leap she made out of the camp? Right over Graypatch's 'ead, an' 'er all cut t' pieces too!"

The urgency of the situation hit Flagg like a thunderbolt. Sitting up silently, he placed a paw across Mellus's mouth and shook her awake. The badger saw something in Flagg's eyes that made her go completely still. He gestured forward with his paw, whispering one word. "Searats!"

Stealthily the two friends stood up, fitting arrows to their longbows.

The two searats were standing some distance away, their backs to the hunters as they sneaked in upon a bed of fern, spears raised, ready for the kill. Flagg and Mellus drew back the shafts upon their bowstrings to full stretch. The otter nodded to Mellus, and she called out in a loud gruff voice, "Ahoy there!"

The two searats turned in the direction of her voice as the arrows left the longbows with a vicious twin hiss. Both rats fell instantaneously, the sharp oak shafts standing out of their necks a half-length.

Regardless of nettle and bush, the otter and the badger crashed through the woodland into the bed of ferns. They stood aghast at the wounded, scarred, bloodstained form of Hon Rosie lying on the ground. She pulled herself up onto one paw, smiling crookedly through her ripped and battered face.

"H-hello, you ch-chaps. 'Fraid they've k-killed me . . . Wot . . . !" Collapsing back, the brave hare lay stretched among the ferns.

Mellus was down beside her, ripping up her garments, bandaging, wiping blood from Rosie's face and massaging her paws as she instructed Flagg.

"Have you got a knife?"

"Yes, marm—one of Friar Alder's best. Is she dead?"

"No, not quite. There's a chance. Cut some poles—no, wait, use the longbows. Chop some vines, anything. We'll use our belts . . . Got to make a stretcher. Here!" She ripped off her belt and threw it to Flagg. The helpful otter took off his own.

"Gotcha, marm. Leave it t' me!"

He set about his task swiftly, glancing urgently back to where Mellus was busy with Rosie among the ferns.

"You can't die, d'you hear me, Rosie? Wake up! If you die, I'll kill you! Oh, I'm sorry dear. Live! Live for Clary and Thyme. Live!"

Rufe Brush and Oak Tom headed the party that had set out from Redwall at dawn. They were all heavily armed and determined to help Mellus and Flagg against the searats. Cutting off the path, they entered the woodlands. Tom and Treerose swung off into the foliage to scout ahead. Gabe Quill brandished a big bung mallet angrily.

"I'll searat 'em, the filthy vermints!"

Rufe turned to him. "Keep your voice down, Gabe . . . Owch! Watch where you're pokin' that lance, Burgo. Pooh! Are you chewin' wild garlic again?"

"Burr, aye, zurr. Found some o' the pesky stuff o'er yonder. Oi carnt aboid the smell tho' I dearly do luv ets taste. 'Pologies 'bout 'ee larnce, zurr."

"Chuck ee larnce aways," Foremole whispered in Burgo's ear. "You'm cudd slay emenies with thoi breath!"

"Over here, straight ahead," Oak Tom called out from a high hornbeam. "It's Mellus an' Flagg bearin' a stretcher."

The Redwallers flocked around Rosie, gabbling questions at her rescuers.

"Is she dead?"

"Coo deary, she'm bad cuttup!"

"Where did you find her, Flagg?"

"Any sign o' Clary or Thyme?"

"D'you think she'll live?"

Mellus silenced them with a growl. "Stop all this silly chattering. We must get this hare to Redwall as speedily as possible. You squirrels, will you get back to the Abbey as quickly as you can. Tell Sister Serena, Simeon, the Abbot and Sister Sage to have all their medicines ready and a room in sickbay cleared out. Right, off you go!"

The three squirrels went off through the top terraces of the woodlands like greased lightning. Ready paws gripped the stretcher, steadying Rosie as the group broke into a fast trot.

Graypatch limped badly from an arrow that had pierced his leg. He gazed around at the smashed cage, the smoldering embers of last night's fires and the carcasses of dead searats that littered the ground like fallen leaves. They were piled in a heap in the middle of the camp. He prodded the lifeless forms with his sword. Somewhere beneath that heap lay two hares and a squirrel. The searat Captain shook his head and slumped down upon a rock.

"Three hares and a squirrel did all this?" he murmured disbelievingly.

Deadglim shambled over. He leaned on a broken spear, nursing the place where his left ear had been. "Eighteen left alive, Cap'n. Well, it would be a score, but two went after the hare that got away."

Graypatch massaged his leg, wincing. "Eighteen, is that all!"

"Aye, Cap'n. What's yer orders?"

Graypatch stared into the surrounding forest. He had come to hate Mossflower country; the whole thing had been a catalogue of disaster since they arrived. He had stolen the *Darkqueen* and set sail from Terramort with a crew of a hundred able-bodied searats, and now he was sitting in this landlocked hell of greenery with only eighteen left.

"Tell the crew to pack up, lock, stock 'n' barrel. We're pullin' out o' this stinkin' place. I'm goin' to find the *Darkqueen*, get 'er seaworthy an' sail out to the open sea, where we can breathe again!"

A slow smile formed upon Deadglim's coarse face. "Aye-aye, Cap'n Graypatch. I'll do that with pleasure, sir!"

Treerose paced the corridor outside the sickbay.

Abbot Bernard came out with a basin and a stained towel. "Ah, Treerose. See if you can get some clean warm water and a fresh towel for me, pretty one."

Treerose's voice betrayed great anxiety. "How is Rosie, Father?"

The Abbot wiped his paws on his wide sleeves, a smile creasing his kindly face. "D'you know, I didn't believe it at first, but she's going to be all right. Thanks to your warning, the creatures who got her here so fast, and the marvelous skills of Simeon and Sister Sage. Yes, Treerose, she's going to be around for quite a number of seasons yet to come. So you stop that crying now and get me fresh water and a clean towel."

Mother Mellus came out to stand in the corridor with the Abbot. "What was all that about, Father?"

"Oh, nothing really. It just surprises me how overnight

that young squirrel has changed from a spoilt brat into a really nice helpful creature."

Mellus patted the Abbot's frail back. "Hmm, then we must be doing something right, the way we bring our young ones up at Redwall, eh!"

The Abbot bowed gallantly. "The way you bring them up, Mellus."

Saxtus lay on his back in the strawberry patch with the Dibbuns. Bagg and Runn chattered incessantly as they decimated the latest crop of ripe fruit.

"Have all the searats gone now, Sax'us?"

"Suppose so. We haven't seen them for a while."

"An' they're not comin' back to 'ttack the Abbey again?"

"I hope not. Why d'you ask?"

"Oh nuts! I wanted 'em t' come back so I could fight 'em!"

"No you don't, little one. We've had enough fighting and killing. Isn't much nicer lying here filling your tummy with strawberries in the sun?"

"Mm, s'pose so, but I can't get at the biggest 'n' juiciest 'n' squashiest ones."

"Why not?"

" 'Cos you're lyin' on 'em. Hohohoho!"

Saxtus got up slowly, feeling the cold juice running down his back. "Well, thank you for telling me so soon!"

Grubb plonked himself down and began stuffing strawberries three at a time. "Oi sees 'ee winds blowed all 'ee strawbly trees away agin."

Sister Sage was creeping from the sickbay with Simeon on tip-paw. They had done all they could with the hare's dreadful injuries; now they decided it was best that she sleep and recuperate. The hinge squeaked as Sister Sage opened the door.

Rosie opened one eye and peeked through the bandaged slit. "Never died after all, wot . . . good . . . show!"

Simeon leaned on Sister Sage's arm. "Incredible! Totally unbelievable. I've heard of cats having nine lives, but that Rosie, she's the limit!"

Sister Sage shut the door as quietly as possible. "Or the absolute bally limit, as Colonel Clary would have said."

37

"Do you know where we are now?"

Mariel and Rawnblade shook their heads. They were completely lost on their guided tour of the tunnels of Terramort.

Joseph pointed ahead. "Go up there—careful now because it's the end of this particular tunnel—and you'll see a couple of gorsebushes. Just part them and tell me what you see."

As they carried out his instructions, Mariel drew in a sharp breath. "It's Fort Bladegirt, right across on the next hill!"

Joseph nodded. "I can take you to another branch of this same tunnel that brings you out on the other side of the fort, or yet another which will bring you out at the back of Bladegirt. Well, does it give you any ideas?"

"A three-pronged invasion?"

"You took the words out of my mouth, Lord Rawnblade. Anything else you'd like to see?"

"Yes, Father. I'd like to see these other two exits. I'm beginning to get a few ideas myself."

"Hmm, I thought you would. Come on then, follow me."

Down below in the main cave, Dandin, Durry and Tarquin were making friends with the freed slaves of the Trag society. A young shrew and some of his companions sat questioning them.

"Where do you come from?"

"Redwall Abbey in Mossflower country."

The youngster gazed at them with shining eyes. "Redwall Abbey, Mossflower country. Does it look as nice as it sounds?"

Tarquin strummed his harolina. "You can bet your fluffy bedsocks it does, young thingummy. Here, Dandin, give me a trill on your whistle while I tune me jolly instrument up an' I'll tell 'em all about it."

Dandin tootled away on his ancestor's flute until between them he and the hare had a rollicking air going. The Trag members tapped their paws on the rocks to the infectious music as Tarquin sang.

"On the old brown path from north to south
Is a place you'd love to stay in.
Come one, come all, to old Redwall,
And hear what I am sayin'.
There's an orchard there that's fat and fair
With apple, berry, plum and pear.
There's a pond with fish and all you'd wish
To grace a supper table dish.
They've a nice soft bed to rest your head,
Or sleep beneath the trees instead.
If you meet the Abbot then be sure to shake him by
the paw.
On the old brown path from north to south
It's peaceable an' free where
Our Abbey stands amid woodlands,
I'm sure you'd love to be there!"

There was loud cheering, and Tarquin was requested to sing the ditty twice more. Durry leaped up and danced with a vole and a dormouse. Afterward they sat about talking. Redwall was the chief topic of discussion among the freed slaves, most of whom had never known or could not remember a place they called home.

"Do you have lots of nice things to eat at Redwall?"

"My spikes y'do! Summercream woodland puddens, deeper 'n' ever pies, strawb'rry flans, blueberry scones, raspb'rry muffins, cheeses you couldn't count, an' cordials, teas, wines an' October ale that me 'n' my ol' nuncle Gabe makes in our cellars!"

"And every creature is free there, Mr. Woodsorrel?"

"Free as the air, young feller, peaceful as the flowers that grow an' happy t' wake up among friends each dawn, wot!"

"Will you take us there, Dandin? Oh, please say you will!"

Dandin held up his paws. "Of course. You have my promise on it, though Mother Mellus'll probably grab you all and bathe the lot of you on sight!"

A small hedgehog sat enraptured with every word he had heard. "Mother! You mean they have a mother there? I can't remember having a mother. D'you think she'll be my mother too?"

"What's your name, young 'un?"

"Barty. That's my sister Dorcas. She's younger than me, I think."

Durry patted their soft unformed spikes. "You can live with me an' Nuncle Gabe. I'll teach 'ee t' be cellar 'ogs."

When Joseph returned with Mariel and Rawnblade a full meeting was called. Freed slaves crowded into the big cavern.

Rawnblade expressed surprise at the numbers. "Quite a sizable army, Joseph. I didn't think there was so many."

The bellmaker indicated a crowd packing the ledges at the rear. "Our Trag warriors who stole three of the searat ships have brought us many oarslaves who wish to join us. All of these have been landed from the three ships we captured. There must be close on a hundred new arrivals, though we are still far below in numbers compared to the searats."

Mariel stood alongside her father. "Not to worry, we've got their ships. It's the rats who are trapped on this island and not us. Besides, we'll have the advantage of cover and surprise. Lord Rawnblade, would you like to outline our plan?"

The badger took a charred stick from the fire and drew upon the rockface. "This is Fort Bladegirt. We will attack tonight when they are sleeping. These three tunnels come out into the hills both sides and behind the fort. Mariel, you and your friends will lead one-third of our force to attack from the left. Joseph my friend, you will lead the other third from the right, that way they will be under pressure from both sides. My Mariel will tell you what to do."

Mariel took over, flattered that such a warrior as the Lord of Salamandastron was consulting her judgment, recognizing in the mousemaid a fellow warrior spirit.

"Use bows and slings. Don't attempt to climb the walls into the courtyard. Stay well hidden and use the ground above the tunnel entrances—that way we can send arrows and stones down at them—but remain silent, don't give the searats any noisy or standing targets to fire back at, and keep slinging rocks and firing arrows as hard as you can. Tarquin, once the rats are occupied in fighting us on both sides you will attack the front gates of the courtyard. Take the rest of the force with you, and make as much noise as possible. You will have a battering ram to smash away at the gates with. We will besiege them from three sides. Tarquin, your squad will be armed with spears, bows and long pikes. Got that?"

"Understood, old scout. What happens then?"

"I come from the back!" Lord Rawnblade explained. "I will pick my moment—it will be when most of the searats are defending the front gate from your battering ram. Outside the tunnel at the rear of the fort is a big boulder on the hillside. I will send it down the hill to smash through the rear courtyard wall. Joseph, the moment you see the boulder start to roll, bring your force down from the right to back me up. Mariel, you bring your creatures down from the left to join Woodsorrel. I'm banking on the rats doing an about-turn and coming to face me. If the ram hasn't battered the gates down, you must prop it against them and use it as a ladder. Well, that is the plan: first they'll be attacked from the left and right, then from the front and back. Once we are inside the courtyard we can force our way into the fort itself, then it's good luck to whoever finds Gabool."

By unanimous decision the plan was voted a good one.

Joseph stood to have a final word with the occupants of the cavern. Gray-furred as he was, the bellmaker stood tall in their eyes, the suffering and indignities he had put up with etching his strong face, righteous vengeance ringing out from his voice like the sound of his own great bell.

"Hear me. This is the time I have waited for; we will rid the earth of searats for all seasons to come. No more are you slaves, you are the fighters of Trag. If victory is ours tomorrow, we have ships to sail away from this accursed island. Let us leave this place deserted, as a monument to the death and misery it has caused to creatures everywhere!"

When the wild cheering had died down, the two small hedgehogs Barty and Dorcas called out. "We're going to Redwall Abbey to live!"

Rawnblade picked them both up, one in each huge paw. "If I know the good creatures of that place . . . you're all going there!"

The cavern echoed and re-echoed to the wild applause of Trag warriors, none of them knowing what the morrow would bring, but each one fervently wishing his or her desire to go and live in the fabled Redwall.

38

Graypatch and his band were lost.

They stumbled about in the vastnesses of Mossflower Woods, not knowing which direction to take next. Each place they arrived at looked the same as the spot they had started from.

Oak Tom sat high in a chestnut tree, watching them. He tested the point of his lance and shook his head. "Wouldn't leave 'em in charge of a Dibbuns' spring outin', any of 'em!"

Deadglim slumped wearily on the ground. "Belay, Cap'n, you sure you know the right course fer *Darkqueen*?"

Graypatch turned on him and vented his temper. "I did when we started out, but you wetnosed idiots a-wanderin' here an' yon scroungin' fer vittles have set me off course. I'm as lost as the rest o' yer, an' it's your fault, not mine!"

Dripnose threw himself down beside Lardgutt. "Yah, what's the use? I'm stayin' 'ere until somebeast finds the right way!"

Graypatch sat down with him, his voice dripping sarcasm. "Oh, you are, are yer? So be it. I am too, matey. This way nobeast'll find the *Darkqueen* an' we'll all sit right 'ere an' rot!"

Fishgill came up with a suggestion. "Cap'n, why don't we split into three groups? We could each set course a different way, mark the trees as we go an' all make our way back 'ere when somerat finds *Darkqueen*."

Graypatch thought about this for a moment, then stood up. "Fishgill, matey, that's the first decent idea to come out o' this load of lunkheads. Right, you take five an' go thataways. Dripnose, up on yer claws, take five an' head the other way, over there. I'll take the other five an' go straight ahead. Don't ferget an' use your blades to mark the trees, otherwise you'll be lost forever in this hellridden forest. Right, let's get goin'."

Oak Tom watched them go before leaping down to scar false routes widespread on the treebark with his lancepoint. The squirrel carefully noted the direction taken by Graypatch and his party, then set out after the five led by Deadglim. Pushing through the brambles and tripping over tree roots, Deadglim and his rats unwittingly made their course south, back the way they had come, completely lost and in their confusion taking a bumbling path toward Redwall Abbey.

"Turn round and follow Fishgill!"

Lardgutt pointed into the leafy canopy. "It's a voice from up there."

Deadglim clawed nervously at his sword. "What d'yer want from us?"

"I'm from the Abbey," the mystery voice called back to him. "We don't want you attacking us again. You're headed for Redwall if you keep on in this direction. Turn round and follow Fishgill. He's traveling in the direction of your ship *Darkqueen*!"

Lardgutt carried on south, calling up in a sneering voice, "Aaahh, you could be trickin' us. I think this way's the right way!"

The javelin hissed down from the branches, slaying him on the spot.

This time the voice was loud and menacing. "Take my word for it, fools die! There are many of us up here. Turn round and follow Fishgill, if you value my advice!"

Deadglim did a swift about-turn. "We're going, look, we're going! Leave us alone and we won't be back!"

A mocking laugh rang out through the trees. "Go then. Quickly!"

Oak Tom plucked the javelin from Lardgutt's carcass as the pounding paws of Deadglim's party receded into the distance. Before nightfall they would join Fishgill's party, in the Flitchaye territory. Oak Tom took one look back to the south, where his friends Rufe Brush and Treerose would be giving Clary and Thyme a decent burial at the deserted searat camp. Setting his jaw grimly, he took off through the woodlands on the trial of Graypatch and the remaining five.

The searat Captain did not know whether to be delighted or disappointed. He stepped out of the foliage and onto the path, leading north with his companions, having traveled in a huge semicircle.

"Well, at least we're clear of all that tangle fer a while, mateys. Maybe now we can get some proper bearin's."

A rat named Stumpclaw strained his eyes northward up the path. "Ahoy, Cap'n. There's a ford up ahead. I can see the sunlight on its waters!"

Relief flooded through Graypatch's body. He sat down by the side of the path, a tear forming in his single eye.

"If it's water it'll run to the sea, mateys, an' it'll take us to *Darkqueen* if it's the right stream. Stumpclaw, take these buckos an' scout the lay o' the water, will yer, matey. Ole Graypatch is weary, I'll be restin' me bones 'ere awhile till you get back."

On a spruce bough not too far distant, Oak Tom sat watching.

Graypatch let the summer sun play on his face as he lay back and relaxed. The stream must lead up to *Darkqueen*, and then down to the sea. Maybe a few more dawns would see him in command of his own ship once more, running south before the breeze, away from Mossflower and the seas where Gabool's vessels hunted.

Sleep was just about to embrace Graypatch when loud screams rent the still air. Silently Oak Tom trailed him as he made his way cautiously to the ford. Using the trees to the side of the path as cover, Graypatch sneaked up to within a short distance of the water.

Iraktaan stood over the carcass of Stumpclaw, his vicious beak dripping red. "Iraktaan kill. Kraaaaak!"

Behind him in the swift-running weed-streaked waters of the ford, the bodies of the three who had made it to the water bounced and bobbed in a grotesque parody of life, though it was only the ripping jaws of the pike shoal which moved them.

Graypatch cut east into the woodlands, avoiding the killer heron and following the course of the stream, voicing his thoughts aloud as he went.

"I'll find the *Darkqueen*, sure as eggs is eggs. Foller the stream—that's all ye do, matey, foller the stream. Haharr, I'll sit aboard me ol' ship an' wait fer the others. No chance Graypatch is goin' t' get lost amid all that forest agin. No sir!"

As the sun grew hotter Graypatch knelt to drink from the stream. He sucked long and noisily, feeling the cool flow of fresh water crossing his chin. Suddenly lifting his face clear of the stream, the searat Captain felt his neck hairs rising. Without turning he knew there was somebeast behind him. A vague blur showed on the surface of the swift-running water, masking the stranger's identity.

Instinctively the searat's claw reached for his sword. "Who are yer?"

The stranger's voice was as cold as north wind on wet stones. "My name would mean nothing to you, rat!"

Graypatch played for time, slowly inching the sword from his belt. "What d'ye want with me, then? I mean yer no harm."

A blow from a lance butt sent him sprawling into the stream. He stood up in the shallows, spluttering. His face was a mask of vengeance. Oak Tom stood on the bank, lance held loose but ready.

"The time for your reckoning is due, searat. Now you must pay for the lives of two hares. Tell me, how does it feel, standing there without your crew to protect you?"

Graypatch swallowed hard, his own voice sounding squeaky in his ears. "Leave me alone, I only want ter get out o' here. Let me go and I won't bother ye anymore. I just want t' get to the sea!"

Oak Tom raised the lance. "Then you shall go to the sea!"

Graypatch had his sword free now, but the squirrel's face was so full of vengeance and rage that the searat's natural boldness and cunning deserted him completely. The sword fell from his nerveless claws into the water as he turned and ran with the flowing stream.

It was fully three days later that Graypatch made it to the sea, floating faceup with Oak Tom's lance standing out from his corpse like a mast with no sail. The two gallant hares of the long patrol had been avenged and Redwall Abbey was freed of further trouble. All with one swiftly thrown lance.

Two hours after dawn next day, set up by a full Redwall breakfast, the creatures of the Abbey began to set their home right again. Fire damage was repaired, crops and orchard tended back to their former fruitfulness, the pond was weeded and cleared of charred fire-swingers, and the main gate had a team attending to it, armed with carpenter's tools and headed by Saxtus.

"Brother Hubert, Cockleburr, lend a paw with this new timber, please. Baby Grubb, I won't tell you again; put that hammer down."

"Burr, oi wants t' nokken 'ee nailers in, Sax'us."

"Well you can't, you're too small. Ah, Foremole, will you and your crew start sawing here—this part where the bottom of the gate is heavily charred. That's it, about there!"

"Yurr, Burgo, Drubber, do 'ee 'old gate still whoile oi saws."

Saxtus picked up some large clout nails. "Baby Grubb, drop that hammer. This instant!"

"Gurr, go boil yurr 'ead, bossy ol' Sax'us!"

"Owowowooch! Come here, you little ruffian!"

Grubb hid behind Sister Sage, who was pushing Hon Rosie's wheelchair. Saxtus hopped about, clenching his paw.

Sister Sage remonstrated with Grubb. "That was a very naughty thing to do, Dibbun."

"Arr, but maister Sax'us tol' oi t' drop 'ee 'ammer."

"Maybe he did. Still, it was no excuse for dropping it on his footpaw."

"Hurr, may'aps it weren't, tho' 'ee do darnce noicely, doant 'ee?"

Hon Rosie held her ribs and winced as she chuckled. "Whoohahahooh! You're an absolute savage, young Grubb!"

Grubb climbed onto the chair and sat upon Rosie's lap. "Yurr, Sax'us daresn't get oi naow, miz Rose."

Simeon felt the smooth grain of the newly planked oak. He pressed his nose against it and breathed in deeply. "That will make a stout door. Pity it loses its fragrance with the seasons and the weather, Bernard."

The Abbot led him away to the shade of the threshold wallsteps. "I feel that everything is going to be all right now, Simeon."

"Good, your senses are improving, my friend. I too can sense something."

"Oh, something I've missed? It's not that mole Burgo and his wild garlic again, is it?"

"Haha, no. I sense that we should do something about continuing construction on our bell tower. I've been meaning to tell you, I had a wonderful dream last night."

"Sshh!" the Abbot interrupted. "Don't mention Dandin or the others. Here comes Mellus. She looks in a happy mood this morning—let's try and keep her that way. Good morning, Mellus. Another beautiful day."

The badger nodded. "It was, until I spotted those two wretches over there. Bagg and Runn—look at them, covered from nose to tail with green gatehouse paint. I'll scrub the hides off the pair o' them!"

She took off at a trot, chasing the two green perils of Redwall.

"Sometimes I think she's only happy when she's got dirty Dibbuns to hurl into bathtubs!" Simeon whispered in the Abbott's ear.

39

Late the previous night six searats had been posted on guard duty by Captain Riptung—Felltooth and the rats who had swum out in vain pursuit of the *Waveblade*. Felltooth was not the most popular searat at Bladegirt, a fact that his mates kept reminding him of.

"Please sir, Cap'n sir, can I swim out an' bring that naughty ship back? Yer great turnipbrain, there was no chance o' catchin' *Waveblade* an' you knowed it."

Felltooth defended his unsuccessful action indignantly. "Ah, sharrap! I was tryin' t' get that craft back fer the likes of you 'n' me, matey. Don't yer realize, we're marooned on Terramort now!"

"Aye, well nex' time let some other dopes do the swimmin' an' you keep yer trap shut, cabingob. Ideas an' decisions is fer Cap'ns—that's why they're Cap'ns, see!"

The crack of the rock was audible in the darkness as it struck the speaker. He dropped without a sound. Felltooth leaned over him.

"Ere, are you all right matey? Yaaaagh!"

An arrow had gone right through Felltooth's ear. He straightened up and ran for the fort, screaming aloud, "Attack! Attaaaaaack!"

Still half-asleep, the searat horde were rousted out by Hookfin, Riptung and Grimtooth. They hurried into the courtyard surrounding Bladegirt, snatching weapons as they went.

"Stir yer stumps, y'dozy layabouts. We're under attack!"

"Come on, out there, every ratjack of ye. Move!"

"Pick up those weapons. Never mind yer fancy clothes—yer goin' to a fight not a dance!"

High in the rocks Dandin and Mariel drew back their bows, glancing along the line of Trag warriors as they drew bowstrings tight in unison. Durry Quill nodded. "Now!"

The arrows zipped off like a flight of angry wasps, straight down into the teeming courtyard, where even despite the night they could not miss among the large numbers of milling rats. As the archers dropped down to fit more shafts to their bows, a line of warriors behind them stood up whirling slings. Again Durry nodded. "Now!"

The rocks hurtled down, chunking into the searats below.

From a lower floor window Gabool the Wild grabbed hold of a passing searat, hauling him in bodily over the sill.

"What in the name of Hellfangs is a-goin' on out there?"

"Majesty, we're bein' attacked!"

"I can see that, idiot! Who is it doin' the attackin'?"

"Sire, I don't know, but we're bein' cut down by arrows an' rocks from both sides, left an' right!"

Gabool hauled the unfortunate off with him toward the banqueting hall. "It's the badger—I know it is. You stay outside the door an' sing out t' me as soon as y'see the badger. Hear?"

The terrified searat nodded dumbly, though no sooner

had Gabool gone into the banqueting hall and slammed the door than the young searat sneaked off back to the courtyard, where a hard-slung rock put an end to all his fears.

On the far hill Joseph was marshaling his troops to snipe from two different directions of the hillside, causing great confusion among the searats. They would turn to fire their bows in one direction, only to be hit from behind as they did.

Riptung ran up and down the courtyard in the dark, laying about with the flat of his sword as he yelled out, "Up there in the hills to yer left, dolts. Can't yer tell by the way those arrows 'n' stones are comin' in? 'Ere, gimme that bow, you!" He snatched the bow and arrow from a bewildered rat. Pulling the shaft taut on the bow, he held it as a row of archers ducked down. Riptung let the arrow fly as the slingbeasts stood up, and was rewarded with a faint cry from high on the hillside.

"See, that's the way to get 'em! Now get down behind the wall and use yer tiny brains. Up an' down! Quick like, same's they're doin' to us. There ain't that many of 'em, judgin' by their volleys."

Gradually the three Captains got the searats into some semblance of fighting crews, using all their cunning in reply to the surprise invasion.

Dandin caught a stray searat who had moved out of the wall cover. He glanced anxiously at Mariel. "Where's Tarquin got to?"

As if in reply a cry rang out from below. "Eulaliaaaaa!"

Whump! . . . Bump! . . . Thud!

The battering ram had begun its work on the front gates. Tarquin had his forces screaming and yelling as they charged with the ram.

"Trag! Trag! Trag! Eulaliaaaa! Trag! Trag! Trag!"

The massive treetrunk, still matted with earth and grass, pounded its blunt head against the quivering timbers of the gates.

Grimtooth dashed around to Riptung. "They're

smashin' the gates in, matey! Take your force from this side an' stand 'em off. I'll get Hookfin to do the same!"

Soon the searats were massed halfway between the fort building and the gates. They fired arrows upward in a curving arc. The shafts fell on the ram crew, slaying several with their first volley. Tarquin ordered his archers to return fire. "Give 'em blood an' vinegar, chaps. Fire!"

Gabool could see only the sea and the rocks below from the big banqueting hall window, but he darted around the slit windows on the other walls, the noise of battle ringing in his ears as he peered out at the dark shapes scurrying below. Dashing to the slit window on the far side, he stared out at the back hillside in horror. The badger had emerged from somewhere high upon the hill and stood there like some giant out of the worst nightmare, framed against the night sky, battlesword stuck in the ground beside him, clad in warhelm and breastplate.

Gabool stood framed in the big window, screaming threats and challenging the enemy who had haunted his waking dreams so long. But Rawnblade was only concerned with the task of the moment. Setting his paws against the vast boulder, he sucked air into his lungs, feeling his mighty chest swell against the metal breastplate. He pitted his weight and strength against the monolithic ball of rock; it budged slightly, then settled back. This time the badger threw his back against it, digging his blunt claws and wide footpads hard into the earth. He crouched and grunted with exertion as sweat trickled across his striped head, forcing his bulk into the boulder. This time it moved out of its depression in the stony soil. Feeling the mass move, Rawnblade attacked it with primeval ferocity. Roaring and bellowing, he hurled all his weight into the side of the formidable stone, sinew and muscle bunched as flesh hit rock. The boulder began to trundle away like some dread juggernaut, slowly at first, then gathering speed on the sloping hillside. Lord Rawnblade seized his battlesword. Throwing back his head he howled the war cry of Salamandastron to the night sky.

"Eulaliaaaaaa!"

The boulder crashed through the hill gorse, spinning and bouncing, a mighty stone ball of destruction, with the badger Lord charging in its wake. With a thunderous rumble it smashed through the wall, sending an explosion of sharded masonry high in the air. Either side of it sections of wall fell like wheat before a scythe. Several rats guarding the back wall stood paralyzed with fright as Rawnblade came bounding through the dustcloud in the shattered breach, followed by Joseph the Bellmaker and a chanting mass of Trag warriors.

"Trag! Trag! Trag! Redwaaaaalll!"

The rats at the main gates stopped shooting arrows. They turned to see what was happening at the back wall.

Riptung dashed through them. "Come on, they've burst through the walls back there!"

Reluctantly the searat archers turned to face the latest peril. Hookfin and Grimtooth shoving and pushing them toward the foe.

"Push 'em back, or we're done for, mates!"

"There ain't that many of 'em, we've got 'em outnumbered, buckos. Charge!"

Spurred on by desperation, the rats clashed with their attackers. Steel clashed against steel as both sides met like two waves crashing together. The bigger, more powerful searats in their barbaric finery did not intimidate the young Trag fighters, who threw themselves upon their hated oppressors with insane ferocity, hacking and cleaving as the melee swayed back and forth; but the rats were experienced skirmishers, each searat and his mate taking one Trag warrior between them, slashing and stabbing from back to front. Soon it became evident that Joseph's force would be routed, without reinforcements.

Rawnblade was fighting his own fight. The Bloodwrath had come upon him, his one aim was to get inside Bladegirt to find Gabool. Oblivious of Trag difficulties, he fought his way toward the fort, seeing nothing through the fiery red mist that engulfed his eyes but the building which contained his sworn enemy. Searats flew before the blade of Verminfate like butterflies caught in a gale.

Outside the main gates they heard the noise as the back wall was broken by the boulder. Within moments the searat arrows stopped raining over upon them. Mariel, Tarquin, Dandin and Durry lifted their heads and listened. The pounding of receding paws and the shouts that followed told them the battle was being joined inside.

Durry did a little dance of impatience. "Use the ram as a ladder. Quick, quick!"

Mariel weighed up and cracked and splintered gates. "No, there's twice as many of us now. Let's see what we can do against these gates. Right, Tarquin!"

"All paws now, every Tragjack of you, grab the ram. One, two, hup!" the hare roared out in his best parade ground voice.

Rank upon rank of willing paws gripped the battering ram, lifting it high above their heads with a rush of strength and energy. Tarquin shouted out commands from the front.

"Righto, chaps. Back up. Back, back, back—a bit more! Come on, you lot on the end, stop bunchin' together and back up. We need a good long run to gain momentum, wot! That's it, laddie buck. Back, back . . . Ah, that's more like it. Halt!"

Mariel stood with Dandin and Durry at the front of the ram, gazing down the long run toward the gates. Tarquin joined them, throwing his shoulder under the log and lifting it high.

"Listen up now, chaps. When I give the word, altogether, fast as y'can. Ready . . . Chaaaaaarge!"

Dust pounded and flew from under the thundering paws. Eyes wide and mouths agape, screaming and yelling bloodcurdling cries, the army of rammers with the log swaying madly above their heads tore onward to the gates in one single mad rush.

Whakkarraboom!!!

There was no sound of splintering timber, just a tremendous *whump*! Door, timbers, locks, bars and bolts, even the two impressive stone gateposts, were knocked flat as if hit by a thunderbolt. Carried on in the momentum of the heroic charge, the rammers clattered across the fallen gates and over the courtyard, the battering ram still held high.

Swept on in the rush, with the blood singing through his eardrums like a high-pitched siren, Durry Quill yelled aloud, "Eeyahoooo!"

The battering ram hit the rear of the searat hordes, scattering them like ninepins. Over the clamor of battle Joseph laughed in relief. The reinforcements had arrived in a spectacular manner.

Riptung knew the tide had turned. He strove madly to group a fighting force about him, but the searats ignored his cries, each fighting with the strength of despair. The searat Captain whirled his curved sword with long-born expertise, taking out a vole and a field-mouse, only to find himself confronted by Dandin. The blade of Martin the Warrior flashed in the young mouse's paws as he closed in to attack. Riptung parried, frantically backing to get creatures between himself and the cold-eyed swordsmouse. The searat tried every move and trick he knew, but his assailant kept coming on, battering the curved corsair sword aside ferociously until he had Riptung backed up to the wall. Above the clash of battle Riptung swung his sword high for a downward slash, screeching in Dandin's face, "You'll never take me alive!"

Dandin slew him with a strong upward swing. "I don't want you alive, rat!"

Hookfin saw that the battle was lost. He sneaked away before the total rout of all the searats, skirting the edges of the fray until he found the section of the back wall that the boulder had smashed through. Without a backward glance he slipped out onto the hillside, with a sigh of relief that died upon his lips. Sitting in front of him on a rock was the impassive vole Tan Loc. Hookfin froze. Drawing his long sword, Tan Loc whetted it against the rock, speaking in a flat voice without even looking at Hookfin. "I've been waiting for you."

• • •

Back at the battle, Joseph found himself fighting for his life. A searat was choking him from behind as Grimtooth swung his cutlass in front. The bellmaker parried each thrust as he fought to shake off the rat, who clung behind him like a leech. Grimtooth slashed furiously, knowing the death of a leader might turn the tide of battle back in favor of the searats. He smiled grimly as the gray-haired mouse began to weaken, and closed in for the kill.

"Redwaaalll!"

Mariel leaped off the back of a falling rat, swinging her Gullwhacker. Grimtooth turned. Catching the full force of the blow between his eyes, he dropped like a log. Durry Quill took the strangler from behind with a rock from the wall debris.

Tarquin fought his way through to them, a broken lance clutched in his paws.

"One more good sally an' they're finished, chaps, I say, wot!" He turned this way and that, bobbing up and down. "Where's me old boss got to? Anybeast seen Lord Rawnblade?"

Mariel struck off into the mêlée. "No. Come on, let's find him!"

They were joined by Dandin as they dodged around skirmishing groups.

The steps up to Fort Bladegirt were littered with dead searats. Durry picked his way between them, pointing with his dagger at the big oak door, which had been hacked almost to splinters and hung crazily on one hinge.

"Ha! Betcher Rawnblade did this wi' that great tree-chopper o' his."

Mariel strode past Durry into the building. "We'll see who gets Gabool!"

40

Saxtus gazed out from the ramparts of Redwall. The sun cast cloud shadows onto the path and across the greenery of the woodlands; fleecy clouds scudded across the sky on a warm breeze. The days of summer season were numbered now.

Simeon joined him, his paws feeling along the battlements until he came in contact with Saxtus.

"The autumn will arrive soon, Saxtus."

"How did you know what I was thinking, Brother?"

Simeon chuckled and patted Saxtus's paw. "I didn't, it was just an educated guess. Creatures often think I have wondrous powers, but it's just experience and observation. Though I do sense that you have more reason than the change of seasons for standing up here. It comes to me that you are watching the road. Would I be wrong in supposing that you are awaiting the return of certain friends?"

Saxtus searched the blind herbalist's wise old face. "You are right, of course, but it doesn't take a genius to know that. Dandin and Durry were my best friends—

Mariel too, for the short time she was with us. I had a dream, you see, the night before last. It was of a great battle, I saw them fighting with searats, like the crew who attacked our Abbey, but there were many many more than that."

"Was it through Martin the Warrior that this dream came?"

"Ah, now you do surprise me. What makes you say that, Simeon?"

"Oh, we are old friends, the spirit of the Abbey and I. Martin has visited me more than once in the land of sleep. You must always heed his warnings. What did you see of this battle?"

"It was not very clear. I saw an old gray mouse, quite a big fellow. He was being attacked by two searats. I cried out in my dream for Martin to help him. Mariel and Durry Quill rescued him. There was lots of fighting, a great battle—things weren't very clear though, and it all faded after a while, Martin too."

"I say, yoohoo! You two up there, what's the matter? Don't you want to try my seedcake?"

It was Hon Rosie waving from her wheelchair. Friar Alder and Cockleburr were pushing it, both their faces pictures of strained patience.

"We'll talk about this another time," Simeon whispered to Saxtus. Turning in the direction of the wheelchair, he waved. "Seedcake, did you say? I used to be a fair cook at making that myself. Hold on, we'll come down and try some. Give me your paw, Saxtus."

Lunch was being served in Great Hall. As they entered, Mellus nudged Foremole, murmuring in a low voice, "Here's another two victims being brought in to sample the dreaded seedcake. What Rosie made it with I don't know."

"Burr, you'm can say that agin. Oi near broken moi diggen claws just picken up a sloice, marm."

Rosie leaned from her chair, scanning the table. "I say, where's me jolly old seedcake gone? You haven't scoffed it all, have you? Well, that's the bally limit. I suppose I'll have to bake another."

"Er, no seeds left, marm," Friar Alder interrupted swiftly.

Cockleburr tugged the Friar's sleeve. "Perishin' puddens, Friar. There's a great box of seeds at the back of the floursacks, I found it meself this m—Oof!"

Alder elbowed his assistant sharply in the stomach and carried on smoothly. "Oh, those seeds, you mean. They've got damp and were beginning to sprout, I was meaning to leave them out for the birds. Oh dear, not a single seed in the kitchens or the storerooms. What a shame!"

Underneath the table, Grubb and Bagg were using the remains of the seedcake as building blocks. "We'll have to get miz Rosie more seeds if we wanna make a model of the Abbey," Bagg grumbled as he looked about for more.

"Hurrhurr, Froir Alder'll scrangle 'ee iffen you'm mention et."

"I s'pose so. I heard 'im say to the Habbit that he hopes miz Rosie'll get better afore she kills us all wi' seedcakes."

Saxtus wandered through to watch some creatures working on the great Abbey tapestry. Brother Hubert was supervising the design from sketches he had found in the gatehouse. He tossed a hank of light brown thread to Sister Serena.

"This color should suit if you're starting the face of the Warrior."

Saxtus sorted a thread out of a slightly darker tone. "Excuse me, Brother, but I think this shade is the correct one."

Hubert held it up to the light, inspecting it carefully. "Hmm, you could be right, Saxtus, but how do you know that this is the color of Martin's face?"

"I sort of sensed it."

• • •

Lord Rawnblade Widestripe strode through the entrance hall of Fort Bladegirt, the sword Verminfate sending out showers of sparks as he clashed it against the stone columns leading to the main stairway.

"Gabool, it is I, Rawnblade the badger. Show yourself!"

The rumble of the badger Lord's challenge echoed back at him from empty chambers and deserted corridors as he mounted the stairs, his keen dark eyes searching everywhere. Rawnblade sniffed, but the odor of searat permeated the air throughout and he could not distinguish the scent of his enemy. Kicking aside the debris of cast-off clothing, useless weaponry and stale food the rats had left behind, he ascended the wide stone stairs.

Heedless of whether the rats had won or lost the battle, Gabool listened to the sounds of the badger ringing through his fort as he nerved himself up for the confrontation he knew would inevitably come. Gripping both sword and dagger, the Searat King ranged about his upper chamber, holding a muttered conference with himself.

"Hahaar, I'll sleep tonight. Once I'm rid of the badger, I'll destroy that useless bell. Aye, that's it! Kill the badger an' roll the bell off the high cliffs inter the sea. What'll be left to worry me then? I've seen 'em all off—Graypatch, Saltar, Bludrigg. Look out, badger. You're next, an' the bell to follow yer! Then they'll see who's the Ruler of Terramort—me, Gabool, King of Searats. I'll build a new fleet, each craft bigger an' faster than *Darkqueen*. They'll scour the coasts for slaves, fine silks, wine an' the best of prime vittles. Haharr, Gabool won't need no bell to announce hisself; they'll know who I am wherever they see my ships hove in an' hear me name."

"Gabool, you spawn of Hell, where are you?"

The deep thunder of Rawnblade's voice vibrated upward from the banqueting hall. Gabool pressed an ear to his room door.

"Keep searchin', badger. I'll lead you a merry dance before I'm done with yer. Gabool ain't feared of a stripedog no more. Oh no, matey!"

• • •

Rawnblade stood before the great bell. It was exactly as he had imagined it. Only a bellmaker with the skills of Joseph could create such a wonder. His hefty paw stroked the stained and discolored surface of the brazen object as he walked around it, reading the mysterious badger hieroglyphics near the belltop, smiling with satisfaction at the message only a badger Lord could interpret.

"That is yet to come. . . . But meanwhile!"

Rawnblade smashed a wooden stool with one blow of his sword. Picking up a severed stool leg, he began belaboring the bell.

Bongboombongaboombongbong!

As he struck the bell, Rawnblade breathed upon a section of the metal and rubbed it clean. He continued to smite the great bell, harder and louder.

Boombongboomboombongbooooongggg!

Peering at the polished section, the badger watched Gabool enter the banqueting hall and begin creeping up on him, sword raised to strike. Rawnblade stopped beating the bell and turned slowly.

"So, you like my music, eh, rat?"

Gabool leaped forward, his sword flashing down like lightning. Rawnblade swung his battlesword sideways, the power of the sweep knocking Gabool's blade flying; it clattered into a corner. The searat stood helpless, his paws deadened by the numbing force of the blow. Rawnblade nodded to the curved sword lying on the floor. "Pick it up and have a proper try!"

Mariel came dashing into the banqueting hall with Joseph, Tarquin, Dandin and Durry. The mousemaid swung her Gullwhacker, shouting, "Stand and fight, rat!"

Gabool cackled harshly. "The bellmaker's brat, eh? Go away, mouse. I've killed you once. You're naught but a ghost!"

Mariel's jaw tightened as the Gullwhacker whirled above her head. "You're wrong, seascum. I'm no ghost! I beat you once and I'm going to do it again, this time for good!"

From the corner of her eye Mariel saw the badger Lord move to attack.

"Gabool's mine, Rawnblade!"

The badger turned his head in her direction. As he did, Gabool plunged the dagger into his chest and sped through a door on the other side of the room. As the door slammed they ran to the badger Lord. He was standing straight, with the dagger protruding. Before anybeast could speak, Rawnblade pulled the dagger out and tossed it aside.

"Nearly grazed my fur when it pierced the breastplate—not bad steel for a searat dagger!"

Tarquin was tugging and shoving at the door. "Blighter's locked it!"

"Out of the way, Woodsorrel. Hurry!" Tarquin barely had time to leap aside as a stroke from Verminfate split the door in two halves. Lord Rawnblade kicked them flat.

"Don't interrupt me next time, mousemaid!"

The stairs in front of them spiraled downward. Keeping one paw against the side wall, they hurried around the dizzying curves.

Gabool slammed the door closed and barred it. Chuckling to himself, he moved an old carpet from a corner of the room and spread it over the hole in the floor. Standing on the far side of it, he went into a crouch, claws stretching forward. Soon he heard his pursuers arriving. There was a rending crash and the door swung lopsidedly on a single hinge. Rawnblade thrust it aside as he stepped into the room, brandishing his sword. He glanced about at the bare walls.

"The running's over, rat. There's nowhere for you to go."

"Aye, so 'tis." Gabool sneered. "You're well backed up by your friends and fully armed too. I thought badgers were true warriors. Why don't yer throw down that great doorcleaver an' meet me in paw t' claw combat, searat fashion. Or are yer just a great cowardly stripedog?"

The red mists of Bloodwrath clouded Lord Rawnblade's eyes as he flung his sword aside and came at Gabool with a mighty roar.

"Eulaliaaaa!"

For an instant Gabool's blood froze within him at the sight of the huge badger charging forward. Then Rawnblade stood on the carpet. He plunged down into the hole with a sharp bark of alarm, falling flat on his back at the bottom of the pit. There was a scuttling noise and Rawnblade shouted aloud, "Stay away!"

Mariel and her companions hesitated in the doorway.

The massive black scorpion rattled out at breathtaking speed. It was on Rawnblade before he could move. His eyes went wide with horror at the sight of the loathsome beast perched on his breastplate. Clicking claws held menacingly wide, it began to bring the venomous barbed sting on its tail up over its back to strike at the badger's unprotected face.

Suddenly some unseen force galvanized Rawnblade into instant action. His paw shot up, grabbing the scorpion by the curve of its tail, and with a mighty bellow he jumped upright. Whirling the evil creature around, he flung it swiftly from the pit. The black scorpion shot up at an angle, striking the ceiling and dropping down—straight into the face of Gabool the Wild.

From the doorway they watched in horrified fascination as the searat leaped frenziedly about the room, feebly struggling with the angry creature locked onto his throat with both claws. It covered his face, muffling the gurgled screams as the lethal tail sent its hooked sting slamming over the top of his head into the base of the skull, whipping back and forth as it stabbed in a maddened frenzy.

Rawnblade heaved himself out of the pit in time to see Gabool fall to the floor, his limbs twitching spasmodically as poison flooded through his crazed brain. The King of the Searats shuddered one last time and died, his body arched back like a straining bow.

Dandin rushed into the room as the scorpion turned its attention to Lord Rawnblade. The young mouse swung the sword of Martin the Warrior.

Once! Twice! Thrice!

The two halves of the terrible creature toppled awkwardly back into its pit, still clicking and striking with its poisonous tailsting.

Rawnblade shuddered. He rubbed his paws together vigorously, as if trying to cleanse himself of the scorpion's touch.

Tarquin addressed his harolina consolingly. "Well, me old twanger, you never got to brain Gabool, after all. Matter o' fact, none of us did. What a shameful waste of such jolly good weapons!"

Joseph put a paw around his daughter's shoulders. "Evil destroyed evil, and good triumphed. Come on, Mariel. Let us leave Terramort. The nightmare is over."

Mariel hugged her father fondly. "Let's go to Redwall!"

Four ships lay ready to sail from the cove at Terramort. Captain Durry Quill stood at the helm of *Waveblade*, renamed *Gabriel* after his favorite "nuncle." Captain Tarquin L. Woodsorrel now commanded the *Hon Rosie*, formerly the *Blacksail*. Captain Dandin rested his paw on the tiller of *Nightwake*, renamed the *Abbot Bernard*. The *Crabclaw* had been restored to her former name, *Periwinkle*, at the wish of her new Captain, Joseph the Bellmaker. He stood proudly with Mariel and Rawnblade on her swaying deck, watching the crew of former oarslaves tying down the final lashings of the great bell. Above them a huge hole gaped in the seaward side of Fort Bladegirt, where the bell had been lowered to the *Periwinkle*'s deck. Dark smoke curled from the breach in the fort as Rawnblade nodded his head in satisfaction.

"I've never used fire on anything in my life, but I was glad to put the torch to that evil building. It will never burn away its memory, but maybe someday in the seasons to come the wind and rains from the seas will scour its blackened stones clean."

Joseph patted the deckrail. "Good old *Periwinkle*. Remember when we first set sail in her, Mariel? Now we can complete that voyage and deliver Lord Rawnblade's bell to Salamandastron, where it belongs."

But the badger Lord had other ideas. "No, friend Joseph, this bell must go to Redwall Abbey, and I will tell you the reason why. When I was down that pit with the scorpion on me I was in the grip of Bloodwrath and did not know what was going on. The creature would have killed me. However, I was saved by Martin the Warrior. It was his spirit that entered me and enabled me to act so quickly. He saved my life, so I must repay him."

Dandin touched the hilt of the sword. "Good old Martin! So it was he who really slew Gabool—or was it him through you, sir, or was it just a bad-tempered scorpion? We'll never know. What do you say, Mariel?"

"I say, here, take this little swallow and hang it where my father can see it. Give me your sword. You won't need it for a moment."

Armed with the sword of Martin the Warrior, the mousemaid stood high on the bowsprit and shouted her orders to the little fleet.

"Hoist anchors and set all sails! There's a running tide and fair wind to take us to the shores of Mossflower country and Redwall!"

The great bell gave out a mighty boom as Rawnblade struck it. The sound echoed around the headlands, mingled with the joyful cheers from hundreds of free creatures as the breeze filled the sails and carried the four vessels out onto the seas in golden summer sunlight.

41

The seasons turned and autumn arrived in due course. Though Saxtus and his friend Simeon kept up their vigil on the ramparts of Redwall, there was still no sign of the returning travelers. The Abbey orchard was now in burgeoning fruitfulness, and each day the crop gatherers were busy with ladders, long poles and industrious energy as they picked and basketed the plums, apples, damsons, pears and berries of many different varieties. The kitchens were working at full capacity, cooking, preserving and storing the fruits. Gabriel Quill's cellar was also a hive of activity; cordials, wines, squashes and October ale were being squeezed, brewed and fermented. The days of autumn continued fine and warm, though darkness started to draw in earlier. Peace and plenty had returned to the Abbey; every creature was happy.

Well, nearly every creature . . .

The three little Dibbuns, Bagg, Runn and Grubb, were totally dissatisfied with their lot and feeling highly mutinous. Two, three, sometimes even four scrubbings a day were commonplace for them during harvesttime. They had been caught in different color changes by Mother Mellus and the good Sisters who cared for them, purple from blackberries, crimson from redcurrants, yellow from greengages, green from gooseberries and generally filthy from climbing trees, falling into bushes, being covered in dust from the cellars, or appearing coated in oven grime and ashes from the kitchen ovens.

Besides being sent to bed early for cheeking some venerable Abbey dwellers, the three miscreants were now being instructed in sewing by Brother Hubert, so that they could repair their own ripped clothing. Hubert had also hinted darkly that they would soon be attending gatehouse school and Abbey history study.

This news was the final clincher, being met with awful scowls and rebellious mutterings, and culminating in the terrible trio swearing a deathly oath underneath a dormitory bed, where they were hiding from their latest misdeeds. They were leaving the Abbey the very next morning to seek their fortunes far afield, or as Grubb succinctly put it, "Sumplace where gurt beasties doant keep scrubben an' barthen us'ns!"

Dawn came soft and misty with warm sunlight, turning the low-lying shrouds of mist from white to pale yellow. The three Dibbuns let themselves out by the north wallgate and trundled up that path, rustling the carpet of brown leaves brought down by autumnal night winds. Each of them had a kerchief bulging with food swinging from a stick across his shoulder, and their mood was decidedly carefree as they strode out with a will.

"Wait'll ol' Ma Mell's finds us'ns are gone. I bet she shakes 'er head an' says 'oh dearie me' a lot then, eh?"

"Heeheehee, she won't 'ave nobeast to chuck inna tub an' scrub no more."

"Hurr, oi 'spect she'll scrub Gab'l an' Froir an' the Habbit. Serve 'em roight!"

"An' we'll be far, far 'way an' all mucky f'rever. Hahahaha!"

"An we won't go t' bed no more an' learn hist'ry off Bruvver Hoobit."

"Burr aye, an' woant they all be a-cryen fer us. Boohoohoo, 'ee'll say, whurr be all they luvverly Dibbuns a-gone?"

"Aaahhhh, will they? Never mind, we'll come back when us'ns are big 'uns, eh?"

"Oh aye, an' we'll spank 'em all an baff'em an scoff everythin'!"

"Hurrhurr, that'll teach 'em a lessing!"

Late breakfast turned into early lunch as they sat at the side of the path, telling each other what tyrants they would be when they returned to the Abbey fully grown. Suddenly Runn squeaked with fright. The three Dibbuns sat petrified at the sight of a giant armored badger who had strolled up out of the mists.

With a strange light in his dark eyes, he swung his massive sword high and placed it into the carrier straps on his back. The badger knelt down, bringing his wide-striped head close to their terrified faces. His voice was growling, deep, but gentle as he could make it.

"Well well, what have we here, three marauders lying in wait for poor honest travelers?"

"U-u-us'ns be oanly Dibbuns, zurr."

"Dibbuns, eh? A likely story. You look more like bloodthirsty rogues to me. All right then, supposing you are Dibbuns, where are you from?"

Bagg found his tongue. "Please sir, Redwall Habbey, sir!"

Rawnblade lifted them carefully in his hefty battle-scarred paws. "Redwall Habbey—I think I may know that place. You'd better come with me. I'll soon find out if you're telling me the truth."

The badger made his way through the hordes of Trag warriors eating breakfast at the side of the path. He halted by a wide flat wooden cart with a great bell upon it. The three Dibbuns sat gazing at their reflections in the burnished metal surface of the bell as they perched upon Rawnblade's paws, their legs swinging over the big blunt claws. Lord Rawnblade lowered them toward Dandin and Durry, winking at the two friends as he did.

"I've just captured these three searat Captains. They were waiting down the way apiece, probably to ambush us and steal our bell."

Dandin and Durry played along with the badger.

"It's as well you did. They look like born killers to me."

"Aye, these searats are all the same, y'know."

Grubb tried reasoning with his captors. "Oh gurraway, oi'm a moler an' they be two hotterfolk. You'm be Dan'in an' maister Quill, oi knows 'ee!"

Rawnblade burst out laughing. "Hohoho! Well said! We'll take you back to Redwall with us."

Bagg held a paw to his snout, confidentially whispering to Rawnblade, "I wouldn't if I was you. Ma Mell's will chuck you all inna tub an' scrub you sumfink awful!"

The orchard workers had halted for a midmorning break and jugs of cider and slices of plumcake were passed around.

Mother Mellus searched around the berry bushes worriedly. "Anybeast here seen three Dibbuns, Bagg, Runn and Grubb?"

Saxtus stood up helpfully. "Do you want me to go and look for them?"

The badger plumped down wearily next to Simeon and accepted a beaker of new cider. "I'd be most grateful if you did, Saxtus. I've run my aching old bones ragged searching for those three rips."

As the young mouse trotted off on a tour of the Abbey grounds Mellus refilled Simeon's beaker.

"What a fine young creature our Saxtus is. I remember he wasn't any great trouble as a Dibbun, always a fairly serious and obedient little thing. Not like some I could name."

The blind herbalist smiled. "You're a proper old fraud, Mellus. You wouldn't know what to do with yourself if all our Dibbuns were quiet, serious and obedient. It makes the seasons happier having a few little pickles around."

• • •

Having searched in the most likely hiding places, Saxtus mounted the wallsteps and scoured the ramparts. Starting at the south wall, he worked his way along to the east battlements, covering every recess and niche, each moment expecting to come upon the three little ones hiding in some favorite corner. He had hidden up here many a time with Dandin and Durry when they were small; all the best secret hideouts were known to him.

Saxtus could feel the anxiety beginning to gnaw at him. He had searched every possible place and still there was no sign of the missing trio. He leaned his back against the northwest walltop corner, looking down into the Abbey grounds, mentally ticking off each place he had covered. The three little ones were definitely missing, but there was no need to upset Mother Mellus yet—they might still be somewhere in the vicinity. Saxtus turned to look up the path. For a moment he could scarcely believe his eyes, he felt his whole body begin to shake and tremble with excitement. Paws twitching and teeth chattering, he blinked and rubbed his eyes to reassure himself he was not witnessing a mirage. He was not! He stood for some time, exerting all his willpower to gain control of himself.

Refreshment time was over in the orchard. Picking up their baskets, the harvesters were about to go back to work. Saxtus's voice rang out level and loud from the ramparts.

"Father Abbot, Mother Mellus, bring everybody with you. Come up here and look at this!"

Mellus and the Abbot, with Simeon between them, rounded the corner of the Abbey building, a crowd of Redwallers following them.

"Saxtus. Hi, Saxtus, what is it?"

"Have you found the Dibbuns, Saxtus?"

The young mouse turned and called back to the swelling band of Redwallers, "Come up here, this is very important, I think you should all see this!"

Now every creature in the Abbey was striding across the lawns, from the orchards, kitchens, Great Hall, Cavern Hole, dormitories and gatehouse, overcome with curiosity.

"I hope it ain't more searats, marm!"

"In the name of all fur, what is it?"

"Hoi, Saxtus, what's all this about?"

But Saxtus had turned his back on them and was staring out at the path from the north, ignoring their shouts.

Mellus quickend her pace. "Ooh, he was always very aggravating as a Dibbun was that one!"

Every creature in the Abbey was now ranged along the wall staring dumbfounded at the sight before them. It was Gabriel Quill who broke the silence. Scrambling up onto a battlement, he waved his paws wildly as he shouted, "They've come back! Oh, Durry me heart, it's me, yer ol' nuncle Gabriel!"

The hedgehog's call seemed to trigger everything. A mighty roaring cheer rose from the walltops; caps and aprons were flung in the air as the Redwallers danced up and down, waving and cheering at the top of their lungs, stamping their paws and howling pure joy to the skies.

"They're back! Oh look, they're back! Hooraaaaaay!!!"

On the path the horde of Trag warriors with the great bell in their midst ground to a halt at Rawnblade's signal.

Mariel stood atop the bell. She loosed her Gullwhacker and began swinging it in circles above her head.

Tarquin winked at her. "Go on, old gel, let 'em know you jolly well did it!"

The mousemaid swung the heavily knotted rope down with both paws.

Boooooommmmmm!

The deep melodious sound echoed out across the brown and russet woodlands in the fine autumn morn.

"Eulaliaaaaa! Trag! Trag! Trag! Redwaaaaalll!"

The answer to Redwall's cheers rent the air as the warriors roared out their battle cry. Sitting on top of Lord Rawnblade's war helmet, Grubb joined paws with Bagg and Runn, who were perched on the badger's shoulders.

Between them they yelled as loudly as any battle-hardened soldier.

Abbot Bernard stood in front of the open gateway, paws tucked into wide habit sleeves. His voice quivered noticeably as he addressed the four travelers who stood with Lord Rawnblade at the head of the army.

"You have come a very long way to be at Redwall Abbey. . . . Welcome home!"

42

Extract from the writings of Abbot Saxtus:

The seasons turn slowly with the earth, Redwall stones grow aged and mellow, and I thank fortune that we live peacefully within our Abbey. The old ones are still with us, I am happy to say: Joseph, Simeon, Hubert and old Abbot Bernard. I sat with them this afternoon, on the rickety remains of the wooden bellcart in the orchard. We talked of bygone times as we lounged about in the warmth of this long summer. Bagg, Runn and Grubb brought us dandelion and burdock cordial to drink. You would not believe what big, well-mannered otters the twins are, and Grubb, always ready with a joke and a smile, he never changes. I know because he put otter hotroot in my beaker. Bernard and his friends were recalling the Feast of the Bell Raising. What a day! Mariel's father was so proud when we named the bell after him, the Joseph Bell, though he would not sit at the head of the table—no, Joseph insisted on sitting with Tarquin and his wife, Rosie. Ah, that was a feast my stomach still remembers. Cellarmaster Durry Quill and his assistant Old Gabriel produced the finest October ale I ever drank, Friar Cockleburr made a bell-shaped fruitcake as big as the Joseph Bell itself, Friar Alder and his Trag trainees did us proud too—there were more trifles, tarts, puddings, salads, cheeses and breads than you could shake a twig at. Oak Tom and his wife, Treerose, say that the feast might have lasted a whole season had it not been for Flagg the otter, Rosie and Tarquin and Mellus and Rawnblade. My word, you should have seen those creatures eat, you would have thought they were facing a seven-season famine!

Well, the bell was finally raised, though a lot more things happened during the three days of that feast, I can tell you. Lord Rawnblade explained the badger symbols around the top of the bell to us all. Would you believe it, they told of the coming of the bell to Redwall, even predicting its name, Joseph. The badger rulers of Salamandastron are truly mysterious beasts. Someday I may take a trip there to study the mountain and its caves. Rawnblade gave permission for Rosie and Tarquin to range the lands freely, and they have formed an organization called the Fur and Foot Fighting Patrol. Last I heard they had twelve members, all their own young ones. Rufe Brush did a strange thing on the third morning of the feast, he took the sword of Martin the Warrior, strapped it to his back and climbed to the roof of the Abbey. Yes, right up to the very top of Redwall—what a climb! Rufe placed the sword on the arm of the weathervane and tied it there; what a curious thing to do. Brother Simeon told me that Rufe had been spending a lot of time staring at our grand tapestry of Martin, so it occurs to me that our warrior may have visited Rufe in his dreams. Rufe Brush is now our bellringer, still as strong and silent as ever. I am very close to Rufe. He is a true friend to me, always ready to step in and settle disputes, though they are few and far between at Redwall. I think Bagg will become the new Foremole. The old fellow spends his days drinking, eating and playing with the Dibbuns; he is a great favorite among the little ones. I miss Dandin and Mariel very much, and sometimes I dream of them. They went off, you know. The peaceful Abbey life was not for them, they said. One morning we awoke to find they had gone south in search of adventures. Joseph merely smiled and said that they would return someday, but Mother Mellus moped about for half a season; she loved that pair very much. Sometimes I wish that I had not been born with a sense of duty and my serious nature. I would have liked to travel with them, but it was not to be. When Bernard stepped down, everybeast immediately called for me to take on the robe of Father Abbot. What could I do? Wherever my friends Mariel and Dandin are, my heart is with them. May the way be fair before them and good fortune attend them both.

I am sitting on the bell tower steps as I write. It is cool and shady in here, quiet too. The roof and all of the woodwork, stairs and doors and beams are made from the timbers of four ships that were dismantled by the side of the ford which crosses the path to the north. Some of the wood was used to build a bridge over the ford, to protect travelers from the pike that swim in the waters there. I have only to look up and I can see the great Joseph Bell overhead. It is truly the pride of our Abbey, a thing of great beauty. Ah well, Rawnblade rules Salamandastron and I must rule here. I love my Redwall Abbey, it is a place of peace and plenty. Soon my friend Rufe will come to ring the bell for suppertime. There will be lots of good things to eat and drink in Cavern Hole, and I will sit in my great chair, surrounded by all of my dear companions, Dibbuns playing beneath the table, Mellus, Sage and Serena, old as they are, still shooing the little ones to bath and bed, and me, discussing with the ancient Simeon what I can sense about the earth, the seasons and the feelings of other creatures. He says I am becoming quite good at it. Old Abbot Bernard will just chuckle into his elderberry wine and recall that Simeon used to say that about him. So I hope you will forgive me, my friends. I must go now and attend to my duties as Father Abbot.

There, I've done it again! Bumped my head on that great knotty thing hanging at the end of the bellrope. I'm always doing that, I must learn to duck my head. Though I think I do it purposely, because that piece of rope reminds me of a little mousemaid named Storm who turned up at our Abbey one summer. Have you guessed what the rope is? Then you must have been taking lessons from Simeon. It is the weapon called Gullwhacker. Before Mariel and Dandin went, they tied it to the end of the bellrope as a reminder to other creatures for all the seasons to come that this was how they brought the great Joseph Bell home to Redwall.